East Is East

East Is East

T. CORAGHESSAN BOYLE

VIKING

VIKING
Published by the Penguin Group
Viking Penguin, a division of Penguin Books USA Inc.,
375 Hudson Street, New York, New York 10014, U.S.A.
Penguin Books Ltd, 27 Wrights Lane, London W8 5TZ, England
Penguin Books Australia Ltd, Ringwood, Victoria, Australia
Penguin Books Canada Ltd, 2801 John Street, Markham, Ontario, Canada L3R 1B4
Penguin Books (N.Z.) Ltd, 182–190 Wairau Road, Auckland 10, New Zealand

Penguin Books Ltd, Registered Offices: Harmondsworth, Middlesex, England

First published in 1990 by Viking Penguin, a division of Penguin Books USA Inc.

1 3 5 7 9 10 8 6 4 2

Grateful acknowledgment is made for permission to reprint excerpts from the
following copyrighted works:
The Way of the Samurai by Yukio Mishima, translated by Kathryn Sparling.
Translation copyright © 1977 by Basic Books, Inc., Publishers.
"I don't care if it rains or freezes" by Don Imus. © Imusic, Inc., 1981.
"Ain't No Mountain High Enough" by Nicholas Ashford and Valerie Simpson.
Copyright © Jobete Music Co., Inc., 1967

LIBRARY OF CONGRESS CATALOGING IN PUBLICATION DATA
Boyle, T. Coraghessan.
East is East: a novel / T. Coraghessan Boyle.
p.   cm.
ISBN 0-670-83220-0
I. Title.
PS3552.0932E18   1990
813'.54—dc20   89-40804

Printed in the United States of America
Set in Janson
Designed by Fritz Metsch

For Georges and Anne Borchardt

Those who wish to live horribly and die horribly are choosing a beautiful way of life.
—Yukio Mishima, *The Way of the Samurai*

"Bred and bawn in de briar patch, Br'er Fox, bred and bawn."
—Joel Chandler Harris, *Uncle Remus*

Acknowledgments

A portion of this work first appeared in *Rolling Stone*.
The author would like to thank the following for their assistance:
The John Simon Guggenheim Memorial Foundation; the University of Southern California; Tom Rohlich; John McNally; Rob Jordan; Kevin McCarey; David McGahee; Marie Alix; Clarence, Sarah and Dodds Musser; and Len Schrader.

Contents

Contents

Tupelo Island

PART I

Small Matters

. . . .

HE WAS SWIMMING, ROTATING FROM FRONT TO BACK, THRASHING
his arms and legs and puffing out his cheeks, and it seemed as if
he'd been swimming forever. He did the crawl, the breaststroke,
the Yokohama kick. Tiring, he clung to the cork life ring like some
shapeless creature of the depths, a pale certificate of flesh. Sometime
during the fifth hour, he began to think of soup. *Miso-shiru*, rice
chowder, the thin sea-stinking broth his grandmother would make
of fish heads and eel. And then he thought of beer—bottles like
amber jewels in a bed of ice—and finally he thought of water, only
water.

When the sun went down, taking all the color with it and leaving
behind a surface as hard and cold as hammered pewter, his tongue
was swollen in his throat and the deepest yearnings of his gut
gnawed at him like imperious little animals. His hands were bloated
and raw, the life ring chafed at his arms, gulls swooped close to
appraise him with their professional eyes. He might have given up.
Might have eased into the dream of bed and supper and home,
slipping into the broth of the sea centimeter by centimeter until
the ring floated free and the anonymous waves closed over him.
But he resisted. He thought of Mishima and Jōchō and the book
he'd taped round his chest, beneath the now limp and sodden

turtleneck. Enfolded in a panoply of Ziploc bags, bound to him with black electrical tape and repository of four odd green little American bills, it tugged at the place where his heart beat.

One should take important considerations lightly, Jōchō said. *Small matters should be taken seriously.* Yes. Of course. What did it matter if he lived or died, if he washed ashore and discovered a simmering pot of noodles with pork and green onion or if the sharks nibbled his toes, his feet, his shins and thighs? What mattered was, was . . . the moon. Yes: the small slip of a perfect moon cut like a parenthesis into the darkening horizon. It was rising, white and pristine, delicate as a fingernail paring. He forgot his hunger, his thirst, forgot the teeming teeth of the sea, and made the moon his own.

Of course, at the same time, he knew he would make it, which made Jōchō's advice a lot easier to stomach. It wasn't only the birds—the pelicans and cormorants and gulls beating west to their roosts—but the smell of the shore that told him as much. Sailors talk of the sweet wafting odor of the landfall that awakens them thirty miles out to sea, but on this, his maiden voyage, he'd never noticed it. Not on board the *Tokachi-maru*, anyway. It was here, fixed to the surface, the twenty short years of his life raveling out like the threads of a frayed cord, that it struck him. Suddenly his nose was an instrument of vigorous and minutely calibrated sensitivity, houndlike and true: he could discern the individual blades of grass on the black shore that lay somewhere ahead of him, and he knew that there were people there, Americans, with their butter-stink and their pots of ketchup and mayonnaise and all the rest, and that beneath them there was dead dry sand and mud seething with crabs and nematodes and all the unseeable particles of decay that it comprises. And more, much more: the musk of wild animals, the healthy domestic stench of dogs and cats and parrots, the metallic odor of spray paint and fuel oil, the faintly sweet scent of the exhaust of outboard engines, the perfume—so rich and potent it made him want to sob—of night-blooming flowers, of jasmine and honeysuckle and a thousand things he'd never smelled before.

He'd been ready to die, and now he was going to make it. He was close. He knew it. He stirred his legs in the darkening waters.

. . .

"SHOULDN'T WE HAVE A LIGHT OR SOMETHING?"

"Hm?" His voice was a warm murmur at her throat. He was half asleep.

"Running lights," Ruth said, her own voice pitched low, almost a whisper. "Isn't that what they call them?"

The boat rocked softly on the swells, serene and stable, rocked like a cradle, like the big lumpy bed with the Magic Fingers massage in the motel they'd stumbled across her first night in Georgia. There was a breeze too, salt and sweet at the same time, gentle, but just strong enough to keep the mosquitoes at bay. The only sound was of the water caressing the hull, soothing, rhythmic, a run and trickle that played in her head with the strains of a folk song she'd forgotten ten years ago. The stars were alive and conscious. The champagne was cold. He didn't answer.

Ruth Dershowitz was lying naked in the bow of Saxby Lights's eighteen-foot runabout. (Actually, the boat belonged to his mother, as did everything else in and attached to the big house on Tupelo Island.) Saxby was stretched out beside her, the drowsy flat of his cheek pressed to the swell of her breast. Each time the boat dipped beneath her, the friction of his fashionable stubble sent small fires burning all the way down to her toes. Five minutes earlier Saxby had knelt before her, adjusted her hips on the broad, flat plank of the seat, stroked open her thighs and moved himself into her. Ten minutes before that she'd watched him grow hard in the dimming light as he sat across from her and tried, unsuccessfully, to inflate a plastic air mattress to cushion them. She'd watched him, bemused and excited, until finally she'd whispered, "Forget it, Sax—just come over here." Now he was asleep.

For a while she listened to the water and thought nothing. And then the image of Jane Shine, her enemy, rose up before her and she banished it with a vision of her own inevitable triumph, her own inchoate stories jelling into art, conquering magazines and astonishing the world, and then she was thinking about the big house, thinking about her fellow writers, the sculptors and painters and the single walleyed composer whose music sounded like slow death in the metronome factory. She'd been among them for a week now, one week of an indefinite stay—a succession of months that came alive in her mind, months with little gremlin faces and hunched shoulders, leapfrogging into the glorious, limitless, sunlit and rent-free future. No more waitressing, no more hack work, no more restaurant reviews, *Parade* banalities or *Cosmo* dreck on safe sex, sex in the shower or waking up at his house. She could stay as long as she pleased. Stay forever.

She had connections.

The thought lulled her, and before she knew it she was drifting off, drawn down into the murk of the unconscious by the champagne, the blanket of the night and the luxurious undulations of the boat, and soon the streaking white forms of sea creatures moved through her dream. She was in the water, floating, and a dozen pallid shapes rushed at her like torpedoes and she cried out . . . but it was all right, she was in Saxby's boat and the stars were alive and she was awake—for an instant—before she fell back into her dream. Porpoises, they were only porpoises, she saw now, and they frolicked with her, poked their bottle snouts between her legs and hoisted her onto their slick and streamlined shoulders . . . but then something went wrong and she was alone in the water again and there was something else there, a shadow rising from the depths, sinister and quick, and it hit her, hard, with a thump that woke her. "Sax?" she said, and at first she thought a boat had run into them because of the lights, because of the lack of lights—she wasn't thinking clearly—"Sax? Did you feel that?"

Saxby was a heavy sleeper. She'd been with him once in California when he slept through three blasts of the clock radio, an earthquake severe enough to knock the pictures off the wall and a practice session the university marching band had held on the field behind his apartment. "Wha'?" he said, "huh?" and his head slowly lifted itself from her chest. "Feel what?"

And then all at once Saxby froze. She was lying back, watching him, when she felt his muscles go tense and heard his grunt of surprise—"What in hell?"—and then she looked up and locked eyes with an apparition. A face, ghostly and astonishing in the blanched light of the moon, hovered over the stern; beneath it, a pair of impossible hands clung to the engine mount. It took her a moment, but then she understood: there was a man there. Clinging to their boat, at night, in the middle of Peagler Sound. She saw him, yes, hair in his eyes, something odd about his features, saw the look of fuddlement and exhaustion on his face, and watched as it turned, as if in slow motion, to one of horror. He gave a yelp—a yelp that transcended the puny limitations of language and culture—and then, before she had time even to recollect her own nakedness, he was gone.

In the next instant she and Saxby were on their feet, fumbling to get into their clothes and tangling their limbs as the boat lurched and heaved beneath them. "Goddamn it!" Saxby cursed, clutching his shorts in one hand and tearing at the anchor rope with the other, "you sorry son of a bitch! Come back here!"

Whoever he was—ghost, voyeur, prankster, errant surfer or castaway—he had no intention of doing anything of the kind. Just the opposite: he was in full flight. Ruth could hear him flailing in the water, and now, sitting heavily and groping for her T-shirt, she could just barely make him out: the dark wedge of his head driving against the black water, a flash of something white—a life jacket? a boogie board?—and the foam, phosphorescent with plankton, trailing behind him like a chimerical tail.

Cursing, Saxby raked the anchor over the side and flung it to the bottom of the boat. The smell of the mud, fecal and corrupt, rose to her nostrils. "What's with this jerk, anyway?" Saxby muttered, and his hands were shaking as he pulled the starter cord. "Is he some kind of pervert, or what?"

Ruth was seated in front, still watching the shadow of the distant swimmer. "He looked"—she didn't yet know what she wanted to say, didn't yet realize what it was about him that had struck her— "he looked different somehow."

"Yeah," Saxby grunted as the engine whined to life, "Chinese or something." And then he goosed the throttle, the boat swung round on its axis and they shot off in the swimmer's wake.

The breeze caught Ruth's hair as she wriggled into her shorts. Her heart was pounding. She was confused. What had happened? What were they doing? There was no time to think. The waves thumped under her, she clutched at the seat and felt the spray in her face. They were closing fast on the thrashing swimmer when she twisted round and cried out to Saxby.

She was afraid suddenly, afraid of Saxby for the first time in all the months she'd known him. He was decent, kind, easy-going, she knew that, a guy who drank Campari and soda and felt self-conscious about the size of his feet, and yet there was no telling what he'd do in a situation like this. "Son of a bitch," he spat, and she could see him gritting his teeth in the cold light, and for an instant she pictured the hapless swimmer pounded flat beneath the smooth glistening fist of the hull. "No!" she cried, but he cut the throttle just as they pulled even with the dark twisting shape in the water.

"Let me get a look at this shithead," Saxby said, and the beam of his flashlight came to life.

For the first time she saw the intruder clearly. There he was, struggling in the wash of the boat, no more than five feet from her. She saw a drift of reddish hair, his odd distorted features, the unfathomable eyes that threw back the light in alarm, and then he was kicking away from the boat, frantic, as Saxby swung the tiller to stay with him. He was panicking, this man in the water, flailing and gasping, fighting at the life buoy under his arm, and all at once she knew he was going to drown. "He's drowning, Sax," she cried, "he fell off a ship or something." The engine sang, throttle up, throttle down. The waves slapped at the hull. "We've got to save him."

She turned to Saxby. His anger was gone now, his face composed, contrite even. "Yeah," he said, "you're right. Yeah, of course," and he rose to his feet, rocking back and forth with the motion of the boat, holding his flashlight as if the strength of its beam could hoist the drowning man aboard.

"Throw him a line," she urged. "Hurry."

The man in the water, thrashing and blind, reminded her of the little two-foot alligator Saxby had gigged one night in the beam of a flashlight on the pond out back of the big house. The thing was floating, inert, no more animate than a stick or a clump of weed but for the fire its eyes gave back in the light, and then Saxby struck and it folded up like a pocketknife, gone, sucked down into the matted depths, only to come back at them like a switchblade, mad and stung and toothy and dying. "You grab him, grab his arm," Saxby said, forcing the boat in tight.

But the drowning man didn't want his arm grabbed. He stopped dead, flung the life buoy from him and shouted up at her, shouted in her face, shouted till she could see the glint of gold in his teeth. "Go 'way!" he cried. "Go 'way!" And then he vanished beneath the boat.

And then there was nothing. No sound, no movement. The motor sputtered, the boat drifted. Exhaust washed over them, bitter and metallic.

"He's a nutcase," Saxby said. "Must of broke out of Milledgeville or something."

She didn't respond. Her knuckles were drained of blood, her fingers seared into the pale chipped wood of the gunwale. She'd never seen anyone die before, never seen anyone dead, not even her grandmother, who'd had the good sense to pass on while she was in Europe. Something rose in her throat, a deep wad of sorrow and regret. The world was crazy. A moment ago she'd been wrapped in her lover's arms, still and serene, the night spread over them like a blanket . . . and now someone was dead. "Sax," she turned to him, pleading, "can't you do something? Can't you dive in and save him?"

Saxby's face was inscrutable. She knew every fiber of him, knew where to hurt him and where to make him feel good, knew how to snip out his soul, wring it in her hands and hang it out like a hankie to dry. But this was something new. She'd never seen him like this before. "Shit," he said finally, and he looked scared now, that was all right, that was a mode she recognized, "I can't see a damn thing. How can I dive in if I can't see him?"

She watched the beam of the flashlight play dully over the surface, and then she heard something, a faint splash, the sweet allision of breaking water. "Over there!" she shouted and Saxby swung the light. For a moment they saw nothing, and then the shore, with its close dark beard of Spartina grass, leaped into view like a slide clapped into a projector. "There!" she cried, and it was him, the swimmer, standing now, the sea lapping at his belt loops, a limp white shirt hanging from him like a rag.

"Hey!" Saxby bellowed, angry again, enraged. "Hey, you! I'm talking to you, you jackass. What are you trying—?"

"Hush," Ruth warned him, but it was too late: the intruder was gone again, already enveloped in vegetation, thrashing through the reeds like a gutshot deer, already anonymous. The sea lay flat beneath the beam of the flashlight. The picture was empty. It was then that the life buoy drifted into view, just beyond her reach, in a wash of reeds and plastic refuse. "Let me—" she grunted, stretching for it, but Saxby anticipated her and powered the boat forward. And then she had it, a prize fished out of the water and dripping in her lap.

She turned it over and there they were, the bold red ideographs that spelled out the name of the *Tokachi-maru*. She couldn't read them, of course, but they were a revelation nonetheless. Saxby hovered over her, peering down at the thing as if it were treasure. The light was in her lap, the breeze gave her a scent of the shore. "Yes," she said finally, "Chinese."

The Tokachi-maru

· · · · · · ·

HIRO TANAKA WAS NO MORE CHINESE THAN SHE WAS. HE WAS A Japanese, of the Yamato race—or at least on his mother's side he was, no one would question that—and he'd left the *Tokachi-maru* amid strained circumstances. The fact is, he jumped ship. Literally. This wasn't a case of cozying up to a barmaid or falling down dead drunk in some back alley while the ship weighed anchor; this was deliberate, death-defying, a leap into the infinite. Like his idol Yukio Mishima, and Mishima's idol before him, Jōchō Yamamoto, Hiro Tanaka was a man of decision. When *he* jumped ship, he didn't entangle himself in verbal niceties: no, he just jumped.

On the day in question, the *Tokachi-maru* was steaming north along the coast of Georgia, bound for Savannah with a load of tractor parts, DAT recorders and microwave ovens. It was a day like any other, the wind brisk, the sun baked into the sky, the 12,000-ton freighter ironing the waves as if they were wrinkles in a shirt. All but six of the forty-member crew sat straight-backed over their western-style lunches (corned beef hash, sardines in oil, scrambled eggs and home fries, all wedded in a single pot and seasoned with A.1. sauce and Gulden's mustard). Captain Nishizawa was in his cabin, sleeping off his preprandial *sake*; Chief Mate Wakabayashi and Able Bodied Seaman Kuma were in the chart room and at the helm, respectively; Ordinaries Uetto and Dorai were on watch; and Hiro was in the brig.

Actually, Hiro was in a storage closet on the third deck. It was sixty-four feet square, or about the size of the apartment he had occupied with his grandmother prior to signing on the *Tokachimaru*, and it was illuminated by a single jittery 40-watt bulb. Hiro had been given a wooden bowl and a pair of chopsticks for his alimentary needs, a bucket in which to relieve himself and a futon to spread on the cold steel floor. There was no ventilation, and the little room stank of fumigant and the Bunker C fuel the huge steam turbines burned day and night. Twenty mops, twenty buckets and sixteen flat-headed brooms hung from hooks screwed into the walls. A scatter of odds and ends—paint scrapers, empty Sapporo boxes, a single Nike tennis shoe spattered with tar—lay where the last storm had strewn them. The door locked from the outside.

Though he was conscientious, well mannered and inoffensive, and so silent and circumspect as to be nearly invisible among his shipmates, Hiro found himself confined to this hateful steel room, his diet limited to two balls of white rice and one tin cup of water daily, because of an uncharacteristic act of defiance: he had disobeyed the direct order of an officer. The officer was Chief Mate Wakabayashi, a survivor of the Battle of Rarotonga who carried shrapnel in his lower back, legs, arms, feet and at the base of his skull, and whose temper consequently tended to be short. He had issued a direct order to Hiro to cease and desist constricting the windpipe of First Cook Hideo Chiba, who at the time lay thrashing on the galley floor beneath Hiro's full and outraged weight. And that was a good deal of weight: at five foot ten, Hiro, who was inordinately fond of eating, weighed close to two hundred pounds. Chiba, who was inordinately fond of drinking, weighed less than a wet mop.

The moment was chaotic. Second Cook Moronobu Unagi, who had once parboiled the face of an OS in a dispute over a bottle of Suntory, was screeching like a parrot: "He's killing him! Murder, murder, murder!"; the Chief Engineer, an intense silent man in his seventies, with bad feet and ill-fitting dentures, tugged ineffectively at Hiro's shoulders; and half a dozen deckhands stood around jeering. Chief Mate Wakabayashi, in his pristine white uniform, scurried up to where the combatants lay entangled on the galley floor, delivered his stentorian order, and was immediately flung into a pot of clear broth as the ship chose that moment to plunge into a trough. Soup—it was a twenty-gallon pot—cascaded onto the floor, searing Hiro's back and permeating Chiba, who already stank enough for three men, with the essence of reduced fish. Through it all, Hiro held his grip.

And what had driven so mild a man to so desperate a pass?

The immediate cause was a pan of hard-cooked eggs. Hiro, who'd signed on the *Tokachi-maru* as Third Cook, beneath the drunken and foul-smelling Chiba and the drunken, leering and unctuous Unagi, was preparing a dish of *nishiki tamago* as an appetizer for the evening meal. The task consisted of shelling a hundred hard-boiled eggs, carefully separating the yolks from the whites, very finely chopping and seasoning each, and finally reuniting them—tenderly—in half-inch layers in a succession of stainless-steel pans. Hiro had learned the recipe from his grandmother—and he knew some thirty others by heart—and yet this was the first time in the six weeks since the ship had left Yokohama that he'd been allowed to prepare the dish himself. More usually, he acted as *sous chef*, errand boy and galley slave, scrubbing pans, polishing the gas ranges, cleaning mountains of defrosted squid, cuttlefish and bonito, chopping seaweed and peeling grapes till his fingers went numb. On this particular afternoon, however, Chiba and Unagi were indisposed. They had been drinking *sake* since breakfast in celebration of *O-bon*, the Buddhist festival of ancestral spirits, and Hiro had been left to himself while they strove to commune with the shades of the departed. He worked hard. Worked with pride and concentration. Eight trays lay before him, exquisitely prepared. As a finishing touch, he sprinkled the dishes with black sesame seed, just as his grandmother had taught him.

It was a mistake. Because at that moment, just as he held the shaker inverted over the last tray, Chiba and Unagi staggered into the galley. "Idiot!" Chiba screeched, slapping the shaker from his hand. The shaker clattered off the gas range. Hiro averted his face and hung his head. Through his sandals, deep in the soles of his feet, he could feel the *ta-dum, ta-dum, ta-dum* of the screws churning through the sour green waves beneath them. "Never," Chiba seethed, his sunken chest and fleshless arms trembling, "never use black sesame on *nishiki tamago*." He turned to Unagi. "Did you ever hear of such a thing?"

Unagi's eyes were slits. He rubbed his hands together as if in anticipation of some rare treat, and he bowed his head with a quick snap. "Never," he breathed, waiting, waiting, "except maybe among foreigners. Among *gaijin*."

Now Hiro looked up. The underlying cause of his explosion, the cause of all his torment in life, was about to surface.

Chiba leaned into him, his monkey face twisted with hatred, flecks of spittle on his upper lip. "*Gaijin*," he spat. "Long-nose. *Ketō. Bata-kusai*." And then he unfolded his clenched fist, studied the palm of his hand for an instant, and without warning struck a savage blow to the bridge of Hiro's nose. Then he turned to the pans of *nishiki tamago*. Raging, in a mad flurry of skinny wrists and snapping elbows, he overturned them on the floor, one after another. "Offal!" he shouted. "Dog shit! Fit for pigs!" Through it all, Unagi regarded Hiro through half-closed eyes, grinning.

This is the point at which Hiro lost control. Or rather, he didn't lose control exactly, but attacked his tormentor in what Mishima would call "an explosion of pure action." The *nishiki tamago* was on the floor, the twenty-gallon kettle rattling its lid, Unagi grinning and Chiba spouting invective, the moment suspended as the tintinnabulation of the last pan hung in the air, and then the First Cook was swimming in chopped egg and Hiro's fingers were locked on his throat. Chiba gasped, the turkey flesh of his neck turning red under Hiro's white, white fingers. Unagi screamed: "Murder! Murder! Murder!" And all the while Hiro hung on, ignoring the jeers, the scalding soup, Chiba's hot foul breath and the face that

swelled beneath him like a blood blister, oblivious to Wakabayashi
and the Chief Engineer, fighting like a rabid dog against the pull
of the eight men it took to separate him from his tormentor. He
was beyond caring, beyond pain, the words of Jōchō pounding in
his head: *One cannot accomplish feats of greatness in a normal frame of
mind. One must turn fanatic and develop a mania for dying.*

But he didn't die. He wound up instead in the makeshift brig,
staring at the walls and breathing Bunker C fumes, awaiting the
Port of Savannah and the Japan Air flight that would take him home
in disgrace.

Gaijin. Long-nose. Butter-stinker. These were the epithets he'd
endured all his life, crying to his grandmother on the playground,
harassed in elementary school and transformed into a punching bag
in junior high, singled out and bullied till he was driven from the
merchant marine high school his grandmother had chosen for him.
Foreigner, that's what they called him. For while his mother was
a Japanese—a firm-legged beauty with round eyes and a fetching
buck-toothed smile—his father was not.

No. His father was an American. A hippie. A young man in a
cracked and rubbed-soft photo, hair to his shoulders, the beard of
a monk, eyes like a cat's. Hiro didn't even know his name. *Obāsan,*
he pestered his grandmother, what was he like, what was his name,
how tall was he? "Doggu," she said, but that wasn't his real name,
it was a nickname—Doggo—after a character in an American comic
book. "Tall," she said sometimes, "with little colored glasses and
a long nose. Hairy and dirty." Other times she said he was short,
skinny, fat, broad-shouldered, or that his hair was white and he
walked with a cane, or that he wore denims and an earring and
was so dirty and hairy (he was always dirty and hairy, no matter
the version) that he could have grown turnips behind his ears. Hiro
didn't know what to believe—his father was like a chimera out of
a children's tale, larger than life in the morning, smaller than a
thimble in the evening. He might have asked his mother, but his
mother was dead.

This much he knew: the American had come to Kyoto in his

hippie rags, with his granny glasses and his rings, to devote himself to Zen and find someone to teach him to play the koto. Like all Americans, he was lazy, stoned and undisciplined, and he soon lost interest in the Zen regimen of prayer and contemplation, but still he haunted the streets of Kyoto, vaguely hoping to learn the rudiments of the koto and bring it back to America with him, as the Beatles had brought the sitar from India. He was in a band, of course—or at least he had been—and it was the oddness of the instrument that appealed to him. Five feet long, with thirteen strings and movable bridges, it was like nothing he'd ever heard, humming and strange, a zither the size of an alligator. He would electrify it, naturally, and lay it flat on a table like a pedal steel guitar and then he would rotate his shoulders and flail his unshorn head, plucking frenziedly at the strings and astonishing the audiences back home. But it was the devil to play, and he needed a teacher. And a job. He was out of work, out of money, and his student visa was about to expire.

That was where Sakurako Tanaka came in.

Hiro's mother was bright, very bright, a high school graduate whose test scores were among the best in her class—a girl for whom even the august Tokyo University was not an impossibility—charming, pretty, ebullient and, at nineteen, a failure. She didn't want Todai or Kyoto University or any of them. She didn't want a career with Suzuki or Kubota or Mitsubishi and she most emphatically didn't want to bury herself in the kitchen or the nursery. What she wanted, desperately, with an ache that ate at her like the gnawings of hunger, like the insomnia that hollowed out her nights and drained her mornings, was to play American rock and roll. Onstage. With her own band. "I want to play Buffalo Springfield, Doors, Grateful Dead and Iron Butterfly," she told her mother. "I want to play Janis Joplin and Grace Slick." Her mother, a housewife in a nation of housewives, was firmly opposed to it. The music was foreign, devil's music, grating, sensual and impure, and the proper place for a young woman was in the home with her husband and children. Sakurako's father, a salaryman who'd worked all his life for Kubota Tractor, who dined, golfed and vacationed with his colleagues and had a plot reserved in the company cemetery, exploded at the mere mention of rock and roll.

The upshot was that Sakurako left home. She took her bleached jeans and her guitar and went to Tokyo, where she made the rounds of the clubs in the Shibuya, Roppongi and Shinjuku districts. It was 1969. Female guitarists in Japan were as rare as loquats in Siberia. Within a month she was back in Kyoto, working as a bar hostess. When Doggo stepped through the door, yenless, with his hair and beads and jeans, with his boots and tie-dyed shirt, his fingertips callused from the friction of the cold steel strings of his guitar, she was lost.

He allowed her to feed him and buy him drinks, and he told her about L.A. and San Francisco, about the Sunset Strip and the Haight and Jim Morrison. She found him a *sensei* who taught shamisen and koto to the geisha of Pontochō, the ancient district of Kyoto, and in his gratitude he moved in with her. The apartment was small. They slept on a mat and smoked hippie drugs and made love while listening to scratchy records of hippie bands. Hiro had no illusions about it. His mother was a bar hostess—she knew a hundred men, coquetry was her business—and the picture of her life played like a grim documentary in his head. She became pregnant, the room shrank, rice suddenly tasted odd and the odor of cooking saturated the walls, and then one day Doggo was gone, leaving behind the cracked photo and a sound of plucked strings that chimed through the interstices of her solitude. Six months later, Hiro was born. Six months after that, his mother was dead.

And so, Hiro was a half-breed, a *happa*, a high-nose and butterstinker—and an orphan to boot—forever a foreigner in his own society. But if the Japanese were a pure race, intolerant of miscegenation to the point of fanaticism, the Americans, he knew, were a polyglot tribe, mutts and mulattoes and worse—or better, depending on your point of view. In America you could be one part Negro, two parts Serbo-Croatian and three parts Eskimo and walk down the street with your head held high. If his own society was closed, the American was wide open—he knew it, he'd seen the films, read the books, listened to the LPs—and anyone could do anything he pleased there. America was dangerous, yes. Seething with crime and degeneracy and individualism. But they'd driven him out of school in Japan—he was lower than the *Burakumin*, who collected the garbage; lower than the Koreans, who'd been brought over as slaves during the war.

And so, Hiro went to sea on the *Tokachi-maru*, the most decrepit, rust-eaten hulk to fly the Japanese flag, went because the ship was bound for the U.S.A. and he could go ashore and see the place for himself, see the cowboys and hookers and wild Indians, maybe even discover his father in some gleaming, spacious ranch house and sit down to cheeseburgers with him. And so, Hiro became Third Cook rather than the officer he might have been had they let him finish merchant marine high school, suffering the abuse of Chiba and Unagi and all the rest—even here, even at sea he wasn't free of it—and so, he consulted Mishima and Jōchō and struck down his enemies and wound up in the brig, humiliated, living with the groans and pleas of his attenuated gut and two balls of rice a day.

In his extremity, he thought of food, day and night, dwelled on it, dreamed of it, apotheosized it. On the day of his escape, he dreamed of breakfast: miso soup with eggplant and bean curd, steamed white radishes, raw onions, mustard with rice. And lunch—not the western-style slop Chiba concocted to show off the fact that he'd once shipped on a freighter out of Tacoma, Washington—but the rice and egg dish—*tamago meishi*—his grandmother would make him when he came in from school, or the sweet bean and barley cakes she'd buy him at the confectioner's or the delicate *sōmen* noodles she stirred in great swirling mounds in her iron kettle. He was dreaming of those noodles, staring morosely at the mops lining the walls, when he heard the heavy footfall of his warder on the companionway steps.

They were approaching the Port of Savannah and Hiro knew

he'd have to make his move soon. He'd read deeply in *The Way of the Samurai* for days, getting Mishima's and Jōchō's words by heart, and now he was ready. The book—in its plastic womb and with the odd little green bills and his father's picture nestled safely between its leaves—clung to him with tentacles of black electrician's tape, the tape his friend Ajioka-san had slipped him in the night. In his hands he held a stout oaken mop, its head soaked heavy with the water they'd given him for washing.

The footsteps, the weary, dragging, footsore steps of Noboru Kuroda, the slug who mopped up the officers' quarters and served them at table, halted outside the door. Hiro stood back, envisioning the slumped shoulders and concave chest, the hopeless hands and perpetually bewildered expression of old "Just-a-Minute" Kuroda, as they called him behind his back, and he waited breathlessly as the key turned in the lock. In a sort of fever he watched as the handle rotated and the door pulled back, and then he charged, the mop thrust before him like a lance. It was over in an instant. Kuroda's tired old jowls seized with surprise, the wet mop speared him in the solar plexus and he went down on the worn linoleum, gasping and floundering like a yellowfin jerked from the somnolent depths. Hiro was briefly sorry for the loss of the rice balls, which were now mashed into Kuroda's shirt, but this was no time for regrets. He stepped nimbly over the wheezing old man and darted up the companionway, his feet quick, liberty pounding in his veins.

Below him, on the second deck, the crew was at lunch, puzzling over their plates and struggling to pluck the odd bit of sardine out of the mélange of hash, eggs and potatoes Chiba had inflicted on them. Above him was the superstructure, and its ascending decks: the ship's office and main electrical and gyroscope rooms on the fourth deck; the radio room on the fifth; the captain's cabin, where even now Captain Nishizawa lay in a *sake*-induced stupor, on the sixth; and, finally, the bridge. From the bridge, high-flown and airy, a pair of observation decks protruded, hanging out over the water on either side of the ship like extended wings. They were catwalks, actually, supported from beneath by steel struts, and from them you could see ten miles on a clear day. It was for these that Hiro was heading.

He rattled up the steps past the ship's office and on up past the radio room and the captain's cabin, moving quickly but with resolution. He wasn't fleeing blindly, not at all: he had a plan, as Mishima, in his gloss on Jōchō, had advised. *One may choose a course of action*, Mishima said, *but one may not always choose the time. The moment of decision looms in the distance and then overtakes you. Then is to live not to prepare for that moment of decision?* It was. And he was prepared.

On up the steps he raced, past the chart room where Chief Mate Wakabayashi glared savagely at him and lurched out the door in pursuit, past the helm where Able Bodied Seaman Kuma stood fixed at the wheel, and out onto the port wingdeck, where OS Dorai gaped at his advancing form as if he'd never before seen a man moving upright on his own two legs. And then, with Wakabayashi raging behind him and Dorai immobile before him, Hiro paused to draw his penknife. Thoughts of all those American movies with their tattooed gangs and the feints and thrusts of their knife fights must have shot through Dorai's head, and he stepped back a pace or two, but the knife wasn't a weapon at all. It was a tool. In two quick strokes Hiro slashed the cord binding the white life ring to the rail, and while Wakabayashi thundered along the deck and Dorai cringed, Hiro became airborne.

It was a sixty-eight-foot drop from the bridge to the water, and from that height it seemed a hundred and sixty-eight. Hiro never hesitated. He fell into the empyrean like a skydiver running before the chute, like an eagle plunging from its aerie, but there was nothing to sustain him in that indifferent element, and the sea rushed up at him like a bed of concrete. He hit feet first, letting the life ring fly, and still the force of the concussion nearly ripped Jōchō from his body. By the time he bobbed to the surface, his lungs heaving for the sweet, sweet air, the *Tokachi-maru* had passed him by, sliding across the horizon like a liquid mountain.

Under full steam, it would take the ship nearly two miles and three and a half minutes to come to a full stop. She would come back for him, Hiro knew that, as he knew that even now all hands were scrambling across the decks shouting "Man overboard!," but he also knew that the tightest turn she could make was almost a mile across. He stroked hard, his feet churning in the brine, arms hammering at the chop. He had no thought of heading west toward the distant shore—they'd expect that of him—but instead he watched the sun and pushed himself due south, the way they'd come.

The water was warm, tropical, gleaming with a thousand jewels. He watched the birds overhead, watched the clouds. He clung to the life ring and kicked his legs. And the sea sustained him, embraced him, wrapped him up like the arms of a long-lost father.

⟍*T*⟍hanatopsis House

. . . .

RUTH HAD WATCHED THE STORM GATHER ALL MORNING. IT WAS SO
dark at 6:30 she nearly slept through her wake-up call, and she
pulled on her shorts and top in the gloom. She came down for
breakfast at 7:00, taking her place as usual at the silent table, and
even then it seemed as if the night had never ended. Owen Birkshead, the colony's director, had lit the lamps in the corners, but
everything beyond the windows was flat and without definition.
Inside, it was muggy and close, the air so thick you could almost
pat it into place like a down comforter. There was no rumble of
thunder, no flash of lightning or streak of rain, but she could feel
the storm coming with a deep physical intuition that connected her
with the newt beneath the rock and the spider drawn up in the
funnel of its web. Of course, she couldn't mention it to anyone,
couldn't say, "It feels like rain" or "We're really in for it now." No.
She was, by choice, sitting at the silent table.

When Saxby's mother, Septima, now in her early seventies and
snoring raucously from the master suite behind the breakfast parlor,
had set up the trust for Thanatopsis House on the death of her
husband some twenty years earlier, she'd followed the lead of other,
more established artists' colonies like Yaddo, MacDowell and Cum-
mington. One of the traditions she'd adopted—and particularly

adhered to—was that of the silent table. At breakfast, it was thought, artists of a certain temperament required an absolute and meditative silence, broken only perhaps by the discreet tap of a demitasse spoon on the rim of a saucer—in order to make a fruitful transition from the realm of dreams to that exalted state in which the deep stuff of aesthetic response rises to the surface. Others, of course, needed just the opposite—conviviality, uproar, crippling gossip, lame jokes and a whiff of the sour morning breath of their fellow artists—to settle brains fevered by dreams of grandeur, conquest and the utter annihilation of their enemies. For them, Septima had provided the convivial table, located in a second parlor separated from the first by a paneled corridor and two swinging doors of dark and heavy oak.

Even on this morning, when the turmoil of the storm was building inside her, when she felt light, almost weightless, when she felt giddy and excited for no good reason, Ruth chose the silent table. She'd been at the colony two weeks now—fourteen mornings—and in that space of time she'd never, even for an instant, thought of sitting anywhere else. Aside from Irving Thalamus, whose trade-in-stock—urban Jewish angst—throve on confusion, the name artists, the serious ones, all chose the silent table. Laura Grobian sat here, and Peter Anserine, and a celebrated punk sculptress with staved-in eyes and skin so pale she looked three days dead. Ruth reveled in it. She pretended to read the Savannah paper—delivered on the previous afternoon's ferry and always a day out of date—while she watched Laura Grobian, with her concave cheeks and haunted eyes—her famous haunted eyes—to see how she spooned up her cold cereal and how the unflagging hours of the night had treated her. Or she'd study Peter Anserine, recently divorced, with his long nose and prominent nostrils, as he hacked and snorted surreptitiously over his food and the book—always European, and never in translation—that seemed attached to him like some sort of growth. And, too, she got to see who was breakfasting with whom at the convivial table, as they had to pass through the silent room on their way. Ruth watched and brooded and plotted, and when it got to be too much, when the table was deserted and she could put it off no longer, she pushed herself up from her chair and walked the quarter mile to her studio in the woods. Saxby, of course, slept till twelve.

It hadn't yet started to rain when Ruth gathered up her things— the satchel with her notebooks, breath mints, her compact and hairbrush and one of the fat pulp romances she devoured in secret— folded the day-old newspaper under her arm, plucked an umbrella from the stand in the front hall and sallied out the door. This was her favorite part of the day. The path, set with flagstones and planted in some bygone era with jonquils and geraniums, took her through a stand of bearded oak and pine and within a good sniff of the marsh. The misery of writing was at hand, it was true, but the smell of the mudflats and the open ocean that drove in twice a day to swallow them stirred memories of her girlhood in Santa Monica—her simple, ingenuous and carefree girlhood, uncomplicated by the mania for fame (and its unfortunate concomitant, work) that had set in when she reached sixteen. And though at this time of year the heat and humidity were unrelenting—the entire state, as she often said, was like a shower stall in a dormitory—and she knew that the mosquitoes and deerflies lay in wait for her beneath the trees, she couldn't help feeling exhilarated. Here she was, at Thanatopsis, writing—or trying to write; the colleague of Laura Grobian, Peter Anserine and Irving Thalamus—and yes, of the walleyed composer too, who, despite appearances, was the most famous of all the twenty-six artists now in residence.

Ruth, known to her intimates as La Dershowitz, was thirty-four, though she admitted only to twenty-nine. She'd been writing since her junior year in high school, when John Beard, her English teacher, as interested perhaps in her triumphant breasts and pouting smirk as in her adolescent poems and stories, encouraged her during the long hours of their late-night tutoring sessions. She'd put in time at most of the better summer workshops, courtesy of her father, and she held a shaky B.A. in anthropology from Sonoma State. She spent a year at Iowa and another at Irvine without

managing to come away with a degree from either, and she'd published four intense and gloomy stories in the little magazines (two
in *Dichondra*, the editor of which she'd met at Bread Loaf, and one
each in *Firefly* and *Precious Buttons*). Money had become a problem,
waitressing a terminal disease. When she met Saxby, who was
flunking out of the oceanography program at Scripps, she fell in
love with his dimples, his laugh, his shoulders and the idea of the
big house on Tupelo Island. And now she was here. For good. Or
at least for a good long while.

She came up the densely shaded path, already wet under the
arms, the satchel jogging at her shoulder, and saw that she'd left
the windows of her studio open. (Each of the artists at Thanatopsis
ate, slept, bathed and relieved him- or herself in the big house, but
was assigned workspace in one of the thirty studio-cottages scattered
about the property, and each was strictly enjoined from visiting
any of the other cottages during the hours of the workday—that
is, from breakfast at 7:00 till cocktails at 5:00. The cottages ranged
in size from Laura Grobian's five-room Craftsman-style bungalow
to the single-room structures afforded to lesser lights, and Septima
had named each of them after a famous suicide in remembrance of
her own husband's untimely demise.) Ruth was in Hart Crane. It
was a one-room affair, very rustic, with an old stone fireplace, a
wicker loveseat, two bent-cane rockers and a single capricious electrical outlet. It was also the farthest from the main house of any of
the colony's studios. And that was all right with Ruth. In fact, she
preferred it that way.

At first the open windows took her by surprise—she'd always
been careful to lock up behind her, not only for fear of an overnight
deluge, but out of respect for the depredations of raccoons, snakes,
squirrels and adolescents. For an instant she imagined her typewriter stolen, manuscript gutted, graffiti on the walls. But then she
remembered the previous afternoon and how utterly disgusted and
sick at heart she was over the whole business—typewriters, manuscripts, art, work, love, pride, accomplishment, even the pro-
spective adulation of the masses—and how she'd left the windows

open to taunt the Fates. Go ahead, she'd said, impaled on the stake
of a wasted afternoon and her own despair, tear it up, ransack the
place, liberate me. Go ahead, I dare you.

Now she felt differently. Now the work fit was on her. Now it
was morning and now she had to sit down to her desk like everybody
else in America. She mounted the three time-worn steps to the
porch, pushed through the unfastened door, dropped her satchel
on the loveseat and confronted the ancient Olivetti portable that
seemed to stare accusingly at her from the desk beneath the open
window. It was still there. So too the page she'd been working on,
still jammed in the machine and curled up like a wood shaving with
the humidity. For a moment she fussed over the greedy, deep-
throated pitcher plants she'd dug up in the swamp—they loved
flies, the fat bluebottles that sizzled against the rusty grid of the
screen and drove her to distraction—then heated herself a cup of
coffee on the hot plate, stepped outside half a dozen times to check
on the progress of the storm, and finally, when the boredom threatened to shut down her mind, she settled down to work.

She tried. She did. But she just couldn't seem to concentrate.
The story she was working on was a multiple point of view thing
about a Japanese housewife who'd tried to drown herself and her
two young children in Santa Monica Bay after her husband deserted her. It had been in all the papers. The children had drowned,
while the woman, her lungs heavy, her throat raw and her eyes
stung with salt, was pulled from the water and resuscitated by a
seventeen-year-old surfer. Ruth had the surfer's point of view
down, no problem. But the children's, that was harder. And the
mother's—what had been going through her head?

Ruth worked for an hour, or what seemed like an hour—she had
no way of marking time and she was glad of it—retyping the first
paragraph over and over till she could barely make sense of it. Her
heart just wasn't in it. She kept thinking of Saxby. The night before
they'd taken the ferry to the mainland and driven into Darien for
drinks and dinner. On the way back he'd pulled off the road and
they'd made love on the hood of the car. He lay back against the

windshield, hard all the way, in his cock, his thighs, the washboard muscles of his abdomen, and she'd climbed atop him, soft and flowering. And then she thought of the storm. And then of the big house, thirty-seven rooms and servants' quarters, once the center-piece of a cotton plantation, slaves beading sweat in the fields, mules and factors and all the rest, Saxby's forefathers astride their buggies, whips in hand. She thought of *Gone With the Wind*, *Roots*, *The Confessions of Nat Turner*, and then she went back to her story, straining to focus on her character, the distraught woman cut off from her culture, her heavy-lidded eyes, fine hands and fingers, and all at once the face of Hiro Tanaka—frozen with fear in the cold crepuscular light of Peagler Sound—rose up before her.

Chinese. She'd thought he was Chinese. But then she'd never traveled any farther east than the sushi bars of Little Japan or the chop suey houses of Chinatown, and to this point in her life she'd never had any need to differentiate one nationality from another. If the sign outside said Vietnamese, then they were Vietnamese; if it said Thai, then they were Thai. She knew Asians only as people who served dishes with rice. Chinese. How stupid of her. Here she was, trying to conjure up a Japanese housewife from a newspaper account, and a real living breathing Japanese—a des-perado, a ship jumper and fugitive—practically throws himself in her naked lap and she thinks he's a waiter from Chow Foo Luck.

It was strange. She couldn't get the image of him out of her head. Where was he? What was he eating? What was he thinking? He'd been ashore a week now and he was still at large, hiding out, buried somewhere in the weeds. There were reports of him everywhere— Saxby swore he'd seen him running for the bushes out back of Cribbs' Handi-Mart—but where was he? The whole island was in an uproar, from the blacks at Hog Hammock to the veiny retirees of Tupelo Shores Estates. The newspaper account had made him out to be something of a desperate character, a violent and reckless sort who'd broken out of the ship's brig, assaulted several of his shipmates and taken a suicidal plunge over the side. The Coast Guard had given up its search after two eyewitnesses from the artists' colony—Ruth couldn't help feeling a little stab of disappointment when she wasn't mentioned by name—had seen him come ashore on the southeast tip of Tupelo Island. The authorities were pursuing the matter. He was believed to be armed and dangerous.

Ruth had had to fight for the paper—this was the biggest thing to hit Tupelo Island since the swine flu epidemic, and everybody wanted to be in on the action. The paper arrived, a day late as usual, two mornings after the encounter on the bay. In the interim she and Saxby had spoken by phone with reporters from the *Atlanta Constitution*, the *Savannah Star* and the bi-monthly *Tupelo Island Breeze*; a special agent of the INS from Savannah who identified himself as Detlef Abercorn; the county sheriff (or "shurf," as the locals had it); and a Mr. Shikuma, president of the Japan-America Society in New York. Mr. Shikuma, in a flurry of thank-yous and apologies, had wanted to congratulate them on identifying Seaman Tanaka and to assure them that the young sailor, though mentally deranged, would cause no one any irreparable harm.

Actually, Ruth liked the attention. She hadn't been herself since she and Saxby had arrived at Thanatopsis House. Perhaps she'd felt intimidated by the Peter Anserines and Laura Grobians, perhaps she'd felt threatened by her contemporaries, as she had at Iowa and Irvine. Certainly she felt awkward about her special relationship with Saxby and the sort of gossip and backbiting it was sure to provoke: *Ruth Dershowitz? Who is she anyway? I mean, what has she written? Or does she even have to write—isn't she the son's latest squeeze, isn't that it?* In any case, she'd held her peace with the others—she hadn't said much of anything to anyone. Oh, she'd exchanged banalities over cocktails or dinner with whoever sat to her left or right, but she hadn't committed herself at all—the ground was shaky yet and she was still learning to walk. But on the night they came in off the bay, she couldn't help herself.

It was late, past two, and the only light in the big house came from the billiard room on the second floor. They took the stairs two at a time, Ruth struggling to match Saxby's long strides. She was out of breath when he flung open the door and tugged her into the room. She saw wainscoting, a chandelier, lamps in the corners. It took her a moment, blinking like someone roused from a sound sleep, to identify the usual crowd of insomniacs.

Irving Thalamus was there, sitting at the card table, his fingers fidgeting as he tried to fight down the impulse to look up and give away his hand. A poet named Bob sat across from him. Bob had a book out from Wesleyan and he was very serious, though he looked more like a beer distributor than an assistant professor at Emory, which he was. Next to Bob, hunched over a Diet Coke and scratching herself unconsciously, was Ina Soderbord, a square-faced, big-shouldered blonde from Minnesota who wrote as if she were in the throes of delirium tremens. In the corner, enfolded in her metronomic silence, the walleyed composer nodded over a book, while the punk sculptress, in leather shorts and a T-shirt the size of a pup tent, leaned over the billiard table in a blaze of light.

Before anyone could greet them, before anyone could glance up with a casual "hello" or "what's up?," Saxby was spewing out the story in his usual hyperbolic style, the encounter on the bay no less stupefying than an encounter with outerspace aliens. But they all loved Saxby. Loved him for his wit and the square of his shoulders and his utter lack of interest in things artistic. Ruth clung to his arm.

"No, I swear it," he was saying, "the guy looked like Elmer Fudd, except with hair, and Ruth and I were getting romantic— or we'd already got romantic and were thinking about getting romantic again—I mean, I'm naked, for christ's sake—don't blush, Ruth; is she blushing? Anyway, it's a little disconcerting. We're out there on the water, and if it was a seal or a tuna or even a whale, I could understand it, but a Chinese Elmer Fudd? And with hair?"

Ruth stepped aside, two steps back and one to the left, and watched their faces as Saxby waved his arms and mugged and ran his voice up and down the register. They were spellbound. When Sax was finished, when he'd left the frightened interloper thrashing through the Spartina grass like a spooked buffalo, Irving Thalamus set down his cards and looked up. "You want to take order now?" he said in falsetto, his face expressionless. "You like egg loal or Chinese wegetable?"

"Maybe he was trying out for the Olympics or something," Bob said, and he was about to expand on this notion when the punk sculptress cut him off. "You people are really fucked," she snarled, slamming down the cue stick. She stood glaring at them from the center of the room. "You're as bad as the crackers. Worse." She drew herself up, as if to spit on the floor, and stalked out of the room.

"What's with her?" Saxby said, helping himself to a handful of peanuts from the bowl in the middle of the card table. "I mean, it's not like we're in the East Village here or something. This is Georgia"—and he thickened his accent—"the sweet ol' downhome Peach State, and I'd say finding a Chinaman in the middle of Peagler Sound is pretty damned incredible—I'd say, for a fact, that the Chinese population of the Sea Islands just soared from zero to one."

Irving Thalamus broke open a peanut with an authoritative crack, and everyone turned to watch him as he bent over it to extract the dicotyledonous kernel from the shell. "No sense of humor," he observed in his smoker's rasp, and Bob began to snicker.

It was then that Ruth felt herself letting go. She was over-wrought, desolate, flooded with conflicting emotions: How could they be so blasé? There'd been a shipwreck. She'd watched an exhausted, half-hysterical survivor flounder to shore and flail through the bushes in a panic. And all they could do was make Chinese jokes. How many others were out there even now, crying out for help, the black unforgiving waters closing over them? "We've got to call the police," she said suddenly. "And the Coast Guard. A ship went down, I know it, it's obvious. Did anyone listen to the radio tonight?"

They were all watching her—even the walleyed composer, who jolted awake with a snort at the mention of radio. "Radio?" she echoed, and then they were all talking at once. "Did anyone?" Ruth repeated.

Peter Anserine had. Ina Soderbord, who had the room next to his, had heard him listening to some news program around eight. But he'd been asleep for hours now, and who wanted to wake him?

Suddenly Ruth was furious, the whole thing—Thanatopsis House, the cynicism, the pressure, the backbiting—too much for her. In an instant, the carefully constructed edifice of her reserve fell to pieces. She was part of it now, centerstage. "I don't believe it," she blurted, and she felt light-headed with the intensity of her emotion. Saxby was there, his arm around her shoulder. "It's okay," he said, but she wasn't through yet. "People could be drowning out there and you, you—you make jokes!"

Tears had started up in her eyes, but she fought them down. She was angry, hurt, confused—she really was—and yet, in some unassailable pocket of her psyche, she was play-acting too, and she knew it. *If they'd only listen*, she thought, *if they only knew . . .* Standing there at Saxby's side, her legs tanned and long and slim, her whole body trembling with her daring and anger and hurt over the way they'd ignored her as if she were nobody, as if she were nothing, she knew she had them. She'd got their attention now, oh yes indeed. The smirk was gone from Bob's face, the walleyed composer looked freshly slapped, and even Irving Thalamus, he of the poker face and deadpan eyes, had changed his expression. If he'd been catty before, now he was an old tom catching a whiff—faint and distant, a molecule on the breeze—of sexual advertisement. "Do something," she demanded. "Will *somebody please do* something?"

The next thing she knew she was sitting at the card table, hunched beside Thalamus, spent, while Saxby and Bob went off to phone the Coast Guard, the sheriff, the local VFW post and the volunteer fire department. "Hey, it's all right," he said, and she gazed at the lizard's flesh that sank his eyes, watched him brush back the black morass of his pompadour. He was fifty-two. He was an institution. His lips were dry and hard, his teeth compact, sharp, white. "You did the right thing. Sometimes we all need a swift kick in the ass, right?"

She looked up at him, miserable, but not so miserable, and he took her hand and shook it, his face composed again in its mask of irony.

But now she was in Hart Crane, writing, or trying to write, and all at once the Japanese woman came back to her, the sad doomed heroine drinking in death, the surf yellow in the sick light, her babies lost and gone forever. She had it, the whole scene, and the words were on her lips, at her fingertips, when the first flash of lightning snatched at the trees. At the same moment she became aware of the breeze. Pregnant and cool, it shook the screens and toyed with the papers on her desk. Ruth couldn't resist it. She pushed back the typewriter and got up to stand at the window and watch the sky deepen overhead. For a long moment she stood there, watching the branches heave and the leaves fan from green to gray and back again, and then something stirred in the deepest recess of her stomach and she thought of lunch.

That stirring was her internal clock. Each day between twelve and one, Owen Birkshead, the inveterate Boy Scout, would slip up on each of the cottages, his tread as light as a Mohican's, a cat's, a ghost's, and hang a lunch pail on the hook beside the door. He played a little game, striving for silence and invisibility so as not to disturb the artists at work, and Ruth played her own little game with him. She waited till her stomach informed her of the hour and then she sat frozen over her typewriter, her ears perked, waiting for the telltale creak of the lunch bucket on its hook or the odd crunch of leaf or twig. And then she would turn, smiling radiantly, and call out "Hello, Owen!" with all the forced cheer of a sitcom housewife. Sometimes she caught him, sometimes she didn't.

Yesterday had been odd. Not only hadn't she caught him, but there was no lunch. From the first warning rumble of her digestive tract to its increasingly outraged burbles and yelps, she got up every ten minutes throughout the long afternoon to check the hook, only to find it hanging empty and forlorn. At dinner Owen insisted he'd delivered her lunch—and where was the insulated container, he wanted to know. Had an animal taken it perhaps? Had she looked in the bushes round the place? She'd wagged a finger at him, conscious that Peter Anserine, nose in book, book in hand, was listening. "Don't give me that, Owen," she'd said, teasing him, "you screwed up. Admit it. In twenty years no artist has gone hungry at Thanatopsis House—and now *this!*" She held a good long hiss on the final syllable and then laughed.

Owen reddened. He was forty, looked like Samuel Beckett, right down to the combative nose and stiff brush cut, and he was as meticulous as a drill sergeant—a gay drill sergeant, if such a combination exists. "I delivered it," he insisted. "I distinctly remember it. *Distinctly.*"

It was no big deal. But she ordered her day around that lunch— and it was a good lunch too, pâté, crab salad, sandwiches of smoked turkey or provolone with roasted peppers, homegrown tomatoes, fruit, a Thermos of iced tea, real silver and a linen napkin. Before it was the Calvary of the morning; after, the naked cross of the afternoon, winding down to the resurrection and ascension of cocktail hour. Now she wondered, with a sharp pang, if the storm would keep him away, if there was some arcane and venerable rule that forbade cottage lunches during electrical storms, and she had a vision of her fellow artists gathered over a sumptuous spread in the big house and lifting their glasses to the storm that crashed romantically at the windows.

It was at that moment, the moment in which she saw the lifted glasses and glowing faces, that the storm broke. Lightning lit the room; the ground shifted beneath her feet. And then the rain came, combing through the treetops with a whoosh, a sharp smell of the earth and wet rank vegetation running before it, the roof and eaves and screens suddenly alive with it. A second concussion shook the cottage, then a third, and her papers were tumbled to the floor. She rushed for the windows, first the one before the desk, then the one in the corner by the fireplace, and then—she stopped dead.

There was someone on the porch.

A shadow flew across the screen door, there was the dull glint of a lunch bucket, and she cried out. He stopped then and she saw him as he was that night on Peagler Sound, his face splotched with welts and scratches, the red clay of his wet hair, his eyes startled and rinsed out. He saw her. Their eyes met. And then he started back, the lunch bucket cradled in his arms, as slick and wet and glistening as a newborn baby.

Hog Hammock

. . . .

ON THE DAY AFTER HE'D JUMPED SHIP AND CONTEMPLATED THE SMALL matter of his own extinction on the breast of the black heaving Atlantic, Hiro Tanaka awoke in a matted tangle of marsh grass. The sun was high, and while he'd slept, exhausted, it had burned his face and hands and the soles of his feet. He was lying on his back in several inches of salt water, suspended above the muck by a pale white tapestry of roots. These were the roots of the marsh grass, *Spartina alterniflora*. If he had cut through them with the penknife he'd thought to shove back in his pocket prior to taking the plunge from the wingdeck of the *Tokachi-maru*, he would have found himself up to his neck in the ooze. But he wasn't thinking about the roots or the ooze or the penknife or the myriad thin seamless cuts the razor-edged blades of the grass had inflicted on him as he staggered ashore in the night. His thoughts, after the initial surprise of waking to birdsong and mudstink instead of rolling decks and Bunker C fumes, focused solely on his alimentary needs.

First off, he was thirsty. Or not merely thirsty, but maddened with the kind of implacable thirst that shrivels Joshua trees and lays waste to whole villages in Africa. He hadn't had so much as a sip of sweet water since old Kuroda had brought him the tin cup and his balls of rice two days earlier. Salt clung to the hairs of his nostrils and eyelashes, encrusted his tonsils and adenoids, choked off his throat like a pair of strangling hands. He felt as if he were gagging, choking to death, and a wave of panic broke over him. Suddenly he was on his hands and knees, the water cool on his wrists, the sun burning, and he was bringing up stomach acid and bile. The taste of it, astringent and sour, set his throat afire, and though he knew he shouldn't do it—he'd seen the movies, seen *Lifeboat* and *Mutiny on the Bounty*, knew that sea water made you go stark raving mad and was a prelude to cannibalism and autophagia and worse—he bent to the water and drank, drank till he felt bloated and sick. Then he flopped over on his back and lay flat and volitionless on his bed of roots, as the stirrings of his second vital need began to gnaw at him.

He'd been in the brig a week, and in that time he'd lost twenty pounds or more. The turtleneck swam on him, his wrists were like the knucklebones of a pig, his eyes had sunk into his head and his jowls had evaporated. Two balls of rice a day. It was inhuman, medieval, barbaric. And it had been, what—two days?—since he'd got even that. Lying there in the stinking grass beneath the alien sun of a wild and alien country, wet and exhausted and starving, he felt his consciousness pull apart like a piece of taffy, till he was thinking with his brain and his stomach both. While his brain took note of the vacancy of the sky and squared off the boundaries of his distress, his stomach spoke to him in the terms of sharpest denunciation. Cavernous and hollow, rumbling, gurgling and raging, it accused him with each futile contraction. He was a fool, an idiot, a shit-for-brains. Why, even at that moment he could be tucking in his napkin on the Japan Air flight to Narita, asking the flight attendant for a bit more rice, another morsel of Norwegian salmon, just a drop more *sake*, courtesy of the Japanese embassy. Of course, they'd be waiting for him at the airport with a set of handcuffs, half a dozen charges ranging from assault and battery to dereliction of duty, and a humiliation that knew no bounds—but could it be worse than this? His stomach spoke to him: What joy in dignity, in life even, without food?

Like most Japanese, Hiro regarded his stomach—his *hara*—as the center of his being, the source of all his physical and spiritual strength. If a westerner were to talk of people who are kindhearted or coldhearted, of heartbreak or heartease, a Japanese would modify the conceit to feature the stomach—in his eyes, a far more vital organ. A heart-to-heart talk would be conducted stomach to stomach, *hara o awaseru*, while a blackhearted cad would be blackstomached, a *hara ga Kuroi hito*. Two inches beneath the navel lies the *kikai tanden*, the spiritual center of one's body. To release the *ki* or spirit in the act of *hara-kiri* is to release it from the belly, the guts, the only organ that counts.

For Hiro, though, the *hara* took on an even more exaggerated importance, for he lived to eat. Harassed at school, tormented on the playground, he took solace in the pastry shop, the noodle emporium and ice cream stand, feeding his strength and determination even as he quieted the cravings of his gut. In time, eating became his sole sensual expression. Oh, he'd had the odd carnal encounter with bar hostesses and prostitutes, but he'd never enjoyed it much, never been in love—he was only twenty, after all—and life offered only work, sleep and food. And food was what he needed now. Desperately. But what could he do? He'd been in the water for eight hours, thrashing at the waves like a marathon swimmer, and now he was too exhausted even to hold his head up. He thought vaguely of chewing a bit of marsh grass to assuage the storm in his gut, and then he closed his eyes on the image of old Kuroda's shirt and the lingering loss of his last two balls of rice.

When he awoke again the sun was dipping into the treetops behind him. At first he was disoriented, the erasure of sleep giving way to color, movement and the reek of mud, but the water brought him back: he was in America, in the U.S. of A., starving to death, and the tide was coming in. He felt it warm against his chin, his shoulders, the swell of his abdomen. With an effort, he pushed himself up on his elbows. He was feeling dizzy. The girdle of black tape cut at his flesh and he felt a sharp throb in the shin of his left leg—had he banged it against the underside of the boat when those butter-stinkers attacked him in the dark?

He didn't know. He didn't care. All he knew was that he had to get up. Had to move. Had to find a human habitation, slip through the window like a ghost and locate one of the towering ubiquitous refrigerators in which Americans keep the things they like to eat. He was conjuring up the image of that generic refrigerator stuffed with the dill pickles, Cracker Jack and sweating sacks of meat the Americans seemed to thrive on, when he became aware of a subtle but persistent pressure on the inside of his right thigh. He froze. There, perched on his torn pantleg and studying the sunburned flesh of his inner thigh with a gourmand's interest, was a small glistening purple-backed crab. It was, he saw, about the size of a mashed ball of rice.

He was going to eat that crab, he knew it.

For a long moment he watched it, afraid to move, his hand tensed at his side. The crab hunched there, unaware, water burbling through its lips—*were* those its lips?—and combing the stalks of its eyes with a single outsize claw. Hiro thought of the crab rolls his grandmother used to make, white flaking meat and rice and cucumber, and before he knew it he had the thing, a frenzy of snapping claws and kicking legs, and it was in his mouth. The shell was hard and unpleasant—it was like chewing plastic or the brittle opaque skin of fluorescent tubes—but there was moisture inside and there was the thin salty pulp of the flesh, and it invigorated him. He sucked the bits of shell, ground them between his teeth and swallowed them. Then he looked for another crab.

There was none in sight. But a grasshopper, green of back and with a fat yellow abdomen, made the mistake of alighting on his shirt. In a single motion he snatched it to his mouth and swallowed it, and even as he swallowed it, his *hara* screamed for more. Suddenly he was moving, stumbling through the stiff high grass, oblivious to the slashing blades that cut at his feet and shins, his hands and arms and face. He moved as if in a trance, the olfactory genius that had visited him at sea come back again with a vengeance.

Dictatorial and keen, it led him by the nose, led him across a snaking inlet and into the shadow of the moss-hung trees at the edge of the marsh. He smelled water there—old water, stale and dirty water, the standing water of swamps and drains and ditches—but water all the same . . . and way beyond it, at the periphery of his senses, he caught a single faint electrifying whiff of fat sizzling in the pan.

. . .

IT WAS THE GOLDEN HOUR OF THE DAY, THE SUN GONE SOFT AS A big dab of butter, and Olmstead White, the grandson of the son of a slave who was the son of a slave who was a free man of the Ibo tribe in West Africa, was fixing supper. He was sixty-eight years old, his limbs as dry and sinewy as jerky, his face baked hard by the morning sun flashing off the sea. He'd been born, raised and schooled on Tupelo Island, and in all his life he hadn't been to the mainland more than two dozen times. His garden stood tall with corn and staked tomato plants, he raised hogs, fished and crabbed and shrimped and oystered, and he did odd jobs for the white people at Tupelo Shores Estates when he needed a bit of pocket money for a chew or a drink or a new battery for the vanilla-colored transistor radio that brought him the Braves games in the cool of the evening. His brother, Wheeler, with whom he'd lived through all the mornings, afternoons and evenings of all his bachelor days, lay six months buried in the family plot out back of the garden.

On this evening, while the Braves game whispered huskily through the tinny speaker, Olmstead White sliced a cucumber and tomato, fixed a side dish of poke greens and was deep-frying a dozen sweet fresh oysters, shucked and floured and dipped in corn-meal and cayenne pepper. He wasn't thinking of Wheeler partic-ularly, or of his nephew Royal, Eulonia's boy, with whom he sometimes watched the hilarious antics of MTV late into the night—oh, the haircuts, he loved the haircuts—nor was he paying much attention to the announcer's dead and buried voice as the Braves blew yet another one. He was thinking nothing, really, his mind in a state of suspended animation as the grease crackled, the birds called in the trees and the screens glowed with the sun. As usual, and without thinking, he prepared a small plate for Wheeler. Later, in the twilight, when Gant and Murphy and Thomas and the rest of the bush leaguers had rolled over and played dead against the indestructible New York Mets, he would set the dish on his brother's grave and retrieve the empty one from the night before.

Like his friends and neighbors at Hog Hammock, Olmstead White spoke in the Gullah dialect of his ancestors, a dialect rich in borrowings from the Hausa, Wolof, Kimbundu and Ibo of West Africa. Along with the dialect came the dim linguistic memory of that faraway continent and the tribal rites and superstitions that had bloomed there in the eternal days. Olmstead White was deeply superstitious, as who wouldn't be in a world without reason or explanation, a world seething with spirits and hexes and voices in the night? He believed in haunts and specters, believed in hoodoo and juju and spells and curses and hags who put the mouth on you and made you wilt like a stalk of celery left out in the sun. He did his best to placate Wheeler's spirit with gifts of clothing, a deck of cards, the odd magazine and a choice bit of his evening meal, each and every night. The plate was always on the ground the next morning, and it was always licked clean. Was it the raccoons, the opossums, the hogs, the hounds, the crows that gorged on that food? Maybe so. But only Wheeler knew for sure.

Well, the bacon fat sizzled and popped and the sweet oyster smell made a fancy Charleston kind of potted-palm restaurant out of the two-room clapboard shack—painted blue and with a blue pyramid slashed on the chimney to ward off hags—and Olmstead White thought nothing and the stirring fork moved in his hand as if by its own volition. The room was hushed. A fly buzzed at the screen. It was then, as the fly struggled and the world slowed down like a worn old carousel, that he came to himself and sensed another presence inhabiting the hazy space of the room. His back was to the door, his hand stirring, the radio whispering and Dale Murphy going down on strikes and nothing had changed, nothing at all, but as sure as he knew he was alive and breathing he knew there was someone—or something—there with him.

He moved like a man coming out of a coma, like Br'er Rabbit stuck to the tarbaby, his hands trembling as he remembered Varner Arms and how he was found dead in his own kitchen, blood spattered on the walls and hag's hair—wild black hanks of it—scattered across the linoleum like a greeting from the darkest pit. His shoulders were rigid, his neck like a flagpole planted deep in the earth. But slowly, ever so slowly, he swiveled his gray-bristling chin till he presented his profile and one wild eye to whatever or whoever stood in the doorway behind him.

What he saw there, through the contracting lens of that one wild eye, froze his heart. What he saw was Wheeler, his brother Wheeler, risen from the grave and with his skin gone the color of leaf mulch, Wheeler, wearing the red cotton button-up shirt and denim overalls he'd left draped over the hard slab of the tombstone not three days ago. "Wheeler!" he cried, jerking around awkwardly and throwing up his arms in extenuation, "I didden mean it, I didden, I never should of called you them low mizzable things on the day you done pass on, but I—" and then he stopped cold. This wasn't Wheeler standing there in his kitchen with a look on his face like he'd just gone and taken a dump in his own pants . . . this wasn't Wheeler with the overalls pinched round the gut and stuck halfway up his shins and the slanting eyes and iron-straight hair hanging in his face . . . this was, this was some kind of Chinaman or something. But what was a Chinaman doing in Olmstead White's kitchen in Hog Hammock on Tupelo Island? It mystified him. It baffled him. In the end, it upset him more than any six hags and apparitions could ever have. "Who you be?" he roared.

For his part, Hiro was no less shocked than the black man who stood twitching and jerking before him. In a delirium he'd staggered out of the salt marsh and up onto solid ground, his dead mother and his lost father dancing round him like fairies, root beer floats and slurpies and stone jugs of cold *sake* in their fluttering hands, and he'd found a rain puddle there, nothing more than diluted mud really, and he'd buried his face in it. By then the smell of cooking fat was overpowering and near and he pushed himself up and went for it at a trot. That was when he'd found the gravestones—crude rock slabs poking up out of the weeds like something he'd seen in a spaghetti Western. The first of the markers caught him in the shin; the second grazed the side of his face as he went down. When he untangled his feet and pushed himself up, he saw the shirt and pants, an overturned plate, a string of dried peppers and a weathered deck of cards. He didn't think, couldn't think, the smell of deep-fried fish—oysters, yes, oysters—driving all else before it, and in half a minute he'd exchanged his torn and filthy clothes for the shirt and overalls. He was hopping, actually hopping as if in some child's game, as if he were in a sack race, as he shrugged into the overalls and slashed through the garden toward that supreme and dictatorial smell.

But now, here he was, in strange stolen clothes in a stranger's house and the stranger was shouting at him. Worse: the stranger was a black man, a Negro, and he knew, as every Japanese does, that Negroes were depraved and vicious, hairier, sweatier and even more potent than their white counterparts, the *hakujin*. They were violent and physical, they were addicted to drugs and they thought only with their sexual organs. He'd seen one once, in the streets of Tokyo, a *bēsubōru* player named Clarence Hawkins, first baseman for the Hiroshima Carp. An awesome man, like a walking statue. But he had no heart—no *hara*—and he wasn't a team player. Here was a man who could have hit a home run with every swing of the bat and yet he refused to take practice with the others, refused the calisthenics and the drill of the thousand fungoes and running in the outfield and the cold baths that demonstrated team spirit and a will to win and guts and determination. The pitchers gave him nothing to hit and the umpires called everything a strike, even if it bounced, and within the year he was back in America. That was a Negro. And here was another, shouting at him in his incomprehensible gibberish.

"Shipwreck!" Hiro shouted back, waving his arms in imitation of the *gaijin*. "I am starving. Please, I beg you, give me something to eat!"

Olmstead White heard him, but for all the good it did, Hiro might as well have been talking Japanese. "Somesing eat" was all that came through, and even that didn't register, so alien was Hiro's accent—and even if it had, the sequel would have been no different. Feeling trapped in his own kitchen, feeling scared and embarrassed and angry, delivered from the haunts and hags and into the hands of a stranger—an Asiotic Chinaman, no less—Olmstead White reacted in the only way he could. Before him, on the table, lay the butcher knife, the one he kept honed for punching through the stiff bristle of his Christmas hog and the soft underbelly of opossum and deer. He looked at Hiro, looked at the knife, and snatched it up.

Hiro could sense that the situation had deteriorated. The veins stood out in the Negro's neck and the whites of his eyes were swollen. He kept shouting and there were flecks of spittle on his lips. It was obvious that he hadn't understood a word. And now he had a knife in his hand, the blade ugly with use. Behind him, the oysters sent up their ambrosial aroma.

It looked bad. It did. Hiro should have turned and fled, he knew that, and he knew too that the blade was sharp and the old man tenacious, a wild beast surprised in its lair. But the oysters exerted their influence, and he recalled the words of Jōchō: *A true samurai must never seem to flag or lose heart. He must push on courageously as though sure to come out on top. Otherwise he is utterly useless.* "Somesing eat," he repeated.

What happened next came as a surprise to them both. Untended, the oysters smoldered, calcified, approached critical mass; in the next instant they burst into flame with a sudden startling rush of air while a thick black plume of smoke billowed up from the pan, growing thicker and blacker even as it rose. Instinctively, both antagonists went for the pan. In the process, Hiro, who despite the loss of twenty pounds was still a broad-beamed young man, jostled the elderly Olmstead White, and Olmstead White, suffering from a touch of arthritis in his right hip, lost his balance, and in losing his balance, thrust out a hand to brace himself. Unfortunately, that hand didn't make contact with the tabletop or the corner of the stove. Instead, it came down squarely in the center of the pan of flaming grease and incinerated oysters, and Olmstead White let out a howl that would have unraveled the topknot of even the staunchest of samurai. The pan tottered a moment on the edge of the stove and then slammed to the floor in an explosion of flame.

In an instant, the shack was ablaze. Jaws of flame chewed at the floorboards, the walls, devoured the dirty yellow curtains. Hiro took to his feet. He was out the door, across the porch and into the crude graveyard before he caught himself. What was he doing? Had he gone mad? He couldn't leave the old Negro in there to burn to death, could he? He turned, Jōchō's injunction on his lips—you had to act, without hesitation, or you were lost, disgraced, a coward—and started back for the house. It was then that the Negro appeared in the smoke-shrouded doorway, his hair singed, his right hand the color of steamed lobster. Hiro stopped again. What stopped him this time, what deflated the balloon of his resolve and rendered Jōchō meaningless, was the object cradled in the old man's good arm. For Olmstead White stood there on the porch, the shack an inferno behind him, fumbling with a double-barreled shotgun and a box of bright yellow shells.

And then Hiro was running again, running from the thunder of the shotgun and the hiss of the flames and the shouts and cries of the aroused neighborhood. All at once there were people everywhere, screaming, running, crying, scrambling over one another like ants pouring out of an anthill. He dodged a fat old woman with a face like a Nō mask and veered away from a pair of startled boys in dirty shorts, and then he was cutting through a dusty yard, scattering chickens and hogs and howling brown babies in white plastic diapers. Running, he glanced over his shoulder and saw the flaming shack in the distance above a sea of black faces and gyrating limbs. It was a scene that made him catch his breath, a scene of utter horror and depravity, dusky faces and sharp white teeth, the cannibals of his boyhood picture books dancing round their hideous cookfire. Hiro ran, no hunger worth this, ran into the deepening shadows and through the muck and puddles and the strange tropical vegetation, ran till at long last the shouts and the curses and the barking of the dogs fell away from him like so much sloughed skin.

.   .   .

ALL THE NEXT DAY HE CROUCHED IN THE BUSHES, CHEWING ROOTS and leaves and the odd handful of sour berries, while voices flared round him and dogs whined and grunted at the leash. Vicious, vengeful, outraged, they were hunting him, these black men of the bush, looking to flush him out, settle the score, lynch him as they were lynched by the *hakujin*. At daybreak a grim-looking Negro with red-flecked eyes came within five paces of where he lay trembling in a thicket of holly and palmetto. The man had a gun, and he was so close Hiro could have reached out and unlaced his shoes. He was terrified. He was miserable. He was hungry. Day bled into night and he fumbled through the dark bush, putting as much distance as he could between himself and the porch lights and barking dogs.

The truth is, he didn't know where he was or where he was going. All he knew was that he was starving and that the *gaijin* authorities would be after him and that if they caught him he'd be imprisoned and sent home in disgrace. He wandered aimlessly, his feet battered and bleeding, mosquitoes and ticks and chiggers and gnats drawing yet more blood, venomous reptiles lying in wait for him. He was a city kid, an urban dweller, raised by his grandmother in the serried flats of Yokohama. Of the forests and mountains of Japan he knew little, and he knew even less about the wilderness of America. He knew only that it was vast and untamed and seething with bear, lion, wolf and crocodile. Unseen wings beat round his head in the darkness. Shrill voices screeched through the hollows of the night. Something bellowed in the swamp.

On the third day—or was it the fourth?; he'd lost count—he

staggered out of the woods in a swirl of mosquitoes, the too-tight shirt and overalls tattered and stiff with dried mud, and found himself on a blacktop road. It was a miracle. Pavement. The smell of it alone reassured him. If he followed it, he reasoned, the road would lead him to civilization, to some tidy little farmhouse where he could risk showing himself and beg for food in exchange for doing odd jobs, maybe sleep in the barn like in those black-and-white movies with the clanking jalopies and the smiling long-nosed old ladies in bonnets and dresses that hung to the floor. Or he could find a diner or a McDonald's like the ones in Tokyo—he thought of the little green bills he'd tucked away in Jōchō's book, buried deep now in the deep pocket of the Negro's overalls—and he could purchase a meal, fries and a Big Mac, Chicken McNuggets and a shake. But he couldn't just stroll on down the road as if he were shopping for shoes in the Ginza. They'd catch him in a minute, the Negroes, the police, and how could he explain what had happened in that shack and what the smell of those oysters could do to a desperate man?

The sun arced over the road before him. He looked to his left, expecting barns and silos, rowhouses, streetlights, taxicabs, and there was nothing but blacktop and trees; he looked to his right and saw more blacktop and more trees. For a long moment he stood there, rooted to the spot with indecision. And then he flipped an imaginary coin and began working his way up the road to the right, not daring to walk along the blacktop itself, but tearing through the brambles and kudzu in the ditch that paralleled it. He had no plan, really, had never had one, not since he'd run afoul of Chiba and Unagi, anyway. He thought vaguely of heading inland, to New York or Miami or San Francisco, where he could lose himself among the mobs of *gaijin* mutts, where he could be, for the first time in his life, like anyone else. But geography—the geography of the West, at any rate—was not one of his strong suits. He did know that the Port of Savannah was in Georgia and that Georgia was in the South where the Negroes harvested cotton and the *hakujin* made them use separate toilets and drinking fountains, but he had no idea where he was in relation to Beantown or the Windy City, and he didn't have even a clue that he was stranded on an island and that the only way off it was via Ray Manzanar's ferry and that Ray Manzanar was related to half the people on the island and knew the other half as well as he knew his own kith and kin. Mercifully oblivious, faint with hunger and too weak even to lift a hand to brush away the horde of mosquitoes that settled on him like a second skin, Hiro forged on.

After a time, the thicket ahead began to brighten with sun, and the tangle of branches became noticeably thinner. He paused, up to his ankles in the standing water of the ditch, and peered through a chink in the wall of vegetation. There was something unnatural, something red, just ahead of him and to the left, something bright and comforting and familiar. He moved closer. What he saw made his heart leap up. There, in the window of a freshly painted clapboard building just off the road, a bewitching and seductive red neon sign spoke to him in a universal tongue: COCA-COLA, it announced, COCA-COLA, and he went faint with gastric epiphany.

He lurched forward, as overcome as he'd been by the scent of the Negro's fateful oysters, beyond all sense and caring, till at the last moment he caught himself. All at once he dropped down with a grunt and hunkered low in the water. He was a mess. The stolen clothes were in tatters, he reeked as if he'd been dead a week, he was filthy and cut and torn in a hundred places. And his face—he was a Japanese, or half a Japanese—and they'd see that in a second and they'd know who he was and what he'd done and then the police would come and he'd be thrown in jail and brutalized by the half-breeds and child molesters and patricides that infested the dark *gaijin* cells like mold. COCA-COLA, flashed the sign, COCA-COLA. But what could he do?

Cautiously, he emerged from the ditch and sat heavily in a clump of waist-high grass. There was no one in sight, not a car in the gravel lot, and from this angle he could see that the door of the shop stood wide open. He had to get cleaned up, had to disguise himself somehow, had to get in there and buy out the store before someone showed up. Yes. All right. He would wash the mud from his clothes as best he could, and from his feet too. But when he glanced down at his feet and calves he saw that they were nearly black with some sort of clinging shapeless things—sea slugs, they looked like. He had never encountered leeches and didn't know that they were sucking his blood—or rather that they secreted an anticoagulant so that his heart pumped blood into them, as if they were extensions of his own veins and arteries—nor did he realize that in casually peeling them off he risked dislodging their mouth parts and causing an infection that could suppurate, turn gangrenous and threaten the limb itself. No, he merely pulled them off, wistfully regarding the plump writhing morsels of their compact bodies—he'd always had a weakness for sea slugs—before dropping them back into the ditch. He didn't need them. Food—real food— was in sight.

Next, he stripped off his clothing and attempted to wash the overalls in the ditch. The red shirt was beyond hope, and so he tore off a strip of it and wrapped it around his head, Ninja style, hoping it would help disguise him. Then he wrung the overalls out, shrugged back into them (no mean feat—it was like pulling on a wetsuit six sizes too small), and turned to the pages of Jōchō. The bills were still there, along with the cracked and bleached photo of his father. He smoothed them out, wondering at the arcane codes and symbols—a pyramid? wasn't that supposed to be Egyptian?— only half believing that this was the real article. It was so—so whimsical, like the play money of a children's game. There was a picture of a man in a wig on three of the notes, and he was wearing a high collar and a benign expression. THIS NOTE IS LEGAL TENDER FOR ALL DEBTS, PUBLIC AND PRIVATE, Hiro read. FEDERAL RESERVE NOTE. THE UNITED STATES OF AMERICA.

He shrugged. Akio Ajioka, the BR aboard ship and his only friend in the world, had traded him the bills in exchange for two bottles of Suntory whiskey and a stack of thumbed-over *manga*. "This is the real thing, mate," Akio had said with a grin, "this is what they use in Times Square, Broadway and Miami Beach."

Akio wouldn't lie to him, he knew that. After a moment he stood and smoothed out the wrinkles in his pants. Clutching the bills in one hand and Jōchō in the other, he crossed the gravel lot to the store.

Inside, it was cool and fresh-smelling, lit only by the sunlight filtering through the windows. Hiro saw racks of food, junk food mostly, in garish plastic packages and brightly colored cans. There was a freezer, and against the back wall, two glowing huge coolers full of beer and soda, a shrine to thirst. Behind the cash register, a young woman—very young, sixteen, seventeen maybe—sat nursing a baby and watching him out of a pair of wide green eyes. "Kin Ah help y'all?" she said.

Food. Hiro wanted food. And drink. But he didn't know how to respond. *Kinahhelpyall* didn't compute, not at all, but he wanted desperately to ingratiate himself, get through the exchange and then bow his way out the door, vanish into the bushes and gorge himself till he burst. He knew he had to have his wits about him, had to demonstrate his savoir-faire, convince her that he was all right, that he belonged and knew the ways of the *gaijin* as well as they knew them themselves. Already the pressure was killing him. He was sweating. He couldn't seem to control his facial muscles. "Somesing eat," he said, trying to sound casual, and he snatched a loaf of bread and a bag of nacho chips from the shelf, all the while bowing and bowing again.

The girl took the baby from her breast—he saw the little fists clench, the feet kick, caught a glimpse of the pink wet nipple and the pink wet puckered mouth. "Bobby," she called toward the back, "we got a customer."

Hiro cradled the bread and nacho chips to his chest. He moved ponderously down the aisle, the wet overalls pinching his crotch, bowing automatically. He was moving toward the cooler, his tongue dry as chalk. Be cool, he told himself. Act natural.

The girl had set the baby down in its crib behind the counter and was leaning lazily over the cash register. "Y'all must be a toorist?" she said with rising inflection.

Toor-ist, toor-ist, Hiro thought, swinging open the door of the cooler, the miraculous refrigerated draft on his face, the six-pack of Coke in hand. What was she saying? He hadn't a clue, but he knew he had to answer, knew he had to say something or he was doomed.

It was then that Bobby stepped out of the back room, wiping his hands on an apron. Bobby was nineteen, as fair and beautifully proportioned as an archangel, but with an IQ so low it prevented him from unfurling his wings. He had trouble with simple sums and he couldn't read the newspaper or punch the cash register. His job was to stock the shelves and watch Bobby Jr. whenever Cara Mae had a customer. He stood there in the doorway, blinking at Hiro.

Say something, Hiro told himself, say something, and all at once he had an inspiration. Burt Reynolds, Clint Eastwood—what would they say? Americans began any exchange of pleasantries with a string of curses, anyone knew that—and even if he hadn't known it, even if he were an innocent, he'd seen Eastwood in action. "Mothafucka," he said, bowing to the girl as he shuffled forward to dump his booty on the counter. And to the bewildered boy, in the most amenable tone he could summon, he observed: "Cock-sucka, huh?"

The girl said nothing. She remained motionless behind the cash register, her jaws poised over a tiny pink wad of chewing gum. The boy blinked twice, then scurried across the room and snatched up the baby as if it were in danger. All the while, Hiro grabbed for Slim Jims, Twinkies, anything, and built a mound of cans and bottles and bright shiny packages on the counter before him.

The girl rang up the purchases. "Ten seventy-three," she said, and her tone was icy.

"Shitcan," Hiro said, grinning now and bowing again, as he produced the four bills and laid them out on the counter. "Toilet. Make my day, huh?"

The girl crushed the gum between her teeth. Her eyes had narrowed. Her voice hit him like a slap in the face. "This is only eight."

"Only eight?" he repeated. He was bewildered.

She let an exasperated hiss of breath escape her. The baby, pressed to his father's shoulder, began to fuss. From outside came the sound of squealing brakes, and Hiro glanced up to see a gleaming new oversized pickup nosing its way up to the store.

"Ah need two seventy-three," she said, "more."

All at once Hiro understood. The little green *gaijin* bills were insufficient. He'd have to part with something and he needed it all, needed everything in the store and more. Didn't they realize? Couldn't they see he was starving? Outside, the engine coughed and died. "Some," he said, pushing away a package or two.

"Je-sus," the girl said. "Ah'll be goddamned."

And then the boy spoke for the first time. "You a foreigner or somethin'?" he said.

Someone had come into the store. Hiro could feel the heavy tread on the floorboards and he watched the girl's face brighten. "Hi ya, Sax," she said.

Hiro didn't dare look up. It could have been the chief of police, the Coast Guard, one of the long-noses from Immigration Akio had told him about. Heart pounding, he concentrated on the girl's hands as she separated his things, put some of them in a brown paper sack and held out three small coins to him. He took the coins and bowed again. "Thank you, thank you," he said, and in his gratitude, his relief, his joy at the prospect of the feast awaiting him and his redemption from the slow death of the swamps, he slipped into Japanese. "*Dōmo*," he said. "*Dōmo sumimasen*."

The girl gaped at him. And then he turned, hurrying, and saw the tall *gaijin* with the colorless hair and cold ceramic eyes, the one who'd tried to run him down with his boat, and in the next instant he was out the door, tucking the package under his arm like a football and bolting for the woods in a mad desperate headlong flight. He never paused, never hesitated, though the butter-stinker was out in the lot behind him shouting, "Hey! Wait a minute! Come back here, will you? I don't . . . I-just-want-to-help-you!"

Help me, Hiro thought, the blood singing in his ears as he flung himself into the ditch and staggered through the scum and into the waist-deep quagmire and the cover of the trees beyond, yes, sure, help me. He knew them. Americans. They killed each other over dinner, shot one another for sport, mugged old ladies in the street.

Help like that he didn't need.

The Squarest People
in the World

. . . .

THERE WERE NO TWO WAYS ABOUT IT: HE WAS GOING TO HAVE TO
go down there. Not that he wanted to. Anything but. The thought
of driving to Tupelo Island in this heat—and with a broken-down
air conditioner no less—so he could stand around in the haze in-
terrogating a bunch of snuff-dipping inbred cracker morons who
could barely wheeze "uh-huh" or "naw" without growing roots and
bark, was enough to make him wish he was back in L.A. Or almost.

Detlef Abercorn stood at the window gazing out at the flat dead
sky that hung over Savannah like an old dishrag. It was a gray
humid high-summer morning, sunless but stifling. He hadn't read
the paper yet, had barely blown the steam off his first cup of coffee,
and already his shirt was wet through. Ten minutes earlier he'd
breezed into the office, blown a kiss to Ginger, the new receptionist
with the freckled cleavage and congenitally parted lips, switched
on his monitor, taken a perfectly innocent sip of coffee—and
watched an IAADA alert claw its way across the screen.

An IAADA—Illegal Alien, Armed, Dangerous and Amok—was
the highest priority designation in the INS electronic mail file. In
Los Angeles, the innermost circle of INS hell, IAADAs went out
routinely, what with Guatemalans shooting at Salvadorans, Hmong
tribesmen microwaving dogs, Turks and Iranians setting fire to

carpet stores and the like—but here, in the mossy old somnolent backwater of Savannah, they were unheard of. The place wasn't exactly a hotbed of international intrigue or even a semi-major port. Nothing ever happened here. Ever. That's why he'd transferred.

It was the Nip, of course—he corrected himself: the Japanese—who'd jumped ship the week before. He'd been monitoring the situation from the beginning—he'd interviewed the ship's captain over the phone and obtained and filed a copy of the Coast Guard report—but it was no big deal. They'd classified the AWOL sailor as IA—Illegal Alien—and left it at that. If he made it to shore, the yokels would have him in the county jail before he could shit twice, and if he gave them any trouble they'd string him up and skin him like a rabbit. But then the report came in that he had made it to shore—there were eyewitnesses, a couple from the artists' colony he'd attacked in Peagler Sound—and Abercorn had dug deeper. From the Chief Engineer of the Japanese ship—a desiccated old fart about a hundred and twelve years old who looked as if he'd been hatched from an egg—he learned that the man at large was armed with a knife and had attacked half the ship's crew before throwing himself over the rail, and so he'd had the regional head upgrade the designation to IAAD, Armed and Dangerous. Still, it was no big deal. A Nip in Georgia? These people ate weasel, picked their teeth with their feet, grew right up out of the ground like weeds, like kudzu; the poor dumb Nip—Japanese—wouldn't last a day, six hours even. Abercorn was sure of it. And then the weekend had intervened and he made the rounds of the discos, drank too much, got lucky, learned most of everything about a girl named Brenda who used blusher on her breasts, and forgot all about the AWOL Nip on Tupelo Island.

But now things had gotten out of hand. An IAADA. He sighed. He'd been looking forward to a long quiet morning with the new le Carré and a pot of fresh-dripped Folgers, with nothing, absolutely nothing to do, except listen to the girls in the main office type up the odd student visa and whisper about the scandalous sex lives of people they barely knew. Yes. And now this. He turned wearily to his desk, lit a cigarette and typed in a request for more information. The screen immediately began to fill:

TANAKA HIRO. JAPANESE NATIONAL. BORN KYOTO 6/12/70. MOTHER TANAKA SAKURAKO DECEASED 12/24/70. FATHER UN-KNOWN. LAST KNOWN RESIDENCE GRANDMOTHER TANAKA WAKAKO 74 YAMAZATO-CHO NAKA-KU YOKOHAMA. ARMED AND DANGEROUS AND AMOK TUPELO ISLAND MID-GEORGIA COAST AD-VISE EXTREME CAUTION. ESCAPED BRIG AND ASSAULTED OFFICERS TOKACHI-MARU FREIGHTER JAPANESE REGISTRATION 1300 HOURS 20 JULY. UNPROVOKED ATTACKS ON EYEWITNESSES LIGHTS SAXBY DERSHOWITZ RUTH WHITE OLMSTEAD FIRST DEGREE BURNS ARSON HOUSE FIRE TOTAL LOSS.

Jesus, was he setting fire to houses now? This was bad news. Worse than bad. The guy must be a psychopath, he thought, a terrorist, a Japanese Manson. And it got worse: he'd been at large a week and already the list of sightings filled the screen. He was everywhere, from Peagler Sound to Hog Hammock and Tupelo Shores Estates and back again, popping up out of the bushes like a jack-in-the-box, terrifying old ladies and stirring up the war veterans and coon hunters till gunfire crackled across the island in an unholy storm from morning till night. He'd cursed a bunch of people at the local grocery, filched three pairs of ladies' undergarments from a clothesline at the artists' colony and made off with a tin dish of dogfood the sheriff himself had set out on his back porch. It had to stop. Detlef Abercorn knew what was expected of him.

The thing was, he'd had no experience with anything like this. He'd spent his twelve years in L.A. raiding sweatshops in Eagle Rock and chasing skinny busboys around tofu-spattered kitchens in Chinatown. What did he know about swamps and hollows—what did he know about Georgia, for that matter? Sure, it was up to the local authorities to make the nab, but he was supposed to be the expert, he was supposed to cast the net, advise them—advise them, what a joke: he could barely make out a word they said down here. Even worse, he'd never had a problem, not that he could remember, with the Japanese. Tongans, yes. Ecuadorians, Tibetans and Liberians, Bantu, Pakistanis and Sea Dyak, everybody and anybody. But not Japanese. They never entered the country illegally. Didn't want to. They figured they had it all and more over there, so why bother? Plenty of them came in to run factories and open banks and whatnot, but all that was done at the highest levels. And Detlef Abercorn didn't work at the highest levels.

No matter. An illegal was an illegal, and it would be his ass if he didn't catch him.

. . .

IT WAS RAINING BY THE TIME HE REACHED THE PARKING LOT. OF course, he thought, what else? The tires on his old battered turd-brown Datsun were bald as melons and the wipers were so frayed they might as well have been bottle brushes for all the good they did. It was going to be a rough trip.

Before it began, though, he had to swing by the apartment, cram his overnight bag with underwear, dental floss, SPF 30 maximum protection sunscreen, calamine lotion and a snakebite kit, dig his hip waders and rain slicker out of the trunk in the storage cage downstairs, and then find a Vietnamese grocery—*the* Vietnamese grocery, probably the only Vietnamese grocery in the whole slow-talking, tobacco-spitting, godforsaken state—on De Lesseps off Skidaway. He was going to rendezvous there with Lewis Turco, an ex-LURP and part-time special agent who'd lived in Borneo, Okinawa and the Pribilof Islands, and he was going to take Turco with him to help sniff out the amok Nip on Tupelo Island. Or rather, he would let Turco do the sniffing while he sequestered himself in the local motel with a couple six packs, John le Carré and the prospect of the upcoming four-game series between the Dodgers and the Braves.

The shirt didn't matter—it was sweat-soaked anyway—but still he wasn't prepared for the typhoon that hit him as he dashed across the lot to the car. By the time he got the door open he was wet right on through to the elastic band of his BVDs. There was no sense in even starting the car—he couldn't go anywhere till it eased up, not with these wipers—and he didn't relish the idea of bolting back to the office, where he'd just look ridiculous in front of Ginger and the other girls, not to mention the button-down types who saw to the main business of the place. They'd always looked at him as if he were a freak anyway, a kind of subspecies not much higher on the social scale than the odd refugee applying for a green card. So he just sat there, not daring even to turn on the radio for fear of running down the battery, fuming over this crazed, inconsiderate, raging pain in the ass of a Japanese Nip—he hated the son of a bitch already, hoped they tarred and feathered him and sent him home to Nagasaki or wherever in a box—and listening to the thousand tiny frustrated fists of the rain as they beat at the roof of the car.

In the end, he was over an hour late to pick up Turco, whom he'd never met and had only that morning spoken to for the first time on the phone. What complicated matters, after the rain had eased up and he'd gone home to pack his bag and dig out his waders, tape recorder, notebooks and the rest, was that he couldn't find the place. He'd only been in Savannah six months and he'd always been lousy with maps. There were all these one-way streets and this endless succession of old squares that you had to drive all the way around, each one, one after another, and they all looked alike. He finally found De Lesseps, but he couldn't locate the store, which, as it turned out, was stuck up in the ass end of an alley anyway. After he'd gone up and down the street twenty times he finally pulled up alongside a red-faced yokel at a stoplight and motioned for him to crank down his window. There was a strong, faintly astringent smell of freshly shucked oysters on the air, of sea sludge and fish scales and worse; the rain pattered down. "Tran Van Duc's Grocery," he shouted, "you have any idea where it is?"

The red-faced man leaned toward him. He was wearing a suit and his wispy blond hair was parted in the middle. He was fat, Abercorn saw now, bulbous, an elephant seal heaved up out of the sea and wedged, as a joke, into the impossibly narrow confines of the cab of his mini-truck. He mumbled something in a heavy accent that sounded like "Roy's hair" or "rye chair."

"I'm sorry," Abercorn said, trying his best to control his winning smile, the smile he wore like a necktie when he needed to, "but I didn't—rye chair?"

The man looked away in exasperation. Mist rose from the pavement. "Rye chair," the man repeated, turning back to Abercorn and pointing a thick finger to the towering, unmistakable, aniline red-on-yellow sign—TRAN VAN DUC—that hovered over the alley not fifteen paces from them. Then the light changed, and the man was gone.

The store was tiny, a central aisle of loosely stacked cans and two low wall-length freezers, and it smelled worse than the fish-stinking pavement outside. Abercorn pulled the door shut behind him and took in the entire place at a glance: a pair of shrunken ageless Asian faces staring up at him in horror, the cans of pickled this and salted that, the strange little fishes in frozen plastic envelopes, the dried spices and chilies and sauces no one would ever buy. He'd raided a hundred places just like it in Arcadia and Pacoima and San Pedro, and he knew that the two behind the counter had residence permits but the twenty in the basement didn't and he knew too that they had to be bringing in more than fish sauce to survive, but that was somebody else's problem. "I'm looking for Lewis Turco," he said.

Nothing. No reaction. He might just as well have been talking to himself, humming, singing, gargling, he might as well have been a dog or a monkey. The couple behind the counter—a man and a woman, he saw now—didn't flinch. They were holding their breath, controlling their heartbeat—their eyes didn't even blink. "Lewis Turco," he repeated, lingering over the syllables, "I-look-for-Lew-is-Tur-co."

"Yo," said a voice behind him, and a man in fatigues stepped out from behind the bead curtain at the back of the store. He was short—five-five or so, Abercorn guessed—and he wore a noncommital expression. His shoulders were too wide for his height and he had a weight lifter's build, strong in the chest and upper arms. He wore a beard and his long flat greasy blond hair was tied back with a leather thong. "Abercorn, right?" he said.

Detlef Abercorn was six-five, he wore his hair short, and at thirty-four he preserved the same lanky narrow-hipped build he'd grown into as the pitching ace of his high-school baseball team in Thousand Oaks, California. "Yes," he said, smiling, "and you're Lewis Turco."

Turco wasn't smiling. He sauntered up the aisle like a cowboy, each stride too long, too wide, sauntered as if he were sprinting up the side of a hill in slow motion, and then he halted abruptly at the counter, wheeled on the wooden couple and said something in a burst of what Abercorn took to be Vietnamese. They came to sudden life, as if they were wired, and the man ducked behind the counter to produce a tightly bound and visibly swollen Army-issue backpack, from the frame of which dangled an entrenching tool, a baton, a pair of handcuffs and several esoteric-looking devices Abercorn didn't recognize, while the woman handed over a cellophane package that appeared to contain some sort of foodstuff—dried meat or roots or something.

Just to hear himself, Abercorn said, "It's a bitch, huh?"—meaning the rain, Georgia, the INS and the rat-crazy, house-burning, Japanese son of a bitch holed up with the slugs and centipedes on funky, dripping, hopeless Tupelo Island.

Turco didn't respond. He'd shouldered the pack and taken the parcel of food from the woman, and now he was studying Abercorn with a cagey look. "Jesus," he said finally, "what happened to you, man—napalm, car wreck or what? Don't tell me you were born with that?"

Abercorn stiffened. He'd heard it all his life and all his life he'd been touchy about it—who wouldn't be? He was a good-looking guy, good bone structure, strong nose and chin, hair as thick as a teenager's. But he knew what Turco meant, knew what he'd had the bad grace to bring up—most people, anybody with any sensitivity, anyway, would have left it alone. What Turco was referring to were the white patches on his face and hands—a lot of people thought it was scar tissue or eczema or something, but it wasn't. There was nothing wrong with him, nothing at all, just that he had less pigment than normal, less melanin in his skin and hair. He'd been born an albino. Or part albino. His coloring was fair to begin with, but the albinism—or vitiligo, as the doctors called it—manifested itself in dead-white patches that mottled his entire body—even his hair. He'd been able to dye his hair, of course, but there was nothing he could do about his skin. And even that wouldn't have been so bad, but for his face. He'd got used to it now, but as a kid it used to drive him crazy—he looked as if he'd been splashed with paint. A rough oval, two inches across, framed his right eye and six paper-white blotches dribbled across his jaw, bleached the bridge of his nose and made his left ear glow in the dark. And his eyes, his eyes weren't blue or gray or green or brown: they were pink, like the eyes of a white rat or a guinea pig. "Beagle Boy," they called him in elementary school, and later, when he got taller and stronger and knocked them down with his big-league curveball, they called him "Whitey." But now he was an adult, and no one, ever, called him anything but Detlef.

He felt the eyes of the Vietnamese on him and the blood rose to his face. "What's it to you," he said, holding Turco's eyes, "I'm part albino, okay?"

Turco stood his ground, smiling now, smiling up at him with the serenity of a man who's never made a mistake in his life. He was taking his time. "Hey, no offense intended, man. It's like I've seen a couple dudes over there that caught it, their own people dropping the shit on them—typical fuck-up—it's like this jellied gasoline, right? Sticks to you like glue. But hey, if I'd known you were so sensitive about it—"

"I am not sensitive," Abercorn said, but even as he said it his voice rose to give him away.

In the car, while the wipers beat uselessly at the smear of rain and they settled in for the seventy-minute drive down to Tupelo

Island, Abercorn, not yet realizing that they'd have to wait three hours for the next ferry and that there were no motels on the island and never had been, began to soften a bit. He had to work with this guy, after all. And Turco was going to do all the grunt work while he, Abercorn, sat in the motel and coordinated things. "Listen," he said after a while, the tinny strains of some moronic country song whining through the speakers, "this Japanese guy. I mean, in L.A. we never had to deal with the Japanese. What do you think?"

Turco was chewing a stick of whatever it was the woman had given him. It was black and hard and had a forbidding alien smell to it. "Piece of cake," he said, chewing. "What you got to realize about the Nips is they're the squarest people in the world, I mean the hokiest, bar none. Shit, even the paddy Burmese are downtown compared to the Japs. They're all part of this big team, this like Eagle Scout thing where everybody fits in and works real hard and makes this perfect and totally unique society. Because they're superior to everybody else, they're purer—that's what they think. Nobody but Japanese in Japan. You fuck up, you let the whole race down."

Rain beat at the windshield. Turco gestured with the pungent black stick of whatever it was. "Even the far-out types, the rebels, the punks with the orange hair and the leather jackets—and there are precious few of them, believe me—even they can't break the mold. You know how they get down, you know how they really thumb their nose at society and show what bad characters they are?"

Abercorn didn't know.

"They all go down to Yoyogi Park in Tokyo on Saturday afternoon from one to three and turn up their boom boxes and dance. That's it. They dance. All of them. Squarest people in the world."

Abercorn digested this information a moment, wondering how it applied to the case at hand, the case that had put him in this car, in this storm, with this root-chewing ex-LURP beside him. The whole thing was a real shame. Ninety-nine percent of the illegals just came in and disappeared—they got a tourist visa and vanished, rode in underneath a bus, breezed in for a semester of college and wound up collecting Social Security. It was a joke. The borders were sieves, colanders, picket fences without the pickets. But when somebody came in and made a lot of noise and started raising hell with the people who bought new cars and registered to vote, red lights started flashing all the way on up the line to Washington, and that's where the Detlef Abercorns came in. "So, uh, what do you think we ought to do?" he said. "The Nips—the Japanese, I mean—tend to be pretty fanatical too, don't they? *Hara-kiri, kamikazes*, the human wave and all of that?"

"Yeah, I've been to the movies too. But the fact is, like I told you, they're just plain square. You know how you catch this clown?"

Abercorn didn't have a clue. But he figured if the barefoot crackers and their hound dogs couldn't bring him in, they were in for a real ordeal. He thought of the soldier they'd found in a cave in the Philippines, still fighting World War II thirty years later. "No," he said softly.

Turco gestured at the pack on the seat beside him. "You know what I got in there? A boom box. Sanyo. Biggest shitkicker you ever saw, puts out enough amps to kill every woodpecker out there stone dead in two minutes flat. I've got a couple disco tapes, Michael Jackson, Donna Summer, that kind of shit, you follow me? I'm going to track the fucker, no different than if this was 1966 in the Ia Drang Valley, cross a trail, any trail. Then I'm going to set this thing on a stump and crank it up."

Was he kidding? Abercorn couldn't tell.

Turco turned to him with a grin that showed off all his teeth, black now with the stuff he was eating. "Hey," he said, reaching back to pat a conspicuous bulge in the pack, "I'm Br'er Fox and this here is my tarbaby."

Queen Bee

OWEN'S WAKE-UP CALL—THREE SHARP BUT REVERENTIAL KNOCKS accompanied by a gently insinuating whisper—startled her from a dreamless sleep. "*Es la hora,*" he whispered through the door, and Ruth forced open her eyes. "*Despiértese, señorita.*" It was one of his Spanish days—that much registered, though she was groggy and hungover and it didn't much matter whether she was summoned in Spanish, Norwegian or Navajo: all she wanted was to go back to sleep.

At 6:30 each weekday morning Owen Birkshead made the rounds of the still and shadowy halls of Thanatopsis House, performing the delicate task of rousing the slumbering artists without compromising their dreams. Depending on his whim, he would summon them in one of the Romance languages, sweet on the early-morning tongue, or in crisp and businesslike German or even Russian. One morning it would be "*Guten Morgen, Fräulein; ihre Arbeit erwartet Sie,*" and the next, "*Buon giorno, signorina, che bella giornata!*" Once, he'd even tried Japanese—"*Ohayō gozaimasu!*"—but he was afraid that the harshness of his accent would scuff the glossy patina of the artists' dreams, and so he gave it up.

"Yes," Ruth gasped, "I'm up," too fuddled to throw back her usual "*Sí, señor, muchas gracias; yo me despierto.*" She'd been up late, too late, and she'd drunk too many bourbons. She listened as the faint shuffle of Owen's footsteps retreated down the hallway, and she heard his knock and the whisper of his voice at the next door: *"Es la hora, es la hora."* She closed her eyes and felt the pain hovering there on the underside of her eyelids. Her throat was parched, her temples felt as if twin spikes had been driven into them, and she had to pee. Urgently. But even as she lay there she knew that the walleyed composer—Clara Kleinschmidt—had beaten her to the communal bathroom round the corner and that the half bath at the far end of the hall would at any moment resound with the thunder of Irving Thalamus's potent morning micturition.

But it wasn't the urgency of her need or the pain either that ultimately drove her from her bed: it was guilt. Wholesome, fruitful, old-fashioned, gut-wrenching guilt. She had to get up. She was a writer, after all, and writers got up and wrote. Her enemies—and here the specter of Jane Shine, in all her phony, scheming, hateful and shy-smiling beauty, seized her like a pair of hot tongs—would already be up and at their typewriters and monitors, already out of the blocks and hurtling down the inside track to usurp her rightful place in *Harper's* or *Esquire*, at Knopf or Viking or Random House. Besides which, it was so much easier to make use of the guilt if you were working well—and she was, finally, working well.

The transformation had begun on the night she'd flared up in front of the little group gathered in the billiard room, though she hadn't realized it at the time. In fact, the ensuing week had been worse than the first. At least during the first week she had the excuse of disorientation, but as the second week dragged on, she felt increasingly bored and out of touch. She continued to sit at the silent table, brooding and defensive, the evenings with Saxby her sole release. But something had happened, some subtle alteration had taken place among the fixed stars of the Thanatopsis firmament, and Ruth's was on the rise. For one thing, she had the patronage of Irving Thalamus. He'd noticed her that night, oh yes indeed, and his attentions—the ironic glances, the little jokes and nudges—became her safety net. By the third week he'd lured her from the silent room to establish her as his chief ally at the raucous, gossipy and sacrilegious table in the convivial room. Together they would pass through the doleful, dingy corridor of the silent room—smirking, always smirking, a joke on their lips—while Laura Grobian dwelt in the trembling deeps of her hollow-eyed middle-aged beauty and Peter Anserine and his young disciples frowned ascetically over their incomprehensible texts. And at night—and this was the root and cause of this morning's hangover and the hangover she'd had two mornings ago and the one she'd have tomorrow morning too—he brought her into his after-hours circle, where she could really shine, where she could thrust and parry, charm, ridicule, demolish and redeem, where she could become her old self—La Dershowitz—once again.

In a way, she almost felt sorry for her rivals. In the aftermath of that fateful night on Peagler Sound, none of them was really in the running. Ina Soderbord was attractive, she guessed, in a big, blocky, heavy-breasted, white-eyebrowed sort of way, but she inhabited her own little corner of interplanetary space and spoke in the breathless, lisping pant of the brain-numb ingénue. Gravity had not been kind to Clara Kleinschmidt and she had a sad sour smell to her, the smell of inherited lace, hope chests and the lingering loveless death of the game show and rocking chair. And the punk sculptress—Regina McIntyre, a product of Ladycliff and Mount Holyoke, Ruth learned after some probing—was too consumed in self-loathing to speak, but for the occasional vitriolic outburst, and her personal style was strictly for the leather crowd. Neither Irving Thalamus nor Bob the poet was the type, not to mention Sandy De Haven, a late and supremely interesting addition to the group, twenty-six, bleached locks dangling in his eyes as he bent over the billiard table, his first novel due out in the fall from Farrar, Straus and Giroux. No. Ruth was supreme here, queen of the hive.

As her confidence improved, so did her work. She revised an old story and sent it off to *The New Yorker* with Irving Thalamus's blessings, and her Japanese piece suddenly began to take off, to blossom, to feel like something bigger than a mere short story. That's where the second thing came in, the other factor that turned Ruth's life around at Thanatopsis, as serendipitous in its way as Irving Thalamus's tutelage—the appearance, on her studio porch, of Hiro Tanaka. Hiro Tanaka, the outlaw, the renegade, the terror of Tupelo Island, filcher of Clara Kleinschmidt's panties, castigator of Bobby and Cara Mae Cribbs, eluder of the sheriff and the INS, Hiro Tanaka, lunch bucket thief. He was her secret, her pet, her own, and it gave her an edge on all of them.

. . .

SHE'D CAUGHT HIM IN THE ACT, CAUGHT HIM THERE ON HER PORCH on that rainy afternoon ten days back, caught him with the evidence in his hands while the trees strained their backs and the earth shook and the stink of sulfur fell like a blanket over the trapped and stifling air. Lightning flashed, rain raked the trees. He hesitated—she could see it in his eyes, recognition and confusion both: *he'd seen her naked, her breasts, her navel, her secret hair*—and for a moment the dull shock of animal surprise left his face. Food was one thing, the first thing, yes, and this was the second.

She wasn't afraid, not a bit. He was just a boy, scared and dirty, his eyes feverish, clothes torn, a scrap of frayed red cloth knotted round his head. He didn't even look Japanese, with his tan irises and dull reddish hair, or did he? There were the epicanthic folds she remembered from anthropology, the round face and stutter nose, the bow legs and the too-deep tan of his scraped and bitten limbs. Blink once and he was Toshiro Mifune; blink again, and he was something else.

He stirred something in her, he did. It all happened so fast that first day, so adventitiously, she didn't have time to think it out: she just saw him there, hungry and scared, and she wanted to fold him in her arms. He was the motherless fawn she'd found as a girl out back of the cabin at Lake Arrowhead, the squirrel the cat had got, the sunken-eyed orphan in a nameless village crying out to her from the black and white ad in the glossy magazine. She had no other motive but sympathy, no other desire but to help—or if she did have, it was buried deep, in the deep soil of the unconscious where plots and schemes and counterschemes have their first quiescent life. And if he was a fawn, and if he was pitiable, and if the lunch bucket was his salvation, she didn't want to scare him off.

The rain lashed him. His hair was knotted with burrs, his nostrils crusted over, his lips cracked. He cradled the lunch bucket and took a step back. What could she do to convince him, what could she say? Take it, and welcome to it, I'm on a diet anyway, my bed is dry and warm, there's plenty more where that came from, I want to help you, I want to keep you, I want to make you my own. She said nothing. He said nothing. But her expression must have told him all that and more, and as he backed off and the rain sobbed from his face and fed the green of the world around him till it threatened to swallow him up, she slowly, gradually, breathlessly lifted her hands to the level of her waist and spread her palms. And then he was gone.

The next morning Ruth was awake and washed and dressed by the time Owen made his rounds. "*Bonjour, mademoiselle,*" he whispered, tapping at her door. She answered him before the words were out of his mouth—"*Merci, je suis réveillée*"—and in the next moment she pulled open the door and regaled him with a dizzy wide-lipped parody of a vamp's smile. Humbled, he could only gape as she flipped her bag over one shoulder and sashayed down the hall to breakfast. She was excited, so excited she'd barely been able to sleep. Not only over the Japanese sailor and the expectation that he'd be back again and that she'd aid and abet him, hide and nurture him, her own breathing secret, but over the new factor— or rather, factors—in the equation: Detlef Abercorn, the tall young square-jawed agent from the Immigration and Naturalization Service, and his comical little henchman, Turco.

They'd arrived the previous evening, bedraggled and wet, at the height of the storm's second assault. The rain had tapered to a drizzle through the long festering afternoon, and fell off altogether as Ruth made her way back to the big house for cocktails. The colonists were all gathered in the parlor—even Septima, in her shimmering silver chemise and antediluvian pearls—when the storm broke loose again with a gush of rain that rattled the windows and for a long scintillating moment cut the electricity. "Oh, we must have the candles lit," Septima cried, clapping her hands together like a child. Her voice floated over the sudden crepuscular hush of the room, warbling and authentic, the stately breathless voice of refinement and Southern breeding. If the colonists, immersed in the generic gabble of the convivial room and cocktail parlor, ever forgot for a moment where they were, Septima's caressing and unimpeachable accent brought them back.

Saxby had left that morning for Savannah to collect the equipment for a new fish study he was contemplating—Ruth didn't know any more about it than that: it was a fish study, plain and simple—and it was Bob or maybe Owen who appeared a moment later with a candelabrum in full festive blaze. A cheer went up, another round of cocktails was drunk, and when the lights were restored it was unanimously decided to forgo them in favor of candlelight and the romance of the storm, which beat now at the darkening windows with all the fury of the Atlantic in turmoil.

Just as Owen stepped into the room to announce dinner, there came a knock at the outer door. The front parlor, where cocktails were served, gave onto the foyer and the regal front entrance. No one ever knocked—all had free entrée—and the thunderous, rude, impatient booming at the front door took them all by surprise. The noise level dropped off to zero, conversations died; all heads turned to peer through the parlor doorway to the foyer, to which Owen, his shoulders thrust forward and with an officious look on his face, was proceeding. Ruth, who was then in the first stages of the metamorphosis that would make her the cynosure of Irving Thalamus's clique and rescue her forever from the oblivion of the silent table, followed him.

Owen threw back the door, a wild busy smell of drizzling nature flooded the vestibule, and Abercorn and Turco, the one too tall, the other too short, stomped dripping into the room. "Hello," Abercorn said, extending his hand to the bewildered Owen and flashing a flawless smile, "I'm Detlef Abercorn, Special Agent of the INS, and this"—indicating Turco, who glared round him suspiciously—"is my, uh, assistant, Lewis Turco."

Ruth felt her heart catch. This was the man she'd spoken to on the phone a week ago—spoken to blithely, pleased with the attention—the man to whom she'd divulged every relevant detail of her encounter with Hiro Tanaka on Peagler Sound. And now here he was, horning in on her secret. She wasn't calculating, not yet anyway, had no dream of Hiro as anything more than a creature that needed to be stroked and appeased and comforted—an exotic and fascinating creature, yes, but not yet her own, not yet her sword and wedge and bludgeon to lay all of Thanatopsis House at her feet. She wasn't calculating, but she knew that she wouldn't—couldn't—cooperate with this tall and very wet man in the cheap detective's overcoat.

Owen gaped at them, for once at a loss for words.

"I wonder if you could help us," Abercorn began, and as the murmur of conversation started up again behind her, Ruth lingered there in the doorway, watching and listening, as Abercorn poured out his tale of woe and Owen blinked in confusion. As it turned out, Abercorn and Turco had waited three hours for the last ferry, and on finally arriving discovered to their regret and embarrassment that there were no accommodations available on the island. They needed a place to spend the night before going off in pursuit of the armed and dangerous alien who'd been terrorizing folks hereabouts—Abercorn actually said "folks hereabouts," though it was obvious to anyone he was a sweaty-palmed city-bred Yankee who was about as folksy as Bernhard Goetz. Sheriff—he pronounced it "sher-iff," not "shurf," though he was trying hard—Sheriff Peagler had told him that there might be a bed or two available here, and he'd be more than happy to pay whatever they liked—he was on official government business, after all, and the alternative was, well, flashing his smile and wincing comically at a peal of thunder, the alternative was to go on out there and drown.

And so Ruth was up early, the first one at breakfast and the first to trot off to work, up before Abercorn could pin her down with any more questions. The woods were still, the morning fragrant with the previous night's rain. The sun had risen golden and glorious from the chop of the cold Atlantic, and as she walked the path to her studio it seemed to melt into the hard unyielding posts of the slash pines. She walked slowly, breathing it all in, but still she arrived at her studio nearly an hour and a half earlier than usual. It was just past seven, and as she sat down at her desk and stared numbly at the curling page in the typewriter, she could think of nothing but lunch. Would he show up? And if he did, what would she do and what would it lead to? She envisioned her Japanese in bed, envisioned herself in Japan, a country of office buildings, claustrophobic streets and tiny feet, and then finally, to pass the time, she settled down to work.

Hiro didn't show up that day. Perversely. It was almost as if he knew she wanted to reach out to him but that he had some kind of cultural thing—some kind of weird Japanese machismo or whatever—that kept him from her. And that evening, since Saxby was still in Savannah and she was just beginning to flex her wings in the billiard room, and because she was bored too and felt like it— the secret, *her* secret making it all the more delicious—she sat down in the parlor over cocktails and chatted with Abercorn. He'd spent a fruitless day interviewing the blacks at Hog Hammock—"I couldn't understand a word they said, I mean not a single word," he said, "and after a while it was embarrassing"—while his assistant had snooped around in the woods with a boom box. She shared a good laugh with him over that, over Turco's boom box. "Yes," she said—she couldn't help it, couldn't help fooling around with him, just a little bit, just for practice—"I thought I heard Donna Summer out there somewhere today."

And where was Turco that evening? Was he tracking down the criminal even as they spoke? "Oh, no," Abercorn had said, "he's not that fanatical. No, he just doesn't like roofs." "Roofs?" she echoed, her lips drawn tight in an incipient smile. "You're not going to believe this," he said, and he lifted a can of warm Coke to his mouth and then put it down again, "but last night, when it was raining?" She nodded. "He takes off out of the room with his backpack and pitches his tent out there in the bushes someplace." And then they had a good laugh over that one, and Ruth looked into Abercorn's pink eyes and thought he was kind of cute in a way.

Two days passed. Abercorn mooned around Thanatopsis House and some of the artists—Regina McIntyre, in particular—began to grumble. Turco was invisible, out there in his tent, creeping through the marsh, putting his loathsome all into deracinating Ruth's secret before it had a chance to bear fruit. In the lull of the afternoon, she heard disco music, distant, faint, deadly. The lunch bucket remained on its hook.

And then, on the third day, Hiro appeared again. It must have been an hour at least after Owen had crept up to the porch and hung the aluminum container on its hook—she'd heard him, heard the groan of the second step, the loose one, but she hadn't turned, hadn't moved, and she covered herself with a furious burst of typing. A line of *x*'s marched across the page, and then another, before she glanced over her shoulder to catch the back of Owen's bristling head receding down the trail to Diane Arbus, where the precocious Sandy was hard at work on his second novel. Ruth lost track of the time, though her stomach grumbled and she got Hiro's face confused with that of her failed and hopeless heroine, and she was in another world, the cries of the doomed children echoing around her, the tide pulling at her feet, when the stair creaked again.

She froze. Slowly, she told herself, slowly. She gave him her profile and held it, and then she looked full-face over her shoulder. He was there, in the doorway, derealized behind the grid of the screen. The red headband was gone—he was wearing something else now, something tan and twisted—and he was naked to the waist, both straps of the coveralls dangling forlornly behind him. He made no move toward the lunch pail.

"I want to help you," Ruth whispered.

He didn't move, didn't speak, just stood there. His face seemed softer somehow, as if he were exhausted or about to cry . . . and she had a sudden leap of intuition: he was just an overgrown child, scared, hurt and hungry.

"Take the food. I left it for you. Take it," she whispered, afraid to raise her voice, afraid he'd bolt.

She saw him swallow hard. He shuffled his feet. And then he lifted the lunch bucket from the hook and cradled it to him.

"Listen," she said, whispering still, whispering like a hunter in a blind, "they're after you, do you understand? Two men, they're in the big house."

He said nothing, but his face looked softer still. He was finished, she could see it. He'd had it. He was ready to give up, throw in the towel, slip the handcuffs over his wrists.

"I won't let them take you," she said. "I'll get you clothes, food, you can stay here, out of sight." She lifted one leg and very slowly swung the chair round to face him. She'd made do with an ordinary face and figure all her life, had triumphed with it, had left a legion of men stunned in her wake, because she had the indefinable something they all wanted and because she knew it. Now, at thirty-four, she had all that and twenty years of experience too, and she was irresistible. "Come in here," she said, and she was still whispering, but her voice had an edge to it now, peremptory and sharp. "Open the door. Sit and eat"—she made the motions with her hands and mouth—"and then you can rest there on the couch. I won't hurt you. I give you my word."

For a long moment he stood there, his eyes riveted on her. He was bigger than she'd remembered, sadder, his eyes gone hollow and cheeks sunk in on themselves, but when he reached for the door she froze again. Maybe he *was* dangerous, she thought. Maybe the reports were true. He was a foreigner, after all. He had different values. He could be a fanatic. A maniac. A killer.

The door swung open and he took a tentative step into the room. He clung desperately to the lunch pail. His eyes were wild. He nearly cried out when the door slammed shut behind him.

Then she saw what it was knotted round his head: shiny nylon, a thin band of white elastic: Clara Kleinschmidt's panties. She couldn't help herself, couldn't hold it any longer—the armed and dangerous alien was an overgrown kid with Clara Kleinschmidt's panties wound round his head—and suddenly she was laughing, laughing so hard she thought she'd choke.

Later, after he'd devoured the lunch, a box of saltines, two apples and a string of Medjool dates her mother had sent her, he fell face forward on the white wicker settee and slept the sleep of the dead. For a long while she just watched him, studying him as a medical student might have studied a corpse or an artist a model. She examined his limbs, his blistered back and scarred feet, the snarl of his knotted hair, the dimensions of his face, even the string of saliva that dangled from his half-open mouth. He was a mess. A real mess. A week and a half of crouching in the swamps hadn't done him much good. His flesh—every visible inch of it—was a crusted quilt of bites and scabs and pustules; an infected contusion had swollen the lobe of his right ear—the upward one—to twice its normal size; and a long hyphenated slash trailed away from his eyebrow like the exaggerated makeup of a clown or whore. His face was puffy, his skin sallow and sunburned. The only article of clothing he wore—a pair of ill-fitting overalls—was torn, seam-split, pinched in the rear and stiff with filth. Worst of all was the odor he brought with him, rank and elemental, the stink of rotting meat, of something dead along the road.

She didn't know how long she sat there watching him—he never moved, but for the rise and fall of his breathing, and the sun slid imperceptibly across the sky. It was cocktail hour (or thereabout: the angle of the sun as it struck the western window and illuminated her pitcher plants told her that much) when she finally made up her mind to get him some clothes, soap, hydrogen peroxide—she was afraid he'd decompose without it. She thought of a piece of fruit—a pear or banana—its skin speckled, jaundiced, blackening finally and collapsing on itself. She pushed herself up, eased out the door and made her way back to the big house.

If she'd hoped to slip in unnoticed, luck was against her. It was a day of unadulterated sunshine and sweet wafting ocean breezes, and her fellow colonists had taken the cocktail hour outside. They were gathered on the patio, glasses glinting in the sun, as she came up the walk. "Ruthie!" Irving Thalamus called, his face lit with chardonnay. "La Dershowitz," raising his glass high, "fictioneer extraordinaire, come and drink some vin ordinaire!"

She had no choice, really: she needed him, and he'd begun, in a big way, to notice her. She crossed the sunstruck lawn, aware of the turned heads and the lull in the chatter, moving in her inevitable way, the heroine of her own movie, picturing herself in that dazzle of sunlight, in her tight jeans and clingy blouse. "Irving," she said, moving into his embrace and exchanging a salutatory kiss that lingered half a beat too long, and then she was nodding to Ina Soderbord and Sandy De Haven and Regina McIntyre and chattering nonstop until someone stuck a glass of wine in her hand and she could pause, for a second, to drink. She let the moment subside and then she was pleading the need to bathe and change for dinner— she'd been working so well she'd missed the time—and her empty glass was on the serving cart and the oaks leapt up at the edge of the two-acre lawn and the sun sat in the windows of the great gabled three-story house and she was up the steps and in.

She was thinking she could get the Band-Aids and antiseptic in the communal bathroom—nobody in the foyer, three quick steps and up the stairs—but what about pants, shoes and socks, a clean shirt? She could rifle Saxby's room—he'd never notice—but Saxby had the washboard front and fall-away hips of the athlete, and she knew his pants would never fit. Ditto Sandy and the austere and long-shanked Peter Anserine. There was Bob the poet, but he was too short, and Detlef Abercorn, who'd been given a back room on the third floor, but he was too tall. She could always buy something in Darien, but she'd have to wait for Saxby and the ferry and she'd have to make explanations—and she didn't want to make explanations, not even to Saxby.

In the bathroom she found iodine, hydrogen peroxide, Vaseline, a box of flesh-colored Band-Aid strips, two bars of lilac-scented soap molded in the shape of gaping alligators, and a hand towel. She was bundling everything up in the towel, listening for footsteps, when she thought of Irving Thalamus. He'd be perfect—not that he was as paunchy as her Japanese, but he was about the same height and he did carry a comfortable little middle-aged spread. A flutter of laughter rose to her from the patio below. She'd have to hurry—no telling when one of them would be up to evacuate a bladderful of wine or gin or repair their makeup. She opened the door slowly, the towel tucked under her arm, and she looked both ways before stepping out into the hall.

She could feel her heart going. There were no locks on the doors—not even an inside latch for nighttime privacy. It was Septima's belief that her artists were to be trusted implicitly with mere material things, and given the freedom to roam about and exercise their libidos with no more restraint than mutual consent. "There are no marriages at Thanatopsis," she'd explained to Ruth on welcoming her to the colony, "we don't recognize the institution. Here," and she'd beamed at Saxby, who stood behind Ruth, rubbing the inside of her wrist, "here we believe in lettin' the artist express him or herself, in whatever way he or she pleases." Yes. And now Ruth was alone on the second floor, the appropriated toilet articles tucked under her arm, expressing herself in a stealthy and antisocial way.

Her own room was on her left, but she passed it, passed Clara Kleinschmidt's room and Peter Anserine's—if anyone asked her what she was doing, she was going to the bathroom, the little one at the end of the hall, to wash up, not wanting to monopolize the full bath in case anyone might want to shower before dinner. And then she passed Owen's room and ducked round the corner. Ahead of her was the door to the back stairway; to her left, the bathroom. And to her right, the door to Irving Thalamus's inner sanctum. She hesitated, heard the laughter and tinkle of glass again, and then she was in.

Hurry, she told herself, *hurry*, and she fought down her resent-

ment over the size and appointments of the room—her room was
like a shoebox—and went directly to the cherrywood armoire.
Hurry, screamed a voice inside her and her hand trembled with
nervous excitement—this was like the movies when the hero breaks
into the killer's apartment and the killer always, always comes back
to surprise him—as she fumbled through the jackets and shirts and
pants still wrapped in plastic from the dry cleaner. Nothing no-
ticeable, she thought, nothing he'll miss. In the drawer below she
discovered his underwear—briefs, silk from the feel of them, in
pink and red and royal blue. She thought about that for the fleet-
ingest instant, about his hairy abdomen and the tight band those
skimpy briefs would make, about his cock and balls swollen against
the material, and then she had what she wanted—a pair of Bermudas she'd never seen him wear—so what if they featured flaming
yellow parrots and chartreuse palm trees?—and a plain white
V-necked T-shirt. She slid the drawer back in, closed up the armoire and reached under the bed for a pair of battered tennis shoes.
He'd never miss them.

And then suddenly a roar went up from the patio below and her
heart froze. There was a shriek and the sound of shattering glass
and then a burst of laughter. She thought she heard a door slam.
She had to get out. But what to do with the evidence? She couldn't
just . . . the pillowcase. But no, he'd be sure to miss that. And
then her eyes fell on the wastebasket, a cheap straw thing lined
with the generic black plastic bag. Breathlessly, she bent to lift out
the bag and dump its contents back into the naked straw basket,
hurry, hurry, starting at every sound, the seconds ticking off and
what if he caught her and what would she say? Still, even under
duress, she did manage to notice the discarded letter from his agent
and the card, neatly torn in two, from—who was it from?—his
son. She stuffed them into the black plastic bag along with the rest
of her booty, and tentatively cracked the door.

It was a shock: someone was coming. A dark form, movement:
someone was coming.

Ruth snapped the door shut, heart pounding, wild excuses on

her lips—she was looking for the laundry room and blundered in here by mistake; she was helping Owen's Puerto Rican slave—what was his name, Rico?—with the trash, yes, his mother was sick and . . . she could hear footsteps approaching, a heavy tread, relentless, coming nearer . . . and then they paused—stopped, halted, pulled up short—just outside the door. She was dead. This was it. She pictured Irving Thalamus's cold lizard look of surprise, Septima's intransigent nose and Owen's hard censorious eyes, instant justice, the only artist ever drummed out of Thanatopsis House for petty thievery—but wait: she could throw herself into his arms, yes, yes, pretend she'd come for that—and then she heard the sudden sharp wheeze of the bathroom door opposite and knew she was saved. She took a deep breath, waited for the sound of the bathroom latch and cracked the door again. No one in sight. She stepped into the hall and closed the door behind her.

It was at that precise moment that Detlef Abercorn rounded the corner. He was wearing a set of earphones attached to the Walkman in his shirt pocket, and he was on her before she could react. "Oh, hey, hi," he said, too loudly, and he slipped the phones from his ears in a motion so automatic it might have been a tic.

Ruth clutched the garbage bag to her chest and gave him a terrified grin.

He grinned back at her, casually leaning into the doorframe with one long arm. She saw that he was looking down her blouse. "Did I tell you I really enjoyed talking to you the other night? I find you a very"—he hesitated, and she could hear a faint metallic voice whispering through the earphones—"a very sexy woman. Really. And I wondered if—I've got a car and all—I wondered if you might like to get off the island for an evening—tonight maybe—and have dinner or something?"

Ruth was on familiar terrain now, and as the shock of discovery wore off, she recovered her equilibrium. "I'd like that," she said, bending to relieve an imaginary itch just behind her left knee, "sometime. Sometime soon. But tonight I'm afraid I already have plans."

Abercorn didn't seem put off. He leaned closer and gave her a long meaningful look. "Hey," he said, putting some gravel into his voice, "I don't know if I'll be around that much longer."

Ruth saw her chance. "Oh? No luck?"

He shot his eyes in disgust. "The guy disappeared. He could be dead for all we know. Either that or he left the island."

"And your assistant? With the ghetto blaster?"

Abercorn's laugh was quick and musical. "Yeah, well, that's another story." He paused. She couldn't seem to help staring into his eyes—she'd never seen anyone with eyes that color before. "So this is your room, huh?" he said. "I was kind of hoping you might, uh—"

She put her hand on his arm. "You're sweet," she said, "but listen, I've got to run. Really. I just realized I don't think I shut off the hot plate in my studio and—"

"All that genius up in ashes, huh?"

"Something like that," she said, ducking out from under his arm and hurrying down the hall.

But it wasn't over yet.

She came down the stairs two at a time, the black plastic bag tucked under her arm, and her only thought was of Hiro, her pet, her secret, face down on the wicker loveseat in the shady studio in the woods. Would he be there when she got back? Would he wake and think she'd gone for the police? Would Turco boogie through the screen door and conk him with his boom box? The furthest thing from her mind was Saxby. But there he was at the foot of the stairs, crabwalking beneath one precarious end of a six-foot-long aquarium. "Ruthie," he grunted. "I'm . . . back!"

She saw now that Owen was attached to the far end of the thing and that they were trying to maneuver it round the butt of the staircase and down the narrow hallway to Saxby's room. The whole operation halted a minute while Ruth descended the stairs to brush Saxby's lips with a kiss and whisper, "I missed you," and then, flashing light, the aquarium moved on, and Ruth was out the door, down the steps and across the lawn. As soon as she hit the woods, she broke into a run.

She was out of breath when she reached the cottage, knitting needles embedded in her sides. She wanted him to be there, wanted to talk to him, wash and bind his wounds, watch him eat and sleep and recover the lost light in his eyes—but somehow, as she came up the path, she knew he'd be gone. The cottage was unchanged. She saw the familiar porch, the windows rich with sun, the pine, palmetto and oak, and she heard the birds in the trees and smelled the sweet rich breath of the ocean, and nothing had changed. She mounted the steps, breathing hard, and gingerly swung open the screen door: the cottage was empty.

Angry with herself—she should have told him where she was going, should have brushed off Abercorn, should have run both ways—she threw the bag down and fell into the rocker by the window. He was gone. He'd never trust her now. But then so what? What did she care? Let him starve. For a long while she sat there rocking as the shadows lengthened and the calm of evening fell over her books, her typewriter, the hot plate and pitcher plants, all the familiar objects of her little life in this temporary outpost. And then, at long last, it occurred to her—and the thought was as sharp as a pinprick—that he might be testing her. Even now he might be crouched in the tangle out there, watching and waiting. All right, she thought, and got up from the chair, poured some water from the jug into a basin and carried it out onto the porch. She made a separate trip for the jug, and left it beside the basin. Then she fished through the bag and arranged the soap and Band-Aids, the towel and clothing and the rest of it on the rail, stuffed the two letters in her hip pocket and started back, through the cloistral deeps of evening, to Thanatopsis House.

In the morning, the things were gone. He'd returned the basin to its hook beside the fireplace, and she found the rag of the overalls and Clara Kleinschmidt's violated panties neatly folded in the corner. He didn't come for the lunch pail that afternoon, but she left it there on its hook—she joked to herself that she could stand to lose a few pounds anyway—and in the morning it was empty. The same thing happened the following day and she thought they'd established a pattern, a rhythm, but she was wrong. A day passed, and then another, and there was no sign that he'd been there. Lunches spoiled. Owen was perplexed. Abercorn packed up his suitcase and Turco his boom box, and, assuring the colonists that the Japanese was no longer a threat, they climbed into their battered Datsun and drove off to the ferry. Saxby filled his aquarium with rocks, water and plants, and in the small hours of the long thick endless nights made Ruth's blood rush with his lips and his fingers and all the rest of him too. And Ruth established herself in the billiard room and at the convivial table and sat down to her type-writer with a new purpose and a delicious lingering thrill of ex-pectation: he'd be back, her Japanese, any moment now. She knew he would. After all, she thought, how could he resist?

. . .

BUT NOW, NOW SHE HAD A HEADACHE AND SHE WAS HUNGOVER and Owen's wake-up call had taken her by surprise. The morning was stifling, a blanket thrown over her face, and it was August already, the first week nearly gone, and there'd been no sign of Hiro for three days now. She forced herself to get up. She had work to do—she'd never worked so well in her life—and she was anxious to get down to breakfast, reign over the table and clear her head with lukewarm coffee and scalding gossip.

She ran a brush through her hair and pulled it back in a ponytail, made up her eyes and brushed her teeth, then slipped into a pair of shorts and a halter top, no brassiere, and dug her white cork-heeled canvas sandals out from under the bed. As she passed through the silent room, Laura Grobian looked up from her soft-boiled egg and acknowledged her with a dip of the head and a blink of the famous haunted eyes, and Ruth felt a quick little surge of triumph. Then it was through the oak doors and on into the con-vivial room, where she was greeted by laughter, cigarette smoke and shouts of "La Dershowitz!" and "Up so soon?" and "She's feeling it now!"

Bob, Sandy, Irving Thalamus, Ina Soderbord and half a dozen others were gathered at the long dark table, a rubble of thrice-read newspapers, books, manuscripts, egg-stained plates, mugs and ash-trays scattered about them. The big silver rocket of a coffee pot sat on the sideboard, along with a serving pan of waffles and a bowl of fruit compote. Rico was in the kitchen, making toast, eggs and Canadian bacon to order. Ruth ducked her head through the swing-ing door to the kitchen and caught him flipping an omelet behind his back. "Pretty fancy," she said, tailing it with a low whistle.

Rico gave her a gold-capped smile. He was twenty-two, six inches shorter than any man ought reasonably to be, and his big black circular eyes devoured his face in sadness. "No sweat," he said.

"Could you make me a poached egg when you get a chance?" she asked, leaning in and balancing on one leg. The kitchen smelled rich and potent. "And maybe some dry wheat toast, two slices?"

"No sweat," Rico said, and he flipped the omelet again, just to show off.

Ruth poured herself a cup of coffee, laced it with Sweet'n Low and hovered over the table till Irving Thalamus cleared a spot for her. "Sleep tight?" he said, giving her a lascivious look as she sat down beside him and crossed her legs. His eyes were hooded, the lids puckered and dark. He looked as if he should be wearing a burnoose and sandals, counting camels and harem girls somewhere out in the Negev.

Ruth gave him a rueful smile. "Too much booze," she said, "but Sax and I took a little stroll after we left you." She paused. "That revived me, all right. And I slept like a stone."

He dropped his eyes and began to fiddle with his fork, building a little pyramid of scrambled egg in the center of his plate. The card from his son—a freshman at Yale—had been bitter stuff. The son was planning to spend the holidays with the estranged wife in Mount Kisco; Irving Thalamus had apparently written to offer him a room in the house he was renting on Key West. The son had written back to say no, unequivocally, and to add that he considered his father a hypocrite, a narcissistic overpraised hack and a moral dwarf who couldn't keep the patriarchal penis in his pants. The letter from the agent was worse. So bad Ruth had experienced a momentary pang of guilt while reading it—but it was only momentary, because, after all, she was an artist, an intellectual, and she made her own rules. The agent—one of the most venerable in New York—had written to say that Irving Thalamus's publisher, the publisher who'd done his last six books, was advising him against coming out with the new novel. *Dog Days* was an embarrassment. Misguided. Incoherent. The publisher—and the agent concurred, gently and at length—knew that he would see the light. In six months' time, with a little distance, he'd repudiate the work himself. He would. And he had his career to think about now, his future in the pantheon of American letters, and why spoil it with an ill-considered move at this juncture? The agent signed off by trusting that the rest cure in the bucolic atmosphere of Thanatopsis House was doing him a world of good.

"So how's your new story coming?" he said, swinging his hard jaw back to her.

She knew he didn't want to hear the truth, knew that the only answer to that question was to grumble, denigrate herself, whine about the blank page and how useless she was and wonder, awe in her eyes, how he managed to produce one astonishing book after another. She took another sip of coffee, set her mug down and leaned in close to him. "I've never worked better in my life," she said.

"Hey, terrific," he said, "that's great, it really is." His eyes looked wounded.

Bob shouted something about poker that night and then rose to leave the table. Ina Soderbord, wearing a pink sweat suit though it must have been ninety already, got up to leave with him and Ruth raised her eyebrows. Irving Thalamus nodded in affirmation. Then Rico cha-cha'd out of the kitchen, a muted blast of salsa music coming with him, and set down Ruth's plate of egg and toast. She took a moment to upend the egg on the toast and dose it with salt and pepper before she turned back to Thalamus and asked the question that had, by all rules of writerly etiquette, to follow from his: "And how about you? *Dog Days* going well?"

He gave her a strange look, the look of a man who's had his shorts stolen and his mail rifled. But no, how could he know? He'd talked about nothing but *Dog Days* since she'd got here—she wasn't giving anything away. "Oh, that," he said, shrugging. "Fine. Okay." He paused. "I'm on to something new now anyway, something totally different for me, a real departure. I'm excited about it." He didn't look excited. Or he looked about as excited as a middle-aged legend contemplating moving his bowels in the communal bathroom, which is exactly what he was.

She was going to say something banal, like "I'm really happy for you" or "It's the least we can expect from you, Irving," but he turned to her suddenly and his face lit up. "Hey," he said, "you hear the news?"

She hadn't. She pursed her mouth and folded her hands in her lap. She was expecting something juicy, something to chew over and digest and laugh about till lunch, the thrilling little kernel of gossip that would make her whole billiard-room routine for the next week. The last thing he'd given her—and it was too much, she couldn't have invented anything better—was the news that Peter Anserine had climbed the stairs to his room one night only to find Clara Kleinschmidt, lumps and all, reclining across his bed like the naked Maja—and the best part of it was, she didn't leave till the morning. "No," Ruth said, arching her back and darting a quick glance round the room, "tell me."

"I can't believe it," he said. "Guess who's coming—for a *six-weeks'* residency?"

She couldn't guess.

Plates rattled in the kitchen, Bob took Ina's hand and sauntered out the door, Sandy yawned, stretched and stood up. Irving Thalamus leaned toward her, his eyes bright, his grin as sharp as a watchdog's. "Jane Shine," he said. "Jane Shine's coming. Can you believe it?"

Fea Purē

■ ■ ■ ■ ■ ■ ■

I WANT TO HELP YOU, SHE WHISPERED AS HE STOOD THERE IN THE
doorway, the lunch bucket clutched in his hand. They all wanted
to help him. That's why they blasted their shotguns at him and
hunted him with their dogs, that's why they played Donna Summer
in the swamps and tried to run him down in their speedboats. It
was this one's lover, her *bōifurendo*, the beef-eater and butter-stinker,
naked and hairy and with his big dog's prick hanging down like a
sausage, who'd run the boat at him when he was half drowned and
chased him out of the store when he was starving. He'd wanted to
help too.

Still, there was something about her—he couldn't say what it
was, couldn't find the word for it in English or in Japanese either.
She was sitting at her desk, her back to him, and when she turned
he saw her silken legs, long and slim, American legs, and he saw
the movement of her breasts and the weight of them. He remembered those breasts from his night in the water, though he was
terrified and exhausted and fighting for his life at the time. He was
drowning, he was dying, and there were her breasts, naked and
appealing under the pale glaze of moon and stars. The whiteness,
that's what he remembered, the whiteness of her there and below,

skin like milk in a porcelain bowl. He stepped through the door.

He was terrified, though he had Jōchō and Mishima to sustain him—he was sure she'd betray him, screech till her tonsils fell out, rouse up every sweating *hakujin* cowboy and kinky-haired Negro in the county—but then he caught the look in her eyes and saw that she was afraid of him. For a long moment he just stood there inside the door, watching her eyes. And then, when he saw them soften, when he watched the smile play across her lips and heard her laugh, he shuffled into the room and squatted in the corner. "*Arigatō,*" he whispered, "sank you, sank you so much." And then he opened up the lunch bucket and he ate.

She offered him more—apples, dates, crackers—and he took it, took it greedily, though he was humiliated. He crouched there like an animal, filthier than he'd ever been in his life, bleeding in a hundred places, stinking like a hog. And in rags. Stolen rags. Negro rags. Jōchō would have despised him; Mishima would have turned his back. He recalled the words of Jōchō on the importance of grooming and personal appearance—life was a dress rehearsal for death, and you always had to be prepared for it, right down to the smallest detail of your toilet, your underwear, your pedicure, your hands and teeth and the color in your cheeks—and he felt humiliated to the depths of his being. He was polluted. Degraded. Impure. Lower than a dog.

"I'll get you clothes," she said.

He was nothing. He stank. He loathed himself. "*Dōmo arigatō,*" he said, and though he was already squatting, he bowed from the waist.

Then she stood. Stood on those lovely slim ghostly white legs and crossed the room to him. She didn't speak. She hovered over him, her eyes lush and consolatory, and held out her hand. "Here," she said, the voice caught low in her throat, and when he took her hand she pulled him to his feet. "Come, lie down," and she offered him the couch. He gave up then and let her lead him like a child, let her tuck the pillow beneath his head and whisper to him in her sacramental tones until his muscles went loose and he felt himself tumble through the wicker, the wood, the earth itself, and into a realm where nothing mattered, nothing at all.

His dream was of baseball—*bēsubōru*—the game that was his whole life until he discovered Jōchō. He was with his grandmother, his *obāsan*, and she was having a *sake* and he a *botto dogu* and the players on the field were swinging their bats and the pitcher was pounding the ball into the dark secret pocket of the catcher's mitt. And then suddenly he was down there amongst them, standing at the plate and swinging . . . not a bat, but the *botto dogu*, chili, mustard and all . . . swinging it till it began to swell and grow and he felt he could do anything, clout a homer with every swing, soar into the air like a bird or rocket. He turned to wave at his *obāsan*, but she was gone, replaced by a girl with a baby at her breast . . . but no, it wasn't just a single girl, there were hundreds, thousands of them, and every one with a suckling infant and every one with breasts as pure and white as . . . breasts . . . an avalanche of breasts . . .

He woke slowly, gradually, a diver rising to the surface of a murky lagoon, and the sleep clung to him like water. It took him a moment, disoriented by his exhaustion and all that had happened to him—he was home in bed, safe in his bunk on the *Tokachi-maru*, nodding off over a lecture at the maritime academy—and then all at once he knew where he was and his eyes locked open. He saw the crosshatching of the wicker, shellacked and faded, and he saw the flowered pillowcase and his own filthy and battered hand. He heard nothing, not a sound. In the next instant he was up and off the couch, cursing himself, cursing her, and then he tore open the door and ran for the woods, his breath coming in torn ragged gasps. How could he have trusted her, he thought, oblivious to slash of palmetto and tug of briar, his adrenaline surging, expecting at any moment to hear the first startled bellow of the sheriff's hounds at his back. The bitch, the false deceptive white-legged *hakujin* bitch: how could he have been so stupid?

This wasn't fair play—*fea purē*—not at all. This wasn't how the

game was played. This was cheating. She'd caught him with his
defenses down, caught him when he was ready to pack it all in, to
give up and die of shame and ignominy, and she'd seduced him
with her voice and eyes and her pure white body and then stabbed
him in the back. But he'd escaped her. Oh, yes. And he would
never yield again, never—he would be as ruthless and crafty as the
high-noses themselves. No more *fea purē* for him. Nice guys finish
last—Leo Durocher, the great *Amerikajin* manager of the Brooklyn
Dodgers had said that, and Jōchō had said it too.

He tore at creeper and twig, splashed through a scum-coated
channel and startled something in the shallows. Finally, winded,
he threw himself down in the red muck to consider the situation.
For a long moment he held his breath, listening—they came at you
with dogs, bloodhounds, he knew that. Give them a sock, a sandal,
a cigarette butt, and they could track you to the ends of the earth.
He was too frightened yet to be miserable, too exhausted to think
straight. But when he calmed down, when the sun dropped below
the rim of the world and left the trees in haunted gloom and the
birds of the night screeched overhead, he was fully miserable once
again, and he began to wonder if he hadn't been just a bit rash.

Perhaps she *had* meant to help him after all. She said she was
going to get him clothes. He couldn't very well expect her to have
a suit of men's clothes in her cabin, could he? She didn't live there,
he knew that much. She came in the morning and left in the evening.
He supposed she was a secretary of some sort and that the cabin
was her office—and if that was the case, well then perhaps she *had*
gone to get him clothes . . . and food, more food, the meat paste
sandwiches and hard vegetables and fruit he'd discovered in the
lunch pail, the little cheeses wrapped in foil and a wedge of frosted
cake. His *hara* announced itself then and he rose itching from the
muck, a lingering sour troubled taste in his mouth, and struggled
back in the direction from which he'd come.

It wasn't easy. The shadows deepened; the trees stood in ranks,
linked arm to arm, as alike as blades of grass; things swift and
unseen whipped through the scrub at his feet. Twice he toppled

headlong into the bushes, the dirty gauze of cobweb and spider silk caught in his mouth and nostrils, mosquitoes harassing him in all their legions. He'd almost given up hope when the tangle of trees released him to the brief remission of the yard.

He froze. It was full dark now, the night clear and moonless. Not twenty feet away stood the cabin, an absence of definition, a shadow that drew in all the shadows around it. Nothing moved. He listened to the chirr of crickets, the hum of mosquitoes, the violent thump and wheeze of his own internal machinery as it went about the business of keeping him alive. What if they were waiting in there for him? What if they were watching him even now, their dogs at heel, guns drawn, fingers twitching over their searchlights?

Step by tottering step, he approached the mass of shadow that was the cabin. Going to school, living with his *obāsan*, swabbing the galley of the *Tokachi-maru*, he'd almost forgotten his own physicality, and here he was, playing another children's game: red light, green light. He took a step and then froze. Two steps. And then another. When he was close, when he could distinguish the horizontal bar of the porch railing from the clot of shadows behind it, he felt a surge of joy. The clothes: there they were! He reached out to the material, the white T-shirt palely glowing. She'd been true to him after all—she was his ally, his friend, his comfort and support, and she did play by the rules, she did, though he must have been as strange to her as she was to him. In that moment, he loved her.

In the next, he was crestfallen. She'd brought him antiseptic and bandages, water and soap and clothing that smelled of scented detergent and the tumble-dryer—but she'd forgotten the most important thing, the thing that made his gut seize and cry out in peristaltic anguish: she'd forgotten food. The apples, dates and crackers, the box lunch, they were nothing, a distant memory, and a great howling inconquerable hunger took hold of him like rage. The bitch, the stupid bitch, she'd forgotten to bring him food!

All right. But he had the clothes, the soap, he had clear clean potable water. Or at least he assumed it was clear, clean and potable—he could barely make out the basin in the black of the night. He bent his face tentatively to the basin and drank, and to his joy he found the water sweet and fresh, with no taint of the swamp— had water ever tasted so good? Then he stripped off his rags, fumbled for the washcloth and soap and began a long slow luxurious lathering which he interrupted only long enough to stave off the mosquitoes.

When he'd finished, he stood and upended the basin over his head and then filled it again—at least she'd thought to leave the water jug on the porch, he muttered to himself, his gratitude drowned in outrage: *no food—Band-Aid strips, but no food!* He wet his hair, soaped and rinsed it and wet it again. Then he sat on the front steps, still naked, and cut the burrs and thistles and twigs out of it with his penknife. He didn't have much of a beard—a few sparse hairs curling from his chin and darkening his upper lip— and these he tried to cut too, but with less success. Finally, he reached for the shorts and slipped into them with all the satisfaction of a half-grown boy slipping into his *yukata* after a long hot soak.

He carried the T-shirt and the tennis shoes, Jōchō and his penknife into the dark cabin with him. For a moment he stood there in the darkness, smelling her, a sweetness of the flesh and a hint of western perfume that lingered like spice on the air. The cabin was deserted. He remembered the hot plate and the tin of crackers. She must have something here, he thought, anything. And then he took a risk: he fumbled round the place, lost in utter blackness, till he found her desk lamp and switched it on.

The room sprang to life, a dazzle of color and dimension—a room, habitable space, four walls and a roof. He was inside. He'd spent his whole life inside, and now he was inside again. The windows glared at him, opaque with light, and he knew he was visible to anyone standing out there in the night . . . but he didn't care. Not now. Not anymore. All he cared about now was food. And where was it? Where did she keep it? He scanned the room— the rows of books, the typewriter with its curling page, the fireplace, the chairs and loveseat—finally settling on the flimsy little table that held the hot plate. There were coffee things there: a mug, a spoon, a ceramic container with packets of Sweet'n Low and non-dairy creamer, a boldly labeled jar of decaf. And that was it. Nothing else. Nothing to eat.

For the next half hour he sat there in a pool of golden light, treating his wounds and sipping decaffeinated coffee—one cup after another. There wasn't much nutrition in it, he knew—some soya protein in the creamer, maybe—but he loaded his cup with the artificial sweetener and the packets of dry yellowish powder and told himself he was having a rich and satisfying meal. He dabbed gingerly at his torn flesh, examined his poor battered feet like a pensioner in his garret. He squeezed the pus and flecks of dirt from the infected cuts and abrasions that striped him from head to toe, treated them with stinging iodine and soothing peroxide, and applied the Band-Aids one atop the other till his legs and arms and chest were a pale wheeling collage of plastic strips. He took his time, and his heart beat like a clock, strong and steady. To be here, to be inside, in this space separated from the hard ground and naked sky, was a quiet miracle. That it was her space, that she was here during the gathering hours of the day, made it all the sweeter. He felt, at long last, that he'd been rescued.

When he was done—when he'd used all the Band-Aids, drunk all the creamer and emptied all the packets of Sweet'n Low—he flicked off the lamp and stretched out on the wicker loveseat. He would spend the night—this one, at least—under a roof, instead of scrabbling around in the mud like an animal. God, how he hated nature. Hated the festering stink and the wet and the gnats in his eyes and ears and nostrils. The wicker was hard beneath him, but it didn't matter. He closed his eyes and settled himself, the obscene drama of the night, with all its comings and goings, its little deaths and devourings, its spiders and snakes and chiggers, out there where it belonged.

The problem was, he couldn't sleep. He was exhausted, worn-out, as weary and heartsick as any human being on the planet, and he couldn't sleep. He kept seeing her, the woman, the *Amerikajin*, rehearsing her face and her body over and over again: the moment she turned to him, the rustled silk of her voice. And then he was thinking of his *obāsan* and how when he was small and couldn't sleep she would read to him in the glowing little circle of the tensor lamp beside his bed. She hadn't liked Mishima, hadn't liked it when he gave up baseball for Jōchō and his *Hagakure*. And then he remembered the nights he couldn't sleep because of the clenching in his gut over the *ijime*—the bullying—they put him through in high school, and how Jōchō had been his hope and solace.

Hiro was seventeen when he discovered *Hagakure*—or rather, Yukio Mishima's appreciation of it, *The Way of the Samurai*. He was a boy in school, a *bēsuboru* player—there, on the field, he was the equal of anyone—and he'd never heard the name of Jōchō or of Mishima either. He played ball with savage devotion, the harsh unpronounceable names of the *gaijin* stars like an incantation on his lips: Jim Paciorek, Matt Keough, Ty Van Burkelo. They were his inspiration, his hope. You could be a mongrel, a half-breed, you could be anything, and all that mattered was that you got a hit when you stepped up to the plate. That was democracy. That was *fea purē*. That was revenge. Fujima, Morita, Kawakami, the very insects who'd blackened his eyes and broken his nose, the ones who hissed *bata-kusai* at his back as he made his way down the corridor, these were the ones he silenced with his bat. They squinted at him from the pitcher's mound, from shortstop and centerfield, chanting their obscenities and waving their mitts to distract him, till his bat met the ball and their legs fell out from under them. *Bēsuboru*, that was his life.

And then one day, walking home from school and attracting the usual stares on the street—everyone knew at a glance that he wasn't Japanese, that he was something else, something alien, and their eyes flew to him and then dropped away as if he were dead, inanimate, a post, a tree, a smear on the sidewalk—he found himself gawking at a poster in a bookstore window. The poster—it was a blown-up photo, in black and white—showed a nearly naked man in the throes of death. He'd been lashed to a tree, his hands bound over his head, and three stark black arrows protruded from his flesh. One penetrated his lower abdomen, just above the folds of his crude breechcloth, another radiated from his side, while the third was thrust nearly to the hilt in the dark clot of hair beneath his arm. His eyes were half open, staring off toward the heavens in glazed rapture, and his mouth was a fierce dark slash of agony and release. He had the musculature of a hero.

Too shy to go in, Hiro only gaped at the window that first day, fascinated, wondering if the photo was real—there was blood, after all, perfect black streaks of blood dribbling from the wounds like grisly brushstrokes. But then, maybe they were too perfect, maybe the whole thing had been staged—a still from a movie or a play—maybe they *were* brushstrokes. And where would anyone come by such a picture if it was real? People weren't tortured to death these days, were they? And with arrows? He wondered if the man might not be an explorer, captured and executed by some big-lipped tribe in New Guinea or South America. If he was, and there was a book about it, Hiro wanted it.

The next day, he steeled himself and went into the shop. It was a cramped and dark place, row upon row of books on metal shelves affixed to the walls, a smell of newsprint and mold and a fruity false air freshener. Fifteen or twenty customers browsed through the stacks of foreign newspapers or waddled up and down the aisles, arms laden with books. Aside from the rustle of lovingly turned pages, the place was as quiet as a shrine. Hiro approached the desk, where a big-shouldered man in smoked glasses with western-style frames sat behind a cash register. Hiro cleared his throat. The man, who'd been staring out the window at nothing, gave him an indifferent glance.

"The poster in the window, sir," Hiro said, so softly he could barely hear himself, "is that a book? I mean, is there a book about it?"

The man looked at him a moment, as if deciding something. Finally, in a weary voice, he said: "That's Mishima."

It was luck, it was fate, it was magic. Hiro stood bewildered before the rack the shop owner pointed him to—twenty, twenty-five, thirty Mishima titles in duplicate and triplicate and more taking a good slice out of the wall. It was as if his hand was guided: the first book he chose, the very first, was *The Way of the Samurai*. He slipped it off the shelf, pleased by its glossy cover and the drawing of dueling swordsmen that seemed to dance across it. He never even glanced inside: the cover was enough. That and the poster. He laid down his money for the laconic shopkeeper and ducked out the door with his treasure, one eye on the cruel photo of the martyred author.

Like most Japanese boys, Hiro knew the mythos of the samurai as thoroughly as his American counterpart knew that of the gun-slinger, the dance-hall girl and the cattle rustler. The wandering samurai, like the lone man on the horse, was a mainstay of network TV, the movie theater, cheap adventure novels and lurid comics, not to mention classics like *The Forty-Seven Ronin* that were on every school reading list. But after a period when he was eight or nine and ran around all day with a wooden sword and a *hachimaki* looped round his head, he'd outgrown his fascination with the whole busi-ness of topknots and swords: samurai, he could take them or leave them. Still, when he opened Mishima's book, it brought him back. He didn't know then of Mishima's right-wing politics, of his homo-sexuality and grandstanding, or even of his ritual suicide—all he knew was that he'd entered another world.

The book puzzled him at first. It wasn't a story. There were no swordfights, no hair-raising tales of samurai derring-do and acts of redemptive heroism. No. It was a study, a commentary actually, by this man, this Mishima with the arrows in his groin, on Jōchō Yamamoto's ancient samurai code of ethics, *Hagakure*. Hiro didn't know what to make of it. *I discovered that the Way of the Samurai is death*, he read. And: *Human beings in this life are like marionettes . . . free will is an illusion.* He read that it was acceptable for a samurai to apply rouge if he woke up with a hangover and that wetting the earlobes with spittle would control nervousness in any situation. It all felt faintly ridiculous.

But he stuck with it, though it was like a textbook, a manual, like something he might read in a science or navigation class. He kept seeing the picture of the martyred author—only later did he realize it was a pose, Mishima's masochistic homage to an Italian painting of a martyred saint—and he plowed through the book as if it were written in code, as if it were his personal initiation into the arcane rites and ancient secrets that would make their master the equal of anyone. It was a game, a puzzle, a conundrum. *Haga-kure*—Hidden Among the Leaves—even its title was mysterious. In the following weeks he went back to the shop several times— the poster was gone, replaced by a life-size cutout of an old man with the face of a bird and a shock of white hair—to sample Mishima's other books. They were novels, for the most part, and he enjoyed them, but none of them had the tug of the first. There was something there, and he didn't know what it was. Over and over he read the cryptic passages, over and over. And then one day, in the way that the sun suddenly breaks through the clouds in the midst of a storm, he had it.

They'd ganged up on him at the ballfield—six or seven of them— and they'd slapped him around and flung his Yomiuri Giants cap into the sewer. He was in a rage, but the rage gave way to despair. When would it end, he asked himself, and the answer was never. He barely spoke to his grandparents that night, and he was restless: he didn't want to watch the game shows, didn't want to listen to tapes on his Walkman, he didn't want to study or read. Finally, out of boredom, he picked up his dog-eared copy of *Hagakure*, opened it at random and began to read. The passage was about modern society, about how corrupt and weak it had become, and all at once, as if a switch had been flipped inside his head, Mishima's words made perfect sense. All at once he understood: the book was about glory, and nothing less.

The society around him—the society into which he'd tried to fit himself all the years of his life—was corrupt, emasculated, obsessed with material things, with the pettiness of getting and taking, selling and buying—and where was the glory in that? Where was the glory in being a nation of salarymen in white shirts and western suits making VCRs for the rest of the world like a tribe of trained monkeys? Hiro saw it, saw it clearly: Fujima, Morita, Kawakami and all the rest of them, they were nothing, eunuchs, wimps, gutless and shameless, and they would grow up to chase after yen and dollars like all the other fools who made fun of him, who singled *him* out as the pariah. But he wasn't the pariah, they were. To live by the code of *Hagakure* made him more Japanese than they, made him purer, better. It was the ultimate code of *fea pure*—or no, it went beyond *fea pure* and into another realm altogether, a realm of power and confidence—of purity—that transcended the material, the flesh, death itself. He'd been made to feel inferior all his life, and here was a way to conquer it—not only on the ballfield, but on the streets and in the restaurants and theaters and anywhere else he chose to go. He would fight back at Fujima and the rest of them with the oldest weapon in the Japanese arsenal. He would become a modern samurai.

But now, as he lay on the *Amerikajin*'s cramped little couch, using Jōchō as his pillow, all that seemed an eternity away. To rely on Jōchō had become automatic with him, but now he was in America, where everyone was a *gaijin* and no one cared, and he would have to find a new code, a new way to live. His tormentors were back in Yokohama and in Tokyo, they were sailing for New York aboard the *Tokachi-maru*, and he was free—or he would be, if only he could get to Beantown or the City of Brotherly Love. The thought soothed him—he envisioned a city like Tokyo, with skyscrapers and elevated trains and a raucous snarl of traffic, but every face was different—they were white and black and yellow and everything in between—and they all glowed with the rapture of brotherly love. He held that image as he might have sucked a piece of candy. And then he shut his eyes and let the night fall in on him.

. . .

HE WOKE TO A PARLIAMENT OF BIRDS AND THE TREMBLING WATERY light of dawn. This time there was no confusion: the moment his eyes snapped open he knew who he was and where and why. He sat up with a long grudging adhesive groan of his Band-Aid plastic strips and examined his shorts and T-shirt and the ventilated tennis shoes that seemed to leer at him from the floor. He could see at a glance that the shoes were at least two sizes too big, designed as they were for the flapping gargantuan feet of *hakujin* giants. And the shorts! They fit, sure, but they were atrocious, ridiculous, a moronic blaze of color that made him doubt the manufacturer's sanity. What did she think he was—a clown or something? Was she trying to make fun of him? His gaze fell on the little table with its clutter of Sweet'n Low packets and the coffee jar he'd scraped clean in his greed, and he felt ashamed of himself. Deeply ashamed. She'd sacrificed her lunch for him, given him a couch to sleep on, gone out and found him clothes and shoes and Band-Aid plastic strips, and here he was complaining. He was an ingrate. A criminal. His face burned with shame.

Already he owed her a debt—an *on*—that he could never begin to repay, not even if he were back in Japan and working in a factory and he saved every yen he made for the next six years. The thought humiliated him, made him feel even lower than he had the night before when he'd come to her in rags. In Japan, any favor, any gratuitous kindness, however small or altruistic, saddles its receiver with a debt of honor that can only be redeemed by repaying the favor many times over. It has become so ritualized, so onerous, in fact, that no matter what their extremity, people are terrified of being helped. You could be run down in the street and insist on crawling to the hospital rather than have a stranger lend a hand— and the stranger would no doubt run the other way, out of respect for your pain and the impossible burden he'd be laying on your shoulders were he to help.

Hiro had been inculcated with the subtleties and minute gradations of this system all his life, his grandmother the most rigorous *on* appraiser in all Japan—she could instantly translate any gift or favor into the precise material worth of its return, and she had nothing but contempt for anyone who fell short by even a yen.

Help an old woman across the street and you got a hand-knitted sweater, a box of cherry chocolates and an invitation to tea. Accept the invitation and you owed the old woman a two-week vacation in Saipan, where she would sift for the bone fragments of her unburied sons; refuse it, and commit a crime second only to mass murder. The whole society was one vast web of obligation. Fail, break a strand of the web, and you've lost face, 120 million tongues clucking *tsk-tsk-tsk*.

Suddenly, he wanted to hide himself. She'd be coming any minute now, bobbing up the path on her long white legs. What would he say to her? And what if she wanted a cup of coffee? What then? Mortified, his ears stinging, he cleaned up the mess and left her his rags, neatly folded, in humble acknowledgment of what she'd done for him, and then he dashed out the door to hide himself in the bushes.

He was squatting over the battered sneakers in a dapple of sun, feeling every one of his hundred and seven oozing cuts, scratches and infected insect bites and thinking nothing, nothing at all—just existing—when she came up the path. Her hair was drawn back in a ponytail that bounced behind her as if it were alive, and she looked waiflike in a pair of baggy white shorts and an oversized T-shirt. The T-shirt featured the silhouette of a racing scull, oars in motion, and the baffling legend CREW THANATOPSIS. Hiro held his breath, though she could have passed within a foot of him and never noticed, so thick was the vegetation along the path. As she approached the cabin, she slowed her pace, stealthy suddenly, as if she were stalking something. He watched her mount the steps on tiptoe, ease back the screen door and hold it open just a moment too long, and then glance shrewdly round the clearing before stepping inside. The door slammed behind her like a slap in the face.

All that day, Hiro crouched there in the undergrowth, drowsing, swatting mosquitoes, fighting down the importunities of his *hara* and listening to the *tap-tap-tap, tapata-tapata, tap-tap* of her typewriter. When the sun was directly overhead, he was briefly aroused by the sudden appearance of a deeply tanned *hakujin* who noiselessly separated himself from the trees and crept across the clearing, step by silent step. For one joyous instant Hiro thought he'd discovered a means to repay his debt and then some—the man was a rapist, a mutilator of women, an escaped maniac, and he, Hiro Tanaka, would fly into action and give his benefactress the great good gift of her life—when to his disappointment and gratification both, he noticed the familiar glittering treasure of the lunch bucket tucked under the man's arm. The man was lithe and trim beneath the plane of his towering high flattop, and he sneaked up the steps and silently hung the lunch bucket on the hook beside the door. Then he stole away like a thief.

For most of the afternoon, Hiro contemplated that lunch bucket with mixed emotions—he couldn't take it, no, he owed her too much already; but then she'd offered it to him, hadn't she? At least she had yesterday. But who could speak for today? Maybe she was hungry, maybe she felt she had a right to her own lunch—or a cup of decaffeinated coffee with artificial sweetener and nondairy creamer. He couldn't take that lunch away from her, couldn't face her: what would she think of him? As it turned out, she never went near the lunch herself, but more times than he could count she got up from her desk to cross the room and peer through the mesh of the screen to see if it was still there. He felt terrible. He felt like a baited animal, a squirrel or fox lured to the trap. But most of all, he felt hungry.

When she left for the day—when he was sure she'd gone and had forced himself to count backward from a thousand just in case— he stole out of the bushes, snatched the bucket on the run and careened back to his hiding place, the fish-paste sandwich—was that tuna?—already in his mouth. After he'd eaten it, after he'd licked clean the wrapping paper and probed the crevices of the box for the last hidden crumbs, he felt tainted and polluted, like the alcoholic who succumbs to the temptation to take that first forbidden drink. Still, he *was* starving, getting along on a fraction of what he normally consumed, and though he fought it, the scenario repeated itself the following day. And that was when he reached his moment of crisis.

He could not, would not demean himself before her again. What did he think he was doing? Did he intend to crouch forever in the bushes outside the fly-speckled window of the only *Amerikajin* who'd shown him a ray of kindness? What was he going to do— grow a long black beard and eat dirt all his life, live like a caveman or a hippie or something? No, he had to get to Beantown, the Big Apple, to the City of Brotherly Love; he had to blend in with the masses, find himself a job, an apartment with western furniture and Japanese appliances, with toaster ovens and end tables and deep thick woolly carpets that climbed up the walls like a surging tide. Then he'd be safe, then he could play miniature golf and eat cheeseburgers or stroll down the street with an armload of groceries and no one would blink twice. The moment he finished the second lunch, the ultimate and final lunch, he started off down the path for the blacktop road that would lead him to a distant wide sun- streaked highway and all the glorious polyglot cities of the land of the free and the home of the brave.

Behind a Wall
of Glass

. . . .

"NOW, SAXBY, I'M WARNIN' YOU—IF YOU GET ONE DROP OF WATER
on that furniture . . ."

The aquarium had been in place for less than an hour, and already
Saxby was filling it from the green plastic garden hose that snaked
in through the open window. The tank was too long by half a foot,
and when he and Owen hadn't been able to negotiate the tricky
corner in the hallway outside his bedroom, they'd set it up on the
window seat in his mother's sitting room. He'd covered the seat
itself with a double sheet of visquine, but Septima was concerned
for the Hepplewhite highboy that stood to its immediate left and
the three-hundred-year-old mahogany sideboard that loomed up
out of the grip of the wallpaper on the right. "Hush now," he said,
reassuring her, "I wouldn't harm one little thing in this house, you
know that," and he manipulated the hose with one hand while with
the other he arranged his aquatic furniture—the rocks he'd plucked
from the Carruthers' seawall and boiled for hours in the colony's
big stewpots to discourage unwanted algal and bacterial blooms,
and the long wet strands of water lily, pickerelweed, bladderwort
and redroot he'd brought back with him from the Okefenokee.
"Hell, I'd be throwing away my own inheritance if I did."

"Saxby, you stop that now," she shot back with a grin that

exposed the long fossilized roots of her teeth. She loved to hear him go on about his inheritance, even if he made a joke of it—what she wanted above all, what she planned to make him swear to on her deathbed, was that he would stay on in the house after her, overseeing the colony's operations in her stead and living a long and fruitful life in the brilliant company that would call Thanatopsis home on into the limitless future.

"Seriously, though, Mama—it'll be beautiful when I'm done. You'll see."

Septima was sunk in the vastness of a chintz-covered easy chair, her feet propped up on a matching ottoman, and her book—a book-club selection on the history of rice-paper manufacture in Wu Chan Province during the twelfth century—spread face-down in her lap. "I know it will, honey," she said, a faint distracted quaver working its way into her voice, as if, just for a moment, age and infirmity had caught up with her, "but that highboy is priceless, simply priceless, and I remember your grandmother Lights saying—"

He turned to her in that moment, water dribbling from his fingertips, sleeves rolled up past his elbows, and gave her a smile so rich it stopped her in midsentence.

"What?" she said, grinning. "What is it?"

"You," he said. "Look at you: you're treating me like I was six years old again—and believe me, I wouldn't complain if you'd only go back to making me corn muffins and drizzled honey in the mornings and tucking me in at night."

His mother said nothing, but he knew she was enjoying it, this vision of her hulking big sinewy twenty-nine-year-old son as a breathless pigeon-toed little boy who couldn't stop eating corn muffins, who looked up into her eyes as if they contained all the answers to all the questions in the universe and followed her, step for step, through the days and weeks and months of her younger and less complicated life. After a moment he turned back to the tank, shifted the hose, adjusted the filter intake, patted a mound of gravel over the roots of the pickerelweed he'd planted in the near corner. There was the murmur of the water, the soft play of the fronds on his skin, the slow soothing pleasure of doing something, making something, of building a world with his own hands. A period of time was erased—five minutes? ten?—before he spoke again. "So how's Ruth been keeping?" he said, glancing over his shoulder.

Septima set down her book and peered up at him over the wings of her reading glasses. Little ripples of surprise crested on the brittle white beach of her hairline. "You haven't seen her yet?"

"Just for a second. I was bringing the tank in with Owen and she was on her way out the door—said she was going back out to the studio . . ."

"At this hour?"

Saxby shrugged. The water felt suddenly cold on his hands. "She missed dinner? And cocktails?"

"I guess." The tank was three-quarters full now, and its water seemed as gray as a field of stones. "I could always have Rico fix her something—or we could get a loaf of bread and a package of Swiss down at the Handi-Mart."

His mother's eyes had a faraway look. He imagined she was summoning up the hundreds of artists who'd passed through Thanatopsis House in her time—from the minor to the major, from the unknown and unknowable to the celebrated and great—and calculating just how many had ever missed cocktails. He lifted his hands from the cold tank and buried them in a towel. "It's no big deal," he said, "I was just—"

"You don't have to worry about Ruth," she said suddenly.

"Oh, I wasn't worried"—he gestured with the towel—"it's just that she's new here and she feels a little out of her league, I guess—a little overawed, maybe—and I feel bad about it. I told her I was only going to be gone two days, but then two stretched into four and . . ." he trailed off.

"Saxby, honey," she said, and her voice was cloudy again, shivered with age, "stop foolin' with that thing and come on over here and sit with your mother a minute."

The outside of the glass was beaded with condensation, the hose running liquid ice up out of the deep roots of the earth, and he realized it would be three or four days at least until the water warmed up enough to put the fish in. The thought was mildly depressing—the excitement was in the completion, six days of labor and one to kick back and see that it was good—and he took a step toward his mother and hesitated, giving the tank one last critical appraisal. He watched the plants nod and bow in the current generated by the hose and the big humming filtration system, saw the secret caves and hollows and piscine apartments he'd sculpted of rock, ever so briefly admired the scope and magnitude of the thing—six feet long and two hundred gallons!—and then sidled across the room to ease himself down at the foot of his mother's chair. Immediately he felt her hand on his shoulder, the maternal fingers tugging gently at his ear.

"I want to tell you somethin'," she said, her voice trembling still, but infused now with a bright contralto hint of playfulness, "and I want you to listen to me. We don't ever disturb our artists at work, no matter what the hour or how anxious we are to"—she paused—"to show them how much we've missed them. Now do we, honey?"

He didn't answer. He was listening to the slow, steady heartbeat of the pump circulating the dense atmosphere of the little world he'd brought to life behind a wall of glass, and all of a sudden he felt sleepy.

"Workin' through dinner," Septima sighed, and her cool lineal hand massaged the nape of his neck, "that girl must really be on to somethin'."

. . .

IT WAS LATE—PAST ONE—BY THE TIME HE FINALLY DID GET RUTH to bed, and he was a little miffed—just a little; he'd been around too, after all—that she wasn't a whole lot more anxious to leave the billiard room and fall into his arms. They'd had an omelet and a bottle of wine together in the kitchen about nine, and she'd been coy and sexy and he'd tugged at her blouse and pinned her up against the meat locker to rotate his hips against hers and feel his blood surge. "Let's go fool around," he said, and she said sure, but led him instead up the stairs to the billiard room.

The usual crowd was there—Thalamus, Bob Penick, Regina, Ina and Clara, the new guy, Sandy, and a couple of others—but there'd been a change in the interior weather since he'd been gone—that much was apparent the minute they stepped in the door. "Hey, Ruthie!" Thalamus cried, rising up out of his chair at the card table like a lizard skittering off a rock, and someone else shouted "La Dershowitz!" and only then did they acknowledge him, though he'd been gone four days.

Ruth poured herself a waterglass of bourbon—neat—and took a seat between Thalamus and Bob at the card table. Sandy and Ina were playing too—the usual, five-card stud—and so was a guy he'd never seen before, a gawky character with dyed hair and a splotched face who looked as if he'd been put together with spare parts. Regina was draped over the billiard table, rattling off one daunting and professional shot after another, and the two women in the far corner—he didn't recall their names—were absorbed so deeply in conversation they might as well have put a Plexiglas wall up around themselves. And where did that leave him? To sit and listen to Clara Kleinschmidt go on about Schoenberg and the twelve-tone scale till his brain dissolved from boredom?

As the evening wore on, Ruth did get up and pay some attention to him—Why was he brooding? she wanted to know—but she skipped round the room like the Queen of May, and always found her place again at the poker table—beside Thalamus. Saxby drank vodka and brooded, though he denied he was brooding, and made small talk with Peter Anserine and one of his disciples, who'd paid a rare visit to the billiard room; discussed the fine points of bedding irises with Clara Kleinschmidt, who proved to him that she was more than just a composer; and finally, in desperation, challenged Regina McIntyre to a game of eight ball, which he lost without taking a single shot. As he became progressively more inebriated, the elation he'd felt over setting up the aquarium and beginning a new project dissipated like a stain in water. And then it was late and Ruth fluttered up to squeeze his arm and give him a kiss with a lot of tongue in it, the guy with the splotched face shook his hand and introduced himself as the INS agent he'd spoken to on the phone, and Irving Thalamus cuffed him on the shoulder and told him a lewd story about Savannah and a whore he'd once had there. Ruth won thirteen dollars and fifty-two cents.

Later, in bed, after he'd stripped her garment by garment and run his fingers the length of her and showed her how much he'd missed her in the most essential ways, he lit a cigarette and wondered aloud about the sudden shift in billiard-room relations. They were in his room, the room he'd had since he was a boy, just down the wainscoted corridor from his mother's room. The night was close, palpable, breathing in through the screen with a sharp wild whiff of the marsh and the tidal creeks and the slow wet burning death of vegetation. Ruth lay apart from him, her skin silvered with sweat in the light of the moon. And then she leaned into him, her breast flattening against his bicep as she lit a cigarette off his. Her face glowed in the flare of tobacco, she exhaled with a deep sweet luxurious breath, and told him that the billiard room was hers, no problem, and that now—finally—she was really starting to enjoy herself.

He reflected on this for a moment, leaning back against the headboard of his childhood bed, squeezed tight and sweltering against her, shoulder to shoulder and flank to flank. His cigarette glowed hot in the dark. "Miss me?" he murmured.

In answer, she took hold of his penis and smoothed it against her palm, a touch as soft and silken as a fluttering sail. "I'll give you three guesses," she said in her smokiest voice and leaned over to kiss him.

He felt that touch and flexed his thighs, tasted her lips and smelled the heat of her. "What about Thalamus?" he said.

She let her hand go slack. "What about him?"

"I don't know," he said, looking away though he knew she couldn't have seen his eyes in that light, "it's just that he seems awful friendly all of a sudden . . ."

Her hand started up again, proprietary, insinuating. "Jealous?" she breathed.

He set his cigarette down on the edge of the scarred night table and covered her rhythmic hand with his own. He held her there and rose up with a screech of the old bedsprings to kneel between her thighs and bring his face down to hers. Thalamus was nothing, a joke, dried up and juiceless, a string of jerky in a slick plastic wrapper. He could have run him down, could have denigrated him, but he didn't. Instead, he answered her question. Plainly. Simply. Truthfully. "Yes," he said.

She was there beneath him, sweat-slick and venereal, salt skin, breath hot on his face, whispering close. "Don't be," she murmured. "I'm just . . . playing the game. You should know that . . . you, Sax . . . you," and she pulled him down into the place where words have no meaning.

■   ■   ■

NEXT MORNING—OR RATHER, AFTERNOON; IT WAS HALF PAST twelve when he woke—Saxby took a cup of coffee, an egg sandwich and yesterday's just-delivered newspaper into his mother's sitting room. He had a vague recollection of Ruth stirring at first light and bending to kiss him as she hurried off to breakfast at the convivial table, but it was so vague as to dissolve instantly into the glow of the sitting room and the strong vertical shafts of light that penetrated the windows and made a theater of the aquarium. Overnight, the tank had been transformed. The water was clear now, absolutely limpid, filtered free of the detritus he'd stirred up in the act of creation, the plants stood tall and held a trembling virescent light, and the shelves of rock loomed against the deep matte background like reefs six fathoms down. He took a standing bite of the egg sandwich, a sip of coffee, and set his breakfast aside. He was too excited to eat. In the next moment he had his hands in the water, adjusting this rock or that, fanning out the gravel, moving a plant as a painter might adjust a still life. But what gave him the most satisfaction, what made him forget all about the congealing egg, cooling coffee and day-old newspaper, was the expectation that his perfect microcosmic world would soon be tenanted. If he was lucky. And luck would necessarily play a major role in the project unfolding beneath his wet cold hands.

For Saxby was no scientist—a committed, even passionate amateur, perhaps, but no scientist. Academic rigor, required courses in physics, biochemistry, geology and anatomy, these were things he could do without. He'd been to several colleges—his mother admired science, and was willing to support him in anything, though she herself, having been a poet in her youth, preferred the Arts—and he'd done decreasingly well at each of them. His love was animals—aquatic vertebrates in particular—and the curricula of these fine, leafy, heavily endowed and venerable schools just didn't seem to meet his needs. Finally, in his midtwenties and after some six years of errant scholarship, he'd dropped out altogether, well short of the credits for a B.S. degree, and he'd done some traveling—Belize; the Amazon; lakes Nyasa and Tanganyika; Papua New Guinea—before settling down on the West Coast. There, drawing on his trust fund for support, he was able to work for minimum wages at Sea World and the Steinhart Aquarium and as mate on a sportfishing boat out of Marina Del Rey (his job to bait the hooks for pale bloodless jowly men in leisure suits). He'd gone back to school—at Scripps—the previous year, but not in the celebrated oceanography program, as he'd told his mother and, later, Ruth. He'd been more or less a hanger-on there, attending the odd lecture in holothurian morphology and allowing boredom and inertia to fix him in a perpetual late lingering boyhood. And then, at a party, he met Ruth, and Ruth brought him back home to Georgia.

When the sun had shifted in the sky and the egg of the egg sandwich had passed from inedible to emetic, the door behind him creaked open and his mother glided into the room. She was wearing an old painter's cap pulled down over her eyes, a pair of jeans, sandals and an oversized blouse, and she fell into her easy chair as if she'd been shoved. "I swear I'll never get used to this heat if I live a thousand years," she sighed.

Saxby had been wandering. He'd been reprising all the aquariums he'd had as a child, all the guppies, swordtails, mollies and oscars he'd escorted through their brief passage of life, and dreaming of this new project, his inspiration, the one that would bridge his childhood love and the sort of seriousness of purpose expected of a man in his thirtieth year. Now he looked up sharply. "You haven't been gardening again?"

There were telltale stains of earth on both the sagging knees of his mother's sagging jeans. She didn't attempt to deny it.

"Mama, in this heat? You'll kill yourself yet."

She waved him off as she might have waved off a fly. "Be a sweet," she said, "and fetch me a glass of iced tea."

He crossed the room without a word—angry at her; why, if she must poke around in the garden, couldn't she do it in the evening?—and went through her bedroom to the back parlor and kitchen beyond it. This was the old core of the house, the original structure around which Saxby's great-grandfather, DeTreville Lights, had built the house as it now stood. Septima had reserved it to herself, as her private living quarters, when she'd set up the colony twenty years earlier. The kitchen had a low beam ceiling and it was long and narrow, peg and groove floors, thick fieldstone walls over which generations of plaster had been smoothed. It was cool here, the windows shaded by the huge snaking moss-hung oaks that antedated the house. Eulonia White, Wheeler's daughter, was shelling shrimp at the table. "She's been gardening again," he said, and went straight to the refrigerator.

Eulonia White was a well-built woman, fortyish, with bad teeth and a sweet faraway look behind the flashing lenses of her wire-rim glasses. She didn't respond.

Saxby poured the iced tea from a stoneware pitcher, and as he sliced a round of lemon and the scent of it rose to his nostrils, he suddenly realized he was famished. "That shrimp salad you're making there, Eulonia?" he asked.

She nodded, her lenses throwing fire. "She say she gone eat in here tonight."

"How about a little sandwich for me, could you do that? Rye or wheat—check with Rico, I think he's got both in the main kitchen—with some mayo, black pepper, squeeze of lemon. Okay? I'll be in with my mother."

Back in the sitting room, he slipped the cold glass into his mother's hand, and then picked up the dead egg sandwich—famished, absolutely famished—and gave it a tentative sniff. "I just been sittin' here watchin' that aquarium, Saxby," his mother said, sipping at her iced tea, "and I do swear it *is* the prettiest one you've ever gone and created, but I said to myself, Where are the *fee*-ish?"

.　　■　　.

IT WAS CLOSING IN ON COCKTAIL HOUR WHEN HE PUSHED HIMSELF up and left the room. His mother, the empty glass cradled in her hands and her head thrown back so that the painter's cap rode like a raft on the permed white swells of her hair, was snoring lightly from the depths of the chair as he eased the door shut behind him. He snatched a towel out of the bathroom, slipped into his swim trunks and dug his mask, snorkel and fins out of the closet. Then he headed out the back door and across the lawn for the boat, figuring to get some exercise in before drinks and dinner turned his limbs to dough.

The sun was so hot on his back it felt ladled on, but it felt good too. He waved to Ina Soderbord, who was sunning herself in one of the lawnchairs, caught a whiff of the ocean and a faint distant snatch of disco music, and then he was in the shadowy fastness of the trees. The smell of life was stronger here, primal, earthy. Butterflies fell like confetti through shafts of light, birds vanished and reappeared, a chameleon the color of astroturf clung to a mossy stump. He felt good. Felt connected. And he saw the remainder of the day opening up before him in a concatenation of simple pleasures: the plunge into the Atlantic, the drifting eternal silence of the ocean floor, the first fragrant sip of vodka, Ruth, crab cakes and endive salad, brandy, billiards, love. The misery of his long vodka-drenched evening in the billiard room was behind him now. It was nothing, an aberration, a misconception: Ruth was playing the game, that was all, she was networking. When he came up on the boat slip he was jubilant, elated, so full of the moment he found himself kicking up his heels and whistling like Uncle Remus himself, his shoulders alight with corny cartoon bluebirds.

But what was this?—there was someone in his boat. Someone long, lanky, the build of a basketball player, L.A. Dodgers cap, acid-washed face: Abercorn. His jubilation was gone, switched off like a light. "Hello," he said, feeling the mud between his toes, feeling foolish, as if this weren't his boat, his water, his trees, as if this weren't the ground on which his ancestors had been born and breathed their last for two centuries and more.

Abercorn was hunched over a yellow notepad and writing furiously, oblivious to Saxby, the day, the drift and tug of the boat on its painter. He was wearing headphones. Saxby followed the connection past Abercorn's blotched ears, spattered neck and wrinkled collar to the Walkman in his shirt pocket, and figured he was either writing a novel dictated by spirit guides or transcribing the tapes of his interviews with the various boneheads who populated the island. "Hello," Saxby repeated, raising his voice.

When there was no reaction, he tossed his flippers into the boat, and that was all it took: Abercorn jumped as if he'd been attacked from within, betrayed by his own body. He gaped up—damn, if his eyes weren't pink, like a bunny's—and then flipped the 'phones from his ears with a confused wheeze of greeting. "Oh, hey," he sputtered, looking as if he'd just come back from a long way off, "I'm just, uh—I hope you don't mind the boat and all, I was just, it was such a nice day, I—" and then, as if the air had run out of his balloon, he fell silent.

"Sure," Saxby said, hardly less embarrassed than the pink-eyed wonder before him, "no problem. I was just going to take the boat out. For a little swim. That's all."

Abercorn made no effort to rise. Instead, he fixed his suddenly shrewd eyes on Saxby and said, "Mind if I ask you a couple of questions?"

Saxby sighed. The sun was like syrup and everything was drowning in it. "I've only got a minute," he said, stepping into the water, gripping the boat to steady it and then swinging himself nimbly over the side.

Abercorn wanted to hear about the incident at the store—and he wanted more too on that first night on Peagler Sound: What did the Nip look like? how tall was he? did he attack without provocation?—and Saxby obliged him, all the while tinkering with the engine, checking the starter plug, the spare gas tank and the coil of the starter cord. Right in the middle of the store incident, just as Saxby was getting to the good part—how the Japanese guy bundled up his junk food and lowered his shoulder like a fullback and shot past him out the door—Abercorn interrupted him. "You know—could I ask you something?" he said.

Ask him something? Wasn't that what he was doing?

"Something personal, I mean."

Saxby fiddled with the engine. "Sure," he said. "Go ahead."

"It's your accent. I mean, I'm from L.A., and everybody down here sounds like they just stepped out of Dogpatch or something—no offense—but you don't have it. You are from around here, right?"

It was a question he'd been asked a thousand times, and the answer was equivocal: he was and he wasn't. He'd been born in Savannah, yes, and he was heir to half the island, even if he did talk like a Yankee. But the reason he talked like a Yankee was that he'd spent half his life—the formative half—in New York and Massachusetts. That was his father's doing. Grandfather Saxby wasn't even cold yet in the grave when Marion Lights uprooted Septima and her year-old son and moved them up to Ossining, New York, on the Hudson River. The family had from time immemorial owned a controlling interest in a big antiquated factory there that produced yeast, margarine, gin, vodka and the callowest whiskey known to man. Till Marion came along, the family had been content to manage the place from afar, but he had different ideas. He gave over the administration of the Tupelo Island estate (which was then called Cardross, after Cardross Lights, founder of the original plantation that had managed to survive intact through six generations of Lights, drought, flood, capricious cotton prices, carpetbaggers, boll weevils and a host of ravenous developers from the mainland) to a wily old former overseer by the name of Crawford Sheepwater, and moved north to become a Captain of Industry.

Saxby was staring at Abercorn, who'd paused to glance up from his notebook and frame the question, but he was seeing his father, that willful and supremely depressed man. Or at least he became depressed as the years of his exile wore on and he didn't exactly unseat the Rockefellers, Morgans and Harrimans. In the beginning he was almost manic with enthusiasm—when Saxby was six, seven, eight, he saw his father as a whirlwind, larger than life, a Pecos Bill or a Paul Bunyan. He was a flushed face over dinner, a set of tweed shoulders to ride on, a lover of trains and odd jokes. *Saxby,* he would say, in his rich deep Southern Gentleman's tones, *you see that dog out there?,* and he'd point to a shepherd or beagle cavorting across the lawn and Saxby would nod. *That dog's from Ohio, Saxby,* he would say, and no matter how many times he'd heard the joke— and he never got it, not till his father was long dead and gone— Saxby would say, *How do you know?,* and his father, in the tone of a professor addressing a room of veterinary students, would reply, *Why, because he has an O under his tail.*

And then later, just before he locked himself in the back pantry of the big gray-and-white Victorian overlooking the Hudson, he would wander in and out of rooms, an antic gleam in his eye, and announce, no matter the situation or the company or how many times he'd announced it already, that "cunt was cunt." That was his formula. He'd look up from his soup, glance cannily round at the guests and clap his hands together. *You know what I say*, he'd announce, pausing to look Septima in the eye, *cunt's cunt, that's what I say*. And then he locked himself in the back pantry when Saxby and his mother were out shopping and the maid had gone home, locked himself up with a bottle of the cheap whiskey he manufactured for the cheap drunks of this great country and enough Seconal to put his board of directors to sleep for a month.

Saxby was nine at the time. Though his mother had been born in Macon and gone to college at Marietta, she stayed on in the big empty house in Ossining rather than return to the big empty house on Tupelo Island. In her grief and bewilderment, she turned back to poetry—the poetry that had been the romantic bulwark of her youth—and she found solace in it. Six months later, she returned to Tupelo Island and founded Thanatopsis House, "that mysterious realm, where each shall take/His chamber in the silent halls . . . ," a palace of art sprung up from the ashes of her husband's death. Saxby spent three years with her there, and then, because the local educational system was "nothing but white trash and niggers," she sent him north again, to Groton. After Groton, it was the string of colleges that entangled him for years before finally setting him loose in California, another Yankee bastion. And so, Saxby had a foreign accent. He was a Southerner, all right, no doubt about that—but only part-time.

It was a long story. To make it short, he rolled his eyes for Abercorn and thickened his accent till it dripped: "Well, Massa Abacoan, Ah sweah Ah jest doan know—Ah'm jest folks like anybody else."

Abercorn responded with a startled bray of a laugh. "That's good. That's really good." Then he capped his Uni-Ball pen, stuck it in his shirt pocket and gave a little speech about how he'd never been out off the Georgia coast and how he was wondering if maybe Saxby'd mind if he tagged along—since he was in the boat already and everything.

Saxby studied him a moment—the long jaw and glistening teeth,

the toneless skin and unnatural hair—and shrugged. "Why not?"
he said, and fired up the engine.

.   .   .

THE FIRST WEEK OF AUGUST WAS AS SLOW AND SILKEN AND SWEET
as any Saxby could remember, and he fell into the embrace of it—
of home, of Ruth, of his mother—with an inevitability that was
like a force of nature. He was up late each night with Ruth—hoisting
cocktails and dining with poets, painters and sculptors, letting his
mind drift over the earnest declarations of the evening's poetry or
fiction reading, joining in the clubby chitchat of the billiard room
till the close lingering heat gave way to something just a breath
cooler coming in off the ocean. He slept late, through the relative
cool of the morning, took his breakfast with Septima and contemplated the vacant perfection of his aquarium. In the afternoons, he
fished, snorkeled, swam. In the evenings, there was Ruth, and the
day started again.

She was something to watch, Ruth. She worked the cocktail
hour, dinner and the ceaseless ebb and flow of billiard-room dy-
namics like a politician—or maybe a guerrilla. There was a little
joke or routine for everyone, from the unapproachable Laura Grobian to the chummy Thalamus and the lesser lights too. She was
amazing. Body signals, pursed lips, an arched eyebrow or nod of
the head that meant worlds: every time he looked up she was holding
a dialogue with somebody. One minute she'd be having a cocktail
hour tête-à-tête with Peter Anserine and two of his skinny solemn
attendants, and the next she'd be across the room, laughing with
Clara Kleinschmidt till they both had tears in their eyes—and all
the while mugging for Sandy or Regina or Bob Penick or for him—
she never forgot him, no matter how wound up she got—and she
would give him a look that passed like electricity between them.

And then she missed cocktails again one night and he stood
around with a glass in his hand radiating his own brand of wit and
charm, but all the while craning his neck to look for her. When
she caught up with him—she slipped in beside him at the table

halfway through dinner—she was out of breath and her eyes were big with excitement. "What's up?" he'd asked, and she'd taken hold of his arm and pecked a kiss at him, all the while nodding and winking and grinning in asides to half the room. "Nothing," she said, "just work, that's all. This story I'm working on's a killer. The best." "Terrific," he said, and meant it. She paused to slip a morsel of veal between her lips. "Listen," she said, "can we drive into Darien tomorrow? I need to get some things." "Sure," he said, and she was eating, small quick bites, her teeth sharp and even. "Groceries. Crackers and cheese and whatnot—for my studio. You know," she said, giving him a look, "a girl gets hungry out there."

Hungry. All right. He whispered in her ear and when they kissed he tasted the meat on her lips and everyone was watching.

And then, at the end of the week—he couldn't put it off any longer, didn't want to—he had to make another collecting trip, this one in the hope of getting his project off the ground. He was going to collect the fish—the rare, almost legendary fish—that would make him his fortune—or rather, carve him his niche in the annals of the great aquarists: fortune he already had. Ruth didn't want to come with him. Not this time. She was working too well, going with the flow, and she couldn't risk it. She'd miss him—even if he'd only be gone overnight—and she'd come along with him next time. She promised.

He spent a full blazing bug-infested afternoon and the succeeding morning on the Okefenokee, casting nets, drawing seines, setting minnow traps, and he came up with a writhing grab bag of fascinating things—pirate perch, golden top minnow, needle-nosed gar, swamp darter and brook silverside—but not what he was looking for. It was a disappointment, but not a crushing one—certainly not a defeat. He'd hoped to get lucky, yes, but knew realistically that he might have to comb the swamp a hundred times before he scored. After all, Ahab hadn't found the white whale in a day, either. Still, he enjoyed the drive, enjoyed the day out in the wilderness, even enjoyed his solitary night in a motel in Ciceroville, where he watched the Atlanta Braves on a color TV bolted to the wall. At noon on the second day he brought his rented boat in and dumped his catch over the side. (He was tempted, especially by the shimmering silver gar, to bring something back for the lifeless aquarium, but he resisted; he didn't want his little world defiled by just any tawdry thing that happened to catch his eye.) Then he headed back for Tupelo Island, hoping to make the afternoon ferry and cocktail hour.

It was early evening when he rounded the bend of the long sweeping drive and the big house came into view. There was movement on the south lawn, and Saxby saw that the colonists had gathered there for a picnic supper, the women's white summer dresses and men's light jackets like so many pale flowers in a field of saturate green. He caught a glimpse of his mother, straw bonnet with a chiffon veil, erect and regal in a wooden lawnchair, and he waved. Ruth would be there somewhere, and he slowed the pickup ever so briefly, but didn't see her, and then he was rumbling into the garage, a faint pink cloud of dust catching up with him as he killed the engine and swung open the driver's door.

He hadn't had a chance to clean up—his hands stank of perch and darter and of the rich fecal muck of the Okefenokee, and the thighs and backside of his jeans were stiff with the residue of his fish-handling—and Ruth took him by surprise. No sooner had he swung open the door and set his feet on the ground, than she was there, rushing into his arms in a strapless cocktail dress that showed off the flashing lines and tawny hollows of her throat and shoulders. "Sax," she moaned, holding him, kissing him, fish-stink and all, "I'm so glad you're back."

He held her, pressed her to him, hot already, hot instantly, a gas grill gone from pilot to high at the merest touch, and he wondered if he should gently push her away, for the sake of her dress, and he was embarrassed and he didn't know what to say. She didn't speak either—just held him—and that was odd: she was never at a loss for words. And then he felt it, a tremor running through her, seismic, an emotional quake: she was crying. "What?" he said. "What is it?"

She wouldn't lift her face.

"Is something wrong? Did something happen while I was away? What is it, babe?"

Her voice was buried, it was doleful and hoarse. "Oh, Sax," she said, and she paused, and she squeezed him and he squeezed her back. "You've got to talk to your mother, you've got to—for me."

Talk to his mother?

"It's Jane Shine," she said. She looked up at him now—lifted her head from his shoulder and showed him the tears on her face and the cold fierce glare in her eyes. "She can't come here. She can't. She's a bitch. A snob. She's—all her talent's between her legs, Sax, that's all. She's not worth it, she isn't."

He said something, anything, a rumble of disconnected words to comfort her, but she wouldn't be comforted.

Her hands tightened on his biceps and her eyes were hard. "No, Sax, I mean it," she said. "She can't come here."

There was a sudden shout of laughter from across the lawn and Ruth didn't flinch, didn't hear it, didn't care. "It would ruin everything," she said.

R u s u

IT WAS A STEAMY OPPRESSIVE TROPICAL DAY, FLIES EVERYWHERE, the reek of low tide settling in the nostrils like a kind of death, a day on which Ruth didn't bother with breakfast at the convivial table. She didn't feel even faintly convivial, and after greeting Owen with a stony face and wordlessly appropriating two hot buttered rolls from Rico, she started up the path for Hart Crane, though she didn't feel much like working either. What she felt like doing was getting off the island, getting out of there altogether—she felt like dressing for two hours and lingering over an eight-course meal at the best French restaurant in New York and then insulting the waiter, the chef, the sommelier and the maître d'. She felt like kicking dogs, pulling teeth, stepping into one of the endless workshops she'd suffered through as a student and annihilating some starry-eyed fool with scarifying and hurtful words.

Gnats darted at her face. Her feet hurt. It was a rotten day. A cataclysmic day. A stinking deadly washed-out low-tide sort of day, the day on which Jane Shine, in all her cheap and overblown glory, was set to descend on Thanatopsis House.

Ruth worked through the morning on her Japanese story—she called it "Of Tears and the Tide"—though what she wrote wasn't very good and she kept getting bogged down on individual phrases and the sorts of choices that are second nature when you're working well and impossible when you're not. At lunchtime, she was up from her desk the moment Owen stole away, and she lifted the bucket off the hook and ate greedily, hungrily, without a thought for Hiro. She hadn't seen him in a week now, and there was no sign he'd been back. The fruit and cheeses she'd left for him were rotting, the canned goods were untouched, the crackers going soft with mold. And that rankled her too: he'd deserted her. He was a living story, a fiction come to life—she'd imagined him and there he was—and she needed him. Didn't he realize that?

She was worried about him too, of course—that was part of it. He could have drowned, fallen into a bog, could have been treed and peppered with shot by one of the fired-up redneck coon hunters who haunted the porch out front of the VFW post. But no, if he'd been shot she would have heard about it before the gun was cool, no secrets on Tupelo Island. Maybe he'd got away altogether— maybe he'd swum to the mainland or stowed away on the ferry. Or—and the thought depressed her—maybe he'd taken up with someone else, some altruistic soul who even now was feeding him a hot bowl of steamed rice and chopped vegetables with a splash of Kikkoman soy sauce and a handful of crunchy noodles. Sure, that was it: he'd found a soft touch someplace else. Richer food. A better deal. Some old blue-nosed widow with trembling hands who fussed over him as if he were a wandering tomcat. Yes, that was it. For a moment the thought arrested her: he *was* a tomcat, a mercenary, and he didn't give a damn for all the risk she'd taken to get him a clean change of clothes or the sacrifice of forgoing her lunch all this time. Suddenly she saw him in a new light: he'd been using her, that's all, and he had no intention of coming back to her. She'd been fooling herself—there was no cross-cultural attraction there, no communication, no seduction. Damn him, she thought, and she went at her lunch as if she hadn't eaten in a week.

Later, when her mind fell numb and she couldn't stand it any longer, when she figured she'd given Jane Shine all the time in the world to settle in and clear out of her way, Ruth pushed herself up from the desk, glanced bitterly round the room—the blackened bananas, spotty pears, the dusty tins of sardines, anchovies and tuna—and slumped out the door. She was planning to skip cocktails and then have Saxby take her out to dinner on the mainland, putting off the inevitable—she just couldn't face that hypocrite Jane Shine, not now, not today. But when she got to the big house and tried to duck up the stairs, Irving Thalamus shot out of the parlor, drink in hand, and caught her by the elbow. He wheeled her into his arms and dragged a quick kiss across her lips, and then he beamed at her, a little drunkenly, while she strained to look over his shoulder and scan the cocktail crowd for that ski-jump nose, that mass of dark iridescent flamenco-dancer's hair, the extraterrestrial eyes and prim bosom, for that ethereal freak, Jane Shine.

Irving Thalamus squeezed her, smiling blearily and exhaling vodka fumes in her face. "Hey," he said, his smile dissolving momentarily, "no Jane. She never showed."

Ruth felt a surge of hope. She pictured the wreckage of the plane scattered across a rocky slope, twisted shards of steaming metal, flesh for the crows to pluck, the auto crushed like an accordion, the train flung from the rails. *I'm sorry, Ruthie, very sorry,* Septima had told her, *but once the bo-ard has made its decision, I don't presume to challenge it. If they feel Miss Shine is qualified—and I must say her reputation precedes her—then I can only welcome her and make her feel at home, as I do hope I do with all our artists.*

"I thought she was supposed to be here this morning?"

Thalamus shrugged.

"Has she called? Has anybody heard anything?"

"You know Jane," he said.

Yes, she knew her. They'd been at Iowa together, the first year, before Ruth dropped out and tried her luck at Irvine. From the moment she walked into the classroom with her downcast eyes and bloodless pale skin beneath a bonnet of pinned-up hair, Jane was royalty—anointed and blessed—and Ruth was shit. She wrote about sex—nothing but—in a showy over-refined prose Ruth found affected, but which the faculty—the exclusively male faculty—

discovered to be the true and scintillating voice of genius. Ruth fought it. She did. This was her arena, after all, and she did manage to captivate one of the instructors, a skinny bearded hyperkinetic visiting poet from Burundi. But he didn't speak English very well, and perhaps for that reason—or perhaps because he was temporary and wore tribal tattoos on his lips and ears—he didn't carry much weight. At the end of the year, when the second-year fellowships were announced, Jane Shine swept all before her.

In anger and frustration, Ruth had quit Iowa and gone home to California and Irvine, where she managed to produce the story that won her her first acceptance in *Dichondra*. But even that small triumph was soured for her—ruined, squashed, throttled in the cradle—when she came home after a modest celebration with two of her classmates to find that month's *Atlantic* in the mailbox and Jane Shine's story—the very same overwrought sexual saga she'd presented in class at Iowa—nestled there in that familiar hieratic print between a Very Important Article and a Very Important Poem. And then, in quick succession, Jane's stories appeared in *Esquire*, *The New Yorker* and the *Partisan Review*, and then she had a collection out and her picture was everywhere and the critics— the exclusively male critics—fell over dead with the highest, most exquisite praise of their careers on their dying lips. Yes, Ruth knew her.

"What do you mean?" she said.

"She likes to make an entrance, is what I mean. Stir up a little drama, make us stew a bit. She's a killer, she really is. One of the heavyweights."

It was an awkward moment. Worse: it was a moment of grinding despair, of defeat and desolation. She couldn't tear at the edifice of Jane Shine directly—Jane and Irving Thalamus had been at a writers' conference in Puerto Vallarta together and they were soulmates and eternal buddies, if not something even more intimate than that—and to hear her praised, let alone even mentioned, was like having fishhooks jerked through her flesh. Ruth was racking her brain to think of how to say something devastating under the guise of being positive, supportive, unhateful and unjealous, as if she wished anything for Jane Shine but loss of hair, teeth, good looks and whatever trickle of talent she'd ever had, when someone shouted, "Hey, there's a car coming up the drive!"

Ruth froze, a named and very specific dread rising inside her till she felt like the heroine of some cheap horror film being dragged down through a sudden rent in the earth. There, framed in the beveled oblong pane of the foyer window, was a silver Jaguar sports car, gliding to a graceful halt at the curb. The top was down. The wire wheels chopped at the light. There was a man in the driver's seat—square-jawed, Nordic, a flash of blond hair, the fluorescent gleam of teeth—and beside him, glittering like a Christmas tree ornament, was Jane Shine, in a flaming silk scarf and oversized sunglasses. The miniature U-Haul trailer, symbol of all that was grubby and gauche, of hurried moves and tacky furniture, would have given Ruth universes of satisfaction in another context, but attached as it was to that gleaming low silver-flanked wonder of a car, it almost managed to look chic.

"It's Jane!" Thalamus cried, and his voice was a sort of astonished yelp, as if he'd expected anyone else, and then his arm fell away from Ruth's shoulder and he was jerking open the door and careening out onto the porch. At the same time, the square-jawed young man bounced athletically out of the car to swing open the door for Jane. In that moment, Ruth noticed with sinking resignation that the man, Jane's man, was as tall and leanly muscled as a Viking conqueror, and that Jane, far from having sunk into the fat she was rumored to have succumbed to, was as trim and stunning and fresh-faced as a high-school twirler surprised by the miracle of her own flesh. "Welcome, welcome," Thalamus boomed, striding down the steps with his arms spread wide as if he'd personally laid every stone of the big house, as if he'd been born and bred in it, the gentleman planter steeped in juleps and horseflesh, Colonel Thalamus himself. "Welcome to the heart of Dixie!"

Ruth didn't wait to see the great swooping lewd Thalamus/Shine embrace, nor did she wait to see the Nordic slave bend to the

U-Haul and unload more luggage than Queen Victoria took with her on her tour of the Empire, nor was she standing demurely in the foyer to greet her former workshop colleague and congratulate her on her success when Jane Shine, locked in the sweaty embrace of one of the legends of Jewish-American letters, swept up the steps in triumph. No. Not Ruth. The instant Thalamus passed through the door, she turned and fled up the stairs, down the corridor and into her room, where she flung herself face down on the bed as if someone had planted an arrow between her shoulder blades. And there she lay, as the shadows deepened and the cocktail chatter from below gave way to the merry clink of cutlery on china; there she lay, listening with hypersensitive ears and pounding heart to the furtive thump and rush of the Nordic slave as he installed Jane Shine in the very room next to hers—the spacious, sunny, antique-infested double room that had languished unoccupied during the whole of Ruth's stay. She listened like a child playing at hide-and-seek—a child hidden so well that the others have begun to lose interest, to forget her, though they still creep by her hiding place—listened till the sounds of dinner faded away and the sports car coughed to life and rumbled off into oblivion.

. . .

SHE MUST HAVE DOZED. IT WAS NEARLY EIGHT WHEN SAXBY CAME for her, and she had to dress in a hurry if they were going to catch the ferry to the mainland. On weekends in the summer there was a twelve o'clock ferry back, and that would give them two hours or so, after the ride out and the drive to the restaurant, to have a few cocktails, eat and unwind. Ruth felt she needed it. Through the first cocktail—a perfect Manhattan with a twist—she even thought of cajoling Saxby into booking a motel room along the coast somewhere, but then she shook off the notion. She'd have to face Jane Shine sooner or later, and it might as well be tonight, in the billiard room, where the footing was sure.

She had a second cocktail and half a dozen oysters, and her mood began to improve. The restaurant helped. It was a soothing, elegant,

beautifully appointed place in a two-hundred-year-old building on
Sea Island, very tony, three stars Michelin, with a wine list the
size of a Russian novel. And Saxby—Saxby was a gem. He was
sly and steady and good-looking, the candlelight playing softly off
the golden nimbus of his hair, his eyes locked on hers; he was
solicitous, sweet, sexy, worth any ten Nordic types in their Jaguars.
The image of Jane Shine would rise before her over her soup, a
crust of French bread or a morsel of *écrevisse*, and he would banish
it with a joke, a kiss, a squeeze in just the right place. And then,
midway through the meal, he proposed a toast.

Ruth was savoring the cleansing frisson of a *glace* of grapefruit
and Meyer lemon, when a waiter appeared at her side with a bottle
of champagne. She looked up at Saxby. He was beaming at her.
She felt a flush of pleasure as they touched glasses—he was such
a sentimentalist, forever reprising these ceremonial gestures, re-
minding her that they'd been together for eighteen weeks or twenty-
two or whatever it was—but this time he took her by surprise. "To
Elassoma okefenokee," he said.

"To who?"

"Drink," he said.

She drank.

"*Elassoma okefenokee*," he repeated, "the Okefenokee pygmy sunfish." He refilled her glass. His grin was wild, alarming, the grin
of a man who at any moment might bound up from the table and
waltz with one of the waiters. "Not to be confused with *Elassoma
evergladei*," he added, dropping his voice in confidentiality.

An elderly gentleman seated at the next table blew his nose with
authority. Ruth was aware in that moment of the gentle smack of
mastication, the patter of muted laughter. She didn't know what
to say.

"My new project, Ruth," Saxby said, elevating the tapered green
neck of the bottle over her glass. "The pygmy sunfish. It's rare
enough as it is, the whole range occurring between the Altamaha
and Choctowhatchee rivers, but I'm looking for something even

rarer." He paused, groped for her hand. His eyes sprang at her. His grin was demented. "The albino phase."

Ruth was feeling the wine. She lifted her glass to his. "Here's to albinos!" she whooped.

Saxby barely noticed. He was earnest now, his hands juggling out a series of gestures, rattling on about this pygmy fish and how So-and-so had first described the albino tendency and how the field biologists from State were occasionally turning the odd one up in their nets on the St. Mary's and how he, Saxby, was going to collect and breed them and turn the reflecting pool at the big house into a breeding pond so he could ship them out to aquarists all over the world. "They all go to Africa or South America," he said, "but there's a gold mine right here in the Okefenokee and the St. Mary's River. Think of it, Ruth. Just think of it."

She had a hard time with that proposition. She wasn't thinking of fish—as far as she was concerned, fish existed for the sole purpose of being broiled, poached or deep-fried—but she wasn't thinking of Jane Shine either. Saxby's voice was a soothing murmur, the wine good, the food even better, the sound of the waves plangent and lulling beyond the dark lacquered strips of the shutters. She drank to Saxby's project, and gladly. When the first bottle was gone, they ordered another.

Later, standing at the bow of the *Tupelo Queen* and watching the low dark hump of the island emerge from the black fastness of Peagler Sound, she felt the strength rise in her. Jane Shine. What did she care if she was surrounded by Jane Shines—she had Saxby, she had Hiro (he'd be back, of course he would), she had the big house and the billiard room and she had her work. She felt powerful, expansive, generous, ready to bury the petty jealousies that had nagged at her all these years. Art wasn't a foot race. There were no winners or losers. You became a writer for the sake of the work, for the satisfaction of creating a world, and if someone else—if Jane Shine—stepped in and won the prizes, usurped the pages of the magazines, took the best room at Thanatopsis House, well, so much the better for her. It wasn't a contest. It wasn't. There was room for everybody.

What with the wine and her revelation aboard the ferry, Ruth felt almost saintly—a Juliet of the Spirits, a Beatrice, a Mother Teresa herself—as she mounted the stairs to the billiard room, arm in arm with Saxby. The usual crew was there. Smoke hung in the air. Pool balls clattered. As they pushed through the door, laughter darted round the corners of the room and fell off to a wheeze, and then Ruth dropped Saxby's arm and started across the floor for the card table. All eyes were on her. She was looking demure, she knew it, looking shy and sweet and gracious. "Ruthie," Irving Thalamus said, glancing up from his cards.

That "Ruthie" should have alerted her—there was no joy in it, no verve; it was merely an announcement, pared down as if with a knife—but Ruth wasn't listening. She was walking, crossing the room, the corners of her mouth turned up in a wide full-lipped airline hostess's smile of greeting, all her attention focused on Jane Shine. She was vaguely aware of Sandy, off to her left, and of Bob the poet, but the only one she saw clearly was Jane, seated at the right hand of Thalamus, seated in her own spot.

No one said a word. Ruth's feet were moving, her thighs brushing lightly beneath the new red tube dress she'd worn to the restaurant, but she didn't seem to be getting anywhere, the floor was a treadmill, she was in the middle of a dream gone sour. And then, suddenly, too suddenly, she was standing over the card table and Jane Shine was glancing up at her. Jane was in white, in a high-collared linen dress with a thousand perfect pleats, though the room was as hot as Devil's Island. Her Andalusian hair, blackly glittering, teetered over her face in thick loose coils, and her eyes—her icy violet eyes—were shrunk to pinpricks.

"Jane," Ruth said, and her voice sounded strange in her own ears, as if she were shouting underwater, as if it were coming back at her from a tape recorder set on the wrong speed, "welcome to Thanatopsis."

Jane didn't move, didn't speak, merely held her there in the silence that roared with the clatter of insects from the void beyond the windows. "I'm sorry," she said finally, "but have we met?"

. . .

THERE WAS NO BREAKFAST FOR RUTH THE NEXT MORNING—SHE couldn't have digested anything anyway. She was up before Owen, up before the birds stirred in the trees or the night gave way to the first thin gray wash of dawn. But then, she'd barely slept. She'd lain there in her narrow bed in her cramped and chintzy room, seething, raging, her mind pounding on like a machine out of control: *God, how she loathed that bitch!* Saxby had tried to console her, but she wouldn't let him touch her—it was perverse, she knew it, but she had to sleep in her own room, right there on the other side of the wall from her, had to drink in her own hurts and distill them, purify them, turn them into something she could use.

The path to her studio, familiar in daylight, was a pit of shadow, blacker than the trees, blacker than the thicket that rose up on either side of her. She had no flashlight, and the names that came to her were the names of reptiles: cottonmouth, copperhead, diamondback. During the drive out from Los Angeles, Saxby had fascinated her with his tales of unwitting tourists in open-toed shoes, of developers and real estate agents bitten in the lip, eyelid and ear, of moccasins thick as firehoses dropping from the trees. Each of these stories, in the most minute and horrific detail, came back to her now, but they didn't deter her, not for a minute. She edged along that invisible path, hearing, smelling, tasting, all her taps open wide. The danger, the oddness of the hour, the thick simmering swelter of the air made her feel alive all over again.

By the time she rounded the final loop of the S curve that gave onto the cabin, the eastern sky was half lit and Jane Shine was receding, ever so gradually, from the front hallway of her consciousness. The place was still, the air soft. The first light in the windowpanes gave back the phantasmagoric shapes of the trees behind her. A cardinal shot across the clearing. As she mounted the steps, she was thinking of her story, her novella, of the woman

in Santa Monica Bay, and of Hiro and his persecution and suffer-
ings, and of how that was her story too. Yes: the woman's husband,
that was it. He'd deserted her and they were looking for him, the
police were, and he'd run off into the—

She stopped cold. The food was gone—the blackened bananas
and maculated pears, the tins of fish and moldy crackers and all
the rest—and the table was a mess, and there was someone, a form,
a shape, yes, huddled on the couch. A surge of pleasure shot
through her—*Someone's been tasting my porridge*, she thought, *Someone's been sleeping in my bed*—and she eased through the door in
silence, standing there with her back to the wall—just standing
there—until the form on the couch became Hiro Tanaka. But he
was different somehow. It took a moment before it came to her: he
was clean. Free of Band-Aid flesh-colored strips, free of scratches
and blotches and insect bites. And the soles of his feet, one set atop
the other, were clean too—and unmarked. He was still wearing
Irving Thalamus's Bermudas, his haunches glowing in the half-
light with all the inchoate colors of the tropical spectrum, but he
was wearing a new shirt, a generic gray sweatshirt with what looked
like a coat of arms emblazoned across the chest. She tilted her head
to make out the legend: GEORGIA BULLDOGS. And then she spotted
the shoes—not Thalamus's worn-out tennies with their tears and
perforations, but a gleaming new pair of Nike hightops. Ruth
smiled. Tomcat, indeed.

She didn't want to wake him, already picturing the startled eyes,
the jaw slack with horror, Goldilocks up and out the window, but
she couldn't stand there all day and she did want a cup of coffee.
After a while—five minutes, ten?—she tiptoed across the room,
filled the kettle and set it on the hot plate to boil. Then she began
to tidy up, sweeping the crumbs from the table into a cupped palm,
dropping the empty tins into an old supermarket bag she'd stuffed
behind her desk, dribbling water over the stiff pink funnels of her
pitcher plants. The lid of the kettle had just begun to rattle when
she turned and saw that Hiro's eyes were open. He was lying there
motionless, hunched like a lost soul on a park bench, but his eyes

were open now, and he was watching her. "Good morning," she said. "Welcome back."

He sat up and mumbled a greeting. He looked groggy. He dug at his eyes with the blades of his knuckles. He yawned.

Ruth stirred a spoonful of the replenished instant coffee into a mug. "Coffee?" she offered, holding the mug out to him.

He took it from her with an elaborate half-body bow and sipped gratefully, his eyes reduced to slits. He watched her pour herself a cup and then he stood, rising awkwardly above her. "I want to sank you so very much," he said, and then faltered.

Ruth held the steaming mug in both hands and looked up into his strange tan eyes. "My pleasure," she said, and then, seeing his puzzled look, she gave him the textbook reply, enunciating each word as if she needed time to chew and digest it: "You–are–very–welcome."

He seemed to brighten at this, and he held out his hand, smiling hugely. His front teeth were misaligned, overlapping, and the effect was just a little, well, goofy. Was this the first time she'd seen him smile? She couldn't remember. But she smiled back, and she couldn't imagine what all the uproar was about—Abercorn, Turco, Sheriff Peagler, all the old biddies of the island. He was harmless, maybe even a little pitiful—if she'd ever had any doubts, she was sure of that now.

The smile suddenly faded and he began to shift his feet and cast his gaze round the room. "I am called Hiro," he suddenly blurted, and extended his hand. "Hiro Tanaka."

Ruth took his hand and bowed with him, as if they were at the very beginning of a minuet. "I'm Ruth," she said, "Ruth Dershowitz."

"Yes," he said, and the smile returned, blooming with teeth. "Rusu, I am very please to meet you."

The Other Half

∎ ∎ ∎ ∎ ∎ ∎ ∎

SEVEN DAYS EARLIER, HIRO TANAKA HAD STOOD POISED ON THE
shoulder of the tar-bubbled blacktop road that promised him release, the road that would lead to the swift clean highway and all
the anonymous cities beyond it. He hesitated, looking first to the
right and then to the left, the road raveling out into emptiness in
either direction. It looked pretty bleak, he had to admit it. The
secretary and her lunchbox lay behind him now, buried in swamp
and scrub, while directly across from him the waning sun pointed
the way west, where a wild continent and a wilder ocean lay between him and the place he'd turned his back on forever—though
he ached for it now. What he wouldn't give for the yawning
boredom of the corner noodle shop, where nothing ever happened,
except to the noodles. Or the tranquillity of the tiny twenty-mat
park across from his grandmother's apartment, where nature consisted of pruned bushes and cultivated flowers, a trickle of water
pumped over a glaze of cemented stones. He remembered sitting
on the bench there as a boy, reading comics or the latest *bēsubōru*
magazine, the murmur of the water lifting him out of himself for
hours at a time.

But there was no sense in thinking that way—all that was lost
to him now. Now he was in America, where nature was primeval,

seething, a cauldron of snapping reptiles, insects and filth, where half-crazed Negroes and homicidal whites lurked behind every tree—now he was in America, and he had a new life ahead of him. And what he wanted was to turn right, to the north—that was where the great mongrel cities lay, that much he knew—but he'd traveled that road already, to the Coca-Cola store, with its sub-human proprietors and deranged customers, and he hadn't thought much of the experience. And so he turned to his left, and headed south.

This time he strode along the shoulder of the road, defiant, angry. If they came for him, he'd fight. Screw them all, the long-nosed bastards. He was wearing clean clothes for the first time in weeks— *hakujin* clothes—and he'd be damned if he'd plunge into the cesspool alongside the road like a scared rabbit. He'd had it. He was fed up. He was going to walk all the way to the City of Brotherly Love. On his own two feet. And god help anyone who got in his way.

He walked, one foot in front of the other, the sun sinking, the mosquitoes massing, and the road never changed. Tree and bush, creeper and vine, stem and leaf and twig. Birds wheeled overhead; insects danced in his eyes. He looked down, and the corpses of lizards and snakes, wafer-thin and baked to leather, stained the surface of the road. He looked up, and something slithered across the pavement. Before long, the canvas of the tennis shoes began to chafe at his ankles.

And then he heard it, behind him: the ticking smooth suck of an automobile engine, the hiss of tires. He hunched his shoulders, set his teeth. Sons of bitches. *Hakujin* scum. He wouldn't turn his head, wouldn't look. The ticking of the engine drew nearer, the tires beating at the pavement, his heart in his mouth . . . and then it was past him, a whoosh of air, rusted bumper, children's faces pressed to the rear window. Good, he thought, good, though he was slick with sweat and his hands were trembling.

He hadn't gone a hundred yards when a second car appeared, this one hurtling out of the crotch of the horizon ahead of him. He watched his feet and the car came toward him. Dark and long, the teeth of the grille, the high wasteful whine of the *Amerikajin* engine, and then it too shot past him, the memory of the driver's pale numb unblinking gaze already fading, already useless. But what the specter of that second car had done was to mask the presence of a third, and he realized with a sudden jolt that not only had another vehicle crept up behind him undetected, but that it was now braking alongside him, the huge demonic white thrust of its fender right there, right there in the corner of his eye. Be calm, he told himself, ignore it. The tires crunched gravel. The fender was undeniable, gleaming, ghostly, white, the long steel snout of the entire race, nosing at him. Every word of Jōchō shot through his head, but he couldn't help himself. He looked up.

What he saw was a Cadillac, an old one, with fins and glittery molding, the kind of car TV personalities and rock stars maneuvered round the streets of Tokyo. In the driver's seat, hunched so low she could barely see over the doorframe, was a wizened old *hakujin* lady with deeply tanned skin and hair the color of trampled snow. She slowed to nothing, a crawl, and her eyes searched his as if she knew him. Unnerved, he looked away and picked up his pace, but the car stayed with him, the big white fender floating there beside him as if magnetized. He was puzzled, tense, angry: What was she doing? Why didn't she just go away and leave him alone? And then he heard the hum of the electric window and he looked up again. The old lady was smiling. "Seiji," she said, and her voice was a jolt of cheer, strong and untethered, "Seiji—is that you?"

Astonished, Hiro stopped in his tracks. The car stopped with him. The old woman clung to the steering wheel, leaning toward him and gawking expectantly across the expanse of the passenger's seat. He'd never laid eyes on this woman before, and he wasn't Seiji, as far as he knew—though for the moment he couldn't help wishing he were. He shot a quick glance up and down the road. Then he bent forward to peer in the window.

"It's me, Seiji," the old lady said, "Ambly Wooster. Don't you remember? Four years ago—or was it five?—in Atlanta. You conducted beautifully. Ives, Copland and Barber."

Hiro rubbed a hand over the hacked stubble of his hair.

"Oh, those choral voices," she sighed. "And the shadings you brought to *Billy the Kid*! Sublime, simply sublime."

Hiro studied her a moment—no more than a heartbeat, really—and then he smiled. "Yes, sure," he said, "I remember."

.   ∎   .

"YOU'RE SO CLEVER, YOU JAPANESE, WHAT WITH YOUR AUTOMOBILE factories and your Suzuki method and that exquisite Satsuma ware—busy as a hive of bees, aren't you? You've even got whiskey now, so they tell me, and of course you've got your beers—your Kirin and your Suntory and your Sapporo—and they're every bit as good anything our lackadaisical brewing giants have been able to produce, but *sake, sake* I could never understand, how *do* you drink that odious stuff? And your educational system, why, it's the wonder of the world, engineers and scientists and chemists and what have you, and all because you're not afraid of work, back to the basics and all of that. You know, sometimes I almost wish you *had* won the war—I just think it would shake this spineless society up, muggings in the street, millions of homeless, AIDS, but of course you have no crime whatsoever, do you? I've walked the streets of Tokyo myself, at the witching hour and past it, well past it"—and here the old lady gave him an exaggerated wink—"helpless as I am, and nothing, nothing did I find but courtesy, courtesy, courtesy—manners, that's what you people are all about. It's manners that make a society. But you must think me terribly unpatriotic to say things like this, and yet still, as a Southerner, I think I can appreciate how you must feel, a defeated nation, after all. What did you say your name was?"

Hiro was seated at the massive mahogany table in Ambly Wooster's great towering barn of a house at Tupelo Shores Estates. He'd finished the soup course, cream of something or other, and he was gazing out on the gray lapping waves of the sea, nodding agreeably and praying silently that the Negro maid would emerge from the kitchen with a plate of meat or rice, something substantial, something with which he could stuff his cheeks like a squirrel before someone discovered his imposture and ran him out the door. The old woman sat across from him, talking. She'd never stopped talking, even to catch her breath, from the moment he'd slid into the passenger's seat of her car. But now, as he watched the gathering dusk and fought down the impulse to attack the maid in the kitchen if she didn't hurry and bring him meat, rice, vegetables, the old lady was asking his name. He panicked. The blood rushed to his eyes. What was his name—Shigeru? Shinbei? Seiji?

But then she went on without waiting for an answer, nattering about flower arrangements, the tea ceremony, geisha and robots (". . . so unfair really of these yellow journalists, and that's what they are, no one would deny that, least of all themselves, so *un*fair and *ir*responsible to characterize such a thrifty and hardworking, no-nonsense, nose-to-the-grindstone race as yours as *robots* living in *rabbit* hutches, shameful, simply shameful, and it just makes my blood boil . . ."), and Hiro relaxed. His function was to listen. Listen and eat. And at that moment, as if in confirmation of his thoughts, the kitchen doors flew open and the maid appeared, tray in hand, two intriguing wooden bowls perched atop it.

She was a big woman, the maid, big as a sumo wrestler, with nasty little red-flecked eyes and a wiry pelt of hair bound tight to her skull in rows that showed the naked black scalp beneath. Her nose was flattened to her face and she carried a sickening odor with her, the odor of the *hakujin*, the meat-eaters and butter-stinkers— only worse. From the moment he'd stepped in the door with his ragged shoes and dangling Band-Aids and thrown himself at the dish of nuts on the coffee table, she'd regarded him with loathing, as if he were vermin, as if he were something she'd squash beneath her foot if only he weren't under the protection of her dotty old mistress. She saw through him. He knew it. And now, as she came through the doorway, she caught his eye with an incendiary look, a look that said his time was coming, and that when it did there would be no holds barred. Hiro dropped his eyes.

"There's nothing more practical than a futon, that's what I've always said, and I was just saying to Barton the other day—he's my husband, Barton, he's an invalid—oh, thank you, Verneda—I was just saying to Barton, 'You know, Barton, all this furniture, all these gloomy old antiques, they're just such a clutter, so inefficient, I mean the Japanese don't even *have* bedrooms—' " And then the old lady paused a moment, a look of bewilderment surprising her all but immobile features. "But then, where *do* your sick and elderly lie up when they're ailing? . . . I suppose in those excellent hospitals, best in the world, *our* medical profession certainly can't touch them, what with the AMA and all their infighting, our own students having to attend medical school in Puerto Rico and Mexico and all those filthy, horrid, Third World places—"

With an angry snap of her wrist, the maid set the wooden bowl down before Hiro, and he wondered in that moment if he'd come far enough, if she recognized him, if she'd called the authorities and they were even then bearing down on him, but the thought flitted in and out of his head, all his attention focused on the insuperable bowl before him. Meat. Rice. He couldn't hide his disappointment: the bowl was filled with salad greens.

Later, though, with time and patience and the bleary, head-nodding endurance of the conscripted, he was rewarded with yams, several dishes of pale green vegetables boiled beyond recognition, and meat—fresh succulent meat, ribs and all. It was the first hot meal he'd had since his dispute with Chiba aboard the *Tokachi-maru*, and he lashed into it like the indigent he was. The maid had set great heavy ceramic bowls of the stuff on the table, and his hostess, pausing in her monologue only to take a birdlike peck at a scrap of meat or mashed greens, urged him on like a solicitous mother ("Oh, do have a bite more of the okra, won't you, Seiji? Heaven knows Barton and I could never—and the pork too, please, please—"). He filled his plate time and again, scraping the depths of the serving bowls and sucking methodically at the naked sticks of the bones that littered his plate, while the old lady rattled on about kimonos, cherry blossoms, public baths and the hairy Ainu. By the time the glowering maid brought coffee and peach cobbler, he was in a daze.

He no longer cared what was happening to him, no longer cared where he was or what the authorities might do to him if they caught up with him—this was all that mattered. To be here, inside, with rugs on the floors and paintings on the walls, to be here at the center of all this wonderful immensity, all this living space—this was paradise, this was America. In a trance, he followed his hostess from the dining room to the library, and while the maid cleaned up they sipped a sweet and fiery liqueur and filled their coffee cups from a gleaming silver carafe that might well have been bottomless.

At some point, he found himself stifling a yawn, and noticed the clock on the mantelpiece. It was past one in the morning. The maid had long since seen to the needs of the invalid upstairs, taken leave of her employer and departed for the night—to her home on the mainland, as Ambly Wooster informed him, in detail and at length. He'd had no problem with the old lady's accent, really—her speech was carefully enunciated and precise, not at all like the barbaric yawp of the girl in the Coca-Cola store—but this term, *mainrand*, was new to him. For the past hour or so he'd merely leaned back in his chair, letting the liqueur massage him, and he hadn't caught more than a snatch or two of the old lady's ceaseless rant. In fact, if it weren't for his in-bred courtesy, his compulsion to avoid giving offense, his samurai's discipline, he would have drifted off long ago. But now, suddenly, the idea of this *mainrand* sprang up in his head like a sapling disburdened of snow, and he cut her off in the midst of a paean to kabuki theater. "Mainrand," he said, "what is this, sank you?"

Ambly Wooster looked startled, as if she'd wakened from a dream. Hiro saw now just how old she was, older than his *obāsan*, older than the bird that laid the thousand-year-old egg, older than anything. "Why, the shore," she said, "the Georgia coast. This is an island we're on. Tupelo Island." She paused a moment, blinking at him out of her watery old eyes. "What did you say your name was?"

An island. All the warmth went out of him like air from a balloon. So he was trapped, and the highway went nowhere. He cleared his throat. "Seiji," he said.

The old lady studied him a long moment, silent for the first time in the past six hours. "Seiji," she repeated finally, regarding him with a cold eye, as if she'd never seen him before, as if she were wondering how he'd ever come to invade her house, her dining room, the sanctum of her library.

Was there a bridge? he wondered. A ferry? Could he swim to shore? He held her eyes, trying his best to look humble, thankful, needful, all the while certain that she was about to order him out of the house, call the police, have him bound and manacled and flung into that dark foul *gaijin* cell that was his destiny. But then an evil thought crept into his head: what could she do, after all, old as she was and alone in the house with an invalid husband and the deep pulsating silence of the night?

"You'll need a towel," she said suddenly, pushing herself up from the chair to gaze serenely on him, her blue-veined hands dangling at her sides. And then she smiled. "So rude of me—here I've kept you till all hours chattering away like an old mynah bird— what you must think of me, poor man." Then she turned and started out of the room. "Well, come on, then," she said, pausing at the threshold, "I'll show you to your room."

He followed her through the softly glowing house, up the stairs and down a long carpeted corridor, in the middle of which she paused to glance over her shoulder and put a finger to her lips. "Shhhh," she whispered, pointing to a closed door, "Barton." He nodded, vaguely aware of a smell of medication and the soft suck and rattle of labored breathing, and then they were moving again, noiselessly, the old woman's narrow shoulder blades working beneath the thin fabric of her blouse. "Here," she said, swinging back a varnished door at the end of the corridor and stepping aside for him.

At first he thought she was having a little joke—this couldn't be the room; it was huge, the size of a dormitory, big enough for racquetball, gymnastics, a swimming pool. And for all her talk of futons, it was dominated by a huge canopied bed that seemed to float over the carpet like a ship under sail. There was an overstuffed couch too, and an armchair. He could see a bathroom beyond it, a TV, air conditioner, windows that gave onto the sea. Twin reading lamps on either side of the bed bathed the room in a rich golden light. He hesitated, but she took him by the arm and ushered him in. "Sleep tight," she said, handing him a towel, "and if there's anything you need, you just let me know. Nightie-night." And the door clicked shut behind him.

He felt drunk. Exhilarated. So pleased with himself he laughed aloud. The bed—it was amazing, stupendous, big enough to sleep the entire crew of the *Tokachi-maru* and Captain Nishizawa too. He tumbled into it, kicking up his heels, bouncing high off the springs, all the while giggling like a child on a trampoline. In the next moment he was in the gleaming bathroom—as big itself as the entire apartment he'd shared with his *obāsan*—and he was rifling the drawers: soap, shampoo, cologne, an electric razor, aftershave. It was too much. He was dreaming. And then all at once he caught a glimpse of himself in the mirror and the elation went out of him.

It made him catch his breath. Made him look again.

But no, it couldn't be. This wasn't Hiro Tanaka staring back at him—not this raggedy bum, not this derelict with the matted hair and sunken cheeks, with the fingernails like a grave digger's and a patchwork of filthy bandages hanging from him like so much sloughed skin. He was twenty years old and he looked sixty—this was what America had done for him. Suddenly he was frightened. He saw himself through the changeless weary succession of weeks and months and years to come, running, hiding, begging, living like a *Burakumin*—an untouchable—in the anonymous streets of an alien world, too hopeless to get a job, too degraded, too filthy. He'd fallen from grace, and the muddied earth had rushed up to engulf him.

He stared into the mirror and despair overwhelmed him, but then, after a period, he glanced at the shower. It was the first shower he'd seen in over a month. He paused a moment to examine it dispassionately, as if he were a student of showers. He slid back the glass door, studied the gleaming controls, the soap dish, the pale scented bar of French soap that made the whole room smell like an orchard. And he examined the tub beneath it, too—the tub in which you could soak a blistered, aching body for hours at a time. Before he knew what he was doing, he was stripping off the filthy bandages, the ludicrous shorts and sweat-stained T-shirt, and he began to feel better. When he turned the knobs experimentally, water thundered from the showerhead, and the sound of it, the smell of it, made him feel better still. And then, wholly converted, he stepped into the tub and let the water wash over him, and it was cleansing, pure, redemptive and sweet.

. . .

THE DAY WAS TERRIFICALLY HOT, A REAL SLAP-IN-THE-FACE, DOG-under-the-house sort of day, the sort of day when a man just wanted to kick back with a cold beer and a plate of crab and listen to the Braves sweat their sorry asses round the diamond. The thing was, he'd promised those Tupelo Shores people he'd do the lawn and trim the shrubs, and he needed the money. Not for himself—he had his chew, his garden, all the crab and oyster and fat pink mullet his traps could hold—but for his nephew. Royal wanted one of those spike-studded wristbands they all wore on MTV, and Olmstead White was planning to surprise him on his birthday. But then, on second thought, maybe he *could* use a little cash for himself too—he'd managed to save most of his things from the fire, the necessities anyway, and he'd been able to move into the reconverted chicken coop out back without any real hardship—but there were a few things he could use. Like some towels and toilet articles—he liked his eau de cologne and his bay rum, liked to smell nice for the ladies, and all those bottles had gone up like firecrackers on him. And so, heat or no heat, after a lunch of black beans and rice with a chopped onion and a dash of the hot sauce he'd made himself from dried cherry peppers and garlic, he looped his machete round the handlebars of his bicycle, swung a leg over, and started down the hard black frying-pan of the road for the big estates at the other end of the island.

It was a ten-mile ride, nearly all of it as flat as his kitchen table, and normally it was nothing for him—he could have gone twice as far and back again without even breathing hard. But he was a little out of sorts today—maybe it was the heat—and though he coasted whenever he could, each time he dug at the pedals he felt a tightness in his chest, as if somebody had slipped a noose under his arms. He'd start in pedaling and he could feel the noose cinch up on him, squeezing all the air out of his lungs, and he just couldn't seem to draw his breath. His bad hip was acting up too, and his hand, blistered and raw beneath the clean white yard-and-a-half-long strip of gauze, burned as fiercely as it had the day that Chinaman had tried to deep-fry it. Three miles down the road, just past Cribbs' store, he thought he'd turn around and go on back home, he was feeling that poorly, but then he thought of that helpless jabbering old white lady and her laid-up husband, and figured he was the better part of halfway there already, and he kept on going.

He felt better as he glided over the little bridge that spanned Pumpkin Hammock and saw the cooters and mud turtles lined up like dominoes on a log beneath him—he could have spit on them if he wanted to—and he thought of himself and Wheeler as boys spearing turtles with an old window hook and the taste of the soup and gumbo his mama would make and the way they nailed the hollow shells up along the south side of the house till the place was shingled with them. And then he was passing Hollieway's Meadow, where the live oaks grew up in clusters out of the stumps of the old trees they'd taken down to build ships for the Confederate navy, his bony old knees pumping, and the noose eased up a notch or two.

He'd taken a pet screech owl out of one of those stumps when he was a boy, an unfledged chick, the runt out of a clutch of three. It was going to die anyway, trampled under by the spiky feet of its siblings, its head pecked till it was one big blister. He'd given it fish, which it didn't like, and mice, which it did. He remembered his mama thinking he was crazy, dicing up a mouse with his daddy's long knife, but he clipped that owl's wings and it grew up to love him, till the dog got it, anyway. That must have been sixty years ago, and now, as he glided through the gates of Tupelo Shores Estates and turned left on Salt Air Drive, he wondered at the memory of it, at the power of human recollection that could take him off his bicycle and out of the heat and send him back through all those long worn-out years. But then he wobbled into the Woosters' driveway and a swarm of greenhead flies came up on him out of nowhere and the noose tightened again and he was back in the here and now. He could taste the sweat at the corners of his mouth.

All right. He would squat and rest a minute in the shade where the grass was deep and cool, and then he'd have a long drink from the hose and get to work. No need to say anything to anybody. They'd see him outside the window, the machete flashing in the sun, and they'd hear him when he fired up the lawn machine, and they'd say, *It's Olmstead White out there working in this heat and maybe we'll just get him a tall glass of lemonade with a finger of vodka in it the way he likes it.*

He squatted, and the noose eased up a little. And then he bent to the hose and the cool water quickened him and he was ready for work, but there was that damn stab in the hip again, and the salt sweat was just like liquid fire on his hand. To hell with the doctor, he thought, and he held the bandage tight with his good hand and he let the water run over the burning one till the salt was gone and the sharpness of the pain fell off a bit. Then he unsheathed the machete and started nicking at the bushes with short quick drops of his wrist.

He must have been at it half an hour or more by the time he worked himself round to the ocean side of the house, where the pool stood behind a waist-high gate all overgrown with wisteria. There was somebody sitting out by the pool, and that surprised him—not just because of the heat, but because the old lady and her husband never paid any attention to the thing, except to let it go green as a duckpond between the pool man's visits. It must be the grandson, he thought, visiting from college. He'd seen the boy now and again over the past few years, hanging round the house, waiting for the ferry, driving his red sports car hellbent-for-leather up and down the street to Cribbs' store—a likable enough kid, even if his eyes were spaced too wide apart and he wore his hair as if it was 1950 still. Hell, and he had to chuckle at the thought, the kid wouldn't know a MTV haircut if it grew up around his ears. The machete flicked and there was a splash and Olmstead White turned briefly to see the froth of the water, the slick kicking limbs, hair flattened out like an otter's, but he thought no more about it.

He trimmed the holly bushes square against the house and then he turned to the pool. He hadn't got to the wisteria last time he was here, and now it was sending out snaking arms every which way and generally looking pretty shabby all the way round. Coming across the lawn, the machete hanging loose in his good hand, he was thinking of his mother, another trick of recollection, as if the day was filtered out of his head and all the past came swarming back to him in its odd and essential details. He was thinking of just this, just one thing, a picture frozen there in his brain: his mama at the stove and himself and Wheeler and his daddy sitting at the table, the mad hag's shriek of a hurricane wind in their ears, windows rattling, claws on the roof, and his mama jiggling the cast-iron pan and flipping corn cakes as if nothing in the world was the matter. He was thinking about that and the tightness was gone, and then he glanced up and caught the grandson's eye, and saw, for the first time, that the grandson was staring back at him as if he'd seen a ghost.

And that was it, the beginning of the end: recognition. This was no grandson—and the noose bit into him with a sudden savage jerk—this was, was . . . there were no words to form the thought, only rage crackling like grease in a hot frying pan. He took three steps forward, the machete poised over his head, and he saw those Chinese eyes, that Chinese nose and mouth and ears come back to haunt him. "Son of a bitch!" he cried—or tried to, the words sticking in his throat, choking him, the noose like a garrote, like two nooses, two garrotes . . . and then something was giving way inside of him and he plunged forward as if into a vast body of water and knew he would never be short of breath again.

. . .

HIRO HAD AWAKENED THAT MORNING—HIS SIXTH UNDER THE Wooster roof—to the smell of eggs, bacon and fried tomatoes, and to the strains of some vaguely familiar symphonic music, some Russian or European thing. He dressed in his freshly laundered shorts—Ambly Wooster, rambling on about textiles, Taiwan, Korea and Jordache, had tried to give him a pair of her grandson's blue jeans, but they'd been too tight to zip up—and then he pulled on the gray sweatshirt, thick cotton socks and Nike hightops that fit as if they'd been made for him, and sauntered downstairs to breakfast.

The music swelled to greet him, and as he turned the corner into the sunstruck parlor, he caught a glimpse of the morning maid, Dolly, darting out of sight like an insect. If the other one, Verneda, was physical and suspicious, Dolly was her opposite: slight and neurasthenic, afraid to make eye contact, her hair a topiary marvel, her skin the buttery tan of the blazer Hiro had worn to school as a boy. She disappeared into the dining room, leaving Hiro to bow deeply to his host and hostess, who were seated at the breakfast table in the bay window overlooking the sea. The glass was pregnant with light. Gulls hung over their heads. Somewhere, beneath the rush of violins, the ocean pounded the shore.

"Seiji!" the old lady cried, giving him a cagey look, her head tilted to one side, a smear of lipstick blotting her crooked smile.

He could see that she was holding back, biting her lip, fighting to dam up the torrent of banality that lashed her tongue like a whip across her palate, teeth and lips through her every waking moment. "*Ohayō*," she said, greeting him in Japanese and struggling with her tongue, her very eyes bulging with the effort to hold it all in.

He bowed again. "*Ohayō gozaimasu*," he returned, and bowed to the husband too. But the husband wouldn't have known that, since he was blind and deaf, propped up in his wheelchair like a man of rags propped up on a broomstick.

On the table were rashers, eggs, toast, butter, coffee, fried tomatoes and marmalade. It wasn't the sort of breakfast he preferred—he liked *ochazuke* himself, a bit of cold rice warmed with green tea—but he couldn't complain. Not after his exile in the wilderness, not after the crabs and grasshoppers and the hopeless spoon-licking repast he'd made of coffee crystals, nondairy creamer and artificial sweetener. But still, the Americans made such a mess of their food—just served it in a heap, with no thought of grace or proportion, as if eating were a shameful thing—and if he weren't starving, he would have turned up his nose at it. He pulled back the chair to sit down.

"Well, don't you notice anything?" the old lady asked, trembling with the effort to contain all those slips of meaning, that rush of words and syllables and phrases.

He paused over the chair, bewildered.

"The music," she said. "The music, Seiji—" and then she caught herself. She was grinning now, her teeth dead and gray, cracked, yellow, too big for her mouth.

And then he understood. The music. It was a routine she'd impressed on him. It meant nothing to him—he liked American music, personally, disco and soul, Michael Jackson, Donna Summer, Little Anthony and the Imperials—but he knew what she wanted. And he needed time here and she was kind to him and he didn't mind, didn't mind at all. He released the chair, stepped back a pace, composed himself, and began, as best he could and with the sweeping muscular movements of the long-distance swimmer, to conduct.

Later, after Barton had been fed and changed and wheeled out into the shade for some air; after Dolly had appeared and vanished again like a domestic ghost, only the faintest click of plate and cutlery giving her away; and after Ambly Wooster had spilled her continents, her oceans, her worlds of breath and gone up to take her afternoon nap, Hiro strolled out to sit beside the pool and grow strong again.

He felt safe here, the space enclosed and cultivated in a proper and proportionate way. And the water—it had been milky the first day, but he'd found the chemicals, the chlorine and acid, and stirred them in, and overnight it had become pellucid—the water soothed him. Throughout the afternoon, as the sun mounted in the sky and the heat rose, he plunged in and out of the pool in the swimming trunks Ambly Wooster had provided for him, frolicking like a seal. And each time he entered the pool, he felt that much cleaner, that much more human, that much further removed from the swamp. He lay back, drying in the sun, and watched the gulls sail across the sky, and when Dolly, eyes averted, slipped up on him with a plate of sandwiches and fruit, he ate with quiet satisfaction and with a deep and abiding gratitude.

America wasn't so bad after all, he began to think. And he even entertained a brief fantasy of staying on here and becoming Seiji, whoever he was, and of looking up his father in the telephone directory and inviting him down. They could swim together, he and his father, and together, with concentration and patience, they could poke holes in Ambly Wooster's breathless monologue and come up for air. But then he knew he was being unrealistic, dreaming, letting his mind drift, knew that they'd pin him down here sooner or later. He was on an island—an island, of all places—and he had to get off it. He thought of asking the old lady to drive him to the mainland in the back of her car, but of course there were problems with that. Just getting her to shut up long enough to put the proposition to her seemed an almost insurmountable obstacle, to begin with. And what would he tell her—that he was a criminal, an outlaw, a vandal? That he wasn't Seiji after all? And where *was* this mainland? From the pool he could see only the open ocean, serene, endless, blue, ocean that rolled over the hump of the world and slapped the shores of Africa. And from the far side of the house he saw another house, and beyond that another house, and then the marsh.

A boat, he thought. Perhaps he could beg a rowboat or a little catamaran, a Sunfish, anything. How far could the mainland be? He was thinking about this theoretical boat, the chance of the waves and the stinking festering cesspool of a marsh that was sure to form a barrier round this elusive mainland, when he became aware that someone was staring at him. He looked up and there he was, the last man in the world he wanted to see.

But no: it was a bad dream. He was hallucinating. It couldn't be. But then the hallucination moved, and he saw that he wasn't dreaming at all, and that the Negro, the cannibal, the madman who'd fired on him with a gun when he was defenseless and hungry and half dead from drowning, was as palpable as the sun in the sky. And worse: that he had a weapon in his hand—a *kendō* sword— and that he was coming at him, eyes rolled back in his head, his mouth a black pit that drained his face. Hiro was awestruck. Terrified. The man didn't look human—he was possessed, hellish— and he was writhing and gasping and choking out a curse in the thick wadded language of the shaman and the witch doctor.

Hiro shot to his feet. There was nothing in all the pages of Jōchō to prepare him for this. He took one look at the transmogrified Negro, raging and kicking and tearing at the earth now, and he had his clothes bundled in his arms and he was leaping the fence like a high-hurdler. He never looked back—as far as he knew his feet never touched the ground. Three bounds and he was out of the yard, over another fence and into the adjoining yard, where a woman whose nose was smeared with some sort of obscene plaster leaped up out of a lawnchair with a shriek that cut through him like a whirling tomahawk, and then he was in the next yard over, fighting off a swarm of dogs the size of stuffed toys. He kept going. Through a clutter of lawn furniture, across patios, leaping pickets, brickwork and chain-link as if he'd been born to it. People shouted at him, but he ignored them. Dogs tore out of the shadows to intercept him, their heads low, and the neighborhood suddenly resounded with their barks and snarls and their mad distracted howls. He kept going.

At some point, breathless, panicked, taking a landscaped slope and bursting headlong through a stand of ornamental pine, he heard the first distant chilling cry of the sirens. They were coming for him. Crouched low, staying with the cover of the trees, he gained the top of the slope and found his retreat cut off by the high rough plane of a stucco wall, an American wall, big but shoddy, the surface peeling in great skinlike patches. It must have been ten feet high, at least. He flattened himself to the abrasive surface, trying to catch his breath, the pandemonium of the neighborhood beating in his ears till it drowned out the distant roar of the surf. He felt naked. Vulnerable. Lost. There was nothing for it but to scale the wall and hope for the best.

It was a small matter. He scaled the wall. Dropping down on the far side, he found himself in a garden: luxurious, overgrown, deserted. There was a pool, and a cabana. In the distance: shouts, barking, the wail of sirens. Slyly, silently, with the stealthy sure athletic tread of the samurai, he crossed the flagstone border of the pool, eased open the door of the cabana, and hid himself in the slatted darkness within.

Later—much later—when the night was a presence and there was no sound but the susurrus of the crickets from beyond the walls and a drowsy hum from the house that commanded the yard, the garden, the pool and cabana, Hiro emerged. Noiselessly—not a ripple escaped him—he bathed himself in the pool, washing away the evidence of his flight, the grass stains, the smudges of dirt and grease. Then he sat in the dark till he was dry, the beat of his heart steady and slow. Carefully, fastidiously, as if it were a ritual, he pulled on the shorts, slipped the sweatshirt over his head, eased into the socks and leather hightops: he was in no hurry. He had a plan. A simple plan. A plan that began and ended with the cabin in the woods and his white-legged secretary. He saw her again— for the hundredth time—as she was that night in the boat, supine and unclothed, and he saw her at her desk, swiveling toward him, offering food and shelter. And then he pushed himself up, found the gate at the side of the house and stalked silently across the lawn. In the next moment, he smelled the tar and felt the hard flat surface of the road beneath his feet.

On an impulse, he bent to touch it. It was still warm.

Still at Large

. . . .

THERE WAS NO QUESTION ABOUT IT NOW: HE WAS GOING TO STAY there with her, under her protection, and he was going to stay indefinitely. Or at least until things cooled down. He'd got himself into some trouble on the other end of the island, at Tupelo Shores Estates, and the locals were in an uproar again. The day after he'd come back to her there was a story on page 6 of the Savannah paper—not much on detail, really, but they hadn't forgotten him: TUPELO ALIEN STILL AT LARGE, the headline read—and a buzz of apocalyptic gossip went round the island. Two days later, the *Tupelo Island Breeze* devoted its entire front page to him.

Ruth might have missed the *Breeze* story altogether, but for Sandy De Haven. She'd spent the day with her exotic refugee—she hammering away at "Of Tears and the Tide," he amusing himself with a paperback in Japanese hieroglyphs he'd produced from god knew where—and she'd come in just at the tail end of the cocktail hour. Sandy was behind the bar in the front parlor, mixing drinks. Bob the poet and Ina Soderbord were no longer a thing—Bob's wife had come down for the weekend, and that was the end of that— and so Ina, white eyebrows fading into white bangs like a mirage, sat at the bar mooning over Sandy. Most of the others had already moved into the dining room, and for this small mercy Ruth was thankful: at least she'd be spared Jane Shine and that sickening little silvery laugh of hers.

"La D.," Sandy said, "what's the poop?" He was already reaching for the vodka, the glass, the glistening bucket of ice.

"Nothing much," Ruth said with a shrug, "—working, that's about it." What was she going to say—that she was harboring a fugitive from justice? She smiled at Ina. Ina smiled back.

"Straight, with a twist, right?"

Ruth nodded, and Sandy handed her the drink. The windows were full of golden light, and for a time, she merely stood there, caught up in the richness of the moment. Saxby was off somewhere with his nets and traps and hip waders, but she'd see him before the night was out—he'd promised her—and Hiro was back at the cabin, lying low. Waiting for her. Depending on her. For the first time in days she felt good, felt like her old self. But then the chatter began to drift in from the dining room and she had to concentrate hard to filter out Jane Shine's maddening titter. When she lifted the glass to her lips, the vodka had turned sour on her. The moment was gone.

"You see this?" Sandy asked, easing a copy of the *Breeze* across the bar. She looked at it a moment before she saw it, and then she set the vodka down. ALIEN INVASION! the headline screamed in 24-point type, and beneath it there was a grainy picture of Hiro, looking sheepishly out from the page. Just under his chin, like some sort of growth, was a card bearing a series of mysterious ideographs and a seven-digit number. He looked lost and hopeless, and if she hadn't known better, she would have guessed he was about twelve years old.

"Pretty desperate-looking character, huh?" Sandy said with a grin.

Ruth didn't answer. She was scanning the columns of print, the boxed stories that set off the eyewitness accounts of Hiro's rampage through the grottoes and flowerbeds of Tupelo Shores Estates. There was an interview with the woman who'd unwittingly harbored him; a statement from the next-door neighbor who claimed the fugitive had terrorized her by running unannounced through her yard; an account of the death, due to cardiac arrest, of one Olmstead White, who was overcome while confronting the suspect who'd attacked him in his home three weeks earlier.

"This Japanese guy's really up shit creek, huh?" Sandy was grinning still. He leaned across the bar, gazing up at Ruth from beneath the dangle of his bleached locks. This was high comedy.

Ina sipped white wine with an ice cube in it. Her voice was breathy and small, considering the size of her frame. "I wish they'd just leave the poor man alone—I mean, just look at him"—and she bent forward to tap the paper with one lacquered nail—"does he look dangerous to you?"

Ruth was reading about Sheriff Peagler and how he'd vowed to put an end to this lawlessness one way or another—the fugitive wasn't even an American citizen, didn't even belong in this country—and no, he wouldn't rule out shooting the expletive-deleted on sight.

"Get these hog farmers stirred up . . ." Ina trailed off.

"Uh-huh, that's what I mean," Sandy said, "it's going to be like something out of *The Chase*." He paused to sip at his screwdriver. "You know that movie? Marlon Brando, Jane Fonda, Robert Redford?"

Ruth looked up at him for the first time. "Yeah," she said, "I mean no. Listen, you mind if I take this, the paper, I mean?"

.   .   .

RUTH SKIPPED DINNER THAT NIGHT. SHE PAID A QUICK VISIT TO the kitchen, where Rico was scurrying around under the supervision of the head chef (Armand de Bouchette, the man who'd made Thanatopsis preeminent among artists' colonies—so far as cuisine was concerned, at any rate), and she filled a pair of insulated lunch buckets with *pompano en papillote*, *artichauts au beurre noir*, steamed baby eggplant, French bread and potatoes in their own essence. "A romantic evening for two, eh?" De Bouchette was standing over her, the toque cocked back on his head, eyebrows lifted in amusement. He was in his late fifties, on the run from a string of bad marriages, a man who liked to sip cognac and spread his hand casually across the buttocks of the female colonists. "You and Saxbee? Or have you maybe been up to something you don't tell us about?"

Ruth kept her head down, busy with the lunch buckets. "Working late, that's all, Armand. Sax is going to join me later—*if* he gets back in time. Real romantic." Then she turned her full-force smile on him, slipped a bottle of wine from the rack above the counter, and left him groping after her retreating flank.

It was nearly seven when she got back to the cabin. The sun was sinking. A breeze drifted in off the ocean. Everything was still. Hiro wouldn't be expecting her till morning, and as she approached the clearing, she wondered how to announce her presence without startling him. She thought of calling out to him from a safe distance—"Hiro, I'm back!" or "It's me, Ruth!"—but if anyone were within earshot, the consequences could be fatal. On the other hand, if she didn't warn him somehow, the minute her foot touched the steps he'd shoot through the roof like a Saturn rocket. She was halfway across the clearing when she hit on a solution—she would start singing, burst into song, and if anyone heard her they would think she was drunk or jubilant or crazed—it was all the same to her. And so, cradling the newspaper and the thermal containers to her chest, she strode across the clearing, singing in a high pure glee-club soprano, belting out the first thing that came into her head: "Oh, where have you been, Billy Boy, Billy Boy? / Oh, where have you been, charming Billy? / I have been to seek a wife, / She's the—"

She caught herself in midphrase—Hiro's head had sprung up in the window like a jack-in-the-box. His face was a mask of pure terror, the face of a man awakening to aerial bombardment, tracers, the mushroom-headed thing itself. But then she caught his eye and saw that he recognized her, and it was all right.

"I brought food," she said, hoping to pacify him with the noun as she pushed through the door, "and this." She set down the silver canisters and held up the newspaper.

Hiro stared numbly at the newsprint stretched taut as a sheet before him. She watched as his eyes fastened on the headline. "You read English?" she asked.

He did. Of course he did. And he was proud of the accomplishment. Americans, with their big feet and blustering condescension to the rest of the world, knew no language but their own. But the Japanese, the most literate people on earth, learned to read English in their schools, from the elementary grades on. Of course, since there were few native speakers in Japan, and since the Japanese system relied on rote learning, the comprehensive skills of the average Japanese were far more highly developed than the conversational.

Hiro looked up from the newspaper. "We learn in school," he said simply.

Ruth folded the paper and handed it to him. He bowed his head and gave her a hangdog look. "They're really after you now," she said. "What on earth did you do to them down there?"

He shrugged. "Nothing, Rusu. Eat food. Listen old lady talk, talk, talk. She never shut up."

He tried a smile on her, the smile of a schoolboy caught out at some prank. There was more to the Tupelo Shores incident than he was letting on—of that she was certain. "Speaking of food," she said, "I hope you like fish."

Over dinner—they sat together at her desk after she pushed aside the typewriter and the clutter of scrawled-over pages that were about to jell into her first novella—he gave her the whole story. He told her of Ambly Wooster's confusion and how she insisted on his spending the night, told her of his joy at having a shower, clean sheets and three meals a day, and of his shock and horror at Olmstead White's unprovoked attack. "No warning, Rusu, nussing—and he has a sword, a *kendō* sword, I sink. He wants to cut me, Rusu, make me bleed."

Olmstead White was dead, and Ruth wondered about the legal ramifications of that. "You didn't touch him, did you?"

Hiro looked away. His face flushed. "I run," he said.

Ruth poured the wine and they drank and talked till the cabin
fell into shadow and all the familiar objects of the place—her typewriter, the hot plate and coffee things, her pitcher plants and the
Hockney poster she'd tacked up on the wall to brighten the place
up—began to lose definition in the deepening gloom of evening.
She told Hiro of her girlhood in Santa Monica—Were there Japanese there? he wanted to know; were there Negroes? Mexicans?—
and he told her of his American hippie father, his mother's disgrace,
the epithets that had trailed him since he was old enough to walk.
She leaned toward him as he spoke: so that was it. His hair, his
eyes, the size of him—he was half an American.

Later, she spoke of her writing—She was an author?; the idea
seemed to surprise him, though he'd sat there all day watching her
at work—and of Jane Shine, and how she'd come to Thanatopsis
to usurp her place. He sympathized. "Very bad sitration, Rusu—
don't let her push you in a circle." And then he told her of Chiba
and Unagi and of his dream of the City of Brotherly Love.

In summer, darkness comes quickly on the islands. The sun pales,
the dense green of the vegetation washes to gray, and night drops
like a curtain. They ate, they talked, and before long fireflies perforated the darkness beyond the windows and Ruth could no longer
make out Hiro's features. "I'll help you if I can," she said finally.
"I suppose that makes me an accessory or something, but I'll think
of some way of getting you off the island and on a train or a bus
going north." She paused to light a cigarette, the match flaring
briefly in the darkness. "You might not find the City of Brotherly
Love, but at least in New York you can disappear—that much I
know."

Hiro's voice was low and troubled and it came to her out of the
darkness. "I can never repay my debt to you, not in a hundred
lifetimes."

"Forget it," she said, "you would do the same for me—anybody
would." She didn't know exactly what she meant by that, but she
could feel his embarrassment, some sort of macho Japanese thing,

she supposed, and she was just talking to cover it. To change the subject, she asked him if he wanted a cigarette.

"No, sank you too much," he said. His voice dropped even lower. "But how, Rusu, can you get me off this island?"

She didn't have a clue. She didn't have a car either, and judging from the look on Sax's face that night on the sound, she couldn't very well let him in on the secret. Or could she? "I don't know," she said, and she realized in that moment that she didn't really want to get him to the mainland, not for a while yet, anyway. "But you can't risk leaving here—the cabin, I mean. Do you understand? They're after you—everybody on the island. And those two men—you remember the disco?—they'll be back, I know they will."

The words were barely out of her mouth when Hiro went rigid. "Shhhh, Rusu," he said, "what was that?"

"What?" she whispered.

"Shhhh. Listen."

And then she heard it: the snap of a twig, footsteps on the path. Suddenly a light played over the front of the house, and Hiro was on the floor.

"Ruth? You in there?"

Saxby.

She was on her feet in an instant—"Yes, yes, I'm here," she called, trying to sound nonchalant, though her heart was boring a hole in her—and then she was at the door, intercepting him at the threshold.

He was wearing a T-shirt and jeans, and his hair had fallen across his eyes. He held the flashlight in one hand, angling the beam so it caught the side of her face. "I looked all over the place for you," he said.

Her circuits were jammed. She couldn't think. "I was here," she said.

"What are you doing?" he said. "Sitting here in the dark? Were you talking to somebody?"

"I was working," she said.

"In the dark?"

"I was thinking. Thinking out loud."

He said nothing, but after a moment he lowered the flashlight and let the huskiness creep into his voice: "Hey," he said, "you're really weird, you know that, Ruth Dershowitz?" And then he took hold of her, the screen door gaping on its hinges, the beam of the flashlight playing crazily off the ceiling. "That's what I like about you."

She wrestled with him a bit, let him kiss her, held him. "Let's go, Sax," she said, whispering into his shoulder. "Let's go back to the house." Pause. "Somehow, I just don't feel like working anymore."

He kissed her again, hard and urgent. "Time for play," he said, and his hand was on her breast.

"Not here," she said.

"On the couch," he whispered, and the flashlight clicked off and dropped with a thump to the weathered planks of the porch. He was struggling with her top, trying to pin her against the doorframe, lift her off her feet and find her mouth with his tongue—all at the same time.

"No," she said.

"Yes," he said.

"Out here, then. On the porch." He had the top up around her armpits, a hand on her hip; she could feel his tongue wet on her nipples. "Out here," she breathed, "under the stars."

And then she swung away from him, caught at his belt and tugged him out of the doorway. In the next moment she was down on the rough planks of the porch and he was on her, breathing hard, and she was making room for him, giddy and hot and beyond caring, the screen door slamming behind them with a sudden sharp slap of punctuation. *He's in there*, she thought, moving beneath Saxby, *in there listening*, and then she was over the top and thinking nothing, nothing at all.

. . .

SHE BROUGHT BREAKFAST FOR HIM THE NEXT MORNING, AND neither of them mentioned Saxby or what had happened the night before. Not right away, at any rate. He was awake when she got there, but he seemed withdrawn, insular, wrapped up in himself like a cat, and his eyes had a dull bludgeoned look to them. The light blanket she'd given him lay balled up in one corner of the loveseat, while he was hunched at the other, dressed only in his lurid shorts—he hadn't bothered to pull on the sweatshirt or socks. And the place smelled of him—for the first time she was aware of that, of his smell—though the odor wasn't unpleasant, not at all. Just different. There'd been a smell of old wood about the place, of fungus and moss and earth—a smell she could only describe as "woodsy"—but he'd replaced it with his own smell. A body inhabited this place now: his body.

As she moved around the place, fussing over the coffee things, setting the table, she could feel his eyes on her. The sky was overcast, close and gray. She'd brought soft-boiled eggs, wheat toast, marmalade and fruit juice. "Are you hungry?" she said, just to make conversation. "I brought some things." He didn't move. After a moment he gave her the faintest nod of his head—a parody of a bow—and rose to his feet. He looked like a waif, looked young, looked angry, sullen, ungrateful. Suddenly she was furious. "What did you want me to do," she said, "—invite him in to play checkers?"

Hiro stood there, shoulders slouched, and turned his wounded eyes on her.

"He's my man. My lover." They were three feet apart. The eggs were getting cold. "You understand that?"

It took him a long moment to answer. "Yes," he said finally, in a voice so soft she could barely hear him.

"You and I," she began, gesturing with a single emphatic finger, "you and I are"—she couldn't seem to find the word—"friends. You understand?"

There was the dull distant throb of a woodpecker assaulting a tree, and then the whine of a chainsaw starting up somewhere. The water on the hot plate came to a boil. Yesterday's page curled over the typewriter.

"Yes," Hiro said. "I understand."

.   .   .

THE NEXT WEEK PASSED WITHOUT INCIDENT.
Hiro spent his days reading the books and newspapers she brought him, rocking in the chair and watching her as she pecked away at the keyboard, scribbled notes or gazed out on the wall of green, waiting for a word or phrase to come to her. He made himself scarce at lunchtime—she didn't know where he went and more often than not didn't even know he'd gone, so furtive had his movements become. But he reappeared, looking hopeful, the moment Owen turned and loped off down the path. And then he went through his daily routine—it was comical, really. He bowed, he smiled, he scraped and writhed and wrung his hands and he wouldn't touch the lunch bucket—wouldn't even look at it—till Ruth had assured him ten times over—and reassured him again—that she wasn't hungry, that she didn't want it, that it was for him and him alone.

In the evenings, when she left him, he made a poor meal of the groceries she'd smuggled in for him—bread and jam, wilted lettuce, a cupful of polished white rice—and then curled up on the couch beneath the thin blanket, and, as she imagined, dreamed of the City of Brotherly Love. In the mornings, he was always waiting for her, neatly dressed in the Georgia Bulldogs sweatshirt or the madras plaid she'd borrowed from Saxby, and the cottage bore no trace of him but for his presence and the lingering faintly yeasty odor of his living and breathing. The books, the blanket and the groceries were hidden away, the floors swept, the mantel dusted, her papers and pens and pencils lovingly arranged on her desk. And there he was, her own pet, waiting for her, a toothy pure uncomplicated grin propping up his eyes and creasing the big joyful moon of his face.

At the same time, very gradually, in the way of a guerrilla band working its way down from the hills to infiltrate the provinces and finally lay siege to the capital, Ruth began to work her way back into the inner circle of Thanatopsis House. Since Jane Shine's arrival, she'd kept a low profile—she had no choice, since she couldn't stomach being in the same room with her. The battle lines had been drawn when Jane cut her that first night and Ruth had been left to fumble over the Iowa connection till Jane's eyes had leaped the ski jump of her nose to settle on her as if on some insect, some legless beggar tugging at the hem of her imperial skirts, and she'd said finally, with a sigh, "Oh, yes, I think I remember you now—but wasn't your hair a different color?" It had taken Ruth a day or two to map out her strategy—and she'd been preoccupied with Hiro, anyway—but now she moved in to do battle in earnest.

Jane was a late riser—she needed her beauty rest, needed time to do her face peels and bust-building exercises, time to run a thousand brushstrokes over her pure white scalp and apply the foundation and concealer and hi-liter, the blusher, eyeliner, mascara and translucent powder that gave her that spontaneous girl-next-door-with-the-Gypsy-hair-and-outerspace-eyes look. And this was the chink in her armor. Ruth began getting up early, anticipating Owen's knock. She dressed as if she were going on a date with a literary critic—hair, makeup, low-cut blouse, the works—and she made certain she was the first at the convivial table each morning and the last to leave. She was charming, clever and seductive, and she made as many oblique but devastating references as she could to La Shine, as they'd begun to call her. And when Irving Thalamus came down, pouches under his eyes, his face as rucked and seamed as the floor of the Dead Sea and a whiff of early-morning bourbon on his breath, she was his girl all over again. She touched him as she spoke, leaned into him, threw back her head to laugh so he could admire her throat and cleavage.

At cocktail hour, she gathered Sandy, Ina and Regina around her—and Saxby too, when he wasn't off stalking the swamps for his pygmy fish—and formed a sphere of influence at one end of the room, while Jane Shine gathered her forces at the other. Sometimes, after cocktails, she'd take dinner with Saxby and his mother in Septima's rooms—this was the *real* inner circle, after all—and then, instead of fencing with Jane Shine in the billiard room, she'd watch an old movie on the VCR or stare for hours into the glowing green vacancy of Saxby's aquarium. She'd preen herself around Septima, conscious of her favor, and she'd think about Hiro and count the days till Jane Shine took her literary freak-show home with her.

It was at the end of the week that Abercorn and Turco showed up again, as inevitable as junk mail. Turco left his boom box at home this time—things had gotten serious and he had a new method now, infallible, couldn't miss. He'd pitched his pup tent in a patch of scrub beyond the north lawn, while Abercorn had been given a closet-sized room on the third floor (and how he'd ever managed to sweet-talk Septima into letting him stay on a second time, Ruth couldn't begin to imagine). Ruth was just coming up the front steps, fagged but exhilarated after working through the shank of the afternoon and making what she felt was real progress on the novella, when she spotted Turco through the foyer window. He was in his fatigues and combat boots and he had Laura Grobian pinned up against the staircase, waving something in her face. Ruth hesitated—*Hiro,* she thought, but then she couldn't very well back down the stairs without arousing suspicion, and so she steeled herself and breezed through the door as if nothing in the world were the matter.

Laura Grobian gave her a frozen smile. She towered over Turco, half a foot taller at least. "—And robotics," Turco was saying, his voice dropping to a snarl, "how do you think our Japanese friends got the lead there? They're cagey, is all. No doubt about it. But you've got nothing to worry about, lady, because we're going to get this one, I'd say within the week, maybe sooner—"

"Laura," Ruth said, gliding through the foyer to poke her head in the mailroom before swinging round to face them, "and Mr. Turco. Back again?"

Turco released Laura Grobian and fastened on Ruth. First he shifted his head, then swiveled his torso and pivoted his legs, and

Ruth couldn't help thinking of a chameleon drawing a bead on an insect. He paused a moment, as if trying to place her, and then he took a step forward and held up the object—it was cotton, she saw, a garment of some kind—he'd been waving at Laura Grobian. "I was just telling the lady here that this whole thing with the illegal is making us look pretty bad, but not to worry—we've got his number now."

The veins stood out in Turco's neck. The camouflage shirt clung to his chest and arms like body paint and he'd obviously worked on that penetrating stare, a little man striving for an effect. Ruth couldn't help herself. "No Donna Summer?"

A flash of anger flattened his eyes, but it passed. He took another step forward, invading her space. "Leg snares," he said, and he unfurled the garment in his hand: it was a designer T-shirt with a chic name splashed across the breast. "And this is the bait—this and a couple pairs of Guess? jeans, maybe some scarves and T-shirts with shit like *Be Happy* and *Keep On Truckin'* printed on them. Anything in English. The Nips are suckers for it."

"Excuse me," Laura Grobian whispered, and then she was out the door and into the golden embrace of the afternoon sun. Turco never even turned his head. He just stood there, inches from Ruth, veins jumping in his neck, his eyes locked on hers. "It'll work," he said. "Trust me."

Ruth gave him a serene smile. Turco and Abercorn. They were incompetents, clowns, and they had about as much chance of catching Hiro as Laurel and Hardy might have had. They would be one more diversion for her, one more wedge to drive between the colony and Jane Shine, one more vehicle on which Ruth could hitch a ride. They'd poke around for a few days and find nothing. Not a trace. And each night, while Sax was engaged elsewhere, she'd bat her eyes at Abercorn, the poor idiot, and console him and sympathize with him and stick her finger in her cheek and offer all sorts of helpful suggestions. Had he looked in Clara Kleinschmidt's closet? The sheriff's henhouse?

"You're right," she said finally, "I'm sure it will." And then, as she floated away from him and started up the stairs, she paused a moment to glance over her shoulder. "Good hunting," she said, and it was real struggle to keep a straight face, "—isn't that what they say?"

Yes, she could feel it, things were looking up.

.   .   .

AND THEN, SUDDENLY AND WITHOUT WARNING, EVERYTHING CAME crashing down again.

It was the night after Abercorn and Turco's arrival, a night that followed a day on which the artists of Thanatopsis House barely advanced their various projects. They were restive, preoccupied, unable to focus or concentrate. An easterly breeze had held steady throughout the day and the whole island seemed newly created from the sea; breakfast had been giddy, lunch forever in coming, and cocktails—people wandered in early for cocktails. There was excitement in the air, the scent of possibility and romance, the sort of incorrigible hopefulness that accrues to the prospect of a good party.

The party—organized by Owen for the dual purpose of paying homage to Septima on her seventy-second birthday and bidding adieu to Peter Anserine, who was going back to Amherst to lecture for the fall term—would feature a Savannah caterer, a dance band and an open bar. Invitations had gone out to the *haut monde* of Savannah and Sea Island and to members of the immediate community, as well as to each of the colonists, and Sheriff Peagler and his brother Wellie—the island's unofficial mayor—were expected to attend, along with a spate of lawyers, gallery owners, art collectors and blue-nosed widows from Tupelo Shores Estates and Darien. A photographer was coming down from Savannah to cover the event for the *Star*'s society page. And the Pulitzer Prize winner in poetry, a onetime resident, was expected to phone. For Thanatopsis, it was the event of the year.

Ruth had been saving an outfit for the occasion, a calf-length black chiffon dress with a lace ruffle at the hip, and a pair of new black pumps. It was a little heavy for the season, maybe—she'd been planning to wear it in the fall—but it was late August, the breeze had cooled things down and she really didn't have anything else—and it *was* a Geoffrey Beene, though she'd gotten it for a song. She'd spent the afternoon quizzing Hiro on Japan—Was it true that steak cost thirty dollars a pound? did he feel awkward using a fork? did they really pay people to squeeze you onto the train?—and then she left him early. "I'll be back in the morning," she said. "Lie low. I'll bring you some treats from the party." And to his inevitable question, she replied: "Soon."

She took a long soak, spent half an hour on her nails. Sax and Sandy were planning to wear tuxedos—the rest would make do with skinny ties and polyester. There would be champagne—good champagne, Bollinger and Perrier-Jouët. Caviar. Lobster. Oysters from Brittany. Ruth groomed herself as if she were preparing for battle, lingering over each detail, seeking the sort of perfection that would make her impervious, invincible—and all the while she was aware that on the other side of the wall, Jane Shine was doing the same. Twice Saxby came for her and twice she turned him away. She moussed her hair, brushed on hi-liter and blusher, did her eyes. When Sax knocked the third time, she told him to go on ahead without her—she'd be ready when she was ready.

The party was an hour and a half old when Ruth made her entrance. She crossed the lawn to the strains of the band playing some sort of Brazilian music—a samba or a bossa nova or something—and the crash of excited voices rose up to engulf her. The tent they'd erected over the dance floor was pitched high and it was open on all sides to the breeze, and as she came up the walk, Ruth could see constellations of Japanese lanterns slowly revolving around the big aluminum stanchions that supported it. She stepped through a bower entwined with cut roses and a black man in black tie and white gloves offered her a glass of champagne from a tray bristling with them. Tara, she thought. The Old South. It was like something out of *Gone With the Wind.*

In the next moment, she saw how wrong she was.

If she'd pictured herself sauntering in to applause and whistles and the flare of flashcubes, Scarlett O'Hara herself, she was disappointed. It was almost as if she were at the wrong party—she didn't recognize anyone. She stood there a moment in the entranceway, getting her bearings, one bare elbow planted in her palm, her wrist elegantly cocked beneath the stem of the glass. Most of the women looked as if they'd bought their gowns by the yard and the men seemed to be stuffed into shirts and jackets several sizes too small for them. Red was the prevailing color for faces, bald spots and exposed shoulders and arms, and the hair color of choice was white. Ruth had expected something magical—or at least something elegant—and instead she'd wandered into the geriatric ball at the 4-H fairgrounds.

She exchanged her empty glass for a full one and moved toward the dance floor, hoping to run into some of the Thanatopsis crowd— or at least someone under sixty. Sidestepping an elderly woman with an aluminum walker and shouldering her way through a group of wispy-haired men with cloying accents and expensive suits— lawyers, she guessed—she found herself on a collision course with Clara Kleinschmidt and Peter Anserine. They were standing together, hunched forward over glasses of champagne and napkins which held some sort of canapé, taking quick hungry bites and talking at the same time. Clara's eyes were moist. She was wearing a long-sleeved, floor-length gown with padded shoulders and a sweep of rhinestones across the breast. From the waist up, it looked like a Russian military uniform.

"Clara, Peter," Ruth said, inserting herself between them, "wonderful party, no?"

"Oh, hello," Peter Anserine said offhandedly, peering down the length of his nose at her. A bit of egg and caviar was stuck to his lip. He seemed glad to see her—or glad for the interruption. Ruth could think of nothing in that moment but the succulent rumor that linked the two of them—the great divorced Brahmin novelist of ideas and Clara, humble Clara—for at least one passionate night.

"Ruth," Clara choked, miserably gobbling at the sliver of toast and fish eggs spread flat in her miserable palm. Her wild eye seemed wilder than ever. And yes, those *were* tears.

"Terrific," Peter Anserine said, "absolutely. Best party I've been to since I left Boston last spring."

Ruth lingered, taking advantage of the moment's awkwardness to draw Anserine out, quiz him when his defenses were down. And did he miss Boston? He was going to be at Amherst in the fall, wasn't he? Was it for the semester or the year? And then back to Boston, or—?

"Well, yes," he said in answer to this last, casting a sidelong glance at the servant slicing by with a tray of eatables, "Boston *is* my town, after all. But then, of course, I'll have to find bachelor digs. To be close to the children."

Clara was absorbed in her food, hunched over still, concentrating on the tricky juggle of napkin, glass and morsel.

"Wonderful," Ruth said, "just wonderful. We're going to miss you here, we really are." There was an awkward interval during which no one spoke. The band broke off and then lurched into a reedy rendition of "Nature Boy," and Peter Anserine gave Ruth a long slow strictly noncollegial look. She shifted her feet, drained her glass and sighed. "Well, I guess I've got to go find Sax," she said. "Have a good one."

And then she was working her way toward the bar, exchanging greetings with people she knew from Darien or her trips to the Tupelo Shores beach with Saxby—looking for Sandy, Irving Thalamus, anybody. She paused to scan the dance floor and take a glass of champagne from a black servant with an immovable face and hair as uniformly white as a cup of detergent. The band had switched to something with a heavy backbeat that felt a lot like reggae, and as the dancers separated from their "Nature Boy" clinches and began to flail their limbs to the spastic beat, Ruth spotted Sandy dancing with a girl she'd never seen before—very young-looking, barely pubescent in fact, but a beauty and born to it. Ruth wondered who she was and felt a small stab of regret as Sandy moved in close, but then Abercorn's dyed pelage and speckled face came into view, riding atop the heads of the others as if thrust up there on the end of a stick, jerking rhapsodically to the beat. And who was it he was dancing with? The crush of bodies closed in for half a beat and then fell back, and Ruth was amazed to see Ina Soderbord opposite him, wriggling her big hips and shoulders and bust as if she'd just been hosed down. And then the crowd drifted into a new pattern and Bob Penick and his wife (hair the color of chicken liver, shiny prom dress with wilted corsage) writhed into view, not ten paces from Ina. They were doing a modified frug, a dance Ruth had learned—and abandoned—in high school.

She finished her champagne—was that her third glass?—and took another from the man with the iron face. (She wanted to tease him the way people tease the guards outside Buckingham Palace—tickle him or blow in his ear or something—but she thought better of it: after all, how much latitude could you expect from an old black man in a starched tuxedo at a white people's party in Georgia?) She was feeling a bit giddy, enjoying herself even if she had been denied her entrance. Abercorn with Ina Soderbord. It was funny: the pale with the paler still. And what if they had children? They'd be eyebrowless, hairless, white as grubs, with little pink fishy eyes, and they'd grow up to be giants upon the earth, with shoulders and tits and feet that would give shoe salesmen nightmares. The boys would buy cheap overcoats and the girls would hyphenate their names—Soderbord-Abercorn—and people would think they were an agricultural product, something to spray on the crops to prevent cutworm. Oh, yes, it was hilarious. And Ruth was giddy. But where was Sax?

It was then that the band pulled the string on the horns and rolled into a piano-thumping boogie-woogie—they were eclectic, all right—and Irving Thalamus's dry sniggering laugh jumped out at her from the direction of the bar. She turned and elbowed her way through the crowd, following the sound as unswervingly as a cat stalking a rustle in the grass. A pair of minor poets and a clutch of old ladies in pink chiffon gave way, and there he was—Thalamus—leaning against the bar and laughing down the front of Regina McIntyre's dress. Regina was showing acres of dead-white shoulder and bosom, and she was wrapped in a black leather dress that gave her the look of an extra in a movie about outerspace vampires. But Ruth's eye didn't rest long on Regina or Thalamus either, because at that moment she spotted Saxby at the far end of the bar, and in the next she felt hot and sick and panicky all at once, felt like Madama Butterfly when they come to take her child away: Saxby was with Jane Shine.

Jane Shine.

It was a blow, and it staggered her. There she was, the woman she loathed more than anyone alive, her enemy, her nemesis, her bugaboo, and she had Saxby in her grip. Flawless, sickening, cool as a model poised on the runway, she was leaning into Saxby, one cold white hand fixed like a grappling hook to his arm. Ruth saw black silk and diamonds, hair on the attack, a roiling cloud of it enveloping Saxby in its fatal nimbus, and all at once she pictured him in the Jaguar, Jane Shine established as the doyenne of Thanatopsis House, her own stay cut mysteriously short. It was too much. She couldn't handle it. She recoiled as if from some un-thinkable horror—Saxby hadn't seen her yet, nor Shine nor Thalamus either—and then Regina's eyes caught hers and Regina smiled—or smirked—and Ruth was fighting her way back through the crush, Thalamus's tentative "Ruthie?" floating somewhere behind her, the piano player up off his stool and banging the keyboard now with his feet and elbows and hams, the crowd roaring, roaring.

Stabbed in the back. Betrayed. A moment ago she'd exulted in Clara Kleinschmidt's tears, above it all, Olympian, La Dershowitz, and now—now she felt the tears burning in her own eyes. How could he? How could he even talk to her? Ruth pushed blindly through the crowd. She felt as if she'd been slapped in the face, humiliated, and there was nothing to do but hide herself, run. She shoved past the old waiter—*Out of my way, Uncle Tom,* she thought bitterly—and he gave her a look, nothing more than a fractional lift of the eyelids, that said *shame,* and the whole group of wispy-haired lawyers did a little dance step to avoid her. She was vaguely aware of the horns ricocheting off the canvas above her as the song ended in a slamming excruciating finale, and then she saw the rosy exit looming up before her.

She was there—*Just let me hold it back,* she prayed, *please god don't let me break down yet*—there under the bower, practically running, when Septima appeared at the other end. Made up to look twenty years younger, her hair tinted and curled, her gown alone worth more than every scrap of clothing in the place combined and her jewelry liberated from the safe deposit box, Septima was making her own grand entrance. On Owen's arm. She seemed to stagger on her heels as Ruth came at her, and she forced her lips into a smile. "Why, Ruthie," she gasped, stopping her with a veiny desiccated hand, a hand that felt to Ruth like the touch of death, "whatever has happened to you? You're pale as a ghost."

A ghost, yes: she was already gone. And what did Septima care? Or Owen—smirking at her, looming up out of the night like an executioner? They probably had her bags packed for her already—she was nothing here, insubstantial, a ghost, and Jane Shine was all and everything. "I—it's nothing," she stammered, her eyes full, "I'm just not . . . I can't—" and then she let it go, shook off the old hag's hand and bolted across the lawn, all the bile of her eighteen years of setback and denial rising in her throat.

Her first thought was to make for her room, slam the door behind her and freeze the world in place—but there were guests on the veranda, in the foyer and the parlor, chatting and laughing, fondling drinks and gobbling their bits of flesh and cheese. She couldn't face them. Not now. Not in this state. And then she thought of the cottage. That was her refuge, her safe house, that was where she reigned, La Dershowitz still—that was where her Hiro was.

She shied away from the house and crossed the lawn in the opposite direction, hurrying, the night moonlit, the path composing itself beneath her feet. Almost immediately the sounds of the party began to fade, soaked up in the insensate mass of foliage, and she was aware of the smaller sounds of the night, the rustling and chattering of things killing, eating, humping. There were fireflies, mosquitoes, she heard the soft breathy call of an owl. Her legs moved, her feet rose and fell. What had she gotten so upset about? So he'd talked to her, so she had her hand on his arm. It didn't mean a thing. Or did it? In that moment the argument fell in on itself and she knew that that hand on the arm did mean something—meant everything—and that he knew it too. He did. And he should have known better. The anger came up on her all over again, burning like acid, all the hotter now that the shock of discovery was behind her. And Saxby would pay for it—oh, how he would pay.

But now, before she knew it, she was coming out of the familiar switchback in the trail and the cottage lay before her, awash in lunar light. "Hiro," she called, and she didn't give a damn if the whole world heard her, "Hiro, it's me. I'm back."

Skittish, he'd fastened the latch from the inside, and she rattled the handle of the screen door. "Hiro, wake up. It's me."

"Rusu?" His voice came back at her from the deeps of the room, sleep-worn and tentative, and then she saw the shadowy form of him rise from the loveseat and reach for his shorts. He was naked, the moon slanting through the windows to reveal the bow of his legs and the awkward dangle of his arms. "I'm coming," he cried, and she watched him fall back into the shadows to lift first one leg and then the other to the dark mouth of the shorts.

"What time is it?" he said, swinging back the door to admit her. "Somesing wrong?"

"No, nothing," she said, turning to face him.

"I should put on a light?" He was right there, right beside her. His breath was musty with sleep, his skin glowed in the moonlight.

"No," she said, whispering now, "no, we won't be needing it."

Parfait in Chrome

. . . .

HE DIDN'T KNOW WHAT SHE WAS SO UPSET ABOUT—REALLY, HE didn't. She wouldn't even look at him, let alone talk to him, for six full days following the party. Saxby understood that it had to do with Jane Shine, and with Ruth's own insecurities, and he understood too that he had to humor her—but what she had to understand was that he was free to talk to anyone he pleased. Just because Ruth wet her pants every time somebody mentioned Jane Shine didn't mean he had to treat the woman like a leper, did it? He liked her. She was—*he thought of her hair, her eyes, her throat, the ever so faint lisp that made her sound as if she were translating from the Castilian*— interesting. And besides, that's all he'd done—talk to her—and if Ruth was going to get so worked up about it, why had she sent him on ahead of her in the first place? What did she expect—that he'd go deaf, dumb and blind? That he'd stand in a corner wearing dark glasses and holding up a sign that said PROPERTY OF R. DERSHO-WITZ till she got there?

All right, it was true—he had gotten a little carried away, what with the champagne and the music and the general high-spirited roar of the festivities, and for long stretches at a time he'd forgotten Ruth altogether. He was enjoying himself—was that a crime? She was late. She was dressing. I'll catch up with you later, she said.

And so he found himself standing at the bar, all dressed up and nowhere to go, and he found Jane Shine standing there beside him. "Hi," she said, and he returned the greeting, social animal that he was, and she took a breath and said that Irving had told her he was interested in aquaria—that's how she put it: "interested in aquaria"—and he was hooked. She'd had several tanks as a girl, and her ex-husband had taken her up the Orinoco in a pirogue and there they'd met Herbert Axelrod himself. The patron saint of aquarists was on a collecting trip, and he took them back to his base camp for a dinner of *piracuru* and onions and showed them a tank crowded with a new species of characin he'd discovered just that morning.

To Saxby, it was the voice of heaven.

When it began to get late and Ruth still hadn't appeared, he crossed the lawn to the house, went up to her room and knocked for the fourth time that evening. There was no answer. He put his head in the door and saw that she was gone. Puzzled, he checked the two upstairs bathrooms, made a quick circuit of the parlor and veranda, and cut back across the lawn to the party, figuring he'd somehow missed her in the crush. He circulated through the crowd, looking for her, and he took a glass of champagne, and when somebody put a plate of food in his hand, he ate. She wasn't on the dance floor, and she wasn't at the bar. He had a bourbon on the rocks, and then another. He talked with Sandy, Abercorn, Regina and Thalamus. Thalamus had seen her an hour or so ago, he thought, heading away from the bar—had he looked on the dance floor? Saxby assured him that he had, and then he downed another bourbon while contemplating the mystery of it all. He went back to the house and asked everyone he ran into if they'd seen her, and he checked the bathrooms again, and the kitchen. She'd vanished.

Back at the party, he had a bourbon with Wellie Peagler and washed it down with a glass of champagne. Wellie was representing a group of investors who wanted to build a golf course and resort on the island, and before he knew it, Saxby was arguing passionately for the inviolability of Tupelo and the claims of historicity, and he snatched a glass of champagne from a passing tray and told Wellie he could take his investors and shove them up his ass. Wellie didn't flinch—just gave him a paternal smile and introduced him to a big pale blustery character who said he was a venture capitalist and they had a drink to that—venture capitalism, that is—and they had a drink to nine irons and holes in one. And then, before he knew what was happening, a girl he'd had a brief thing with when he was home to visit his mother two Christmases ago took him by the arm and led him out onto the dance floor. The rest was a blur, though he did remember standing at the bar at some indeterminate hour talking to somebody he couldn't recall about something he'd forgotten, when his mother put a hand on his arm and asked him where Ruth was.

Ruth. The name came back to him as if from some coat closet of memory. Ruth's face rose before him, and it was knit with fury. He looked at his mother and shrugged.

Was she all right? his mother wanted to know. Was she feeling ill? Had they quarreled?

He defended himself in all his innocence—no, no quarrel; he'd been looking for her all night—and he was about to have another drink when Septima put her arm in his and announced in a quavering voice that she was tired. She kept a tight grip on him as she said her unending goodbyes, and then she led him across the lawn, up the steps and into the house, where she put him to bed and sleep came like a guillotine.

In the morning, he had a headache.

Rico made him some poached eggs and a Bloody Mary, and he ate the eggs and drank the drink and felt worse. It was two in the afternoon when he mounted the stairs to check on Ruth. The enigma of her disappearance had settled on him while he was numbly slicing egg and watching the yolk run, trying to decide whether his stomach could handle that much gravity. Ruth, he thought. Jesus Christ, what happened to Ruth? As he mounted the stairs, he felt a sense of impending crisis, ominous and inescapable, but chalked it up to misfiring neurons and the egg that lay there like death on his stomach. Ruth wasn't in her room. Her cosmetics—jars of this and that, mascara, lipstick—were scattered all over her dressing table, and her bed was unslept in. Or it had been slept in and remade. It *was* two o'clock, after all. She would be at her studio at this hour, working. For a moment he thought of hiking out there to clear up the mystery surrounding the party—and any little misunderstanding that may have arisen from it—but his legs felt like wax and he went back to his room to lie down a bit and let the world readjust itself to him.

He woke for dinner, feeling hollow as a reed. After washing his face and slicking back his hair with a little gel, he lumbered up the stairs to try Ruth's door again. This time, his knuckles had barely made contact with the wood when the door flew back on its hinges.

Ruth stood there before him, small, cold, wicked and glittering, her face drained of blood, her eyes like cut glass. "You son of a bitch," she said.

"But I—"

"Tell it to Jane Shine," she snarled, and the door slammed shut with an explosion that resounded all the way down the hall.

He was about to reach for the doorknob, call out her name, protest his innocence, when he heard the screech of wood on wood and watched the door shudder as some immovable piece of hereditary furniture settled against it. He couldn't resist trying the doorknob anyway. It turned, but the door itself was stuck fast.

So she'd seen him with Jane Shine—so that was it. He felt bad about it, but he was blameless. He was. And as he stood there in the hallway, a stream of dinner-bound colonists making their way around him with nods of greeting and knowing smiles, he began to feel put upon, abused, wronged and shamed, a man condemned without a trial. But Ruth was hot—he knew her temper only too well—and he wasn't about to plead with her through a closed door while celebrated composers and Jewish legends sauntered by and smirked at him. In the end, he stood there speechless for two whole minutes, and then he shrugged and went down to dinner.

During the course of the next several days, he tried to get close to Ruth, tried to make amends, explain himself—though he was guilty of nothing, except maybe playing along with her neurotic games. But she wouldn't talk to him. She turned away from him in public, refused to answer his knock, spent more and more time holed up in her studio. He was depressed about the whole thing, and the more depressed he became, the more he found himself seeking out the company of Jane Shine over cocktails or dinner or around the billiard table in the small hours of the morning. He was playing with fire, and he knew it, but it wasn't just Ruth that depressed him, it was his project too—and Jane Shine, with her knowing smile and luminous eyes and her easy conversance with fishes, lent a sympathetic ear.

The biggest problem with the project was that it just wouldn't fly. If the albino pygmy sunfish had ever existed, it was extinct now, gone the way of the dodo and the dinosaur—or so it seemed. He'd made a standing offer—fifty dollars a fish—to all the entomologists, piscatologists and amateur aquarists dipping their nets in all the backwaters, bayous, rills, puddles, cataracts and creeks in the state, and nothing had turned up. His own nets were seething with all sorts of intriguing things: stickleback larvae and catfish fry, cooters and frogs and newly hatched cottonmouths the size of pipe cleaners, whole glistening fistfuls of *Elassoma okefenokee* (all of them brown, of course, a disappointing and unvarying brown, a brown the color of shit and heartbreak). Not a single milk-white mutant showed its scaly little head. Finally, out of boredom and impatience, and despite his initial resolve, he began bringing home specimens for the aquarium. He couldn't resist. He was a boy in a man's clothes, and this was his new toy.

The first day he dumped in about a hundred *Elassoma*, all of them a depressing uniform brown, though some of the males, in a certain light, showed an encouraging grayish tinge. The fish, barely an inch and a quarter long, all but vanished in the vastness of his two hundred gallons, and he began to think that a smaller tank would have served his purpose just as well. But the tank was inhabited now, and he was excited, lit by the same charge that had electrified him when his father surprised him on his eighth birthday with a ten-gallon starter tank. The next day he added another hundred pygmy sunfish and a sampling of other species too—the warmouth, the flier, the least killifish and the golden topminnow, and a pullulating little swarm of half-inch bullheads to patrol the bottom.

He woke the following morning—the morning of the party—to find thirty of his pygmies floating belly up in a slick of mucus at the surface. He checked the pH of the water, and it was fine—slightly acidic, like the peat-tinctured waters of the swamp itself. Puzzled, he fished out the pale bloated little corpses and dumped them in the flowerbed beneath the window. When he came back later that afternoon, half the fish in the tank were dead and even the bullheads were struggling near the surface—and you couldn't kill them with a hammer. And then he noticed that the water had a distinct yellowish cast to it, as if the fish were swimming in pickling brine or urine instead of the pure filtered well water he'd been careful to provide. Something was wrong, seriously wrong, and he turned to the pages of Axelrod's *Exotic Aquarium Fishes* for enlightenment.

Under the section headed "Invasive Organisms," he discovered that the pristine world he'd created had been infiltrated by undesirable elements. Protozoa—he remembered them from freshman biology, virulent little animalcules with waggling microscopic tails—were blooming in the water—his water—and wiping out the desirable elements. He discovered too that the solution to the problem was permanganate of potash, which would eradicate the protozoa and leave the fishes unharmed, and after driving to a pet shop on the mainland, procuring the chemical and dosing the aquarium with it, he watched most of the remaining fish float slowly to the surface and breathe their last. The next day a swarm of carnivorous water beetles materialized from nowhere to finish off the survivors.

In the absence of Ruth, Jane Shine provided solace. After dinner that evening, he led her down the hallway and into the back parlor, where they stood gazing on the pale massed bodies of the dead.

"It's a shame," she said. "All that wasted effort."

He watched her out of the corner of his eye, her face lit in the soft glow of the aquarium, and he felt guilty. Ruth would kill him. Eat him alive. But he was depressed and discouraged and where was she when he needed her? He sighed. "I guess I'm going to have to tear down the whole thing and start over." He gave her a rueful smile. "God had the same problem. Or so I hear."

"It's so beautiful," she murmured, her eyes fixed on the aquarium.

They watched as a crippled killifish rose feebly to the surface, enfolded in the spidery grip of a water beetle.

Jane turned to him. "It's the plants," she said. "They're coming in on the plants."

"Yes," he said. "I know."

"I'd go to a place like Aquarium City—do you have anything like that around here, in Savannah maybe? Get your plants there. At least you know they're clean."

He nodded. Aquarium City. It was so simple: nature was subversive and untidy, and the kindly folks at Aquarium City would be only too happy to sanitize it for him. Yes, of course. And the way she spoke, clipping off each phrase as if it were too precious to part with, reduced him to helplessness. How could he question that voice? She spoke, and he felt like a toppling tree.

"Otherwise"—she gestured toward the quivering fish—"well, you could wind up with *any*thing in there."

.   .   .

WHEN RUTH FINALLY CAME BACK TO HIM, HE FELT NOTHING BUT relief. Yes, he'd been around the singles bars of La Jolla and Westside L.A., and yes, Jane Shine couldn't have been any more compelling if she'd been soaked in pheromones, but Ruth was what he wanted. Ruth was palpable and real in a way that Jane Shine, with her puffed-up, otherworldly beauty, could never approach. She was pretty in her own way, uniquely Ruth, and he couldn't get enough of her. But it went beyond pretty, way beyond: she was a life force, a tidal wave, and she swept all before her, and yet at the same time there was something vulnerable and uncertain about her and it made him feel strong to be there for her. And her obsession with writing—the whole lexicon of her books and writers and reviews, her lists of who was in and who was out—it was the perfect counterbalance to his fish, an obsession he could relate to, a reason for being. And it didn't matter if the obsession was for stamp collecting or paleontology or Renaissance art—it didn't even matter if she was good at it or not—it gave her a fire and a life that made other women seem dull by comparison. He had his fish, and that was all right by her; she had her writing.

She came up to him at cocktail hour and laid a hand on his arm (blessedly, as the Fates would have it, he was leaning over the bar with Sandy at the time; Jane was nowhere to be seen). "Hi," Ruth said, and that was it, the six days of silence forgotten, Jane Shine a *verboten* subject, the party a distant memory. And without another word she took him by the hand and led him upstairs to her room.

In the morning, before she tripped off to breakfast in the convivial room, she woke him with a gentle rub and lubrication and told him she'd be needing a ride into Savannah that afternoon—for groceries. "Savannah?" he said. "What's wrong with Darien?"

"Oh"—offhand, gazing out the window—"you know, there are some things I want that you're just not going to find at the local Winn Dixie." She turned to him and grinned and he felt the relief again, coursing and strong, washing over him like a hot shower. "Let's face it, Sax—Darien, Georgia, isn't exactly gourmet heaven."

"Okay," he said, shrugging, "fine," and at four he drove her to an address on De Lesseps and had a beer in a place he knew on the waterfront while she pushed a shopping cart around. When he swung by to pick her up an hour later, she was waiting for him on the street, engulfed in brown paper bags. He was surprised by how much she'd bought—eight bags of canned goods—and even more surprised when she declined his offer to help carry the stuff out to her studio. "What do you mean?" he said, glancing over his shoulder at the mountain of groceries as he put the car in gear. "You're going to haul all this shit out to the cottage by yourself? Cans and all?"

Ruth was examining her nails. "I'll do it in shifts," she said, "don't worry about it."

"But it's no problem, I mean I'd be happy—"

"Don't worry about it," she said.

But Saxby did worry about it, all the way down the highway to the ferry and all the way across Peagler Sound and up the blacktop road to the house. How was she going to get eight bags of canned goods out to her studio—and what in god's name did she need them for anyway? She had her breakfast and dinner at the house and each afternoon Owen brought her a gourmet lunch—finest lunch offered by any artists' colony anywhere, or so his mother claimed. It was crazy. Was she expecting a siege or something?

And then, as they were staggering through her bedroom door with the booty, one of the bags split, spilling cans all over the floor, and Ruth stopped him when he bent to pick them up. "I can do it myself," she said, turning her back to him and crouching over the cans as if she meant to hide them. That was odd. And it was odder still when he retrieved the two cans that had escaped her.

"Fried dace?" he said. "Bamboo shoots? What are you, going Oriental on us?"

She spun round on him, and while she didn't exactly snatch the cans out of his hand, she took them firmly from him and dropped them into the unrevealing depths of the bag on the table behind her. "No," she said, smiling then, "not really. It's just that . . . I like to try new things."

"Fried dace?" He shook his head and returned her smile, and then she fell into his arms, but the whole thing was very peculiar, very peculiar indeed.

. . .

ON THE WEEKEND, JANE SHINE WENT OFF TO SEA ISLAND WITH SOME clown in a silver XKE and he watched Ruth come to life again. She practically pirouetted round the room at cocktail hour, and at dinner she couldn't sit still, flitting from table to table like a gossip columnist at a premiere. Saxby didn't mind. He was glad to see her enjoying herself, reasserting her preeminence, shining like a supernova in the Thanatopsis firmament. And he was glad too that she seemed to have forgotten all about the party, letting him off the hook vis-à-vis the Jane Shine incident and any number of related peccadilloes he wasn't necessarily even aware of, but condemned for all the same. While she was clowning with Thalamus at the next table, he laid his aquarium woes on Clara Kleinschmidt, talking to hear himself talk—and to pay her back, in small measure, for Arnold Schoenberg.

After dinner, there was a recital by Patsy Arena, a squat, broad-faced woman of Cuban extraction who looked as if she'd stepped out of a Botero painting. She was new to the colony, having come just that week at the invitation of Clara Kleinschmidt, and she played the old Steinway in the front parlor as if she were tenderizing meat. In all, she was to play three compositions that evening, two of her own and one of Clara's. Owen turned the lights down. Ruth held Saxby's hand. The colonists cleared their throats, twisted in their seats, leaned forward in fear and expectation.

Bang! Patsy Arena hit the piano like a boxer. Silence. *One and two, one and two,* she whispered, bobbing her frizzy head. *Bang! Bang!* she slammed at the keyboard with the ball of her fist. And then: nothing. For three full agonizing minutes she sat rigid, staring at the cheap plastic alarm clock perched atop the gleaming ebony surface before her. Finally the alarm went off—*ding-ding-ding*—and *Bang!* she hit the keyboard. The piece was called *Parfait in Chrome,* and it went on for forty-five minutes.

Afterward, as a kind of dessert, there was the weekly movie (*Woman in the Dunes,* a nod to Owen, who was in one of his Japanese phases). Nearly everyone sat through both the recital and the film, which ultimately had more than a little in common. Life at Thanatopsis, as stimulating as it might have been to the artistic sensibility, was problematic as far as entertainment was concerned—Saxby was aware that most of the colonists found it a grinding bore—and the nightly readings, recitals and exhibitions, as well as the weekly film, were small moments of release in a bleak continuum.

Of course, none of that stopped Ruth from spontaneously rewriting the film's dialogue, much to the amusement of her fellow colonists, or from parodying Patsy Arena's performance later on in the billiard room. She had the whole crew in hysterics. They were red in the face and pounding at their breastbones as she pantomimed the pianist's clumsy assault on her instrument, but then Clara and her protégée hunkered into the room and Ruth deftly threw the ball to Abercorn, who'd been giggling innocently in his beer. "Catch anything in your snares today, Det?" she asked.

The laughter subsided. Clara poured Patsy a drink. Everyone looked at Abercorn.

Abercorn had been mooning round the place off and on for the past week or so. Sometimes he had the other character with him, sometimes not. Ruth's question had a barb in it, and Saxby swirled the ice in his drink, watching Abercorn squirm. He kind of liked the guy, actually—or maybe he just felt sorry for him. Abercorn looked up at Ruth out of his big darting rabbit's eyes. The question seemed to sadden him. "Nothing," he said. He tugged at his nostrils, scratched an ear. "Lewis and I think somebody else is involved."

Ruth looked away. Suddenly she was deeply interested in the way the bourbon in her glass caught the light. At the time, Saxby thought nothing of it—but there was a look on her face, lips pursed, eyes downcast but alert, that he was to recall later. "I don't get it," he said. "What do you mean—like somebody on the island is hiding him or something?"

Abercorn nodded, slowly and gravely, his chin stabbing at the circle of colonists gathered round him. Everyone was listening now. "I can't think of anything else—he's been out there for five weeks, and aside from that business down at Tupelo Shores and the shit he's been able to steal here and there, don't you wonder what he's eating?"

Saxby hadn't given it a thought—at this point the big awkward
Japanese kid who'd lurched out of Peagler Sound that night and
run from him at the market was more amusing to him than anything
else. But now—just for a moment and so quickly that he dismissed
it the moment the thought flashed into his head—an answer came
to him: fried dace.

. . .

THE NEXT NIGHT—SATURDAY—RUTH DIDN'T TURN UP FOR COCK-
tails, and Saxby sat with his mother on the veranda and watched
for her. When Armand rang the dinner bell and still she hadn't
come in from the studio, he ambled into the main dining room and
sat at one of the small tables in back with Septima and Owen. His
mother rattled on about colony business—who was coming in the
fall and how so-and-so had been turned down at Yaddo and how
she wouldn't dream of inviting her—and he closed his ears, shut
down his brain and lifted the fork to his lips. After dinner he retired
to the back parlor to brood over his aquarium. That morning he'd
drained the tainted water, discarded the plants and gravel and
rocks—he was going to give the thing a rest for a couple of days,
and then he was going to start all over again. But he'd learned his
lesson. This time he was going to Aquarium City and he was going
to be patient. No more fooling around: he was going to breed albinos
and he was going to make money. And what's more, he was going
to take his place among the great amateur aquarists of the century:
William Voderwinkler, Daniel DiCoco and Paul Hahnel, father of
the fancy guppy.

He tried the title out on himself—*Saxby Lights, father of the albino
pygmy sunfish*—and then he put on a tape—Albinoni, one of his
mother's favorites—and settled into the easy chair with the latest
National Geographic. He tried to read an article about the declining
resilience of beards among Pacific Coast mussels and its implications
for the future of the shellfish industry, but he couldn't concentrate.
He was restless. There was a reading that night—Bob Penick was
previewing some new poems—but Saxby really didn't have much

use for poetry and would have gone only to please Ruth—and Ruth wasn't back yet. A shadow fell over the house, and he reached to turn on the lamp: it was coming on to dusk.

And then suddenly he was out of the chair, his mind made up in an instant—damn it, he didn't care what the rules were, he was going out there to surprise Ruth. She'd been working for twelve hours straight, for christ's sake—she could have written *War and Peace* backwards and forwards by now. Enough was enough. If he fractured her creative bubble, so much the worse, but she could reconstruct it tomorrow. He was tired of waiting.

Red dirt, green gone to gray: the path lay before him like a coil of smoke. He hurried along, sandflies giving way to mosquitoes, anoles rustling through the deepening clots of undergrowth. Up ahead, he heard the soft *chuck* and plaintive sobbing *will's-widow* of the night-flying bird whose call gives rise to its name, and the branches above him were filled with the roosting chatter of the day birds. It was the hour of evening when the diamondback extracts itself from a hole in the ground, drawn to the scurrying warmth of the quick-blooded mammals on which it preys. Saxby stepped lightly.

And then, as he was coming down the final stretch to the cottage, a shadow settled into the path before him. Thick, furtive, dark with the shades of night. It was probably just a cornsnake, but he and Ruth would be coming back up this path in a few minutes, and he didn't want any surprises. Ten feet from the thing—it was a snake, all right, coiling itself like a lariat, dead center in the middle of the path—Saxby bent for a stick. Crouching, one foot extended and the stick outstretched like a foil, he inched toward the thing and felt his heart freeze within him when it struck at the stick and thrashed its rattles all in the same instant. The chirring was explosive, grating, loud as castanets. But it subsided almost immediately, and the shadow of the snake melted into the undergrowth with the faintest crepitation of leaf and twig.

Saxby dropped the stick and moved on up the path, blood pounding in his ears. Always fun playing with snakes, he thought, setting one foot down after the other with the exaggerated care of a man wading through wet cement. Night was settling in as he came round the final loop in the path, and he cursed himself for having forgotten his flashlight. But Ruth would have one—and if she didn't, they'd cut a stick and sweep the path before them, as he used to do when he was a boy coming home late from some adventure on the other end of the marsh. He was thinking of Ruth, a comical version of the snake encounter already taking shape in his mind, when the cottage came into view.

There was no light.

That was a surprise. At first he thought he'd missed her some-how, but then he remembered his last postprandial stroll out to the cabin and how he'd found her sitting there in the dark. He was going to call out, but something made him stop. She was talking to someone, her voice a murmur, indistinct, a current of admonition or urgency to it, as if she were scolding a child. And then the screen door wheezed open, slapped shut. Saxby froze. There was someone on the porch, and it wasn't Ruth.

The Dogs Are Barking, Woof-Woof

. . . .

WHEN RUTH CAME TO HIM OUT OF THE NIGHT, HE WAS DREAMING of his mother, his *haha*, his *okāsan*, the soft-smiling girl in the mini-skirt who'd brought him into the world and suckled him and looked deep into his eyes. It was a dream of the cradle, an oneiric memory, idealized and distilled from the stack of photographs his grand-mother kept in the bottom drawer of her dresser. The photos flapped through his dream like a riffled deck of cards and he saw his mother standing outside a cram school with her guitar and the strong heavy legs and handsome wide face he'd inherited from her; saw her on the futon, thinner now, eyes fixed on the kicking infant framed by the crook of her arm; saw her alone in a crowded bar, bottles winking like stars behind her. And then her face pulled back and rose like the moon into the sky above him and she was Chieko, the wide-hipped girl he'd met in a dive in the Yoshiwara District, her arms around him, lips tugging at his own like sentient things. . . .

Then the door rattled and he knew the police had come for him with their Negroes and their dogs.

But no: it was Ruth's voice coming to him out of the shadows. Ruth's voice. Fumbling for his shorts, the latch, was something wrong? No. Did she want him to turn on the light? No. She was wearing some sort of musk, a scent that came from a bottle and brought him back to his dream, to Chieko and the scintillating lights of the Yoshiwara.

Ruth kissed him, her lips cool on his own, and he felt her tongue in his mouth. Her dress was chiffon, electric against his skin. He didn't understand—they were friends, she'd told him, only friends, and the big butter-stinker with the hair like rice paper and the leaping pale eyes, he was her lover. But her dress fell to the floor as if tugged down by invisible hands and she held him, her flesh pressed to his, the pure white long-legged puzzle of her involved in him now, and he didn't try to understand, didn't want to, didn't care.

In the morning, in the fullness of the light, she raised her head from his chest and looked into his eyes. He felt her there, poised against him, and he listened to the soft murmur of life awakening in the trees and held on to that cool gray gaze with a prick of emotion that must have showed in every line of his face. She seemed to be deciding something, sizing him up, reviewing the night and the moment and the sudden flurry of her options. "Only friends," he murmured, and it was the right thing to say. She smiled, opening up, blossoming, and then she kissed him and everything fell into place.

She went back to her other house, the big house, before the sun was out of the trees, and later she brought him rolls and fruit and meat cut in strips. While he ate, she sat down at her typewriter and began hammering away at the keys with a furious racket. After an hour or so, during one of the long pauses in which she stared out the window and murmured to herself in a faraway voice, he cleared his throat and asked her what it was she was writing.

"A story," she said, without looking up.

"Thriller?"

"No."

"Love story?"

She turned in her chair to look at him. He was sprawled in the loveseat, thumbing through a news magazine—crack, AIDS, children gunned down in the schoolyard—bored to the very roots of his hair. "It's a tragedy," she said, "very sad," and she pantomimed the emotion with a downturned mouth.

He thought about that for a moment as she went back to her typing. A tragedy. Of course. What else? Life was a tragedy. "About what?" he asked, though he knew he was keeping her from her work and he felt guilty about it.

"A Japanese," she said, without turning her head. "In America."

This was a surprise, and before he had a chance to absorb it, he blurted, "Like me?"

Now she turned. "Like you," she said, and then she was typing again.

At lunchtime he went outside and crouched in the bushes until the *hakujin* with the stiff back and wirebrush hair had hung the lunch bucket on its hook and marched back up the path and out of sight. Ruth wouldn't touch the food at first—little sandwiches of cucumber and sausage, with fresh-cut vegetables and raspberries in cream for dessert—but he insisted. He was half crazed with hunger, but he felt so guilty and he owed her so much—and so much more after last night—that he couldn't see her deprived. She was so skinny, and all because of him. "We share," he said, going down on his knees before her and touching his forehead to the floor, "please."

She laughed when she saw him prostrate himself, and finally she gave in, pushing her typewriter aside and clearing a place on her worktable. They ate in silence, but he saw, with gratitude, with love, that she left him the lion's share. While he was clearing up and she lingered over a cigarette, he broke the silence with a question that suddenly and unaccountably popped into his head: "Rusu, please and forgive me: how old are you?"

She threw back her head to draw at the cigarette, exhaling the answer: "Twenty-nine."

"You divorce?"

She shook her head. "Never married."

He took a moment with this, brushing crumbs from the table,

crossing the room to lean out the door and replace the lunch bucket on its hook. "In Japan," he said, "a woman is married at twenty-four. For a man, twenty-eight."

Ruth was smiling, a sly sardonic look in her eye, and he had a sudden vision of her in the Big Apple, in a townhouse with a bathtub the size of his *obāsan's* apartment, pictures on the walls, chrome and leather furniture and the ubiquitous deep-pile rug, and he saw himself coming home to her there, a salaryman in suit and tie and carrying a neat calfskin briefcase. "And how old are you?" she asked.

He was twenty. Just. But he looked older, he knew he did, and he didn't want to disappoint her with the disparity in their ages. "Thirty-one," he said.

Her eyebrows lifted. Twin plumes of smoke escaped her nostrils. "Really?" she said. "Three years past the limit. I'm surprised at you, Hiro—you ought to be married yourself."

. . .

SHE SPENT NEARLY ALL OF THE NEXT FEW DAYS WITH HIM, RETURN-ing to the big house only to sleep at night. He didn't ask her about that, about the sleeping arrangements, and he was still tentative around her. He wanted her, and he tried to tell her that with his eyes or by casually brushing against her as she rose from her desk. At one point, after watching her work through all the interminable hours of the day, he came up behind her and laid a hand on her shoulder. "Not now," she said, pulling him to her for one of those quick pecking kisses the Americans are so fond of, "I'm still work-ing." Later, when she came back from the big house with dinner for them both, he made a mute appeal—a movement of the hands, a slow melt of the eyes—and she saw it, and acknowledged it, but she told him she wasn't feeling very well. "The heat," she said, and she deflected the whole subject of their involvement with a question about Japan: was it *this* hot over there?

And then one evening she went back to the big house for cocktails and she didn't return. It was seven and his stomach was growling.

It was eight and the sun was gone and he began to give up hope. But then maybe—just maybe—she'd be back in the night. He waited for hours, brooding. What did she want with him, anyway? Was it all a game to her, a joke? And when was she going to fulfill her promise, when was she going to get him out of this stinkhole? He felt bitter sitting there in the dark without her—bitter, and though he wouldn't admit it to himself, jealous too—and he forgot all about his gratitude and the debt he owed her, and he got up from the rocker and flicked on the light over her desk.

There it was: her story. One page in the typewriter, the others scattered across the desk as if they'd been dropped there by a sudden gust of wind, pages x'd out, scrawled over, stained with coffee and ink. How many times had he straightened them up for her, how many times had he arranged her pens and pencils and rinsed her coffee cup? He'd never looked at a word. Not because he wasn't curious, but because he was ashamed to. How could he violate her privacy like that after all she'd done for him? That's how he thought, that's how his *obāsan* had raised him. But now, having sat and brooded in the dark and with the jealousy of the lover on him, he thought differently. He didn't give a damn for her privacy. He sat down, shuffled the pages, and began to read:

> He was a Japanese male in the full flower of Japanese manhood, solid and unyielding, and he came home from the office in the small hours and tore at her kimono. The children were asleep, the Sony silent, the tiny apartment polished like a knife. Michiko went wet at the first touch of him. There was whiskey on his breath, imported whiskey, the whiskey he drank each night at the hostess bar, and the smell of it excited her. She loved him for the moon of his face and the proud hard knot of his belly as it pressed against hers, and for his teeth, especially for his teeth. They overlapped like joy and sorrow, the path to his smile as tortuous as a trail torn across the face of Mount Fuji.
>
> He forced himself into her and a cry escaped her lips.

"Hiro," she moaned, clinging to him, holding fast as if she were drowning, "Hiro, Hiro, Hiro!"

Hiro glanced up from the page. The room looked strange to him suddenly, looked like a cage, the walls closing in on him, the lamplight cinching his wrists. He didn't have the heart to read on.

. ■ .

"WHEN?" HE DEMANDED.

She was unpacking groceries, groceries enough for an army, for a siege, enough to keep an animal sleek in its pen for a month at least. "I told you: Sax's car is a pickup. I need a car with a trunk, to hide you." Her elbows jumped; the cans mounted on the table. "His mother's car is what I'm thinking of. I just have to come up with an excuse to borrow it."

"You stall, Rusu. You want to keep me here. You want to make me a prisoner."

The light, the jungle light, was in her hair, slicing at her eyes. She dug into the backpack for another tin of fish. "You prefer it out there?"

"When, Rusu?" he repeated.

She rattled the bag and turned her head to look at him. "I don't want to keep you here against your will—really, Hiro, I don't. Think of the risk I'm running just by harboring you. I like you, I do. I want to see you get out of here . . . it's just—it's not that easy, that's all I'm saying. You don't want to get caught, do you?"

He stood there looming over her, hands on his hips. He didn't answer.

"She's got an old Mercedes with a trunk the size of the Grand Canyon. It'd be ideal." She showed him her perfect pink gums and irreproachable eyes, and suddenly the fight went out of him.

"Okay," he said, dropping his eyes. "Soon, yes?"

"Soon," she said.

And then, two nights later, she staggered up the steps with another load of canned goods, and he couldn't help noticing her cryptic little smile. "I have a surprise for you," she gasped, thumping across the room to fling herself at the desk and wriggle out of her backpack. She threw out her chest, narrowed her shoulders and eased the straps down her arms. He could smell her, a rich dark scent, perfume and sweat commingled.

"Surprise?" He edged closer, watching her hands as she loosed the string at the neck of the bag. He was expecting a treat—a wedge of cake or a Mars Bar maybe; she knew he loved Mars Bars—but she dug yet another can of fried dace and a cellophane package of withered roots from the depths of the bag. His face fell. How she'd ever got the idea that this—this *stuff*—would appeal to him was a mystery. Dried fishheads, bark shavings in plastic envelopes, flat black mushrooms like patches of sloughed skin, can after can of bamboo shoots—what did she think he was, some barefoot hick from Tohoku or something? Dried fishheads? He would have preferred practically anything—Chef Boyardee, Hamburger Helper, Dinty Moore—but it was too awkward to ask. Beggars couldn't be choosy.

She turned to him, put her hands on his shoulders and pecked another of her airy kisses in the direction of his cheek. "It's all set," she said. "Day after tomorrow. Sax is going out after his pygmy fish and I'm taking Septima's car to Savannah—clothes shopping."

It took him a moment. "You mean—?"

She looked up at him, beaming.

"Rusu," he said, and he couldn't contain himself, joy and discovery lighting him up like a rocket. He clutched her in his arms—he was getting out of here, he was on his way, his life was starting all over—but then he felt her body pressed to his and a sudden sharp sense of loss deflated him. She would take him to the city and he would walk away from her, one mutt more in a mob of them. He would never see her again.

"So," she said, pulling back to study his face, her lips stretched in a grin, "are you happy?"

He didn't know what to say. He was groping for the words—

happy, yes, but unhappy too—when a violent hissing clatter burst on them out of the night. It startled them both. Hiro thought of a blowout on the highway, a truck tire reduced to tatters, but the racket of it went on and on, an explosion of ratcheting and hissing that was like nothing he'd ever experienced. Ruth's eyes leapt. His face felt dead.

"A snake," she whispered, gripping his arm. "It's a rattlesnake." And then: "Someone must be coming up the path."

Rattlesnake. The flat wicked head rose up from some deep place inside him, the cold lifeless eyes. He was a boy again, clutching his *obāsan*'s hand and staring with grim fascination into the venom-flecked glass of the reptile house at the Tokyo Zoo.

"You've got to hide." Ruth's face was aflame. "Out there, in back."

The flat wicked head, the flickering tongue. Did she think he was crazy? He wasn't going anywhere.

"Now!" Her voice was harsh, toneless. "Go!"

Her hands were on him, she was pushing him, the screen door wrenching open and snapping shut behind him like a set of jaws. He stood there on the doorstep, peering into the throat of the night, wondering if he couldn't just crouch there on the porch till the overactive reptile and all its flat-headed cousins crawled back into their holes. He caught his breath and held it. All was quiet. No snakes, no intruders. But he remembered the last time, remembered Ruth and her *bōifurendo* thrashing on the rough planks of the porch, and he slunk over the rail and hid himself in the shadows alongside the house.

Just in case.

.   .   .

IN THE MORNING, HE WAS UP AT FIRST LIGHT. SOMETHING HAD wakened him, a ripple of sound at the periphery of consciousness. His eyes fell open on the familiar overhead beams, tired wood, dead wood, and the sick greenish light that hung over the place like a miasma. He blinked twice, wondering at the noise that had awakened him. The birds were going at it, cursing one another in the trees, and there was the flatulent whoop of a frog or lizard or something and the chittering intermittent screech of a monkey— or did they even have monkeys here? But it was nothing out of the ordinary, nothing different from what he'd been hearing day and night since he'd jumped ship. Nature, that's what it was. All those seething little lives, toads and caterpillars and all the rest . . . what he wouldn't give for the squall of a good disco, voices raised over the din of the drum machine, snatches of laughter and shouts from the bar, the stuttering roar of the big Hondas and Kawasakis pulling up out front . . . but there, there it was again. A sort of pant or wheeze, as of a dog on a choke collar or an old man with emphysema laboring up a flight of stairs.

He heard that wheeze, and lying there, half awake, he thought of his grandfather. He'd slept in the same room as the old man when he was a boy in Kyoto, before his grandfather died and his *obāsan* moved back to Yokohama to be near her people. Hiro was afraid at night, afraid of the moving shadows on the wall and his grandfather's labored breathing, and of intangible things too, of vampires and werewolves and white-boned demons, and of the fox that took human form. His *ojisan* was retired then, from Kubota Tractor, and he had a good pension and a plot reserved in the company cemetery, but still *obāsan* went out to work the night-shift at the glassworks. Sometimes, when he got so frightened he thought he would burst open like a sausage, he would wake his grandfather and the old man would catch his breath and wrap him in his spindly arms. "Don't be frightened," he would whisper, "*inu ga wan—wan hoeyoru wai*, the dogs are barking, woof-woof." Barking, that's all.

And then, incredibly, the wheeze that had woken him turned to a bark—a real bark, distinct and unmistakable, and he thought for a moment his *ojisan* was there with him, woofing softly in his whistling old voice. But then a second possibility occurred to him and he sat bolt upright with the shock of it: it *was* a dog. A police dog. The sheriff's dog. And it wouldn't just bark: oh, no, this dog would bite.

. . .

TWO HOURS EARLIER AND NO MORE THAN A MILE AND A HALF AWAY, Eulonia White Pettigru's boy had wakened to the thin trill of his clock radio and the distant pinched thump of drum and guitar. Royal flicked off the radio and sat up, the dark clenched round him like a fist. He'd slept despite himself, though he knew he'd have to be awake and dressed by four—four, that's what Jason Arms had said—or he'd miss the whole thing. Now he was awake, smelling the world and hearing it too—every least sound, the mice in the kitchen, the bats in the air, even the faintest rasp of the earthworms coupling in the grass outside the window. Breathing deep, trying to fight down the little wheel racing inside his chest, he caught a scent of it: the whole world smelled fresh, new-created out of the dregs of the night, as sweet and charged and piquant as a stick of Big Red gum still in the wrapper.

The luminous hands of the clock radio showed 3:35. *I have more of a right than any of them to be there*, he thought, and his fingers trembled as he fastened the snaps of his spiked wristband. From the back room he could detect the soft stertor of his mother's breathing, the dip and rise of her feathery snores. The image of the granola bars in the kitchen (chocolate chip–peanut butter) came into his head, but only briefly and not very persuasively—he was too excited to eat.

Outside, the smell was stronger, sweeter, leaching through everything and killing all those habitual stinks of crab and hogs and the dog-run out back of the Arms place. Royal threw himself down on the front steps to lace his hightops, and then it came to him: he was smelling pipe tobacco, Yerdell Carter's special blend with cinnamon and rose hips all ground up in it. But then—and his hands froze on the laces—was he late, was he missing it? An undercurrent of waking life suddenly whispered to him out of the dark—the distant snap of a match, a murmur of conspiratorial voices: every-body was in on the secret. A soft curse escaped him and the little wheel in his chest accelerated a notch. He was thinking of the coon hunters his father convoked each autumn under the big old live oak in the front yard, dogs whining, shadows milling, the spit of to-bacco, soft truncated jokes caught somewhere between throat and lips. Royal jerked at the laces, the blood pounding in his ear—*more of a right than any of them*—and then he was down off the porch in a single covetous bound and tearing across the lawn to the Arms place.

Jason was up already, fussing over the dogs with a cup of coffee in his hand, looking important and old, though he was just two years, eight months and eleven days older than Royal. The porch light, a single dull 25-watt bulb, made a yellowish pocket in the night, and before he was halfway across the lawn, Royal could see the dark shapes of the men gathered there, eight or ten of them, squatting in the shadows and solemnly masticating the sandwiches Jason's mother had made up for them in the unlighted kitchen. His eyes told him what his nose already knew: Yerdell Carter was among them, his pipe softly glowing, a deer rifle propped up be-tween his legs. The others (he recognized Jenkins, Butterton, Creed, friends of his father and coon hunters all) hunched over shotguns, embracing the dull gleam of the steel as casually as they might have embraced umbrellas on a day with a threat of rain.

The dew was heavy and Royal came up on them with a squeal of his sneakers. He was breathing hard. Too tall for sixteen, gan-gling, with the tapering long African shanks of his father and the carefully chopped dangle of his bleached and processed hair, he looked—well, *different*—and he knew somebody would have some-thing smart to say about it. Yerdell Carter was the man. After crushing a mosquito with an audible slap, he grinned out of his ruined old face and asked Royal if he was going to catch himself a Chinaman.

Royal didn't answer. His father should have been there in his place, but his father was driving truck in Kansas or Wyoming or some such windblown terminus Royal knew only from videos. His father was driving truck about two thirds of the time, and when he came home, he came home. Royal was sixteen and twenty pounds underweight, a loose gangle of gristle and bone. But where Jason and the dogs were going, he was going too. And nobody was going to stop him.

Jason looked up from his dead father's dogs and offered him a sandwich, white bread and bologna. "Uh-uh," Royal said, shaking his head as if he'd just been offered the body and blood of Christ, the flesh warm still and palpitating. "Ain't hungry."

The night before—six hours ago, that is—he and Jason and Rodney Cathcart had been watching *Rock 'n' Roll High School* on Jason's VCR when Sheriff Peagler came to the door. Jason's mother was in bed already and the three of them just about shit blood when they saw who it was: they'd been smoking pot—all the roaches they'd saved over the course of the summer rolled into one thin miserable number—and the smell of it hung over the parlor like an evil ghost. But the sheriff wasn't interested in pot. He was interested in the two big coon hounds and the little yellow bitch Jason's dead father had paid a hundred and ten dollars for in Brunswick.

The sheriff was a bone-thin white man with deep creases in his face and two hard blue eyes that took hold of you like pincers. He'd been a high-school football star—a wide receiver—and he'd won a scholarship to some college up north, but dropped out after two seasons. He wore a hat and a badge, but he dressed in jeans, T-shirt and boots like anybody else. He knocked once and stuck his head in the door. "Jason," he said, "would you step out here a minute?"

And that was it. That was why there were ten men (and now twelve and soon to be fifteen) gathered out front of the Arms place looking like the start of a coon hunt, and that was why Jason was acting so important and why Royal couldn't hold anything on his stomach: they'd found the son of a bitch of a Japanese Chinaman that had gone and killed his uncle. The sheriff wanted the dogs and he was paying Jason twenty-five dollars for the use of them and himself as handler, but he'd warned Jason to keep it quiet. "I want to catch this malefactor and put him behind bars once and for all," he'd told him, using one of his college words to drive the point home, "and I don't want half the island out there gettin' in my way, you follow me?" But Jason had to tell him and Rodney, what with the sheriff's pickup backing out of the driveway and the Ramones on the TV crunching chords in their black pipestem jeans, and Rodney had gone home and told his mother and maybe his three brothers and six sisters and his grandpa and his daddy too, and now, when the sheriff pulled up at four for Jason and the dogs, there was going to be a crowd.

. . .

THE VOICE WAS BOOMING, THUNDEROUS, LOOSED FROM THE CLOUDS, and it sent him into a panic so absolute and immediate it made the fillings in his teeth ache and rendered Jōchō all but useless. "*Hyro Tanayka, you come own outta there now, nice and easy, and y'all put your hands up own top your head where Ah kin see 'em.*" And behind that voice, the barking of the dogs—rabid, slavery; barking that choked on its own rage and saliva, the barking of killers and man-eaters. Strip the flesh from the bone.

The shorts were off the floor and girding his loins in a nanosecond, no time for the Nikes, and then he was clawing his way over Ruth's desk to get at the back window. Up went the sash, one foot on the desk, the other on the sill, and then he froze. His *hara* dropped, his heart turned to ash. What he saw there was Negroes, Negroes with guns and dogs. And *hakujin* too, with uniforms and badges and more guns and more dogs. He was surrounded. It was all up. It was over.

"*Hyro Tanayka,*" the voice boomed from the front of the house, "*y'all have till a count of ten to come own outta there or Ah cannot hold myself accountable for the consequences! One. Two. Three . . .*"

He knew them. They'd tried to run him down before he'd even set foot on their soil, they'd chased him out of Hog Hammock and Ambly Wooster's house too. They were Americans. Killers. Individualists gone rampant. He hung his head and started for the door, defeated, crushed, expecting no mercy but the law of the jungle and of the mutt and half-breed. If he put his tail between his legs and his hands atop his head, then he could . . . could . . .

But all at once, magically, insidiously, the words of Jōchō whispered to him—*The Way of the Samurai is a mania for death; sometimes ten men cannot topple a man with such conviction*—and he was a Japanese all over again, not a mutt, not a *happa*, not half a *hakujin*, but a Japanese, and the strength came back to him, settling in a fiery ball in his gut. He came through the door—"Don't shoot!" he cried— with his hands atop his head, but with a gleam in his eye.

In that moment, all of them—the sheriff, the state troopers, the red-eyed Negroes, the gawk of a *hakujin* with the speckled face and the runt in fatigues Ruth had told him about—all of them relaxed their grip for the tiniest sliver of an instant. He was on the doorstep, he was on the porch, and they were all gaping at him as if they'd never seen a man with *hara* before. That was all it took, that sliver of an instant, the sheriff dropping the megaphone from his lips, the Negroes and troopers and poor white trash easing up on the trigger . . .

"Make my day!" Hiro suddenly shouted, diving for the floorboards as the astonished, outraged cannonade opened up all around him, shattering glass, splintering wood, ricocheting off Ruth's Olivetti and slicing through the trove of bamboo shoots and fried dace in deadly syncopation. And then, in the next sliver of an instant, in the space between the first round and the second, he bounded over the railing and ran headlong into the first man he encountered, an old Negro with a smoking gun and a pipe jammed between his teeth. The old Negro was a carpet, a rug, a piece of lint. He was gone and there was another, and then a white man, and Hiro ran through them as if they were made of paper, silly astonished faces, black and white, sailing back on their buttocks, guns and cigarettes and spectacles flying up into the air as in some miraculous feat of levitation.

The jungle embraced him. There was another barrage, an anguished shout and a chorus of curses, and Hiro's bare broad feet pounded at the mud of a trail he knew as well as he knew the stairwell to his *obāsan*'s apartment. Then he heard the dogs, the savage joy of the multivoiced roar as they were set loose, but he was a samurai, a killer, a hero, and he was heading for a bog that would choke any sixty dogs . . . nor would he hesitate. He'd plunge headfirst into the muck, live it, breathe it, smear his naked body with it and dwell forever here in the wild, his home primeval, Tarzan the Ape Man, unconquerable and—

Suddenly the whirl of his thoughts choked to nothing. There before him, poised in the middle of the path and with his head and shoulders lowered for action, was a Negro. A boy. Hightops. Jeans. Hair like a New Guinea cannibal. Hiro was running, leaves in his face, a dazzle of sun through the trees, the path beneath his feet, and there was a Negro. He was startled—how had he gotten here?— but there was no time for introductions. Behind him the dogs bayed, guns blazed and hot high voices mounted one atop the other: Hiro lumbered down the path like a bull coming out of the gate.

"Get 'way!" he shouted, swiping at the boy with a jerk of his arm. In the next instant he felt the impact, flesh on flesh, the boy's hands like claws fastening at his waist, his feet slipping out from under him, and then he was face down in the mud, gasping for breath. Before he knew what had happened the boy was on top of him, flailing at him with fists that were hard little sacks of bone. "You gook son of a bitch," the boy cried, and Hiro could smell the sweat of him as he tried to fend off the blows and get to his feet, could hear the dogs closing now, swarming at him, the boy's voice rising to a howl, a shriek, an assault of high piercing syllables that cut through him like bullets: "You killed my uncle!"

The Okefenokee

PART II

Everybody's Secret

. . . .

SHE WAS IN TROUBLE, DEEP TROUBLE, AND SHE KNEW IT THE MINUTE
Saxby stepped in the door. For one thing he was supposed to be
gone by now, long gone, off to the Okefenokee to dip his nets and
scare up his fishes. And then there was the expression on his face—
grim and disappointed, the look of a man revising his options,
altering his world view, the look of the outraged moralist, the
inquisitor, the hanging judge. A tiny chill of recognition brought
her back to the previous night. He'd been waiting for her in the
billiard room when she got back late from the cabin, and though
they'd sat up for an hour and then made love, he'd seemed morose,
preoccupied, he'd seemed distant and untouchable. All this rushed
on her in the moment of waking as he slipped in the door and
pushed it shut behind him.

The room was dark still—she'd drawn the shades before going
to bed, thinking to sleep late—but the light of day, hard and uncompromising, assaulted her even as he shut it out with the wedge
of the door. Brightness trembled at the corners of the windowframe,
the sun insinuated itself under the door. It was Sunday. The clock
read 7:15. "Saxby?" she murmured, awake already, awake instantly. "Is anything wrong?"

Of course there was something wrong—he should have been two

hours gone by now. Saxby said nothing. Just stood there, his back to the door. And then he was moving suddenly, crossing the room in two angry strides to jerk open the shade. Ruth felt the light explode in the room, her eyes pinched tight, squinted—it was an ache, an assault. "They got him," he said. "He's in jail."

She couldn't help herself. He'd caught her off guard and she fell back on her natural defenses. She sat up, pressing the sheet to her breast. Her mouth was small, her eyes big. "Who?" she said.

He looked angry, dangerous, looked as if he'd been gored. "Don't be coy, Ruth. You know who I'm talking about. Your pet. Your houseboy. Or was he more than that, huh? 'I just want to try something different,' you said, isn't that what you said. Huh? Something different?"

"Sax," she said.

He was standing over her now, his muscles cut, backlit against the window. She could see the veins standing out in his arms. "Don't 'Sax' me," he said. "I was there, Ruth. Last night. I saw him."

She shifted her weight, tucked the sheet up under her arms. "Okay," she said, reaching for a cigarette, "all right. I helped him. But it's not what you think." She paused to strike a match, inhale, shake it out and deposit the spent curl of it in the ashtray on the night table. "I felt sorry for him, you know? Like with a stray dog or something. Everybody was after him and he was—he's just this kid, and besides, I needed him—I mean, not at first—but I needed him for this story I'm writing . . ."

Saxby held himself rigid. He was the man in the boat on Peagler Sound, focused and invincible, beyond her control. "How long?" he demanded. "Two weeks? Three? A month? It's a big joke, isn't it? On all of us. Abercorn and that little peckerwood Marine or whatever he is, Thalamus, Regina, Jane—my mother even. But what really burns my ass is you put it over on me too. What, you couldn't trust me with it? Answer me, goddamn it!"

She was busy with her cigarette. It was all she could do to keep from grinning, grinning with guilt and shame and defiance, and that would only make it worse. And she needed Sax on her side, now more than ever. If he knew—and the thought made her stomach clench—then they all knew, and they wouldn't find it very funny. She was an accessory, an aider and abettor. She could go to jail. "I wanted to tell you, Sax—I was going to—" she began, and then she trailed off. The light heightened. The room was silent. "Look, Sax: it was a game. Something I knew that none of them did—not Peter Anserine or Laura Grobian or Irving Thalamus either. I was insecure here, you know that. And this was something I could hold on to, something of my own—"

"Yeah," he said, his voice thick with disgust and self-pity, "but what about me?"

She was angry suddenly. She was in trouble—deep trouble—and he'd put her there. "No," she said, stabbing the cigarette at him for emphasis, "what about *me*?" Here he was, her lover, her confidant, the sweet funny guy with the big feet, and he'd betrayed her. "You turned him in, didn't you?" she said, taking the offensive.

His face changed. She loved him, she did, but he was weak inside, and now she had him. "You, you never told me," he stammered. "I see him there on your porch and I'm thinking about all those cans of fried dace and bamboo shoots—what do you expect me to do? I mean, at least you could have told me."

"You shit, Sax." Now she was crying. Her shoulders quaked a bit and the sheet slipped to her waist. She reached for it, to cover her breasts, but then she let it fall away again. She could see herself as through the lens of a camera, sobbing in the morning light, in bed, naked to the waist, betrayed by her man and at the mercy of the authorities. It was a poignant moment, just like real life. She glanced up at Saxby. He was struck dumb.

"Don't you ever think?" she gasped. "Don't you know what this means? They're going to come after *me* now, they're going to want to question *me*—they could arrest me, Sax." She'd worked herself up now. The bed was trembling, her breast heaving. She was feeling scared, angry, feeling sorry for herself.

Saxby came to her. She felt him ease down on the bed, reach

out to stroke her arm. "Hush," he said. "You know I won't let
anything happen to you."

"I'm scared," she said, and she was holding him. "He was just—
it was like a stray dog or something," and then she was sobbing all
over again.

. . .

SHERIFF PEAGLER STOPPED BY AROUND NOON, A GRIM-LOOKING
Abercorn and grimmer-looking Turco flanking him. There was no
Sunday morning ferry, so they'd put Hiro in an old slave-holding
cell for safekeeping till Ray Manzanar made his eight o'clock run
to the mainland and back. (There was an earlier ferry, at six, but
as the sheriff was to inform Ruth with an executioner's grin, they
were going to need all the daylight they had to comb over the scene
for evidence.) Ruth knew the cell—it was out back of John Berryman, the closest of the studios to the big house, and currently
occupied by Patsy Arena. Saxby had showed her the cell the day
they arrived: it was the sort of thing tourists liked to look at. Actually, there were two cells, stone and crumbling plaster, big oaken
doors with sliding bolts and a barred window twelve feet off the
ground. The planters would immure a new slave in the one—wild-
eyed, feverish, fresh from Goree or Dakar and the scarifying trip
across the pitching wild sea—and in the other, a long-broken docile
doddering old fatherly type, and the old slave would sweet-talk the
new one, calm his fears, indoctrinate him. The cells were in an
outbuilding behind the studio. If it weren't for the trees, you could
have seen it from the big house.

Ruth had had four hours to compose herself, though all Thanatopsis was abuzz with the news. She'd posted Saxby at the door—
Irving had been by, Sandy, Bob, Ina, Regina, even Clara and Patsy,
but Saxby wouldn't let them in. She'd hear the knock, watch Saxby
rise, pull back the door and step into the hallway, and then she'd
strain to hear the whispered colloquy that followed. At eleven,
Septima herself, regal in a blue silk dress with lace trim and pearls,
huffed her way up the stairs. Saxby couldn't deny his own mother,

and he helped her into the room. Ruth was in bed still, feeling like an invalid, though she'd pulled on a blouse and shorts. "I really don't know whatever this is all about," Septima began in her breathy old patrician's tones, "but I do suspect that you are entirely innocent of any wrongdoin', Ruthie—isn't that right?"

Ruth assured her that it was. "If he was in there, Septima—and it burns me to think of all that beautiful old paneling all shot full of holes, and god knows what they did to my typewriter and the manuscript I've been slaving over for the last six weeks—if he was there, you have to know it was totally without my knowledge or consent. He snuck in at night, I guess. Who's to stop him?"

Septima sniffed. She trained her watery gray eyes on something outside the window. "And you never noticed anythin' amiss, Ruthie? Nothin' out of place?"

Ruth was ready for this one. She forced a smile, and she shrugged. "I'm embarrassed to say it," she said, indicating the room, which was a festival of strewn underwear, tops, socks, shoes, spine-crushed books, rolls of toilet paper and tattered magazines, "but you know, I've never been much at keeping things up. It's my artistic temperament, I guess." She looked up at Sax. He looked away. "Sax can tell you: where it drops, it stays."

Sheriff Peagler wanted to know the same thing.

It was noon. They were in the front parlor—she and Saxby, Peagler, Abercorn and Turco—and the door was shut behind them. It was hot—stifling—and though the windows were open wide, there wasn't even the hint of a breeze. The house was quiet. The diehards among the colonists were dispersed in their studios, typing, painting, molding clay and poring over scores; the others were sailing, fishing, taking the air in Savannah.

Sheriff Peagler—Theron Peagler, college-educated and cold as a snake—leaned toward her. He was sitting in a leather wing chair and he held an untouched glass of ice water in his hand. In a minute he would ask Saxby to leave the room. But now he leaned forward to ask Ruth if she'd ever noticed anything out of place in the studio—the furniture moved around, the windows up, anything.

Ruth had spent some time on her makeup, marshaling all the weapons in her arsenal. She had a feeling she was going to need them. She'd glanced at Abercorn when they stepped into the room, but that was it—she really couldn't look him in the eye. Not yet, anyway. She took a minute. Smoothed her skirt. Composed herself. "Septima—Mrs. Lights—asked me the same thing. But you must have seen the place, I mean, even before they started shooting it up"—a dig, a tiny dig—"and it's a real mess. I'm sorry. I'm just not much for housekeeping. I mean, I don't notice things."

This was the point at which the sheriff glanced up at Saxby and asked if he wouldn't mind leaving the room.

Saxby looked at Ruth, and then at the sheriff, and finally he heaved himself up out of the chair and strode across the floor. Ruth counted his footsteps—eight, nine, ten—and listened to the gentle, well-oiled click of the heavy walnut door as it shut behind him. She felt hot and cold suddenly and her heart was singing in her ears. She could hear them breathing on either side of her. There was no other noise.

No one said a word. Hot and cold. Ruth stared at the carpet and for a moment she considered going faint with the heat, but she rejected the notion as soon as it entered her head—it would only incriminate her. They were toying with her, she realized, toying with her, the little pricks. She felt Abercorn's eyes on her, and she lifted her head.

The blotted skin, pink eyes, hair like false whiskers: how could she ever have considered him even remotely attractive? He was trying to stare her down, a crease of rage between his hard pink bunny's eyes. Let him stare. She gave it right back to him.

"Miss Dershowitz." The sheriff was addressing her. She held Abercorn's gaze a second longer than she had to, and then turned to look at the leathery little man in the jeans, workshirt and badge. He looked sly, insidious, a man who'd heard all the alibis and knew all the answers. Her courage failed her. She would break down, that's it. Break down and admit it all.

"About the food. We found—what do you call it—*Oriental* foodstuffs on the premises, seaweed and dried roots and suchnot. How do you explain that?"

"I wouldn't know." Her own voice sounded strange to her, distant. "Maybe he brought the stuff in at night. I don't eat dried roots."

"Cut the shit, lady." Turco's voice came at her like a kick in the side, and she shot her eyes at him; he was perched on the edge of the chair, mouth working in his beard, a little homunculus, the gnome that violates the virgin in the fairy tale. "Just cut it, will you? You been jerking us around here for six weeks now."

Ruth turned away from him. She would break down, yes, but prettily, and in her own good time.

"Enough," Abercorn spat, and Ruth was shocked at the rage in his voice. He was big, powerful in a lank and sinewy way, an athlete: perhaps she'd underestimated him. She felt something stir in her, though the timing was inappropriate, to say the least. "Ruth, listen," and his voice softened just perceptibly, from a snarl to a growl, "we've got enough on you right now to book you as an accessory to manslaughter in the death of Olmstead White, arson in Hog Hammock, harboring a fugitive from justice and giving false information to an agent of the federal government." He paused to let the terminology have its effect. "Make it easy on yourself, will you? I mean, Sheriff Peagler can put the cuffs on you right now, if that's what you want. But there's no need for anybody to get nasty here. We just want to know the facts, that's all."

Abercorn eased back in his chair, as if he were settling in for the first act of a play. "Now," he said, his voice placid, complacent, the voice of a man who already has what he wants, "when did the suspect, Hiro Tanaka, first contact you?"

∎   ∎   ∎

THE REST OF THE AFTERNOON WAS A THING THAT HOVERED AT THE windows and took the breath out of the air, bloated and interminable. Ruth sweated in places she'd never sweated before—between the toes, in the runnels of her ears—and in the usual places too.

Her thighs met in a glutinous embrace, the elastic band of her panties became a towel, a sponge, her breasts lay heavy and wet against her ribcage. Abercorn had read her her rights, and that scared her, and she sweated all the more. In another context it would have been comical, like something out of *Dragnet* or *Miami Vice*, but here, now, it made her sick inside: this was one role she wanted no part of. When he offered her immunity from prosecution if she would tell him everything—and testify to it in court—she jumped at the chance. "After all, Ruth," he'd said, the bunny eyes gone hard with malice, "nobody's after *you*. Though I do want to emphasize just how serious your little, uh—*prank*, let's call it—has been. Is. And what a dim view my office—not to mention my boss and his boss in Washington—takes of obstructing justice and aiding and abetting those elements that would enter the country illegally." He paused to study his nails. "Especially when they commit criminal acts and mayhem."

More terminology.

She bowed her head and agreed with him. He was wise, and she was penitent.

In all, they kept her for nearly two hours. It was a classic grilling, right out of the INS handbook (if there was such a thing). Abercorn had settled down to play the pal, the protector, interceding for her against the grunts and curses and pained incoherent cries of Turco and the steady ferrety pursuit of Peagler, and she'd given him what he wanted. Mostly. She told him about Hiro making off with her lunch bucket and how she'd discovered it and took pity on him. And she admitted the business with the Oriental food—he was like a stray dog. Or cat. Didn't they see that? It was like putting out a salt lick or a bird feeder. On the issue of harboring a fugitive, she was firm: she denied it outright. If he slept in her studio she knew nothing about it—there was no lock on the door, after all. As far as she knew he came only at lunchtime and took the food like a wild animal. And no, she'd never provided him with clothes or money or anything like that: it was just the food, and she left it there on the porch.

And then there came a point at which the three of them fell silent. Flushed and greasy, her hair and makeup devastated, she studied her feet and felt their eyes on her. In that moment she realized she had a headache. A tiny whirring drill began to bore through her skull, front to back, back to front, over and over. "You're free to go now, Miss Dershowitz," the sheriff had said, and Ruth got up and left the room in a daze. Mercifully, the front hallway was deserted.

She made her way to her room, shrugged out of her clothes and let the window fan dry the sweat from her skin. She took an aspirin and two short hits from the pint of bourbon she kept on the night table, and she began to feel better, if only marginally. It was then that she thought of Hiro. He was out there now in the infernal heat of that crumbling cell, awaiting prison, deportation and whatever the Japanese would do to him after that. She thought of the Rape of Nanking, the Bataan Death March, Alec Guinness emerging from the sweatbox in *The Bridge on the River Kwai*, and then she lay face down on the bed and began to massage her temples.

Hiro. Poor Hiro. She *had* made love to him, after all—for the novelty, yes, and because the moment was right—but there was feeling there too. There was. And she ached for him in that parched and blistering cell, Abercorn and Turco hanging over him with their obscene and insatiable curiosity. She ached for him, she did, but she'd been through an ordeal herself, and now, as the afternoon settled in, she closed her eyes and drifted off into a sleep that was depthless and pure.

She woke to a discreet, solicitous tapping at the door. It was five in the afternoon. There was a stale taste in her mouth, the residue of nicotine and bourbon. "Yes?" she called.

It was Saxby, waking her for the second time that day. This time there were no recriminations. This time he was beaming, grinning, puffed up to the roots of his hair with boyish glee. "Ruth! Ruth!" he cried, and it sounded like a dog's bark at the door, and then he was in the room, on the bed, snatching her hands up in his own.

"Ruth!" he cried again, as if she'd been lost for years. His eyes were swimming. He looked delirious. "Ruth!" he shouted, though he was right there, right on the bed beside her. He didn't ask how she was feeling, how the interrogation had gone, whether they were going to shackle her to a bunch of spouse abusers on the chain gang or hang her by her thumbs—he just kept repeating her name, over and over. She wanted to know if he was drunk.

"Drunk? Hell, no: Ruth!"—there it was again—"Ruth!"—and again—"Roy Dotson just called!"

Yes? And so?

"He's found them. My albinos. I'm out the door this minute." And then he was up from the bed, shuffling his big feet, jerking his limbs and tugging at his ears like one of the afflicted.

"Really?" She was grinning back at him now, feeling good, feeling happy for him, though the fish business was an ongoing mystery to her. Why fish? she wanted to ask him. What was the attraction? Seals, she could see, otters, the purple gallinule, for christ's sake—but fish? They were cold-blooded, stupid, gaping mouths and cartoon eyes: she hated fish. Hated aquariums. Hated dip nets and seines, canoes, rivers, lakes, swamps, hated it all. But watching him there in the stippled shadows of the lace curtains, tasting his excitement, she was happy.

Then he bent to kiss her, deep and hard—the kiss of an explorer leaving home, the kiss of a lepidopterist or spelunker—and he was out the door. But then he was back, poking his head round the doorframe. "Oh, yeah," he said, hanging there, his motor revving, fish on the brain, "I almost forgot: How'd it go? With the sheriff and all?"

The question brought her back, and for a moment she was afraid all over again, but then it passed. She was okay. She was in one piece. Hiro was in jail and her novella was shot full of holes—literally—but they weren't going to do anything to her. She could write another novella, forget all about the Japanese and their weird rites and customs, let somebody else portray suicide in the surf and sex in kimonos. She had Sax and Septima and Thanatopsis House, she had Irving Thalamus and Laura Grobian—and Jane Shine was gone for the weekend. No, there was nothing to worry about, nothing at all.

"How'd it go?" She repeated his question, reaching for a cigarette and feeling Olympian, impervious, unscathed, La Dershowitz ascendant. She took a minute with the response, Saxby hanging there in the doorway, the late shafts of the sun gilding the curtains till they seemed solid as pillars. "Fine," she said. "Just fine."

.   .   .

ON SUNDAYS, ARMAND SERVED DINNER AT SEVEN AND SOMETIMES a bit later, depending on his whim and the mood of the colonists. Sunday was, after all, the day of rest, or so Septima reasoned, and long before she'd engaged her current chef she'd pushed back cocktails and dinner by an hour on the Lord's Day, and it was now a Thanatopsis tradition. Sunday afternoons were long and languorous, and no one stirred before six, when the first sunburned and subdued clumps of artists began to gather on the patio or in the front parlor for cocktails. Sometimes there would be music—a poet would sit down at the piano or a biographer would reveal a hidden talent for the clarinet, ravishing the room with the adagio from Mozart's concerto or a Gershwin medley—and the ice cubes would tumble into shaker or glass with a rhythmic click that was salvation itself for the sun-dazed and weary.

It was close to seven when Ruth came down for dinner. She'd scrubbed and showered and scrubbed again, ridding herself of any vestige of the sweaty film that had clung to her earlier that afternoon, clogging her pores and making her feel dirty and vulnerable while Abercorn hung over her with his unfinished face and chummy questions. She was wearing a white Guatemalan peasant blouse embroidered with bright blue flowers and matching full skirt, and she descended the steps and crossed the front hallway feeling light, airy, lustral, feeling unconquerable all over again.

When she entered the front parlor, Sandy was at the piano, stroking the petrosal keys as if they were flower petals, dripping his way through one syrupy Beatles tune after another. The melodies were perfect reconstructions of a thousand memories, syrupy or not, and with the help of their third or fourth cocktails, the colonists were in a mellow mood. Ruth stepped through the door and recognized them all, her friends and fellow artists, her community, her family, poised on sofas and ottomans, hovering over the bar, each and every one of them a joy and a solace.

Irving Thalamus was the first to call out her name, as usual—it was his way, chutzpah thrown up like a screen, the legend crowing—and then a murmur went through the room and they converged on her as if she'd just broken the tape in the marathon.

"You fox," Thalamus said, shaking his legendary head, "you sly fox." And then, turning to the others, "Can she keep a secret or what?" He was beaming at her, embracing her, squeezing her as if she were exotic fruit. "This," he pronounced, "is a *writer.*"

Ruth hugged him back, giving them all a knowing but self-deprecatory grin, and reddening, if ever so slightly. Ina was staring at her in wonder. Bob's eyes were glowing. Regina, in a chartreuse leather halter, looked up from a game of solitaire and one of the cigars she was now affecting, and Sandy broke off in the middle of "Fool on the Hill" to leap a barstool and pour Ruth a conspicuous martini—a whiff of vermouth and three olives, just the way she liked it. Clara and Patsy were there too, hovering at the edge of the press and looking like Tweedledee and Tweedledum in matching pantsuits.

"Hey, La D.: you're just in time," Sandy hollered, elbowing his way toward her with the drink held high, "—we just sent out for sushi."

And oh, they laughed at that, her fellow colonists, mellow and proud, an excess of moisture in their eyes, warming up for the evening, the week, the month to come, with its string of Japanese jokes, its cops and robbers routines, and the audacious, awe-inspiring theme that would underlie it all: *What La Dershowitz won't do for a story, huh?* And all the while the delectable questions—how long, how much, had she slept with him and what did the sheriff say?—hung in the air, awaiting fulfillment.

During the soup course, Ruth managed tête-à-têtes with Irving, Sandy, a myopic poet in a strapless gown with whom she'd never before exchanged a word, and a vacuous, wide-eyed Ina Soderbord. Over salad, Clara and Patsy pressed her for details, and while she tore into the main course—she found that she was ravenous after all the day's excitement—Septima herself wanted clarification of some of the statements she'd made earlier. It wasn't a dinner—it was musical chairs. By the time Rico brought out dessert and the big gleaming coffee urn, Ruth was the center of a group that wheeled out from her like planetary bodies, circling, tangential, held fast by the irresistible force of gossip.

After-dinner drinks were served on the patio.

Ruth was chatting with Bob and Sandy, enjoying the relative cool of the evening, feeling reborn, when she felt a hand slip into her own and looked up into the depthless haunted eyes of Laura Grobian. At fifty, Laura Grobian was the doyenne of the dark-eyed semi-mysterious upper-middle-class former-bohemian school of WASP novelists, famous for a bloodless 209-page trilogy set in 1967 San Francisco. She'd published a few slim volumes since (each phrase chiseled like sculpture—or dental plaster, depending on your point of view) and she'd been photographed by Karsh, Avedon and Leibowitz, her sunken cheeks, black bangs and haunted eyes as fixed an image in the public consciousness as Truman Capote's hat or Hemingway's beard. She dismissed Bob and Sandy with a neurasthenic bob of her head and drew Ruth aside.

"Oh, Ruth," she gasped, fanning herself while bats careened overhead and mosquitoes hovered, "I heard, I heard all about it. How terrified you must have been—"

Ruth gazed on her with wonder. If Irving Thalamus was a legend in his own time, Laura Grobian was supernal, divine, and here she stood in the flesh, not merely acknowledging Ruth's existence, but seeking her out, conferring with her, pumping her! Ruth leaned toward her and dropped her voice to a stagey whisper: "I've never been so afraid in my life, Laura." She paused a beat to see how the haunted-eyed Laura Grobian was taking this little familiarity, and then went on. "Well, the sheriff—he was the worst. He's got those Southern manners, yes, but when he gets you in that room and starts grilling you, let me tell you he's the most powerful and intimidating man I've ever been this close to in my life. You know what he does?"

Laura Grobian's spectral eyes were canny and fixed. She was all ears.

It was at this moment that a vaguely familiar automotive cough and rumble insinuated itself between the buzz of conversation and the shrilling of the insects, and the colonists looked up briefly from their Grand Marnier and Rémy-Martin to the fleeting wash of a pair of headlights. A gleam of silver flitted beneath the lights of the drive, there was the rise and fall of the car's engine shutting down and the elegant thump of first one door and then the other closing on perfection: Jane Shine was back.

Ruth could feel them, the whole group, the whole colony, abuzz as they were with excitement over *her* exploits, *her* daring, *her* immaculate bedeviling of the powers that be, hesitate in the breach of that moment. The chatter died round her and her heart sank. But then Laura Grobian's ruined but exquisite tones floated out to fill the vacuum—"But tell me, Ruth, honestly: you *were* hiding that desperate man all along, weren't you?"—and it was over. As one, the colony turned back to the conversation, to the drink at hand and the company present. Jane Shine was back. So what else was new?

It couldn't have gone any better for Ruth, queen of the hive once again—she was even readying herself to grant the inevitable and gracious billiard-room audience to Jane Shine later that night, or maybe she'd snub her, maybe she would—it couldn't have gone any better, till there came a single wild shout from out beyond John Berryman that grew immediately into a chorus of cries and lamentation and gave rise in the next moment to a parade of footsteps storming the patio. "What is it?" someone cried, and Ruth saw the sheriff's face, wild and white, Abercorn's, Turco's, their mouths drawn tight and eyes rabid, and then the sheriff seized on her, Ruth, as the first face he recognized. "The phone," he barked, "where's the phone?"

She was frozen. They were at her again, at her like hounds. Everything broke down in that instant, faces flapping round her like sheets in the wind. "Phone?" she repeated, stupid, dazed.

"Goddamn it, yes," he snarled, looking on her with hatred, real hatred, before turning away in disgust and seizing on Laura Grobian. And then he was turning wildly away from her too, flailing his arms at the crowd gathered there on the patio with their sweet drinks and snifters of swirling dark cognac. "I need your help, all of you," he cried, and then his voice dropped down to nothing and he finished the thought as if he were talking to himself, "—the son of a bitch is gone and got himself loose again."

*F*our Walls

. . . .

THEY'D CAUGHT HIM. RUN HIM DOWN. OVERWHELMED HIM WITH
their guns and their dogs and their Negroes. They'd caught him,
yes. Oh, yes. Slapped him, handcuffed him, jerked their elbows
into his ribs, his gut, the small of his back. They shoved him,
abused him, humiliated him, made him walk the gauntlet of them
as if they were red Indians in the forest, jeering and spitting and
cursing him for a Jap, a Nip, a gook and a Chinaman. Yes. But
they weren't red Indians. They were white-faced and black-faced,
blue-eyed, kinky-haired, they stank of butter and whiskey and the
loam that blackened their fingernails, and it was they who'd exter-
minated the red Indians with a ferocity so pitiless and primeval it
made the savages seem civilized. Yes. Oh, yes. And they hated
him. Hated him so deeply and automatically it froze his heart: this
was American violence, bred in the bone. This was the mob, the
riot, this was dog eat dog.

The hate. It took him aback, it did. He was like them—that was
the whole point, couldn't they see that? He was a mutt too. But
they didn't see it, didn't care. They cuffed him and shoved him
and spat their curses at him and he saw the hate in their cold rinsed-
out *hakujin* eyes, saw it in the black stony glare of the Negroes: he
was an insect, a snake, something to be stepped on and ground into

the dirt, eliminated. The face of the Negro boy had been almost ecstatic with hate as he crouched there in the path, consumed in his passion, implacable, worse even than the dogs. (They were there too—right there, right in Hiro's face—choking back snarls and drool and breath that stank of meat gone bad, trembling all over with the urge to fall on him and tear him to pieces.) *Uncle!* the boy kept shouting, as if it were some sort of war cry, *Uncle! Uncle!*, his fists clenched, his eyes hard, tongue swollen, his very blood turned to acid with the ferocity of his hate.

And then there was the puffed-up little man in fatigues who pulled the boy off him and forced his wrists into the handcuffs, and the other Negro who called off the dogs, and the spatterface from the INS and the sheriff too: there was no glimmer of humanity in any of them. They'd never smiled, laughed, enjoyed a meal, friendship, love or affection, never petted a dog, stroked a cat or walked a child to school. They were hunters. Killers. And Hiro was their quarry, foreign and strange and worth no more time or thought than a cockroach dropped from the ceiling into their morning grits.

Their hands were on him, firm hands, iron hands, and the cuffs bit into his wrists. The sheriff hauled him to his feet and walked him back down the path, grim and purposeful, jerking impatiently at his manacled forearm while a deputy prodded him from behind. Hiro could hear them hooting and cursing and shooting off their weapons somewhere up ahead, but then the sheriff called out to them in a fiery hoarse shout and the noise of the guns abruptly ceased, lingering for a moment as echo and then fading away to stillness. A hush fell over the morning and all at once Hiro was afraid. He held the fear in a lump inside him, a tumor of fear, and he bowed his head and concentrated on his feet.

The man in fatigues and the boy with the dogs had fallen into step behind Hiro and the sheriff—they were quiet now, the dogs, whining and panting like housepets out for a stroll in the park— and behind them were the agency man and the spidery Negro boy whose towering unquenchable *Amerikajin* hate had brought Hiro down. It was a parade, that's what it was. Grim, silent, angry, a parade in celebration of hate. But Hiro had no time to get philosophical about it—already they were emerging on the clearing at Ruth's place and a murmur went up around him. He kept his eyes on the ground, but he could feel the presence of them, black and white, a mob of them, and he could smell the gunsmoke on the air. No one spoke. No one cursed or abused him. And then suddenly a man dried up like a stick of firewood stepped in front of him—"You Jap bastards kilt my brother Jimmy," he snarled—and Hiro felt a stitch in his side, the elbow to the kidney, and then all the rest of them were spewing it at him—hate—until the sheriff got him in the car and out of there, out of the jungle and down the black macadam road to the cell that awaited him.

And now, here he was, in a *gaijin* cell, fulfilling his destiny.

From the storage room of the *Tokachi-maru* to the big bedroom at Ambly Wooster's to the cramped loveseat at Ruth's to this joyless cubicle of rotten mortar and stone, he was a prisoner in perpetuity, hopeless and defeated. The City of Brotherly Love was an illusion, a fairy tale—he saw that now. And then he thought of Jōchō and Mishima. In defeat, there was only one path to honor, and that was death. Mishima had addressed the soldiers of the Self-Defense Forces on the day he died, exhorting them to join him in rising up to purify Japan, and when they didn't join him, when they laughed and jeered, he'd turned a sword in his own guts and made a mockery of them all. Alone in his cell with the stirrings of his guilt and shame, Hiro fell back on Jōchō. He didn't have the battered and stained little volume—the sheriff had taken it from him, along with the picture of Doggo and the few odd little coins he'd got back from the girl in the Coca-Cola store—but he knew the formula, knew it by heart. The more they hated him, the more Japanese he became.

It couldn't have been much past seven in the morning and the heat was like a weight on him already, pounds per square inch, a measure of his defeat. He sat there on the stone floor and pressed tentatively at his stomach, feeling a sword there, feeling liberation and honor, and something else too: hunger. Stinking and mud-encrusted, bruised, flayed and terrorized, humiliated to the point at which there was no alternative but suicide, he was hungry. Hungry. It was an embarrassment. A joke. The urgings of life crowding in on a funerary rite, a preparation for death gone up in dreams of sweet bean cake and ice cream.

Well, all right. Perhaps he wasn't defeated yet. It was all in the interpretation, wasn't it? *Small matters should be taken seriously*, Jōchō said. Well, then, his hunger was a small matter, and he would take it very seriously indeed—and the larger matter, the matter of his solitary and eternal fate, he would take lightly. As for the smaller matter, he was sure they would feed him something—not even the *hakujin* could be so barbaric as to let a prisoner starve to death. And as for the larger matter, he would have the right to a fair trial, wouldn't he? He thought about that a moment, a fair trial, justices in their funereal robes, a jury of long-noses empaneled to vent their hate on him, Hiro Tanaka, the victim, the innocent, the *happa* from Japan trussed up like a turkey and studying the scuffed tiles of the courtroom floor as if their pattern would somehow reveal the so-lution to his predicament . . . and then all at once a glorious notion came into his head, a notion that tossed off fair trials, fuming sheriffs, dogs and Negroes and gun-toting crackers as if they were so much refuse, the outer wrapping of a morsel so sweet and nour-ishing it inflated his *hara* just to think about it: he would escape.

Escape. Of course. That was it: that was the solution. Two little syllables leaped into his head and he felt the blood beating in his veins, in his tiniest vessels and capillaries. He was a man with *hara*, a modern samurai, and if he'd escaped from the storage closet of the *Tokachi-maru*, from Wakabayashi and Chiba and all the rest, then he had the wits and courage and stamina to defeat all the *gaijin* cowboys in all the endless streets and alleys and honky-tonk bars of the whole Buddha-forsaken country, and he could escape from here too.

For the first time since they'd slammed the door on him he looked around, really looked, letting his eyes linger over each detail. The cell was ancient, filthy, slowly giving itself back to the chaos from which it had evolved in some dim colonial epoch. It was like a stall in a barn, except that there was no water, no straw, no place to relieve oneself—not even a bucket. The amenities consisted of a wooden bench built into the wall opposite and two lawnchairs— aluminum tubing and plastic mesh—propped up in the corner. Above the bench, twelve feet from the ground at least, there was a single barred window that apparently gave onto an interior room beyond it, judging from the light. And that was it, but for the door through which he'd been bundled half an hour ago.

He was sitting on the stone floor where they'd left him, where they'd dumped him in a rush of clattering shoes and urgent feet, his ribs throbbing and a long nasty gash coloring his left shin. When he wet his lips, he tasted blood at the corner of his mouth, and there was a tender spot—and some swelling, it felt like—along the cheekbone beneath his right eye. At least they'd removed the cuffs, though it seemed a small thing to be thankful for after all they'd inflicted on him. He rubbed his wrists. And he scanned the cell again, hopefully, wondering if he'd missed something. He hadn't. He was locked in. He'd been abused and humiliated. There was no way out.

But then he gazed up at that dim high window, and then down at the lawnchairs and back up again, and a picture came to him of a pair of jugglers he'd seen on TV as a boy, one balancing atop a stack of stage chairs while the other offered him a whirl of knives, Indian clubs and flaming torches to spin over his head. If he stacked those chairs on the bench and if he could manage to climb atop them, he could reach the window—and if he could reach the window he could find out what was on the other side and see if one of the bars wasn't maybe just a tiny bit loose. But then why would it be loose? he thought, sitting there still, aching with a dull persistence. And yet, why not? The building was old and disused, a relic of the times when the Negroes were shackled and the red Indians butchered. And this cell—this must have been where the *hakujin* kept their Negroes before they dragged them out to whip and lynch and burn them.

The thought lifted him to his feet.

He stood a moment at the door—a slab of oak, featureless, solid as rock—and then he noiselessly crossed the cell and took up the lawnchairs. They were frayed and dirty and their joints were locked with rust, but he managed to unfold them nonetheless. What followed bore less resemblance to a feat of skill performed in the center ring than an elaborate pratfall. The first attempt landed him on the stone floor and jammed that tough little appendage of bone at the nether end of his spine right up into his mouth. The second attempt twisted a knee, traumatized an elbow and put a permanent bow in the frame of one of the chairs. There was noise, of course—the stiff applause of the chairs clattering from bench to floor, the thump of perspiring flesh against unyielding stone, the small astonished grunts and gasps of pain—but no one came to the door as he lay there panting and writhing. For this, he was thankful.

He stacked the chairs again and again, balancing, teetering, clutching and falling, until finally, on his eighth attempt, as the chairs shot perversely out from under him and his arms flew up over his head, he made a wild snatch at the highflown bars and to his amazement caught hold of them—two of them, that is. For a moment he hung there, gratified, till the bars gave way and he dropped back into the cell, grazing the bench on the way down and reopening the gash on his shin as surely as if he'd been aiming for it. When he recovered, he found that he was still clutching the pitted iron bars as if they were a pair of dumbbells. Above him, the window gaped like a damaged mouth: four bars remained where a moment before there had been six. Better yet, numbers 2 and 3 were in his hands and the gap they left was easily wide enough to squeeze through. On the down side, his brief glimpse beyond the window had revealed a second cell, identical to his own, but for the lawnchairs. Clinging there, poised in the moment between hoisting himself up and lurching back from the window in a storm of dust and mortar pellets, he discovered a familiar bench, a scatter of refuse, and a heavy ancient solid-core door, firmly shut and for all he knew as immovable as the one behind him.

If he was disappointed, he didn't have time to dwell on it, because at that moment the outside bolt slid back with a screech of protest and a low rumble of voices startled him to his feet. He looked wildly around him. The chairs lay crippled on the floor, the window gaped in the most obvious and incriminating way, and the bars—the bars were still clutched in his hands! *Think fast:* isn't that what the Americans say? They throw you a live hand grenade and say, *Think fast.* But Hiro, in that moment, leaped beyond thought and into the realm of pure reaction: even as the door pushed open, he slipped the cold iron bars into the rear waistband of his shorts and sat heavily in the bowed lawnchair, simultaneously booting its mate back into the corner with a discreet jerk of his foot. And then the heat from outdoors hit him like a fist and there they were, the sheriff and the two government men, edging warily into the cell.

For a long moment the three of them stood there in the doorway, watching him as they might have watched a tethered animal, as if trying to gauge how dangerous he might be and how far and suddenly he might leap. Hiro sat there on his iron bars and watched them watching him. The tall one, the spatterface, had the eyes of a rodent, pink and inflamed, the strangest eyes Hiro had ever seen in a member of his own species. Those eyes fastened on him with a look of wonder and bafflement. The sheriff's eyes were the eyes of a white-boned demon, as hard and sharp and blue as the edge of a blade. The little man—and it struck him in that moment how much he resembled the photo of Doggo, with his long blond hair and beard, a hippie for all his military trappings—the little man looked bemused. If the tall one regarded him with awe, as if he'd just dropped down to earth from another planet, and if the sheriff gave him that implacable look of *gaijin* hate, the little man's eyes said *I've seen it all before.* The moment lingered. No one spoke, and though it shrieked for attention, though it hovered over them like a great flapping bird, no one seemed to notice the window.

"Here," the little man said finally, shoving something at him—
a paper bag, a white paper bag with the legend HARDEE's printed
on it in bright roman letters.

Hiro took the bag and cradled it stiffly in his lap. The little man
held out a Styrofoam cup. Hiro reached for it, smelling coffee, and
bowed his head reflexively in acknowledgment of the gesture. He
felt the heavy pitted bars dig into his hams and his heart began to
race.

Then the tall one spoke, his face spattered with the strange paint
of his skin. "Sheriff Peagler," he said, his voice officious and cold,
the voice of the prosecutor calling in the evidence, and the sheriff
reached out to pull the door closed. "Thank you," he murmured,
and he turned to Hiro, the look of wonder replaced now by something harder, more professional. "We'd like to ask you a few questions," he said.

Hiro nodded. He concentrated on their shoes—the sheriff's steel-
toed cowboy boots, the tall one's gleaming impatient loafers, the
scuffed suede hiking boots that embraced the little man's delicate
feet. The shoes edged closer. Outside, beyond the heavy door, a
bird called out in a high mocking voice. And then the three of them
started in on him, insinuating, badgering, hectoring, and they didn't
let up for nearly four hours.

Was he familiar with the Red Brigades? Did the name Abu Nidal
mean anything to him? Where had he learned to swim like that?
Was he aware of the penalties for entering the country illegally?
What was his full name? What had he hoped to gain by attacking
the late Olmstead White? Was it a burglary? An assault? How long
had he known Ruth Dershowitz?

The heat rose steadily. Hiro crouched over the paper bag and
clung to the Styrofoam cup till the black liquid grew tepid. His
hara rumbled, the iron bars cut into his backside like files. And yet
he didn't dare move, not even to sip the coffee—the slightest agi-
tation could collapse the chair, send him reeling in a clatter of iron
and aluminum, the bars he'd pried from the window exposed to

his inquisitors' eyes, and then where would he be? He held himself as rigid as a statue.

His interrogators were insatiable. They wanted to know everything, from what school he'd attended to his grandmother's maiden name and what each of Ruth's lunches contained, right on down to the number of seeds in the pomegranate, and yet, rapacious as their curiosity was, never once did they glance up and discover the naked evidence hovering over their heads. For the first half hour or so they remained standing, circling him, punching their questions at him with quick jabs of their fingers and fists—what time? what day? what hour? why? how? when?—riding a current of body English and cold *hakujin* rage; but then, starting with the tall one, they began to succumb to the heat, and they settled in on the narrow bench beneath the window, buttock to buttock, firing questions in a synchronized barrage and jotting notes in the little black pads they produced from their shirt pockets.

Hiro answered them as best he could, head bowed, eyes lowered, responding with the restraint and humility his *obāsan* had instilled in him. He tried to tell them the truth, tried to tell them about Chiba and Unagi and how the Negro had attacked him and how he'd tried to save the old man when the fire exploded round them, but they wouldn't listen, didn't care, caught the vaguest glimmer of what he was saying and shouted him down. "You went there to steal, didn't you?" the spatterface cried. "You attacked an officer aboard your own ship, took advantage of a senile old lady and her crippled husband, set fire to an innocent man's house when he resisted you—isn't that right?" Hiro never had a chance to respond. The little man was on him. Then the sheriff. And then it was back to the spatterface and on and on and on.

"You're a thief."

"A liar."

"An arsonist."

They knew all the answers: all they needed was confirmation.

What seemed to interest them most, though, what aroused even the increasingly sleepy-eyed sheriff, was Ruth. They wanted to implicate her, and as the morning wore on, it seemed to be all they cared about. Hiro was already packaged, already wrapped up and condemned—he was history. But Ruth, Ruth was an unknown quantity, and they converged on the mention of her like sharks on a blood spoor. Had she given him food, clothing, money, sex, drugs, alcohol? Had she harbored him, tucked him in at night, was she planning to help him escape from the island and evade the law? Had she fondled him, kneaded his flesh, conjoined her lips and her private parts with his own? Was she a communist, a scofflaw, a loose woman? Was she a folksinger, did she wear huaraches, attend rallies, eat lox and bagels? Was she a Jew? She was, wasn't she?

No, he said, no. No to every question. "She doesn't know me," he said. "I take her food, sleep when she go away."

The tall one was particularly aroused. "You're lying," he mocked, glaring like a big spattered rodent. "She harbored you all along, she shared her bed with you, brought you groceries and clothing."

"No. She doesn't." Hiro ached in every joint from holding himself erect. He wanted to tear open the bag and fall on the food, wanted to moisten his lips with the tepid coffee, but he didn't dare. The iron bars were part of him now. The chair creaked when he spoke. The window gaped.

"All right," the tall one said finally, rising and consulting his wristwatch. He looked at the sheriff. "It's noon now. I'm going to want him alone—just me and Turco, after we've talked to her."

The sheriff rose. He stretched and rolled his head back on the axis of his neck, rubbing the cords and muscles there. "Sure. You do what you need to. It's you fellas that're going to have to handle this anyway—it's way out of our league." He sighed, cracked his knuckles and gave Hiro the sort of look he might have given a two-headed snake preserved in a jar. "I've heard about all I want to hear."

Then the little man stood too, and the three of them shuffled their feet in unison as if it were part of an elaborate soft-shoe routine, and then they were out the door and the door slammed shut behind them. Hiro felt the thump of that door in his very marrow, and all at once he found he could breathe again. Gingerly, he lifted first one leg and then the other and eased the adamantine bars away from his flesh, which seemed by now to have incorporated them as a living tree incorporates a rusted spike or the abandoned chain of a dog long dead. He dropped the bars to the floor and worked himself out of the chair, wincing, cup and bag still clutched in his hand. His legs were raw, cramped, bloodless, his buttocks inert, and he felt as if he'd been hoisting sumo wrestlers up on his shoulders, one after another, for whole days and nights, for weeks and months and years . . . but then he looked up at the window and broke out in a grin.

Ha! he exulted. Ha! The fools. They were so stupid it was incredible. Four hours they'd sat there, and never once did they glance up at the window. It was the American nature. They were oafs, drugged and violent and overfed, and they didn't pay attention to detail. That's why the factories had shut down, that's why the automakers had gone belly up, that's why three professional investigators could sit in an eight-by-ten-foot cell for four hours and never notice that two of the bars had been pried from the window. Hiro wanted to laugh out loud with the joy of it.

And then, still standing, he turned his attention to the paper bag. Inside there were two rock-hard biscuits, each wrapped around a sliver of congealed egg and a pink tongue of what might once have been ham. It never ceased to amaze him how the Americans could eat this stuff—it wasn't even food, really. Food consisted of rice, fish, meat, vegetables, and this was . . . biscuits. No matter: he was so hungry he scarcely used his teeth. He bolted the biscuits, which tasted of salt and grit and grease so ancient it could have been the mother of all grease, and he washed it down with the cold coffee.

In the next moment he was scaling the wall again. It took him only two tries this time, his arms flailing, the chairs swaying wildly beneath him. He found toeholds in the rough masonry, and for a long while he clung to the ledge, dangling like a pendant. When he'd finally caught his breath, he was able to replace the two bars he'd removed from the window, even going so far as to mold neat little plugs of masonry crumbs at their base. He knew that the *Amerikajin* agents would be back in the afternoon, and he didn't want to press his luck. He knew too that they planned to take him to the ferry in the evening and thence to the mysterious *mainrand*, where a modern cell awaited him. And why wouldn't he know? They'd discussed their plans right there in front of him, as if he were deaf and blind, as if English had suddenly become impenetrable to him despite the fact that they'd just got done asking him about six thousand questions in that very same language. Oh, they were sloppy. Sloppy and arrogant.

Hiro, however, had no intention of winding up in that mainland cell—or in any other, for that matter. When they were finished with him, when they were hunkered down over their chili beans and barbecue and generic beer, when the hypnotic voice of the TV murmured from every porch and window and even the dogs grew drowsy and stuporous, that was when he would make his move. That was when he would scale the wall one last time and drop catlike into the adjoining cell to try his luck on the outer door, all the while praying that it wouldn't be locked. And it wouldn't be. He knew that already. Knew it as positively and absolutely as he'd ever known anything in his life, knew it even as he let his exhaustion catch up to him and he drifted off to sleep. It was just the sort of detail the butter-stinkers would overlook.

·   ·   ·

HE WOKE TO A SHARP THRUST OF LIGHT AND A SUDDEN ESCALATION of heat as withering as the blast of an oven. His sleep had been deep and anonymous and they took him by surprise, the tall one with the rodent's eyes and his runt of a companion. It must have been late in the afternoon, shadows lengthening in the barn that enclosed the cell, a flash of electric green just perceptible in the moment the door swung open to reveal the great gaping wagon-high entranceway to the barn itself. Hiro sat up. His clothes were wet through, his throat parched. "Water," he croaked.

The tall one shut the door and the day was gone. The little man laughed. He had something in his hand—a tape player, Hiro saw now, Japanese-made and big as a suitcase—and he maneuvered round Hiro to set it beside him on the wooden bench. The little man's smile had changed—it was a cruel smile, unstable, no longer bemused. Were they going to force a confession out of him as the police did in Japan? Were they going to tape it and edit out the groans and screams and cries for mercy? Hiro edged away from the thing. But then, flexing the muscles of his neck and shoulders, the little man reached out to depress a button atop the machine and immediately the cell swelled with music, disco. Hiro recognized the tune. It was—

"Donna Summer," the little man said, flexing and grinning. "You like it?"

This time, they questioned him for what seemed like days, but what actually must have been closer to two hours, Hiro later realized. They asked him the same questions they'd asked him earlier, over and over again. Questions about his politics, about Honda and Sony and Nissan, about Ruth and Ambly Wooster and the old Negro and the accident at the shack. And all the while the disco beat drummed in his head and his voice cracked around the parched kernel of his throat. They held out the promise of water as a bargaining chip—if he cooperated he would be rewarded; if not, they'd watch him die of thirst and never lift a finger. He cooperated. He told them, over and over again, about Chiba and Unagi and Ruth and her lunches and everything else he'd told them a hundred times over, only this time he told it with Donna Summer and Michael Jackson for accompaniment. Every once in a while he would say something that struck the little man and the little man would interrupt him to give the tall one a look and say, "See? What'd I tell you? Squarest in the world." They left him a Tupperware pitcher of tepid water and another Hardee's bag, this one filled to the grease-spattered neck with twists of cold greasy potato and two geometrically perfect hamburgers.

Hiro forced himself to eat. And he drank down the water too, every drop: he didn't know when—or if—he'd see more. There were two deputies outside the door—he'd seen them when his inquisitors had let themselves in and out of the cell. He could hear the soft murmur of their voices, smell the flare of their tobacco. Twenty minutes. He would give them twenty minutes to eat their corn dogs and piccalilli and butterscotch ripple ice cream, twenty minutes to stupefy themselves with gin and whiskey and beer. Then he would make his break.

He counted out each of those interminable minutes, second by second—*one a thousand, two a thousand, three*—and he heard the faint but distinctive hiss of pop-tops, and there was the smell of hot grease and more tobacco, and then the murmur of voices faded away to silence. The time had come. The time for action. The time when a man of action *must make up his mind within the space of seven breaths.* Hiro only needed one. He sprang for the wall, clambering up the slick stones like a lizard, removed the false bars and squeezed through into the adjoining cell. Head first, then shoulders and torso and the right leg, then reverse position and drop lightly to the bench below. His blood was singing. He was moving, acting, in control of his own destiny once again—and the door? His fingers were on the rusted handle, his thumb poised over the latch—it was the moment of truth, the moment on which all the rest depended. He pressed: it gave. Ha!

Rusty hinges. Open a crack. Look. There, leaning back in a chair propped against the door of the first cell, was a deputy, red *hakujin* face and wheat-colored mustache, pointy nose and slivered lips. His head was thrown back, the cigarette smoking between his fingers, the can of beer and grease-stained bag at his side, and his breathing was deep and regular, somnolent, breath caught in the pit of the larynx and released again with the faintest stertor. Yes: the long-nosed idiot was asleep!

Hiro almost swaggered when he realized it: *asleep!* But he contained himself—discipline, discipline—and slipped out the door like a shadow, a ninja, the nimblest assassin ever to float over two feet. But what of the other guard? What of him? He was nowhere to be seen. Stealthy, stealthy. The red cheeks and flaming nose, the air sucked down the tubes and vomited out again: Hiro couldn't resist. He bent over the sleeping deputy and slipped the cigarette from between his fingers, justifying it to himself as a precaution: it was only a matter of a minute or two before the fool singed himself awake. But the chicken—it was chicken, breaded and fried, wings, drumsticks and thighs, in the grease-stained bag—the chicken was another matter. Casually—as casually as Yojimbo hiking up his *yukata* or Dirty Harry scratching his stubble—Hiro leaned forward to pluck a drumstick from the bag, savoring the moistness of it as he eased along the inner wall, looking for a door that would give onto the yard out back.

And what was here? A shadowy vastness, rafters and crossbeams, a smell of urine, fungus, the body functions of animals dead a hundred years. He moved to his left, away from the deputy and the glaring high double doors of the barn's main entrance, flattening himself against the cool stone wall. The place was deserted: an ancient pitchfork against the damp wall, the stalls where livestock had once been kept, the odd strands, like fallen hair, of antediluvian hay. Something stirred in the rafters overhead and he looked up into the slatted shadows to see a pair of swallows beating through the gloom. And the other deputy? Hiro was light on his feet, invisible, a ghost in the place of ghosts. At the end of the line of stalls a weak light leaked round the corner and down a hallway. Hiro made for it.

He turned down the hallway to his right, proud and scornful and ready for anything—he was escaping, escaping again!—and the light swelled to embrace him. There was a doorway there, vacant and bleeding light—a doorless doorway, the wooden slab with its latch and handle apparently lost to some ancient *hakujin* cataclysm. Beyond the doorway he saw green—the virescent glow of freedom in all its seething jungle urgency—and he hurried for it.

But it wasn't as easy as all that.

He paused in the crude stone doorframe, glanced right and left— a driveway, cars, shrubs, trees, lawn—and then made his break, bolting for the band of vegetation that rose up at the far end of the lawn, thick and reclusive and no more than a hundred feet away. He was bent low and scurrying like a crab, already ten steps out of hiding and exposed for all the world to see, when suddenly he froze. There was a dog there, right in front of him, lifting its leg against a tree. A dog. Better than forty dogs, better than the snarling seething pack that had closed in on him at Ruth's, but a dog none-theless—and no lap dog either, but a big raw-boned gangling shep-herd sort of thing that looked as if it had been put together with spare parts. The dog finished its business in that moment and Hiro saw its eyes leap with something like recognition as it loped toward him, a woof—a tiny grandfatherly woof—rippling from its throat. Hiro was planted, rooted, he'd grown up out of the ground like a native shrub, hopeless and immobile. The woof would become a concatenation of woofs, an improvisatory riff of woofing, followed by bared teeth and the bloodcurdling howls and the angry voices of discovery, while through it all the clink of handcuffs played in counterpoint. Was this it? Was it over already?

It might have been, had not the sensory organs of his fingertips communicated a swift tactile message to him: he was holding a half-eaten drumstick. Holding meat. Chicken. Dripping and irresistible. And what did dogs eat? Dogs ate meat. "Here, boy," he whispered, making a kissing noise with his lips, "good boy," and then he was inserting greasy bone in woofless mouth. But even as he did so and even as the dog melted away from him in greedy preoccupation, he heard a ribald screech of laughter and looked up to see three *hakujin*—two men and a woman—emerge from the very line of trees into which he'd hoped to disappear. They were dressed in tennis whites and carrying racquets, and they hadn't noticed him yet—or if they had they didn't remark it, absorbed as they were in themselves. The woman leaned into the men with a bawdy whoop and all three doubled up, spastic with laughter.

Though in that moment he recalled the words of Jōchō—*A true samurai must never seem to flag or lose heart*—Hiro found himself on the verge of panic, mental disintegration and physical collapse. *He*

could not move. He was caught in a bad dream, powerless, his limbs
as useless as a quadriplegic's, and they were coming for him, coming
to devour his flesh and crack his bones. His eyes flew to the points
of the compass: there was the dog, happily frolicking with the scrap
of chicken, and there was the line of trees that promised release—
and there, interposed between him and his goal, were the tennis
players, they who at any moment would look up in stunned surprise
and raise a shout of horror and dismay. What to do? He hadn't a
clue. Move, and he was dead. Stand still, very still, and he was
dead too. All at once the decision was made for him: a pair of stocky
women in bonnets and tentlike sundresses suddenly rounded the
far corner of the barn with a great booming shout. "If it isn't
McEnroe and Connors!" the smaller of the two bellowed in the
direction of the tennis players. "And Chrissie Evert too!" the larger
added in a stentorian shrill.

That was it. That was enough. Suddenly Hiro was moving, head
down, back to them, walking with purpose and determination, as
if he belonged here, just another artist out for a stroll on the grounds.
Directly ahead of him was the parking lot, with its cars and pavement, shrubs and trees and flowers in plucked beds, the big house
rising above it in the near distance: it wasn't the direction he would
have chosen. "Patsy!" a woman's voice cried behind him, "Clara!"
And then one of the men shouted, "Vodka and gin!" This was
followed by a general roar and a spate of lubricious laughter.

"Just heading over ourselves!"

"Join us?"

"Join you? We'll lead the way—better yet, we'll race you!"

Whoops and more whoops.

"Last one"—out of breath—"last one there's a rotten egg!"

Hiro kept going, dog, women and tennis trio fading away in his
wake, certain that at any moment the hue and cry would rise up
to engulf him. The drive curved through the trees in front of him
and a huge forsythia bush rose up to block the house from view.
He saw a Toyota, an American car that looked like a Toyota, and
a Mercedes—a big, royal blue Mercedes sedan—parked at the curb

with its trunk open. And then, as the grass gave way to pavement under his feet and the shouts at his back subsided to a trickle of giggles and guffaws, something Ruth had said came back to him: *It's got a trunk the size of the Grand Canyon.*

The rest was a whirl—deliberate, but a whirl nonetheless. There were more voices, men's voices, and movement off to his left. It was now or never. Fighting the urge to run, he crossed the pavement in crisp, businesslike strides—movement behind the forsythia now, legs, shoes, a gabble of voices—and in one clean motion threw himself into the trunk of the Mercedes as if he were tumbling into bed. Things gouged and poked at him—fishing traps, a camp stove—but he didn't have time to worry about it. He lifted his right hand from the depths of the trunk and took hold of the steel ribs of the lid, and then, as casually as if he were pulling the covers up over his head, he pulled it closed.

The Whiteness of
the Fish

· · · · · · ·

SON OF A BITCH. SON OF A FUCKING BITCH. THE HUMILIATION LEVEL
here was climbing like a rocket. What had it taken them, six weeks
to catch this joker? Six weeks to nail one sorry slump-shouldered
fat-assed Nip who looked like he was about twelve years old. And
now, when it was all over, when he'd been hauled in, reamed out
and locked up like a hamster in a cage, the yokels turn around and
let him go. Yeah. Right. And now what, call out the National
Guard?

Lewis Turco was angry. He was incensed. It was getting dark
and things were looking grim. Nobody knew anything, least of all
the half-wit deputy who'd opened up the door to take the prisoner
to the ferry and discovered an empty cell. Oh, the cell had chairs
in it, all right, stacked up under the window, and the window had
a couple bars left in it too, but it was empty space, one hundred
percent Nipless. And then he'd asked his buddy about that, but
his buddy had been out back taking a leak and so they figured
they'd better tell the sheriff, and now here they all were, running
around like mental defectives, shouting in everybody's face. Mean-
while, the light was nearly gone, the artistic types were milling
around on the patio enjoying the show, the dogs were back over
there in Niggertown and the sheriff looked like he'd just chewed

· 234 ·

off a piece of his own ass and swallowed it. And the Nip—the Nip was probably halfway to Hokkaido. The incompetence of these people. The shit and stupidity. *Jesus.*

And these artists. Christ, they made him want to puke. Aberclown sucked up to them, especially the little Jew bitch who'd been hiding the guy all along—hiding him and then lying about it, just to jerk them off. Big joke. Ha, ha, ha. There she was now, right in the thick of it, cradling a drink and giving everybody that wide-eyed innocent look, pure as Rebecca of Sunnybrook Farm, what would she know about it?

He would have found out. If Aberclown had only let him go, he would have found out a hundred and five percent of everything she ever knew, from her daddy's ATM number to how many hairs she had on her twat—he'd been in on some cold interrogations, men and women both, VC as hard and silent as stones, and nobody knew how to put the fear into them like he did—but with her it wasn't an interrogation, it was a tea party. He'd sat there for two sweaty stinking hours with Aberclown and the sheriff and it was all he could do to keep himself from taking her by the hair and jerking her head back till her throat opened up like a slow drain with a snake down it. Damn. But Aberclown and the hick sheriff treated her like a senator's wife or something and she threw out a couple crumbs and that was it. She hadn't told them the half of it. Why should she? She was an artist, right?

He was standing there, fuming, when he felt a pressure on his arm and all at once he was staring up into the puffy face of another artist, a great big fluty-voiced ass of a woman with a cast in one eye. "What's this all about?" she gasped. "What's happening?"

He couldn't help himself, he couldn't—he felt himself slipping, three toes over the line and whatever you do don't pull that ripcord. "What the fuck you think is happening," he snarled, jerking his arm away from her. "It's Armageddon, they're fucking dogs out there, eating human flesh. Wake up, bitch." The rage was racing in his veins as he watched her shrink away from him.

But what now? The sheriff had disappeared into the house, Aberclown's big speckled face was coming up on his left like something out of planetary alignment and the deputies were standing around with their thumbs up their asses—son of a fucking bitch. He'd been all packed and ready to go, he'd stowed his gear and chowed down his last hunk of overcooked barbecue and a couple warm Budweisers in somebody's greasy back kitchen, and he was looking forward to kicking back at home, smoke some weed, take the boat out, maybe look up that waitress from Shucker's—what was her name, Linda?—and now he was going to have to start all over again.

Just then the lights went on in the house, a spill of silver washing over thirty pairs of dress shoes. Turco squared his shoulders and looked round him: here he was in a crisis situation and what the hell was he doing about it? He was just standing around like the rest of the shitheads, his feet cemented to the flagstones: in a minute he'd have a drink in his hand and before you knew it he'd be an artist himself. "Lewis!" It was Aberclown—now *he* had a hand on him, it was feel-up-Turco night. "Lewis, we've got to get—"

"Get shit," Turco said. "Get fucked."

It was at that moment that Dershowitz threw back her head and laughed—laughed—whooping like the ringer in a comedy club, bending over to pat her breastbone and give her tits a good shake for everybody to see. And the rest of them—the surfer boy with the cute little bleached forelock and the old guy with the hairy wrists—they were laughing too. This laughter—these *artists* with their drinks in their hands and their twenty-five-dollar haircuts and their clean white sculptured teeth—it was too much to take. "Lewis," Aberclown was saying, "Lewis, I'm talking to you—" but it didn't register.

Turco came at them without warning, catching the old guy with an elbow that doubled him up in his own puke and drilling the beachboy with a single shot to the sternum that sent him sprawling, and then he had her, the bitch, had her by the hair, the glass shattering on the flagstones at her feet and her hands caught fast behind her. "Where is he?" he demanded, barking, raging, jerking at the knot of her hair as if he were climbing rope. "Where the fuck is he?"

The moment lingered like a shock wave, and then they were on him—Aberclown, the hairy old geek and the beachboy, the fag with the flattop, everybody, even the lame-ass deputies—and he hurt at least one of them with a chop to the groin and he nailed another with a side-blade kick, but the bitch broke away from him and they got him down by sheer force of numbers. They were yammering like dogs, he couldn't hear them, everybody in on the act now, and she was coming at him like a Harpy, kicking him over and over again with the point of a sharp-toed little red shoe. "My father'll make you pay for this," she yelped, makeup smeared, sunglasses gone, "you bastard . . . if Saxby was here . . ."

Saxby? Who the hell was Saxby? Not that it mattered, because Aberclown had him all wrapped up in his orangutan's arms and there were about fourteen bodies attached to his, hustling him out onto the lawn and into the shadows that were closing over the trees like the curtain falling on the very last act of a play. Or not just a play, a tragedy.

. . .

AT THAT MOMENT, THE MOMENT OF THE ALTERCATION ON THE PATIO, the moment Ruth invoked his name, Saxby wasn't on Tupelo Island at all. He was in his mother's Mercedes, tooling down the highway at seventy-five, heading for Waycross, Ciceroville and the western verge of the Okefenokee Swamp. In the back seat, trembling slightly with the motion of the car, was a dirty yellow gym bag into which he'd stuffed his toothbruth, razor, a change of underwear, three pairs of socks, two of shorts, a T-shirt and a bandanna. Alongside the gym bag, low humps of nylon in the dark, were his sleeping bag and one-man tent. He'd put his traps and waders, a cylinder of oxygen and a roll of clear heavy-duty plastic bags—for fish transport, with twists—in the trunk. The Mercedes wasn't exactly the most convenient vehicle to be taking on a collecting trip, but the pickup was in the shop—Fords! six thousand miles on the damn thing and already it was leaking oil—and when Roy Dotson called to tell him he'd caught a bucketful of albinos in a trough on the back side of Billy's Island, he didn't have time to think about it: this was what he'd been waiting for since he left La Jolla.

He was excited, hurtling through the long shadows of the evening, the radio cranked up high. The music was country, of course—he liked soft rock, Steely Dan and that sort of thing, but once you left the city you got nothing but your hard-core redneck honky-tonk psychodrama—but he cranked it anyway. Albino pygmies. Roy Dotson had them, a whole tankful. And they were his. His for the asking. He felt so exhilarated he beat time on the steering wheel and sang along in a high-pitched, off-key whinny that would have cleared the Grand Ole Opry in ten seconds flat:

> *I don't care if it rains or freezes,*
> *Long as I got my plastic Jesus*
> *Glued up own the dashboard of my car.*

He roared past clapboard filling stations, towns that consisted of three farmhouses and a single intersection, past shanties and dumb-staring cattle and low pink-and-white fields of cotton and on into the twilight, the steel-belted radials beating rhythm beneath him. He was feeling good, as good as he'd ever felt, picturing the reflecting pool out front of the big house converted to a breeding pond, milk-white albinos churning up the surface as he cast food pellets out over the water, orders from aquarists all over the world, a steady stream of offers to lecture and consult . . . but then he thought of Ruth and the picture switched channels on him. He'd felt bad about leaving her like that, but Roy's phone call had lit up all his lights, galvanized him—she'd be all right, he'd told himself, the adrenaline pumping through him as he tore around the house, hurrying to make the six o'clock ferry. And if she wasn't all right—and here he had to admit how hurt he'd been—it was her own fault. She hadn't told him, hadn't trusted him. He'd felt betrayed. Angry. Felt like getting back at her. And so he'd gone to Abercorn—who wouldn't?

But it wasn't as cold as she made it out to be. He'd got Abercorn's promise to go easy on her—and no, there was no question of prosecution, none at all—and he'd sat with her through the questioning till Theron got up and asked him to leave the room. She'd seemed fine when he kissed her goodbye, seemed her old self again. If she'd suffered a little, maybe she deserved it. He believed her when she claimed the Japanese kid was nothing more than a curiosity—he was ridiculous, pitiful, with a face like putty waiting to be molded and a head too big for his body—but she carried things too far. To think that she'd kept the whole thing a secret from him, her lover, her man—and he'd do anything for her, she knew that—well, it hurt and there were no two ways about it.

Still, Saxby wasn't one for brooding. He punched another button on the radio and the small glowing Teutonic space of the cab swelled with the skreel of fiddles and the twang of guitars, and before he knew it he was yodeling along with a tune about truckers and blue tick hounds and Ruth slipped from his mind, replaced by the glowing alabaster vision of a pygmy sunfish gliding through the silent weedy depths of the Okefenokee.

It was dark by the time Saxby reached Ciceroville. He gassed up at Sherm's Chevron and then swung into the parking lot of the Tender Sproats Motel, Mr. Gobi Aloo, Proprietor. The tiny fly-spotted office was deserted, but when Saxby depressed the buzzer connected to the apartment in back, Gobi appeared like a genie sprung from a bottle. The little man's features lit with pleasure as he bundled himself through the door and sidled up to the desk, a smell of curry wafting along with him. "Well, if it ain't the man hisself, Saxby Lights, from Tup-e-lo Island, Georgia." He spoke with the slow drawl he'd developed within days of his emigration from the Punjab, slurring the syllables round the wad in his cheek. "Saxby, Saxby," he drawled, wagging his delicate head, but then, as he did from time to time, he slipped into the light musical cadence of the subcontinent: "And to what do we owe the pleasure? Fish, I would be thinking, yes?"

"You guessed it, Gobe." Saxby could barely contain himself— he was bursting with the news. "Roy's found them. Soon's I check in I'm going straight over there to have a look at what he's got and in the morning we're going to pull some nets and hopefully we're going to get lucky. I mean real lucky. Jackpot time."

Gobi beamed up at him, a buttery little man in a dirty feedstore cap, an overstretched T-shirt and a pair of overalls. If it weren't for the caste mark between his eyes, you might have mistaken him for a sunburned cracker. His drawl thickened with the exchange: "Y'all gone git you some, Ah know it—y'all deserves nothin' less." He turned his head to spit a reddish-brown stream of tobacco and betel-nut juice into the wastebasket under the counter.

On his last two visits to the Okefenokee, Saxby had stayed here, at the Tender Sproats Motel in Ciceroville. It was forty-seven miles from the dock at Stephen C. Foster State Park, on the western edge of the swamp, but it was a five-minute walk from Roy Dotson's place. And that made it convenient. He signed the register Gobi slid across the counter to him.

"Y'all be stayin' one night or two?"

"One night," Saxby told him, pressing a twenty into his palm and getting back a worn single and three nickels in exchange. If things worked out he'd be heading back to Tupelo tomorrow night; if not, Roy had gotten him a special permit and he was going to pitch his tent on Billy's Island for as long as it took.

"Listen," Gobi said, handing him the room key as his voice deepened into the whiskey-cracked gruffness of the cracker and the pioneer, "y'all take care now, hear?"

Saxby didn't bother with the room. He pocketed the key, parked the Mercedes in the slot reserved for number 12, and started up the street for Roy's house. He could barely fight down his euphoria. He felt connected to everything, holy, Whitmanesque, a man on the verge of a special communion with the mysteries of nature and the whiteness of the fish. The night conspired with him. It was perfect, so still and warm and peaceful the sky could have been a velvet glove cupped over the town, and he smelled honeysuckle and jasmine and heard the distant curt bark of a dog and thrilled deep within him to the sizzling pulse of tree frogs and crickets. Porch lights glowed against the suffocation of the night. The streets were deserted. Ciceroville was a dry town in a dry county, and all its population of 3,237 was already settled in for the evening, gathered round the tube with Coke and lemonade and cans of beer that sweated in their hands like contraband.

Roy was waiting for him on the porch. Saxby loped up the walk, his heart banging, and there he was, in the porch swing, his daughter Ally and a picture book in his lap. "Evenin', Sax," Roy drawled.

"Roy." Saxby was so excited he couldn't elaborate on the greeting, the punch of the syllable about all he could manage.

"Saxby, Saxby, Saxby!" Ally squealed, and in the next instant she was down off the porch and whirling in his arms. Roy was still in the porch swing, watching him, a grin on his face. The light over his head fluttered with moths.

"So you got them," Saxby said finally, while Ally giggled and clawed at his arms and he fought to maintain his balance and keep her trusting head and frail arms away from the banister.

Roy nodded. He was thirty-one years old, his forehead sloped back from a face that was primarily nose and he wore his white-blond hair slicked back and drawn up in a ponytail. He worked for the National Park Service and he was second in command at the Okefenokee National Wildlife Refuge. It was he who had arranged for Saxby's special collecting permit—the least a former fraternity brother could do, as he rather dryly put it. "You want to go on inside and have a look at the fish," he asked, "or you want to sit out here and listen to the rest of *Green Eggs and Ham*?"

"Give me a break, Roy," Saxby said, but he'd already set Ally down like a package he didn't want to forget and started up the steps. "Where are they—in the house or one of the tanks in the garage?"

Roy had risen to his feet. "Well, if you really want to see them," he said, "—but are you sure you don't want to watch the Braves game first? It's a twi-night doubleheader."

Saxby let him have his fun, but when Roy lightly bounced down the steps and ambled round the corner of the house, he was right on his heels. He saw that they were heading for the garage, a slouching two-story affair detached from the house and desperately in need of paint, putty, nails, lumber, floor joists, weight-bearing beams and four or five hundred roofing shingles. They passed Roy's pickup and his wife's Honda in the dirt drive, moribund leaves crunching underfoot, the dirt-smeared windows ahead of them glowing with a soft seductive light.

There was no room for the cars in the garage, which housed Roy's bone and taxidermy collections, his traps and tools and cages and an aggregation of household refuse that would make the careers of any twenty future archaeologists: collapsed card tables and staved-in chairs, rolls of stained wallpaper and carpet remnants, cardboard boxes stacked to the ceiling and spilling over with dis-membered dolls, broken crockery, faded magazines and rusted Ginzu knives, rack upon rack of paint cans, empty wine bottles and jars of paint thinner, embalming fluid and formalin. In the midst of it all, Roy always kept a few mesh cages rattling with snakes and turtles and opossums, and half a dozen ancient slate-bottomed aquariums bubbling away under jury-rigged lights. If he found something interesting in the swamp, he brought it home with him.

Now, with Ally sailing on ahead of them and chanting "Saxby's fish, I wish, I wish" in a nasal singsong, they entered this cramped but hallowed space. The first thing to catch Saxby's eye was a stuffed armadillo perched atop a coat tree, and then the mounted paw of a bobcat that had left it behind in a trap, something in a cage with black glittering eyes, and finally the aquariums, dimly lit and yet glowing like treasure from across the room. He was breathing hard—practically panting—as he waded through the slurry of refuse underfoot and made his way to the shining glass

pane in front of which Ally had stationed herself. Crouching down
to peer expectantly through the thick curtain of algae, he saw . . .
a rippled snout and two dead saurian eyes peering back at him.
Ally's laugh was shrill as a fire alarm. "Tricked you!" she screeched.

"Next one over, Sax," Roy coached. "To your right."

Saxby turned his head then and experienced his moment of grace:
there they were. His albinos. Opercula heaving, fins waving, cold
little lips blowing him kisses. They were a small miracle.

He looked closer. None of them—there were eighteen in all—
was longer than the cap of a Bic pen and most of them showed fin
and tail damage from the attacks of their neighbors. Despite their
size, they were an aggressive species, fiercely territorial and antisocial. Roy had provided a few twigs and stones for cover, but it
was a halfhearted effort that didn't begin to protect them from one
another. What was he thinking? Didn't he realize what they had
here? Saxby felt the resentment rising in him, but he caught himself—there they were, albinos, pygmy sunfish as smooth and white
as miniature bars of soap, and that was all that mattered.

For a long while he squatted there in front of the tank, watching
them hang in the water, circle the surface, rise and fall and make
sudden savage runs at one another. They were white, all right, and
it amazed him. He'd known that they would be—intellectually,
that is—but the reality leaped out at him. He'd seen albino catfish,
cichlids as pale and pink as cherry yogurt, blind cavefish bleached
of color through eons of groping in the dark, but this was something
else. This was a legendary whiteness, the whiteness of purity, of
June brides, Christo's running fence, the inner wrapping of the
Hershey bar. He would breed them, that's what he would do,
breed them because they were unusual, rarities, freaks, because
they were white as the sheets and hoods of the Ku Klux Klan,
white as ice, heartless and cold and necessary.

He looked up. Ally was gone. Roy hovered over him. "Can we
get more?"

Roy was smiling his quiet smile. He understood the sort of excitement that made the breath come quick in the presence of a

certain butterfly or slug or a glistening pale little fingernail-sized fish. "We can sure try," he said.

. . .

THE NEXT MORNING THE TELEPHONE ROUSED SAXBY FROM DREAMS of the colorless depths. It rang once and he seized it as if it were prey, as if he'd been lying still there all night so as to lull the thing into giving itself away. "Yeah?" he gasped.

It was Gobi. "Rise and shine, y'all," he crooned in his Indo-cracker drawl. "It's five-fifteen."

Ten minutes later Roy was out front with his pickup and a boat trailer. A long narrow flat-bottomed boat rested atop the trailer, the legend *Pequod II* stenciled on its bow, one of Roy's little jokes. "Mornin'," Roy said, laconic and slow-smiling, and he handed Saxby a Hardee's bag and a Styrofoam cup of coffee, black.

Saxby could have opened the trunk of the Mercedes right then and there—and he almost did, and he cursed himself afterward for resisting the impulse—but he decided not to bother. If he hauled out his waders and traps and the O_2 and the rest of it and transferred them to the pickup, it would delay them a precious few minutes, and he was really stoked to get going. And anyway, he'd want his own car down there at the swamp if he did have to stay on a day or two. In the end, he took the coffee and the bag of fast food and shrugged. "Guess I'll just follow you," he said. "All right?"

A low pale ghostly mist clung to the road all the way down to Fargo, and then, when they swung onto 177 to head into the swamp itself, the mist turned to drizzle. Saxby listened to the swish of the wet tires, watched the boat sway on the trailer ahead of him. He felt a deep sense of peace, of connection, of calm. Deer stood poised at the edge of the road, wading birds feinted and shook their great wings into flight. He was going to get everything he wanted: he knew it.

The drizzle fell back into the mist, the mist thickened, and then they were there. He followed Roy through the parking lot out front of the tourist center and pulled up ahead of him on the narrow spit of land by the boat ramp. On one side of them was the dredged and widened pond in which the rental boats were kept, and on the other, the channel that led to Billy's Lake and the infinite shifting maze of watery trails that snaked through the swamp beyond it. It was drizzling still and the sky hung low over the treetops in a dull metallic wash. The place was quiet but for the handful of fishermen loading their boats with a soft murmur of expectation, and the jays and catbirds that cursed one another intermittently from the trees. The water, peat-stained and tepid, was the color of fresh-brewed tea.

Saxby stood at the door of the Mercedes and watched Roy back the trailer down the ramp. When the trailer was in the water, Roy cut the engine, pulled the parking brake and got out to release the boat, while Saxby ambled to the rear of the Mercedes to fetch his gear. He wouldn't need the oxygen and plastic bags till he headed home with what he hoped would be the nucleus of his breeding stock, but he was thinking of his waders, minnow traps and dip net, as well as the little thirty-foot seine that might just come in handy in a relatively clear patch of water. He hadn't opened the trunk since he'd hastily loaded it some twelve or thirteen hours earlier, but as he fit the key into the lock he could visualize its contents, already leaping ahead to picture them stowed away in the bottom of Roy's boat and the boat itself gliding off under the sure silent stroke of their paddles. The lock accepted the key. The key turned in the lock.

It was the sort of thing that happens every day.

A Jungle

. . . .

WHAT HAD HAPPENED TO HER? WHAT WAS WRONG WITH HER? WHERE was the visionary who woke up rigid, forsaking breakfast to stride boldly through the dripping forest to the nunnery of the studio, the cross of her art? Ruth didn't know. All she knew was that she felt as drained of energy as when she'd contracted mono as a teenager. She had a headache—it seemed as if she'd had a headache for days, weeks, the better part of her life—and her limbs felt tentative, as if they weren't really attached. Maybe she was coming down with something, maybe that was it.

It was dawn, just, the light pale and listless, and she made a groggy but furtive dash for the bathroom down the hall—thank god no one was stirring yet—and then slipped back to her room and fell into the bed as if her legs had been shot out from under her. Thirty seconds more and she would have been gone, pulled back down into the vestibule of sleep, but then the phone rang deep in the bowels of the house and consciousness took hold of her. The sound was faint, distant, the buzz of an insect on the far side of the room—but she knew it was ringing for her. She knew it. Very faintly, and again at an incalculable distance, she heard footsteps—Owen's footsteps—crossing the downstairs hallway to the phone in the foyer. She fought to keep her eyes closed, to shake it off, but the phone was ringing and she knew it was ringing for her.

Three times it rang, four, and then it choked off in the middle of the fifth ring. She couldn't begin to hear the murmur of Owen's voice, but she imagined it, and she listened as the footsteps started up again, as the dull stealthy tread of them recrossed the foyer, mounted the stairs and started down the upper hallway. She sat up. It was her father, she was sure of it. The doctor had warned him—the stress of the courtroom, the late nights, the obsessive tennis and racquetball, the cigarettes, martinis, New York steaks. Her father! Grief flooded her. She saw his face as clearly as if he were standing there beside her, the glint of his wire-frame glasses, the splash of gray in his beard, the look of the *mensch*, the law-giver, the man of wisdom and peace . . . there would be a funeral, of course, and that would mean she'd have to leave Thanatopsis for a week, maybe longer. Black crepe. She'd look good in that, slim through the hips, and her tan would glow . . . but her father, it was her father, her daddy, and now she was naked to the world—

The footsteps halted outside her door, and then came Owen's knock and his subdued rasp—no language games, no chirp of humor: "Ruth, it's for you. Long-distance."

She knew it, she knew it.

"It's Saxby."

Saxby? Suddenly the picture clouded over. Her father was all right, he was okay, as healthy as the Surgeon General himself and sleeping peacefully at one of the better addresses in Santa Monica. But it was—six o'clock? What could Saxby want at six o'clock? Her heart gave a little skip of fear—was he hurt? But no. Why would he be calling if he was hurt—it would be the police or the hospital, wouldn't it? And then she thought of his fish. If he was dragging her out of bed because of some damned little loopy-eyed fish—

"Ruth, wake up. Telephone."

She caught herself. "Yes, yes, I'm awake. Tell him I'll be right there."

The footsteps retreated. She bent to shuffle through the mess on

the floor. She was looking for her terry-cloth robe, and her cigarettes, and maybe something to wrap round her hair in case anyone
was up. She found the robe—she'd borrowed it from a hotel in Las
Vegas on her way out from California, and there was a rich reddish
stain over the left breast where she'd upended a glass of cranberry
juice on it—and she came up with the cigarettes too, but no lighter
and no scarf. She caught a glimpse of herself in the bureau mirror—
sunken eyes, too much nose, a frenzy of fractured little lines tugging
at her mouth—and then she ducked out the door, cradling her
cigarettes, and found herself staring into the huge startled gypsy
eyes of Jane Shine.

Jane was on her way to the bathroom. She was wearing an antique
silk kimono over a white voile nightgown and her feet were prettily
encased in a pair of pink satin mules. Her hair, ever so slightly
mussed from sleep, was thicker, curlier and glossier than any mere
mortal's had a right to be. Her face, bereft of makeup, was perfect.

Ruth was wearing a fifty-nine-cent pair of Taiwanese flipflops,
the stolen robe was six sizes too big and practically stiff with filth,
and her face, as she knew from her glancing appraisal in the bureau
mirror, was the face of one of the walking dead. Sleepy, oblivious,
off-guard, Ruth had stepped out of her room with a vague idea of
the telephone, and there she was, Jane Shine, her greatest enemy,
looking like some forties actress having breakfast in bed on the
backlot of Metro-Goldwyn-Mayer.

Jane's eyes narrowed. Her face was alert but impassive. She
blinked twice, stepped round Ruth as if she were a minor nuisance,
a small but annoying impediment to her majestic progress—a pile
of luggage, a potted palm left out of place by the help—and floated
on down the hall with a gentle swish of silk. Oh, the bitch, the
bitch! Not a word, not an excuse me or beg pardon, not a good
morning, hello, goodbye, drop dead, anything. Oh, the icy arrogant
bitch!

Ruth just stood there, immobilized, rigid with hate. She waited
for the click of the bathroom door behind her, and then she started
down the hallway, clenching her jaws so hard her teeth had begun

to ache by the time she reached the phone at the foot of the stairs. "Sax?" she practically snarled into the receiver.

His voice came right back at her. He was excited about something—fish, no doubt—and her mood, which was poisonous to begin with, took a turn for the worse. "Ruth," he was saying, "listen, I've got to tell you this before anybody else does—"

She cut him off. All he cared about was fish. Lewis Turco had hurt her, had taken her by the hair and hurt her, and all he cared about was fish. "He grabbed me by the hair, Sax, and he called me a bitch in front of everybody, called me a lying Jew bitch right out on the patio in front of everybody." The phone gave it back to her—she could hear the outrage trembling in her voice, a slice of anger that fell away into hurt. "If he thinks he's going to get away with it, he's crazy . . . I'll sue him. I will. I'll file a complaint . . . Sax," she bleated, "oh, Sax."

There was a silence on the other end of the line. Saxby was confused, and when he was confused he got flustered. "What are you telling me, somebody pulled your hair?" And then he made a leap. "You mean the Japanese kid? Is that how he escaped?"

"Japanese kid? I'm talking about Turco. Lewis Turco. The little Nazi jerk that tags around with Detlef. He went berserk out on the patio last night and he"—her voice broke—"he assaulted me. He went for Irving too, and Sandy. You should see the bruises on Sandy's chest. He wouldn't touch me if you were here, he wouldn't dare, but—but—" She felt herself breaking down.

"Ruth, stop it. Listen to me."

Saxby wouldn't allow it, wouldn't listen. He had something to tell her, something more important than the fact that some overdeveloped clod had beat up his girlfriend, some miraculous fish find, the news that would send shock waves through the world of overgrown adolescents who spent their entire lives watching fish fuck in little glass tanks. She was angry. "No, you listen. He attacked me, goddamn it—"

"Ruth, the Japanese kid is here. Hiro. Hiro Tanaka. He's here."

What was he saying? Ruth glanced up to see Owen dart round

the corner for the kitchen. All the anger drained out of her. "Hiro? What do you mean? Where?"

"Here. In the Okefenokee. I opened the trunk of the car and there he was, curled up like a snake. In the *trunk*, for christ's sake."

It was early yet and her head ached: it took her a moment to process the information. Saxby was gone, ferreting out his pygmy fish on the other side of the state. Hiro had escaped. The sky was above, the earth below. Gravity exerted its pull, there was magnetic attraction, the weak force. Fine. But Hiro in the trunk of Saxby's car, Hiro in the Okefenokee Swamp? It was too much. It was a gag, a routine, Saxby was pulling her leg. Even now Abercorn and the sheriff and an army of yapping dogs and shotgun-toting crackers were combing the briar patches and cesspools of the island, and Hiro—the fugitive, the jailbreaker, the big soft kid with the pitiful eyes and overfed gut—was a hundred miles away. In a swamp. *The* swamp. The swamp to end all swamps. Poor Hiro. Poor Detlef. Poor Sax. But no, it couldn't be: it was too perfect. "Are you sure?"

"Of course I'm sure."

"Did you—" she began, and she was going to ask if Saxby had hurt him, if the raging Saxby had emerged, the aggressive, the rough, but she thought better of it. "I mean, did he say anything or did he run away again or what? Did you try to help him?"

Saxby was keyed up, speaking in breathless explosive little bursts. "It was Roy and me. He was in the trunk. By the time I knew what was happening he was gone."

"Gone?"

And then she got the full story. Saxby told her how he'd packed the car yesterday afternoon, too excited to remember whether he'd shut the trunk or not, and how they were out on a spit of land, water on three sides of them, and how Roy was backing the boat down the ramp. He told her how Hiro had leaped from the trunk like a wild-eyed maniac and plunged into the boat pond—"Every time I lay eyes on the guy he's jumping into some mudhole"—and how he'd kept going till he reached the far bank and the swamp beyond. "The guy's a fanatic," Saxby concluded. "A nut case. And if he thought Tupelo was something, he's got a real surprise coming."

Suddenly Ruth was laughing—she couldn't help herself. Laura Grobian came wide-eyed down the stairs to breakfast in the silent room and Ruth was laughing, gagging, nearly hysterical with the news, so weak she could barely hold the phone to her ear. The picture of Saxby standing there dumbfounded with his strapping feet and hopeless hands, of Hiro, his crooked teeth set in the big moon of his face, splashing for his life all over again, churning up the duckweed and plunging ever deeper into the swamp—trading one swamp for another—it was too much. It was like something out of *Heart of Darkness*—or the Keystone Kops. Yes, that was it: *The Keystone Kops Meet Heart of Darkness*. And the irony—that was what really killed her. The plan had worked. Hiro had finally got his wish—he was off Tupelo Island—and he'd made it in the trunk of Saxby's mother's car. It was funny, oh, it was funny.

"It's not funny, Ruth. It's not." Saxby was hot, his voice pinched to a rasp. "Look: Roy's already called the police. I'm calling to warn you. After yesterday . . . I mean, the guy turns up in the trunk of my car and they're going to believe I didn't know about it? Or you either?"

She hadn't thought of it that way. But still it was funny. "You're innocent, Sax—they never hang an innocent man." She knew she would regret it, but she couldn't help herself: suddenly her mood had improved. She was positively giddy. This was fun.

"Goddamn it, Ruth. This is your deal. You're the one who—" Saxby stopped dead. His voice just wilted. Static crackled over the line. Outside, the sun emerged to dig a shallow grave in the mist.

"Sax?"

"Tell me the truth," he demanded, "and no crap now—you didn't help him escape, did you?"

. . .

LATER—SHE COULDN'T POSSIBLY GO BACK TO SLEEP AFTER THAT phone call, and she knew they'd be at her again, the sheriff and

Detlef and that little slime—and him she wouldn't talk to, never, never again—she took a walk out to the studio to survey the wreckage. The overcast had cooled things down a bit and she caught a premonitory whiff of fall in the drizzle that lifted her spirits, but she was pretty well soaked through by the time she came round the double bend in the path. Before she even laid eyes on the cabin she noticed the little things, boot prints in the mud, the undergrowth trampled back here and there, and then, right in the middle of the path, she found half a dozen shell casings, red plastic and bright untarnished brass. She bent for the casings, fingered them, and threw them back down in disgust. Then she rounded the final bend and came upon the cabin.

From a distance it looked just as it had the night before last. There were the oaks, brooding over the roof with their beards of Spanish moss, there were the palmettos and berry bushes, there the steps, the door, the invitation of the windows. Insects hung in the air, birds shot overhead and lighted in the branches: it seemed as if nothing had changed. But as she drew closer she saw the glass glittering on the worn planks of the porch and saw that the screens had been perforated, the screen door shattered. Shell casings littered the yard, splinters of wood, hot bright nuggets of glass. And the porch—it was so spattered with shot it looked as if every woodpecker in Georgia had been at it, and there was a chunk the size of her fist missing from one of the uprights.

All at once she understood what it meant—not in the abstract, not on the telephone with a laugh in her throat and the world somewhere out on the horizon, but here in the actuality, in the wet and the heat and the stink of decay: *They'd tried to kill him.* Crackers, rednecks, Turco, Abercorn: the mob. A chill went through her. This was no joke. The closest she'd been to a gun in her life was in the front row of a movie theater—you just didn't mount guns in the back window of your BMW on Wilshire Boulevard, you didn't pick your teeth with them or hunt widgeons or wild boar or whatever they slaughtered out here in the boondocks. But to have a gun, an actual gun, pointed at you—how could she begin to understand what Hiro had gone through?

Inside, it was worse. It wasn't the shell casings she was finding now, but the bullets themselves. The paneling was pockmarked, there was a hole through the cushion of the loveseat, one of her pitcher plants had been sheared in half. Glass littered the floor, along with the odd twisted bit of lead, and one of the cane rockers was overturned in the corner. About the only thing that had escaped unscathed was her typewriter. There it sat, the eternal page curled over the keyboard.

She almost wished it hadn't survived, almost wished it had been blasted beyond recognition, the platen gouged and twisted, the keys scattered like rice at a wedding. She looked at it sitting there in mute accusation and a sinking, empty, hungry feeling came over her—call it nerves, guilt, the bane of the writer who isn't writing. "Of Tears and the Tide" was just wasted time—she didn't have the stomach to continue it, not now. *They'd tried to kill him.* How could she do justice to that?

But what now? She was living at an artists' colony, surrounded by writers, and she hadn't done any writing in a week. She hadn't expected to work today—and no one would have expected it of her—but in some part of her she was disappointed that the damage hadn't been more dramatic, more sweeping and cataclysmic, the sort of damage that would have precluded any thought of work. As it was, if she really wanted to, if the fit was on her, she could have swept up the glass and sat down to work right then and there, no need even to bother with the man Owen was sending out to patch the screens, replace the glass and putty up the bullet holes.

Just to do something, she got out the broom and dustpan and swept up the shards and nuggets of glass and the odd little flattened bits of lead that hadn't managed to embed themselves in the walls or slice clean on through and into the infinite. Then she dumped the ravaged pitcher plant over the front railing, fed one of the survivors the husk of a bluebottle she found amidst the debris on the windowsill, and finally sat down at her desk—but tentatively, as if she were only trying out the chair.

For a long moment she gazed out through the gaping window and then she gathered up the fat sheaf of scrawled-over Xerox paper that represented the whole of "Of Tears and the Tide," and buried it deep in the desk drawer. Down there, buried even deeper, she discovered the manuscript of an old, half-finished story she'd been meaning to rework. It was called "Two Toes," and it was another thing she'd developed from a news story—this one a piece that had made the national news and galvanized the attention of the whole slumbering and self-obsessed country. Everyone knew it. It was the story of Jessica McClure, the eighteen-month-old girl who'd fallen down a well shaft in Texas and wound up wedged tight in a pipe less than a foot in diameter, and who was rescued after two and a half days of heroic effort on the part of miners, firemen, police and evangelists, albeit at the cost of two toes on her right foot. Ruth didn't understand that exactly—the amputation of the toes, something to do with constricted blood flow—but her idea was to show the girl as a teenager, seventeen, eighteen maybe. Grown up now, living with the memory of those two terrible days and the burden of her brief and fading celebrity, she would have become self-destructive, hateful. Shooting drugs, drinking, whoring around. She would never make the national news again, and she knew it, her life a downward spiral from the age of one and a half on. And what would she do then? She'd marry some tattooed greaseball fifteen years her senior, a drummer in a rockabilly band, and then—but that was as far as Ruth had gotten. And now, reading over what she'd written, sifting through her notes, she felt nothing but despair. The idea stank. She stank. The whole miserable muggy drizzling world stank.

She lurched up from her desk and stepped out on the porch. It was no later than ten, ten thirty, though with the cloud cover it was hard to judge. She wondered if Owen was planning to bring her lunch. They'd seen plenty here over the years, from nervous breakdowns to fistfights to heart attacks and every sort of drunken and debauched behavior imaginable—artists would be artists, after all—but they'd never seen this. Hiro Tanaka, the Japanese desperado; La Dershowitz, his self-sacrificing succorer—or that didn't sound right: protector, then; and the glorious, full-color, Dolby-enhanced Attack of the Rednecks! They'd never seen a studio shot up before. If for nothing else, they'd remember her for that—even if she never wrote another word. In years to come they'd lean over the bar or push back their dinner plates or bubble round the convivial table to corner some newcomer, some ingénue, and allow the incredulity to light up their faces as some one of them, queen of the hive or king of the jungle, gasped, *Don't tell me you've never heard the story of the bullet holes in Hart Crane?*

Yes, Owen would bring lunch, all right. Business as usual. They'd seen everything but this, and it would go down in Thanatopsis legend, but Septima would never allow anything to interfere with the orderly business of creation, let alone the frenzy of the mob, destruction of property, attempted murder, anarchy and Yahooism. The only thing was, Ruth wouldn't be there to eat the lunch Owen would bring her. She was too dispirited. Too anxious, too depressed even to work. And then she had a thought: maybe it was closer to eleven, after all. If so, the mail would be in. Maybe she'd just take a stroll back to the big house and see if there was anything for her. She couldn't work today. Not today. And who could blame her?

.　　■　　.

AS IT TURNED OUT, THERE WAS SOMETHING FOR HER. TWO THINGS, actually. She checked her box in the coatroom, her eyes hungrily scanning the grid of mailboxes, noting as she did every day the volume of mail jamming Laura, Irving and even Jane's boxes while her own remained conspicuously and degradingly empty. They got letters from publishers, agents and editors, high-tone magazines, review copies, fan mail. She got nothing. (For a while she'd toyed with the idea of stuffing envelopes with dummy letters and mailing them to herself, but she was afraid the postmarks would give her

away—to Owen, at any rate. He was the one who sorted the mail—
and any secret, any tidbit about anyone was fair game at Thanatopsis; the place was a jungle, it really was—and if *that* got out
she'd never be able to show her face again.)

She envied Laura Grobian, who got fan mail from all over the
world. When she was alone in the mailroom, when she was sure
no one was looking, Ruth pulled the letters out and fanned through
them, transfixed by the postmarks, the addresses, the exotic foreign
stamps and legends. She was envious of Irving too. And Jane,
though it sickened her to admit it even to herself. Jane got letters
from her publisher, of course, and proofs to correct, and once she'd
even gotten an envelope from *Harper's* that looked and felt suspiciously like an acceptance letter, not to mention the thin blue aero-
grams from Italy that came two or three times a week. As often as
not, Ruth got nothing—and everyone knew it. They probably made
a joke of it—who would want to write her, anyway? She didn't
have a publisher. She didn't have an agent. She didn't have fans
or a mysterious hot-blooded Venetian lover who franked his letters
only with the initials *C. da V.* or even friends. Her mother never
even wrote her.

But today she was surprised.

She spotted the big manila envelope projecting from her box the
moment she stepped through the door, and she knew instantly what
it was. It was the manuscript of "Days of Fire, Nights of Ashes,"
returned from the *Atlantic. The New Yorker* had rejected it promptly,
but she'd prevailed on Irving once again to lend his name and
influence to her cause and she'd held out high hopes for the *Atlantic.*
They'd had it for three weeks. And now here it was, back again,
a dead albatross, refuse in a neat foursquare envelope, one more
dismissal from the world at large. As she snatched the thing from
the box, her second piece of mail fluttered to the floor. It was a
postcard, glossy and inviting, showing the sunstruck beach at Juan-
les-Pins. On the reverse, six lines from Betsy Butler, a poet she
knew from Iowa who if anything was even more obscurely published than she, and therefore someone Ruth could continue to

enjoy. Betsy was on the beach. She had a poem coming out in a magazine Ruth had never heard of. All right. Fine. But there was a P.S.: had Ruth heard the news? About Ellis Disick who'd been at Iowa with them? His first novel had just gone at auction for $250,000, movie rights went to Universal and the book was a main selection of Book-of-the-Month for the spring: wasn't that just too much? Gritting her teeth, Ruth tore grimly into the envelope from the *Atlantic*. Just as she'd suspected, her manuscript, slightly worn about the edges, stared back at her. The rejection slip, signed in a mad indecipherable scrawl, was curt: "Too hot for us. Try *Hustler*."

.   .   .

RUTH SPENT THE AFTERNOON IN BED. SHE LICKED HER WOUNDS, brooded, poked desultorily through a Czechoslovakian novel Peter Anserine had recommended with an emphatic quiver of intellectual fervor animating his Brahmin's nostrils, and ate her way miserably through a two-pound box of tollhouse cookies. She found she was missing Sax—the old Sax, the ardent sexy Sax who lately seemed to have sublimated all his libidinous energy in the pursuit of pygmy fishes—and she very nearly let her malaise overwhelm her desire for cocktails and company. But she struggled back beyond the humiliation of the scene on the patio and the grimness of the cabin to the moment of her triumph over the entire affair of Hiro, and that cheered her. There was plenty of mileage to be got yet from that—and too, this was the day that the new arrivals would be putting in their initial appearances, and it would be a shame to miss that. Ruth spent half an hour on her face, fished through her wardrobe for something red, and came down the big staircase to cocktails as a queen to coronation.

The first person she laid eyes on was Brie Sullivan, who was standing in the foyer amidst a clutter of mismatched suitcases, looking bewildered. Ruth knew Brie from Bread Loaf and she liked her for her myopic pursed-lip expression—she always looked slightly dazed—and her air of the eternal hick and newcomer, and because, like Betsy Butler, she hadn't published much (and judging from her workshop stories, all of which seemed to be about disembodied brains and talking unicorns, she never would). She had a broad smooth forehead and strong hands and hair that flew round her face as if she were caught in a perpetual windstorm. "Brie," Ruth said, offering her outspread palms as she swept down the staircase, her voice rich with noblesse oblige.

Brie's response registered somewhere on the scale between a yelp and a screech, before trailing off into frequencies audible only to more sensitive lifeforms. "Ruthie!" was the rough sense of the sound she produced, and then they were in each other's arms, sisters torn asunder by the Fates and at long last reunited. After a moment they fell back a pace, still clutching one another but attaining enough distance for a quick but keen mutual appraisal. Brie looked good, Ruth had to admit it—but then why wouldn't she, she was only twenty-six. "I'm knocked out," Brie gasped, her dull gray gaze licking about the foyer, darting into the fuzzy purviews of the parlor where the dim forms of the cocktail crowd could be seen hanging protectively over their drinks, and then settling again on Ruth, "—I really am. I'm stunned. The place is fantastic, much tonier than I'd imagined even—"

"Yes," Ruth agreed with a proprietary air, "it's first class all the way here. Septima—that's my boyfriend Saxby's mother?—she keeps the place competitive, that's for sure. They know how to spoil you. The food alone . . ." Ruth put three fingers together and waggled them in appreciation.

Brie was treating her to a broad open-faced look of wonder and unadulterated joy. "I'm so glad you're here," she said in a kind of bark. "I thought I was going to be the only one—" Brie hesitated. "The only . . ."

Only what? Ruth wondered. Talking unicorn? Ditzy blonde? Rank amateur? Was Brie insulting her, was that it? Was she saying that she'd thought it would be all Grobian, Anserine, Kleinschmidt and Thalamus, all celebrity and anointed royalty, but that now she saw there was a peonage here as well and that Ruth was part of it? Like herself? Ruth could feel her ears turning red.

Brie never finished the thought. She squealed something unintelligible followed by "Oh, Ruthie, it's so good to see you!" A second obligatory hug ensued, slightly less fervent than the first, and then Ruth led Brie into the parlor for cocktails.

At the bar, Ruth introduced her to Sandy, Regina, Ina and Bob, each of whom received in return a look of such awe and abasement they might have been Salinger, Nevelson, Welty and Ashbery. Brie then grilled them, as a group and individually both, about the minutest and most banal details of their personal histories, ending up with the *verboten* question: "So what are you working on now?"

Ruth smiled serenely throughout, exchanging occasional glances with her friends and giving them the odd shoulder shrug for their unspoken commiseration. She was the undisputed queen here, after all—or she was so long as the pretender, Jane Shine, remained under wraps. And where was La Shine, with her flamenco hair and phony laugh—choking to death on a bit of pickled truffle in her lofty and well-appointed room? Out for a drive with her Nordic slave? No matter. In giving Brie the great good gift of her patronage—if she was all right in La Dershowitz's eyes, she was all right, period—Ruth felt charitable, saintly even. It was the least she could do.

She let it go on a bit—"And you're a Scorpio too?" Brie was gurgling at Ina in a battle of shoulders and flying hair—and then she cut in and took Brie by the elbow. "You're going to want to unpack," she said. "I'll get Owen for you. But first"—a pause, casual as a yawn—"would you like to meet Irving Thalamus?"

Brie was a game-show contestant, second runner-up for the title of Miss America, she'd won the lottery and hit the jackpot at Vegas. The squeal of sheer wonder, amaze and delight shot directly out of the bounds of human hearing, and Sandy, Ina and Bob smiled softly to themselves, as they might have smiled at the antics of a child or a puppy; Regina fell back on her punk scowl. "Really?" Brie managed when she'd caught her breath, "Irving Thalamus? Is *he* here?"

Ruth led her over to where Irving sat propped up in an armchair with a double vodka and an issue of a literary magazine devoted exclusively to an appreciation of his work. It was good reading, and Irving was absorbed in it, oblivious, frowning behind his patriarchal eyebrows and the diminutive reading glasses perched like a toy on the end of his nose. He obliged them with a smile, and after Brie had made her obeisance—at the height of it Ruth thought she was going to roll on the floor and piss herself—he turned on the Thalamus charm and treated them to an in-depth, line-by-line assessment of the merits and failings of the critics the magazine had solicited to do honor to him.

Ruth got Brie a Calistoga and herself a bourbon, and she sat at Irving's right hand while he went on about a certain Morris Rosenschweig of Tufts University with all the wit, charm and self-deprecating irony of a man who still had something to live for. Ruth watched, and listened, and thought it was a pretty good act.

Clara and Patsy were next, and then a group of minor figures who happened in the door as Ruth was guiding Brie back up to the bar, and lastly, Laura Grobian. Laura was seated alone in the far corner, as usual, a golden high-stemmed glass of sherry catching the light from the reading lamp beside her. She had her notebook with her—she always had her notebook with her; that notebook drove Ruth crazy—and she was writing in it, her head bent to the page. "Laura"—Ruth's voice was steady, chummy, full of cheer— "I'd like you to meet Brie Sullivan, one of our new colonists?"

Laura glanced up at them from beneath the celebrated black bangs and Ruth had a shock. She looked terrible. Looked haggard, confused, looked as if she'd been drinking secretly, living on the street, haunting graveyards. *Cancer*—the word leaped into Ruth's head— *an inoperable tumor. Two months. Three.* But then Laura smiled and she was her old self again, regal, unassailable, the ascetic middle-aged beauty with the devouring eyes and terrific bone structure. She held out her hand to Brie. "I'm pleased that you've joined us," she said.

Brie squirmed, squared her shoulders, blew the hair out of her face. She was working herself up for this one. Laura blinked at her in wonder, and then the flood came. "I'm honored," Brie began, trying to control her voice, but it was pitched too high, unsteady with worship and excitement, "I mean, I'm blown away. I am. I mean the Bay Light trilogy, after I read it, it was the only thing I could read for the longest, for years . . . I think I know every word by heart. I'm, I'm—this is really amazing, it's an honor, it's—it's—"

"Do you know the story of Masada?" Laura asked suddenly, glancing down at the page in her lap and then back up at them— Brie and Ruth both. "Ruth, certainly you must know it?"

Masada? What was she talking about? Was it a quiz or something? "You mean where the Jews killed themselves?"

"A.D. 73, April the fifteenth. Mass suicide. I've been reading about it. About Jonestown too. And the Japanese at Saipan and Okinawa. Did you know about Saipan? Women and children flung themselves from cliffs, cut out their own entrails, swallowed cyanide and gasoline." Laura's voice was quiet, husky round the edges of its exotic ruination.

Brie puffed at her hair, shifted the glass from hand to hand: she was clearly at a loss. Ruth didn't know quite what to say either— this wasn't cocktail-hour banter, this wasn't gossip and publishing and wit—it was morbid, depressing. No wonder Laura always sat alone, no wonder she barely managed to look alive. "How horrible," Ruth said finally, exchanging a look with Brie.

"The U.S. Marines were about to land and the civilians had been abandoned. The rumor was that to become a Marine you had to murder your own parents. Can you imagine that?—that's what they thought of us. The Japanese—*civilians*, women and children— leaped from a cliff into the sea rather than fall into the hands of such monsters."

Ruth said nothing. She took a nervous sip of her second bourbon—or was it her third? What was she driving at?

"I read a story about that once—it was like the people were

lemmings or something," Brie announced, settling on the arm of the chair opposite Laura. "In fact, I think it was called 'Lemmings'—yeah, it was, I'm sure of it. I think."

"Exactly." Laura Grobian held them with her haunted—and, Ruth was beginning to think, ever so slightly demented—gaze. "Mass hysteria," she said, seeming to relish the hiss of it. "Mass suicide. A woman steps up to the edge of the cliff, clutching a baby to her breast, the five-year-old at her side. People are jumping all around her, screaming and weeping. It goes against all her instincts, but she shoves the five-year-old first, the half-formed limbs kicking and clawing at the poor thin air, and then she follows him into the abyss. And all because they thought we were monsters."

Ruth had had a rough day, what with the cabin torn to pieces, the utter collapse of her work and inspiration, the excitement of Hiro's jailbreak and Saxby's phone call, not to mention the scene on the patio last night, and she didn't need this, not now, not even from Laura Grobian—but how to escape? And then, because she couldn't help herself, because the moment was so uncomfortable, she asked the interdicted question: "You're working on an essay? A new novel?"

Laura was slow to reply, and for a moment Ruth wondered if she'd heard her. But then, in a vague and distant way, she murmured, "No. Not really. I just . . . find the subject . . . fascinating, I guess." And then she came back to them, shrugging her shoulders and lifting the sherry glass from the table.

It sounded like an exit line to Ruth, and she was thinking of the routine she could make of this, of Laura Grobian's gloom and doom, and if she'd dare it, when the buzz of conversation in the room suddenly died and all heads turned to the doorway. The two other new arrivals had appeared for cocktails. Both of them. Together.

Ruth watched Brie squinting toward the doorway in expectation of some new revelation, some further miracle of earthbound celebrity, and then watched as her head turned, her brow furrowed and her lips formed the question: "Isn't that—?"

"Orlando Seezers," Ruth said.

The figure was unmistakable. Though Ruth had never met him, she'd seen photographs. He was sixtyish, black, goateed and confined to the gleaming electric wheelchair in which he now appeared. During the campus riots of the sixties he was injured in an altercation with a student who claimed he only wanted to go to class. It was at NYU, as Ruth recalled, on a staircase. Before the accident he wrote bittersweet blank verse about blues and jazz figures and fiery outraged polemics that won him comparison with James Baldwin and Eldridge Cleaver; afterward, he wrote sestinas and a series of very popular comedies of manners centered on life on the Upper East Side.

"And—?" Brie wondered aloud, squinting till her face seemed on the verge of falling in on itself.

"Mignonette Teitelbaum." Ruth didn't know her either, not personally, but Septima had informed her that she was coming with Orlando Seezers—"I heah they are *prac*-tically inseparable"—and she knew *of* her, of course. Teitelbaum—and Ruth couldn't help hearing a breathless "La" affixed to the surname—was six foot three, flat-footed, hipless, breastless and Seezers's junior by some thirty years. She was the author of two books of minimalist stories set in the backwoods of Kentucky, though she'd been born and raised in Manhattan, attended Barnard and Columbia and lived in Europe most of her adult life. Rumor had it they'd met at a dance club in SoHo.

The couple hesitated there on the threshold until Irving Thalamus rose with a mighty roar—"Orlando! Mignonette!"—and crossed the room to embrace them. The buzz started up again. Brie, a look of rapture on her face, began drifting toward the triumvirate of embracing lions as if in a trance. It was then that Laura Grobian took hold of Ruth's arm. Brie seemed somehow to sense the motion and froze. Ruth looked down at Laura, not yet alarmed, but afraid she was about to start up with the Masada business again while the precious minutes of the cocktail hour dwindled away to nothing. "Ruth"—Laura held her with those fathomless eyes—"I'll see you tonight, after dinner?"

"Yes, sure," Ruth said, though the ground had shifted beneath her again. She was Laura Grobian's intimate, yes, but what in god's name was she talking about now?

Laura smiled up at her as if they'd just come back from sailing around the world together. "Jane's reading. Jane Shine's. You haven't forgotten, have you?"

Brie swooped back in on them at the mention of Jane. "Jane Shine?" she gasped, hovering over them as if one of the secret names of Jehovah had just been revealed to her. "She's here too?"

The tectonic plates were really shaking now, grinding up against one another with all their terrible rending force. Off balance, Ruth could only nod.

"Oh, Ruthie"—Brie glanced wildly from Ruth to Laura and back again—"do you know her?"

Where the Earth Trembles

. . . .

VAST AND PRIMEVAL, UNFATHOMABLE, UNCONQUERABLE, BASTION of cottonmouth, rattlesnake and leech, mother of vegetation, father of mosquito, soul of silt, the Okefenokee is the swamp archetypal, the swamp of legend, of racial memory, of Hollywood. It gives birth to two rivers, the St. Mary's and the Suwannee, fanning out over 430,000 leaf-choked acres, every last one as sodden as a sponge. Four hundred and thirty thousand acres of stinging, biting and boring insects, of maiden cane and gum and cypress, of palmetto, slash pine and peat, of muck, mud, slime and ooze. Things fester here, things cook down, decompose, deliquesce. The swamp is home to two hundred and twenty-five species of birds, forty-three of mammals, fifty-eight of reptiles, thirty-two of amphibians and thirty-four of fish—all variously equipped with beaks, talons, claws, teeth, stingers and fangs—not to mention the seething galaxies of gnats and deerflies and no-see-ums, the ticks, mites, hookworms and paramecia that exist only to compound the misery of life. There are alligators here, bears, puma, bobcats and bowfin, there are cooters and snappers, opossum, coon and gar. They feed on one another, shit and piss in the trees, in the sludge and muck and on the floating mats of peat, they dribble jism and bury eggs, they scratch and stink and sniff at themselves, caterwauling and screeching through every minute of every day and night till the place reverberates like some hellish zoo.

Drain it, they said, back in the days when technology was hope. They tried. In 1889, Captain Harry Jackson, a man with a vision, formed the Suwannee Canal Company to dredge the swamp and drain off the water, bugs, slime, alligators, snakes, turtles, frogs and catfish, and convert the rich remaining muck to farmland. He got some capital together, brought in half a dozen huge steam dredges capable of digging a canal forty-five feet wide and six feet deep at the rate of forty-four feet per day. He erected a sawmill to cut lumber for fuel and for profit, and he kept the dredges going round the clock, and the more he dug, the more the water poured in. But he kept at it, and the canal advanced at the rate of some three miles a year. The problem was that by all estimates it would take three hundred miles of canals to effectively drain the swamp, and even a man with vision couldn't expect to live to a hundred and forty. Captain Harry Jackson didn't. He died in 1895, having made a tiny wound in the flank of the unassailable swamp, a wound into which the water flowed as if an artery itself had been severed. The dredges rotted and sank, the sawmill fell to ruin. Leaves and vines and fine young trees closed over it all.

But if they couldn't eliminate the Okefenokee, they could at least rape it. And so the logging company came in. They built two hundred miles of elevated railway trestles throughout the swamp to get at the virgin stands of cypress, they built a town on Billy's Island with a hotel, a general store and telephone connection to the outside world. From 1909 to 1927, the shriek of the saw dominated the mighty swamp. And then the big stands of cypress were gone, and so was the lumber company. The trains backed off into civilization, the trestles collapsed, the hotel, the store, the telephone itself vanished as if the whole thing were a traveling show, a mirage, and within ten years there was nothing left but the rusted hulks of useless machinery, devoured in weed, to indicate that a town had stood on Billy's Island.

In 1937, the federal government did the only reasonable thing and declared the swamp a wildlife refuge, in the process tracking down and evicting the last of the bushwhackers, poachers, gator skinners, moonshiners and assorted inbred primitives and desperadoes who had fled here as to the earth's remotest outpost. The Okefenokee became a refuge for every least thing that swam or flew or crept on its belly, but it was a refuge no longer for the swamp hollerers and law benders. The water rose, the trees thickened, the star grass and bladderwort and swamp haw proliferated, the gators rolled in the muck and multiplied, and the old ways, the oldest ways, the eternal and unconquerable ways, triumphed.

■   ■   ■

OF COURSE, HIRO KNEW NONE OF THIS. ALL HE KNEW WAS THE trunk of the Mercedes, all he knew were shin splints, muscle cramps, aching joints and nausea, all he knew was the dawning realization that the invisible driver up front yowling about his plastic Jesus like some drunk in a *karaoke* bar was the king butter-stinker himself, the *ketō*, the long-nose, his nemesis and rival at love, Ruth's big hairy *bōifurendo* . . . all he knew was the moment of release.

And oh, how he ached for that moment through every lurch and swing and bump of the car, through every hairpin turn and crunch of the tires and through the long sweltering night at the motel— yes, it was a motel, he could hear the cars pulling in and out, the doors slamming, the chatter of voices. Left alone, he tried to tear his way through the wall of the trunk and into the back seat, but there was no room to work and the wall was unyielding, adamantine, a thing the Germans had built to last. And so he ached and tried to massage his muscles and breathe the close stale air with patience and concentration; and so he waited like a samurai, like Jōchō, like Mishima, like a Japanese, for the moment the key would discover the lock.

When the moment came, he was ready. Tired, sore, hungry for the light and air, seething with a slow deep unquenchable rage for all his hurts and wrongs, for the naked cheat of the City of Brotherly Love and the loss of Ruth, he was ready, ready for anything. But when at long last the key turned in the lock and the lid rose above him like the lid of a coffin, the explosion of light blinded him and he hesitated. Shielding his eyes, he squinted up into the face that hung over him, a familiar face, the *bōifurendo*'s face, frozen in shock and disbelief. That was it, that was enough. All the rest was as automatic as the engine that drove his heart or the surge of blood that shot through his veins.

He sprang, taking his adversary by surprise. But there was no need for the karate he'd mastered through assiduous study of the diagrams in the back of a martial arts magazine, no need to grapple, kick or gouge—the *bōifurendo* had fallen back in horror, his eyes hard as nuggets, a look of impotence and constipation pressed into his features. Good. Good, good, good. Hiro came up out of his offensive crouch and darted a glance round him to get his bearings. And then, with the shock of a slap in the face, came his second big surprise: as far as he could see there was nothing but water, muck, creeper and vine, the damnable unending fetid stinking wilderness of America. But no, it couldn't be. Was it all swamp, the whole hopeless country? Where were the shopping malls, the condos, the tattoo parlors and supermarkets? Where the purple mountains and the open range? Why couldn't the butter-stinker have popped open the trunk at the convenience store, at Burger King or Saks Fifth Avenue? Why this? Why these trees and these lily pads and this festering *gaijin* cesspool? Was it some kind of bad joke?

No one moved. Hiro stood there poised on the brink of capture and escape, the *bōifurendo* immobilized, his accomplice up to his knees in the murk and gaping up at him in bewilderment. He could have darted past the *bōifurendo*, dodging round him on the narrow spit of dry land, but there were more butter-stinkers behind him, a whole legion of them with fish poles and pickup trucks and boat trailers, the hate and loathing and contempt already settling in their eyes. There was no choice: hesitate and you are dead. Three strides, a running leap, and he was in his element, in the water, in the water yet again, born to it, inured to it, as quick and nimble and streamlined as a dolphin.

Déjà vu.

But this time the water wasn't salt—it was bathwater, turgid, foul, the swill they flushed down the drain after the whole village has bathed for a week. He slashed at the duckweed and surface scum, powering for the far side of the lagoon before the astonished fishermen behind him could drop their tackle boxes and fire up the engines of their leaping blunt-nosed *hakujin* swamp boats. He reached the far shore—but it wasn't land, actually, it was something else, something that rocked beneath his feet like the taut skin of a trampoline—while the familiar shouts rose behind him and the outboard engines sprang to life with the growl of the hunting beast. No matter: he was already gone.

Yes, but now what? If he'd thought the island was bad, if he'd had his fill of bogs and mosquitoes and clothes that never dried, then this *mainrand* was hell itself. He fought his way through the bush, away from the voices and the scream of the outboards, clawing his way through the tangle, but there was no rest, no surcease, no place to set his feet down or pull himself from the muck. The water was knee-deep, waist-high, two feet over his head, and beneath it was the mud that sucked at him, sank him to the hips, pulled him inexorably down. With each desperate flailing stroke he was sinking deeper. Such an ignominious death, he thought, invoking Jōchō, inflating his *hara*, but going down all the same. Finally, his limbs numb with fatigue, gasping for air and choking on the gnats and mosquitoes that blackened the air around him, he managed to heave himself out of the muck and up onto the slick bony knees of a tree that rose up before him like a pillar of granite.

He lay there panting, too sapped even to brush the insects away from his face, the gloom of the big moss-hung trees darkening the morning till it might have been night. A swamp! Another swamp! A swamp so massive it could have swallowed up Ruth's cabin, Ambly Wooster's subdivision, the big house and all the piddling bogs and mud puddles on Tupelo Island without a trace. Shit, he gasped. *Backayarō*. Son of a bitch. He felt like a mountaineer who's dragged himself up the face of a sheer cliff, inch by agonizing inch, only to find a second cliff, twice as high, rearing above it. What had happened to him? How had he gotten here? Doggo, his *obāsan*, Chiba, Unagi: they were faces he could barely recall. But Ruth: he saw her clearly, in sharp focus, saw her in all her permutations: the slim white-legged secretary, the seductress, the lover, his protector and jailer. She'd shared her food with him and her bed, shared her tongue and her legs, and she was going to smuggle him to the *mainrand*—not this *mainrand*, not the *mainrand* of rot and stink and demented nature, but to the *mainrand* of cities and streets and shops where *happas* and wholes walked hand in hand.

It was then—delivered from the trunk of the Mercedes and thrust back into the swamp—that he had a thought that stopped him cold. For forty-eight hours now, from the time they'd run him down with their guns and their dogs and their glassy cold eyes, through his escape from the holding cell and the swollen stultifying hours of his entombment in the trunk, he'd been circling around the hard knot of an inadmissible question—*Who had betrayed him?*—and its equally painful corollary, *Who knew he was hiding out in the cabin in the woods?* Now the answer came to him, the answer to both questions, wrapped up in a single resonant monosyllable: *Ruth.*

. . .

THERE WAS A WAY THE PADDLE DIPPED INTO THE WATER AND WITH a single deft motion of the wrist dug, rotated and dipped again, a rhythm and coordination that held out the possibility of perfection, and it pleased him. It was tidy. Neat. The stroke conserved energy and expended it too—not like those idiots in their motor launches on the public trails—and it felt good in the shoulders and triceps. It was so quiet too—he could almost imagine himself a Seminole or a Creek, slipping up on gator or ibis or even one of the palefaces who'd driven them into the swamp in the days of Billy Bowlegs.

Jeff Jeffcoat was gliding through a dream. Ever since he was a boy in Putnam Valley, New York, he'd wanted to do this, to push through the greatest swamp in America, skirting danger, unfolding miracles, watching the gator in its wallow, the anhinga in its nest, the cottonmouth curled in the branches of a tree in deadly sema-phore. And here he was—thirty-eight years old, newly arrived in Atlanta to work in the colorization lab at TBS, his wife Julie perched on a cushion amidships, his son Jeff Jr. plying his paddle in the bow—here he was, doing it. And it was glorious—something new round every bend. It was hot, sure, he had to admit it, and the bugs were horrendous despite the repellent that stung his eyes, soured the corners of his mouth and dripped steadily from the tip of his nose along with about half a gallon of sweat. But what was a little discomfort compared with the chance to see an alligator snapper in the wild—a hundred and fifty pounds, big around as a cocktail table—or the legendary black puma or that rarest of rare birds, the ivory-billed woodpecker?

"Dad." Jeff Jr.'s voice was low and insistent, the terse whisper of the scout; Jeff felt Julie come to attention, and his own eyes shot out past the bow to scan the mass of maiden cane and titi up ahead. "Dad: eleven o'clock, thirty yards or so."

"What?" Julie whispered, snatching up the binoculars. She was wearing a hairnet to combat the bugs, a pair of Banana Republic shorts and the pith helmet Jeff had bought her as a joke. She was as excited as he was.

Jeff felt a thrill go through him: *this* was life, this was adventure, this was what the explorers must have known through every waking moment of their lives. "What is it, Jeffie—what do you see?"

"Some—"

"Shhhh: don't scare it off."

The whisper of a whisper: "Something big. See it, up there, where the bushes are shaking?"

"Where?" Julie breathed, the binoculars pressed to her face. "I don't see anything."

Jeff fanned the paddle in the water, ever so silently, the canoe creeping forward under its own momentum. It was probably an alligator—the swamp was crawling with them. Yesterday, their first day out, they went nearly an hour before they spotted their first gator—and it was a runt, two feet or less even—but the moment had been magical. They'd spent half an hour motionless in the canoe, just watching it lying there, as inert as the cypresses towering over it. He must have taken two rolls of film of that gator alone, and every shot would be the same, he knew it—gator in ooze—but he'd gotten carried away. Later, as the day wore on and the gators popped up everywhere, as common as poodles in the park, the family became so inured to their presence that Jeff Jr. had done a very foolish thing. A big gator—ten, twelve feet long—had nosed up to the canoe while they were lunching on the chicken breast and avocado sandwiches Julie had made the night before, and Jeff Jr., bored or heedless or just feeling full of the devil, as boys will, had begun to toss bits of bread and lettuce into the water and the gator had gone for them. That was all right. But familiarity breeds contempt, as Jeff's father used to say, and Jeffie had flung an apple at the thing. Hard. He was a pretty good pitcher, Jeffie was, the ace of his Little League team, and the apple drilled the alligator right between the eyes—and that was when all hell broke loose. The thing had come up out of the water and slammed down again like a cannonballer coming off the high dive, and then it vanished, leaving the canoe rocking so wildly the water sloshed over the side and soaked the camera bag, the picnic basket and Jeffie's backpack. That was a close one, and Jeff Jr. had seemed so upset—his eyes big and his shoulders quaking—that Jeff had forgone the lecture till they set up camp later that evening.

But now they were closing in on it, whatever it was—he could see something thrashing around in the weeds up ahead—and Jeffie suddenly sang out: "It's a bear! A—a—a brown one, a big brown bear!"

A bear! Jeff could feel his blood racing—a bear could turn on them, upset the canoe, deliver them in an instant to the snakes and gators and snapping turtles. He backpaddled hard, his eyes leaping at the vegetation ahead—there it was, a snatch of brown, the maiden cane trembling, a splash, then another—

But it wasn't a bear after all—and they had a good laugh over that one—it was a pair of otters. Otters. "My god," Julie gasped, "you had me scared half to death, Jeffie." She'd dropped the binoculars in her lap and her face was pale under the brim of the pith helmet. The otters darted under the boat, bobbed up again and gave them an inquisitive look.

They were like puppies, that was what they reminded him of, sleek and playful puppies, and they instantly incorporated the canoe into their game of tag. It was a thrill, and they watched them for half an hour before Jeff remembered himself, checked his watch and got them going again.

They were on a schedule, and they had to stick to it—by law. Jeff had made reservations for this canoe trip a year in advance, as soon as he'd gotten a firm commitment from Turner and put the house up for sale. The Park Service allowed only six canoe parties at a time to overnight in the swamp, and competition for those six spots was fierce. Each party had to follow a set itinerary and was required, by park regulations, to arrive at its designated camping platform by 6 P.M., when the rangers closed the park down for the night and all fishermen, bird-watchers and other day trippers were required to return to the dock. The Park Service literature explained that this six o'clock deadline—all paddles out of the water, all overnighters to be on their platforms—had been established for the canoeists' own safety. It was dangerous out here, what with the gators, the cottonmouths, coral snakes and rattlers, and that gave Jeff a thrill too—but he was sensible and punctual and he didn't really like surprises, and he always obeyed the law to the letter, even on the highway, where he stuck doggedly to 55 while the big rigs and Japanese sports cars shot past him as if he were parked in the driveway. The Park Service allowed them eight hours to get from platform to platform, and so they had plenty of time to dawdle and see the sights, but after the otter business they were running late. Jeff dug deep with his paddle.

It was quarter to six in the evening, and he was beginning to stew—had they taken a wrong turn somewhere?—when Jeffie crowed, "I see it, I see it, dead ahead!"—and there it was, the elevated platform that was their second night's destination. The weathered support beams and the crude roof detached themselves from the wall of vegetation, a great blue heron lifted itself into the air with a clap of its wings, and they were there, gliding up to the platform on a burning shimmer of light. Like the platform on which they'd camped the previous evening, this one was three hundred feet square and roofed with porous planks, and it rose a precarious three feet above the water level of the swamp. Its amenities consisted of a chemical toilet, a charcoal brazier and a logbook, in which each overnighter was required to record date and time of arrival and departure.

Jeff Jr. and Julie steadied the canoe while Jeff clambered up onto the platform, alert for snakes or lizards in the rafters—or anything else that crept, crawled or climbed. The previous night Julie had let out a shriek they could have heard back in Atlanta when a coachwhip suddenly appeared from one of the overhead beams, plunged into the potato salad and lashed itself across the floor and into the duckweed on the far side of the platform. This time, they were taking no chances. Jeff was thorough, visually inspecting the beams and the underside of the platform, and poking a stick into each of the overhead crannies where beam and plank came together. Then he turned to the logbook. The Murdocks, of Chiltonberry, Arkansas, had preceded them, and in the space reserved for comment they'd observed: "Skeeter Hell." Before them it was the Ouzels of Soft Spoke, Virginia, and all they had to say was: "Beautiful stars." It was the line above the Ouzels' that caught his eye—someone, described only as "Fritz" and whose handwriting was so pinched and secretive Jeff could barely make it out, had written: "Note: 14′ gator *can* get up on platform." "Can" was underlined three times.

"Jeff, what's taking you so long? I've got to use the ladies'."

"Yeah, sure," he replied absently, wondering if he should mention the acrobatic gator and deciding that he would, but later, after supper, when they were all settled in for the night. "All clear," he called, keeping it simple.

Jeff made a fire with the real oak briquettes he'd brought along from Atlanta, and Julie extracted three princely New York strip steaks from the cooler. They shared a beer and Jeff Jr. had a Coke while the steaks sizzled and sent up a clean searing aromatic smoke that for a while overwhelmed the reek of the mud and disoriented the mosquitoes. The water was shallow out back of the platform—no more than shin-deep—but out front there was a considerable pool, an enlarged gator wallow, no doubt, and Jeff kept his eye on this for the agile gator, who for all Jeff knew liked his steak rare. Jeffie got out his fishing pole, but Jeff and Julie both insisted that he practice his clarinet first—they believed that an individual should be well-rounded, and though Jeff Jr. was only ten, they were already looking ahead to college admissions—and so while the meal cooked and Jeff swirled his half a can of warm beer round a plastic camp cup, the angst-ridden strains of Carl Nielsen floated out over bog, hammock and wallow, tempering the mindless twitter of the birds and tree frogs with a small touch of precision.

After dinner it began to cloud over and Jeff suspended a ground-cloth from the beams to cut the wind from the southeast, where lightning had begun to fracture the sky and the distant dyspeptic rumble of thunder could be heard. Then he built up the fire with an armload of pine branches he'd thought to collect earlier in the day, and the family gathered round to roast marshmallows, swat mosquitoes and tell stories. "Well," Jeff said, settling down beside Julie as the groundcloth flapped and the smoke swirled, "you all know why this great swamp is called the Okefenokee—"

"Oh, come on, Dad—you've already told us about fifty thousand times already."

"Jeffie, now don't you use that tone with your father—"

"—the land of trembling earth, because it's important to the story I'm going to tell, a tragic story, horrible in its way"—and here Jeff paused to let the adjectives work their spell on his audience, while the rumble of the thunder came closer and closer—"the story of Billy Bowlegs, last of the great Seminole chiefs."

Jeff Jr. was sitting cross-legged on one of the flotation cushions. He leaned forward, that alert look he got when he was practicing or doing his homework settling into his eyes and the incipient furrows of his brow. "It's because the peat rises in mats and trees grow on them and stuff and then when you try to walk on it you fall through—like Mom yesterday. It was so funny. It was like"— his tone had begun in the adenoidal reaches of exasperation, but now he was enjoying himself, riding the pleasure of his own authority—"like all these little trees were attacking her or something."

Jeff brought him back. "Right, Jeffie: and what is peat?"

"Um, it's like coal, right?"

Jeff wasn't too sure himself, though he'd devoured every guidebook available on the Okefenokee, but then the lesson had gone far enough anyway and the story was waiting. "Right," he said. "It's important to know because of what happened to Billy Bowlegs after one of the bloodiest massacres in the history of this region. Anyway, this was about in 1820, I think, and Billy Bowlegs was chased into the swamp with about thirty braves after raiding a settler's cabin. He hated the whites with a passion, even though he wasn't a full-blooded Indian—legend had it that his father was a white man, a criminal who escaped from a lynching party and got himself lost in the swamp . . ."

It was then that the first wind-whipped spatters of rain began to tap at the groundcloth and Jeff paused to mentally congratulate himself for having thought to secure the bottom too. There was a flash of lightning followed by a deep peal of thunder and the whole family looked round them, surprised to see that dusk had crept up on them. Jeff wanted a cigarette, but he'd given up smoking—it was unhealthy, and both he and Julie agreed that it set a bad example for Jeff Jr.—so he took out a pack of sugarless gum and offered it round instead.

"That last one was close," Julie said, the glow of the fire playing off her smooth dependable features. She looked good, tough, a pioneer woman who'd fight off the Indians with one hand and burp babies with the other. "Good thing you thought to hang the groundcloth. You think I should put up the tent—I mean with this roof and all?"

He was wise, fatherly, firm. "No," he said, "we'll be all right."
"What about the story, Dad?"
"Yeah. Well. It was a stormy night like this one and Billy Bowlegs
and his men smeared their faces with mud on Billy's Island and
then poled their dugouts to the edge of the swamp. There was a
white family there, settlers, who'd just come from, from—from
New York—"
"Aw, come on, Dad—you're making it up."
"No, no: I read it. Really. Anyway, there were three of them,
husband, wife and son—a boy about your age, Jeffie—and they
had a dog and some cattle, a mule, I think. Farmers. They'd drained
a couple of acres and were trying to grow cotton and tobacco in
the rich soil underneath. They'd been there a couple of months, I
think it was—they hadn't even been able to get a house up. All
they had was a lean-to, on a platform like this, a roof, but the sides
were open—"
"Dad."
Jeff ignored the interruption. He had him now, he knew it. He
gave Julie a furtive wink. "Billy Bowlegs told his men to take the
woman and leave the men for dead. But the rain was coming down
so hard one of the Indians slipped and fell and the musket went
off, just as the rest of them were coming out of the bushes with a
whoop. 'Run!' the father shouted, and all of a sudden there were
tomahawks and arrows everywhere, but the son and mother took
off and the father fired his gun to give them a headstart and then
he ran too. But you know what?"
Jeff Jr. was leaning so far forward he had to prop himself up on
his elbows. "What?" he said in a kind of gasp.
"They ran right out onto a peat island that had torn loose in the
storm and suddenly it was like they were running in a dream, going
as fast as they could and getting nowhere, and there was Billy
Bowlegs, his face streaked with mud, the tomahawk raised over his
head—"
At that moment a gust of wind tore loose the binding of the
groundcloth and it collapsed, dousing them with a wild oceanic

spray. Suddenly it was pouring, whipping in through the opening
and gushing through the colander of the roof. In the confusion, Jeff
sprang to his feet and shot a glance out back of the platform, while
Julie and Jeff Jr. howled and scrambled for their rain slickers, and
what he saw there froze him in place. A figure had materialized
from the gloom, and it wasn't the acrobatic alligator and it wasn't
the bear they'd missed either. Bowlegged, tattered, smeared with
mud and filth, it was the figure of Billy Bowlegs himself.

.   .   .

FOR HIS PART, HIRO DIDN'T KNOW WHAT TO THINK. THERE WAS A
storm coming, it was getting dark and he'd been bitten six or eight
times by every last mosquito on earth, not to mention their cousins,
the ticks, chiggers, deerflies and gnats. Choking on mud and vomit,
carved hollow as a gourd with hunger, he'd staggered out of a bog,
scattering birds, reptiles and frogs, and into a stand of trees where
the water was shallower, the mud firmer. Hours back, when the
sun stood directly overhead, he'd blundered across a raft of bitter
purple-black berries and crouched in the ooze, gorging till they
came back up like the dregs of a bad bottle of wine. For a long
while he lay there enervated, cursing himself, his *hakujin* father and
strong-legged mother, cursing Ruth—she'd betrayed him, the
bitch, used him for her story, her fiction, used him on a whim and
then discarded him like so much human rubbish. The water cradled
him. He closed his eyes on a hail of mosquitoes and slept afloat.
And then, as the sun dropped out of the sky and every animate
thing in the swamp came to him for its hourly ration of Japanese
blood, his senses reawakened. It was a sound that got him going
first—a soft lilting incongruous melody weaving in and out of the
cacophony of roars and grunts and screeches that tore at him without remit. Was it a flute? Was somebody playing a flute out here
in the hind end of nowhere? And then his sense of smell kicked in
and the knowledge of cookfire and meat came to him.

   The storm broke round him as he lurched out of the trees and
up onto the bed of semifirm mud, something like earth beneath his

feet once again—a small miracle in itself—but what lay before him was a puzzle. A crude structure, nothing more than a lean-to really, struggled out of the tangle a hundred feet away, and there were people inhabiting it, *hakujin*, gathered round a fire. Was this a house? Were these hillbillies—or swampbillies? And what was a "billy" anyway—some sort of goat, wasn't it?—and how could anyone, swampbilly or no, actually live here? But then this was America, and nothing about these people would surprise him. Whether they were buffalo skinners, young Republicans or crack dealers, it was all the same to him—he was dying of the wet and hunger and a despair that was all talons and claws and wouldn't let go of him, and he needed them.

Still, dying or not, this was nothing to rush into. He recalled the bug-eyed Negro fighting for his oysters, the girl in the Coca-Cola store, Ruth, who'd lulled him into submission only to turn on him and cut his heart out. He smelled the meat, saw the shelter, imagined what it would be like to dry himself, if only for a minute . . . but how could he approach these billies? What would he say? Pleading hunger was no good, as the Negro had taught him; the Clint Eastwood approach had backfired too, though he'd been satisfied with his curses, proud of them even. The only thing that had worked was dissimulation: Ambly Wooster had believed he was someone called Seiji, and if she'd believed him, maybe these people would too. But he had to be cautious. Living out here—he still couldn't believe it—they had to be primitive and depraved. What was that movie, with the city dwellers in canoes and the hillbillies attacking them from the cliffs?

But now they'd seen him. The lightning flashed, the rain drove at him. There was a man standing there on the platform, wearing a dazed and frightened expression—it looked bad already—and he was yelling something and the other two—a woman and a boy—froze. What was he saying? Oh, yes. Yes. The *hakujin* war cry: "Can we help you?"

Hiro stared at them and then glanced round him at the rain-washed swamp. He was beaten, starved, swollen with insect bites, filthy, saturated, anemic with loss of blood—and it seemed as if it had been going on all his life. He took a chance. Let them shoot him, let them string him up and nail him to a cross, flay the skin from his bones, devour him: he didn't care. Ruth had betrayed him. The City of Brotherly Love was a fraud. There was the swamp, only the swamp. "Toor-ist!" he called, echoing the girl in the store. "Fall out of boat!"

Nothing. No reaction. The two smaller faces flanked the larger and the three pairs of rinsed-out eyes fastened on him like pincers. The wind screamed. The trees danced. "Toor-ist!" Hiro repeated, cupping his hands to his mouth.

What followed was as astonishing as anything that had happened since he'd taken the plunge from the wingdeck of the *Tokachi-maru*: they believed him. "Hold on!" the man called as he might have called to a drowning child, and in the next moment he was down off the platform and splashing toward him through the mire. It was nothing short of a rescue. The man threw Hiro's arm over his shoulder as if he were a casualty of war, as if the rain were a shower of bullets and hot shrapnel, and scuttled back with him to the shelter, where the woman and boy were in motion too, hastily hanging some sort of dropcloth as a protection against the elements. Within minutes the fire was snapping, he was toweling his hair dry and the man was offering him a sleeping bag to wrap himself up in. Then the kettle sang out and a Styrofoam cup of hot instant noodles was thrust into his hand and he was eating while the three fed the fire, stopped the holes in the roof and watched him with bleeding eyes. "More?" the man asked after Hiro had finished, and when he nodded yes, a second Cup O'Noodles appeared as if he'd conjured it.

"You'll need dry clothes," the man said, and before he could even communicate the need to the woman, she was digging through a backpack crammed with shirts, shorts, towels and socks. Backpack? Were they campers, then? And if they were, why weren't they camping out on the clean sweet dry expanse of the open prairie instead of in this sewer? *Gaijin:* he would never understand them,

not if he lived to be a hundred and four. They offered him clothing—a T-shirt that bore a huge childish drawing of a smiling face
and the legend WORLD'S GREATEST DAD, a pair of too-tight underwear
and cut-off blue jeans that would never have fit him if he hadn't
suffered so much privation of the *hara*. Hiro went off into the far
corner to dress, all the while bowing and asserting his gratitude,
calculating *on* and giving thanks so profuse he could have raised a
shrine to them. Did he want more to eat? He did. And then it was
meat snapping on the grill, potato chips, hard-boiled eggs, carrot
sticks, cabbage salad and pound cake. "*Dōmo,*" he said, over and
over, "*dōmo arigatō.*"

They were watching him. Sitting there in a semicircle before
him, hands clasped to their knees, eyes aglow with charity and
fellow-feeling. They watched him eat as a doting young mother
might watch her baby spooning up his mashed peas and carrots,
hanging on every bite. Inevitably, though, now that they'd rescued
and fed him, the questions began. "You're a Filipino?" the man
asked as Hiro fed a wedge of pound cake into his mouth.

Careful, careful. He'd decided that the best policy—the only
policy—was to lie. "Chinese," he said.

Their faces showed nothing. The smoke swirled. Hiro reached
for the last piece of pound cake. "And you were out here on a day
trip?" the man persisted.

Day trip, day trip: what was he talking about? "Excuse and
forgive me, but what is this 'day trip'?"

"In the swamp. As a tourist—like us." For some reason the man
laughed at this, a hearty, beautifully formed laugh that bespoke
ease and health and success in business, and which burst from an
orthodontic marvel of a mouth. "I mean, did your boat overturn,
was anyone hurt? Were you alone?"

"Alone," Hiro said, leaping at the answer provided for him. He
felt that a smile would be helpful at this juncture, and so he gave
them one, misaligned teeth and all. This lying business wasn't so
hard really. It was the American way, he saw that now. He was
amazed that he'd had such trouble with it at Ambly Wooster's.

They were the Jeffcoats, from Atlanta, Georgia. From New York, actually. Jeff, Julie and Jeff Jr. (The boy blushed when his father introduced him.) Hiro bowed to each in turn. And then they were watching him again, but with a look of expectation now. What? he wanted to ask them. What is it?

"And you are—?" the man prompted.

"Oh!" Hiro let a little gasp of embarrassed surprise escape him. "How silly. Forgetful. I am—" and then he stopped cold. Who was he? He'd told them he was Chinese, hadn't he? Chinese, Chinese: what did the Chinese call themselves? Lee, Chan, Wong? There was a place called Yee Mee Loo two blocks from his *obāsan*'s apartment, but the name was ridiculous—he, Hiro Tanaka, standard-bearer for Mishima and Jōchō before him, couldn't be a Yee Mee Loo. Never.

"Yes?" They were leaning forward, smiling like zombies, all three of them, absolutely delighted to be out here in this drizzling hellhole exchanging pleasantries with a mud-smeared Chinaman. Rain dripped from the timbers overhead, fell like shot on the surface of the water before them.

"I am called . . . Seiji," he decided finally—what would they know, Americans; how would they know a Chinese from an Ugandan?—"Seiji . . . Chiba."

And then, feeling expansive, dry and warm and wrapped in a down blanket, his stomach full for the first time in days, he told them the pathetic story of his misadventures in the swamp. His boat had overturned, yes, two days ago—it was a crocodile that attacked him. It dropped from the trees on him and he wrestled with it, but the boat went under and he lost everything, all his bags of meat, his Cracker Jack, his Levi's and his surfboard. And so he wandered, on the verge of death, eating berries and drinking from the swamp, until they rescued him—and he ended by praising them for a full five minutes, in English and Japanese both.

When he was finished, there was a silence. The storm had let up and insects had begun to whine through the fevered air; something bellowed in the night. "Well," the man said, clapping his hands together like a referee, "I guess we all better turn in, huh? It's been quite a day."

. . .

SOMETIME IN THE DEEP STILL VIBRATING HUB OF THAT NIGHT, when the chittering and hooting and screeching had subsided to a muted roar and the new generation of mosquitoes lay waiting to be born, Hiro awoke shivering and discovered that the rain had started up again. He knew where he was at once and knew too that the insulated blanket they'd given him—these *Amerikajin* seemed to have two of everything—was soaked through. The wind had shifted to the north and there was the unmistakable scent of autumn on it. But what month was it? August? September? October? He had no idea. He'd been gone so long, living like a bum on the street, like a barbarian in a cave, that he didn't even know what month it was, let alone what day or hour. Shivering, he thought about that, and began to feel very sorry for himself indeed.

They would be after him soon, he knew that. The *bōifurendo* would go to the police and the tired pointy-nosed little sheriff would round up his Negroes and dogs and take a flotilla into the swamp, speedboats and pontoon boats, canoes and dinghies and floating jail cells. The spatterface and his hard little companion would be there, Ruth, Captain Nishizawa—they'd batter the trees with helicopters, tear open the sky with their sirens and the long-drawn-out blood-thirsty howls of the dogs. If they hated him two days ago, they loathed him now to the depths of their being. He'd made fools of them. And they would come after him with everything they had.

It was a shame. It was. If that Mercedes had belonged to anyone but the chief butter-stinker himself, if it had belonged to an itinerant peddler, an encyclopedia salesman, a hit man, Hiro could have been a thousand miles away by now—in the Big Sky Country, in Motown or at the Golden Gate. But it hadn't, and he wasn't. What he needed, he realized with a jolt of intuition, was a boat. If he had a boat he could paddle his way to the edge of the swamp, strike out cross-country and find a road, and then—then what? More double-dealing? More hate? More *hakujin* backstabbing and Negro viciousness? Yes, and what choice did he have—they were going to hunt him down like an animal. He lay there, wet and miserable, wrapped in his sheet of lies, and he hardened his heart. He knew where there was a boat. A canoe. Sleek and quick and provisioned for an army.

The Jeffcoats slept as one, the gentle stertor of their breathing synchronized, sleep a reward, their goods spread out round them like an emperor's ransom. The canoe lay there in the shadows at the edge of the platform, blackly bobbing. He could have spat in it from where he lay. But what was he thinking? They'd been kind to him, like Ambly Wooster. There was no hate in their eyes, only health and confidence. How could he steal from them, how could he abandon them to their fate out here in the howling wilderness?

How? Easily. They were *hakujin*, after all, *hakujin* like all the others, and after they found out who he was they'd lock him up themselves, twist the handcuffs tight with the cracked porcelain gleam of righteousness in their eyes. He was a Japanese. A samurai. To be ruthless was his only hope.

He was about to make his move, about to slip out of the wet blanket and stir himself to betrayal, when the boy began to moan in his sleep. The sound was incongruous and devastating in the dead black night. "Uhhhhhh," the boy groaned, swallowed up in his dreams, "uhhhhhh." In the space of that groan Hiro was plunged back into his own boyhood, awakened to the demons that haunted his nights and the birdlike embrace of his grandfather, and then a figure rose up in the dark—the father, the boy's father—and Hiro heard the gentle shushing, the susurrus of comfort and security. Father, mother, son: this was a family. He let the apprehension wash over him until it became palpable, undeniable, until he knew that the canoe, his only hope, would stay where it was.

He woke to the smell of corned beef hash and eggs. It was an unusual smell—aside from the slop Chiba concocted, he'd had little experience of foreign foods—but he recognized the habitual *hakujin* odor of incinerated meat. "Seiji!" a voice chirped at him the moment he opened his eyes. It was Julie Jeffcoat. She was in shorts and a shell top that emphasized her breasts, motherly and sexy all at once. "Sleep well?" she asked, crossing the platform to hand him a cup of simmering black coffee. The sun was up. It was hot already. Jeff Jr. perched at the edge of the platform, methodically flicking a lure from the tip of his rod to the far edge of the pond and then drawing it back again, while his father bent over the canoe, stowing away their gear in tight precise little bundles. He whistled while he worked. "Well," he boomed, glancing over his shoulder at Hiro, "ready for some breakfast, pardner?"

Dazed by the assault of cheer and energy, Hiro could only nod his assent. He was feeling a bit queasy—but then why wouldn't he, with all he'd been through—and he hoped the food would help steady him.

Jeff Jeffcoat turned back to his work. Jeff Jr.'s line sizzled through the guys and there was a distant splash. Hiro sat up to blow at his coffee and Julie Jeffcoat presented him with a plastic plate heaped with eggs, hashed meat, puffed potatoes and fruit cocktail from a can. It looked like something Chiba would whip up for one of his western-style lunches. "Ketchup?" Julie asked, and when he nodded, she squirted a red paste over everything.

"Denver omelet, yes?" Hiro said.

Julie Jeffcoat smiled, and it was a beautiful *Amerikajin* smile, uncomplicated and frank, a smile that belonged on the cover of a magazine. "Sort of," she said.

Half an hour later, Hiro watched Jeff Jeffcoat steady the canoe as first Jeff Jr. and then Julie eased themselves into the narrow trembling envelope of the vessel. It was heaped to the gunwales with the neatly stowed paraphernalia of their adventure in the wilderness, with their cooler, their charcoal and starter fluid, their binoculars and fishing rods and mess kit, their tents and sleeping bags and changes of clothing, their paperback books, flashlights, lip balm and licorice. There was no room for Hiro. Jeff Jeffcoat had assured him that they would paddle straight back to the boat launch and get a ranger to come rescue him. He looked pained—

he *was* pained—because they couldn't take Hiro with them. But Hiro—or Seiji, as they knew him—wouldn't be forgotten, he had Jeff's word on that.

Before he shoved off, Jeff Jeffcoat had impulsively sprung from the canoe to shuck his loafers and hand them to Hiro. "Here," he said, "I've got another two pairs in my backpack, and you're going to need these more than I do." Hiro accepted the shoes with a bow. They were Top-Siders, the sort of shoes the blond surfers wore in the beer commercials on Japanese television. Hiro slipped them on, feeling like a surfer himself in the cutoffs and oversized T-shirt, as Jeff Jeffcoat eased back into the canoe and shoved off with a mighty thrust of the paddle. "So long," he called, "and don't worry: they'll be here to get you by noon. I promise."

" 'Bye!" Jeff Jr. cried, shrill as a bird.

Julie turned to wave. "Bye-bye," she called, and her voice was like Ruth's, and for a moment it stirred him. "You take care now."

They'd left him food, of course—six sandwiches, a Ziploc bag crammed with marshmallows, three plums, two pears and a sack of tortilla chips the size of a laundry bag, not to mention the two-liter bottle of orange soda with which to wash it all down. "Sank you," Hiro called, "sank you so much," wondering if *on* could be calculated in the negative, for what wasn't done as well as what was. He owed them a debt, an enormous debt—but then they owed him too. He hadn't bludgeoned them to death, hadn't stolen their food, their canoe, their paddles and fishing rods and charcoal briquettes. When you came right down to it, he'd sacrificed himself for them—and wasn't that something?

He stood there on the platform a long while, watching them as they threaded their way up the narrow channel, paddles flashing in perfect harmony, father, mother, son.

Tender Sproats

. . . .

THERE WERE TWO MOTELS IN CICEROVILLE, "GATEWAY TO THE
Okefenokee Wilderness," and both were on the order of refugee
camps as far as Detlef Abercorn was concerned. The first, Lila's
Sleepy Z, featured a miniature golf course in the middle of the
parking lot and a café with a hand-lettered sign in the window
offering breakfast for 99¢, with unlimited refills of coffee and grits.
It was booked solid. The other place, the Tender Sproats, enticed
the weary traveler with a swimming pool filled to the coping with
what appeared to be split pea soup. Abercorn thought of all those
billboards along Interstate 80 touting homemade split pea soup, as
if anyone in any condition would ever actually want split pea soup
beyond the first spoonful. This was an improvement: here you got
to swim in it. He shrugged and pulled into the lot.

It wasn't as if he was planning to spend much time in the swimming pool anyway. His job was on the line here—his whole career.
Forget the le Carré, the six-pack and the air-conditioned room alive
only to the soothing flicker of the color TV; from here on out it
was more like James M. Cain, a cup of piss-water doused with
iodine, sweat, sunburn and aching joints. He'd had a call early that
morning from Nathaniel Carteret Bluestone, the regional head in
Atlanta. Real early. Six-thirty A.M. early. He was never at his best

at 6:30 A.M., but he'd been out past two tramping all over the island with Turco and the sheriff and about six hundred yapping dogs on the lukewarm trail of Hiro Tanaka and when he picked up the phone he was so exhausted he could barely think.

N. Carteret Bluestone had wanted to know why Special Agent Abercorn was bent on making a mockery of the INS. Had he seen the morning papers? No? Well, perhaps he'd find them instructive. The Nip—Japanese, Bluestone corrected himself—was front-page news all of a sudden. Abercorn tried to explain that the papers were a day late at Thanatopsis House, but Bluestone talked right over him, quoting the headlines in an acidic tone: " 'At Large 6 Weeks, In Jail 6 Hours'; 'Score 1 for the Japanese, 0 for the INS'; 'Jailbreak on Tupelo Island: Alien Makes It Look Easy.' " And what was this about Lewis Turco attacking some woman and making wild—and litigious—accusations? It was a mighty sorry way to run an investigation, mighty sorry.

Abercorn couldn't argue with him there, except maybe to add that "sorry" was far too tame an adjective. He could have offered excuses—it was the sheriff's people who'd let the suspect go; *he* hadn't attacked anybody and couldn't answer for Turco; everybody down here talked like Barney Fife and had an IQ to match—but he didn't. All he said was, "I'll do my best, sir."

Bluestone opined that his best seemed to fall short of the mark. Far short.

"I'll do my damnedest, sir," Abercorn said.

There was a pause on the other end of the line. "You do that," Bluestone said finally. "And this time, handcuff the suspect to your own goddamned wrist. And do me a favor—"

"Yes?"

"Swallow the key, will you, so it comes out with the rest of your shit."

News of the second call, the one from Roy Dotson, didn't reach him till nearly four in the afternoon. And why not? Because he was out in the boondocks, sifting through the mudholes of Tupelo Island, as if anybody believed it would do any good. If they were looking for frogs they would have been in heaven. Or mosquitoes. The temperature was up around a hundred, the sun had ground to a halt directly overhead and he thought he was just about to die from the stink when one of Peagler's deputies came sloshing toward them with the news that they were wasting their time. The suspect had fled the island. And where was he? In a sharecropper's shack? Hitchhiking to Jacksonville? Digging his chopsticks into a plate of shaved beef and onions at a sukiyaki joint in downtown Atlanta? No. He was in a swamp, another swamp, a swamp that made this one look like a wading pool.

And so here he was at the Tender Sproats Motel in Ciceroville, Georgia, Gateway to the Okefenokee Wilderness. It was seven-thirty at night and the neon sign glowed against the darkening sky in a halfhearted imposture of civilization. Lewis Turco was asleep in the passenger seat, reeking like a sewage plant. Mud encrusted his boots, clung to his fatigues, caked his beard and hair. They'd had a falling-out over the Dershowitz incident and hadn't spoken more than ten words to each other all day. The moment the bulletin came through on Tanaka, Turco had dropped his stick (he'd been beating the bushes, literally), and without a word turned and stomped back to the big house, where he flung his gear into the Datsun and settled into the passenger seat. By the time Abercorn got there he was unconscious.

Abercorn pulled up to the motel office and shut down the wheezing engine. He figured he would check in, have a quick shower and a cup of coffee, coordinate with the local sheriff and interview Roy Dotson at his home. Then he would get a couple hours' sleep and start the chase again in the morning. That was the plan. But he was tired, bone tired, and he didn't smell too great himself.

The man behind the counter was short and dark, with the narrow shoulders and fleshless limbs of a child. He had the gut of an adult though, and a well-fed one, and he wore a caste mark beneath the greasy bill of his feedstore cap. His glittering dark eyes went directly to Abercorn's face—he'd burned out there in the swamp, he knew it, and the burn made the dead-white discolorations of his condition stand out more than ever. Suddenly he felt self-conscious. "I need a double," he said.

"Y'all mean a twin?" the little man drawled.

"Double," Abercorn said. "Two beds. One for me and one for— for him." He jerked a thumb over his shoulder in the direction of the car, where Turco's head and upthrust beard could just be made out over the dashboard.

The little man broke into a grin that showed off the bright red stubble of his teeth. He ducked down to spit something into a wastebasket under the counter, and then bounced back up again. "A twee-in, like Ah said. For a minute there—y'all ain't from around Clinch County, am Ah correct in that assumption?"

Abercorn could feel the weariness settling into him like a drug, like the tingle of a good double shot of tequila on an empty stomach. Japanese. He should have stayed in Eagle Rock, busting Mexicans. "Savannah," he managed. "L.A. originally."

"Uh-huh, uh-huh." The little man was nodding his head vig- orously. "Ah coulda sworn it. Thought you was a Yankee—and for a minute there maybe a little, you know, funny. Wantin' a double for two grown men . . ."

Abercorn was dragging, worn thin, but a tiny knot of inspiration flared in his brain. "Punjabi, right?" he said.

The little man beamed. "Chandigarh."

"A twin. I need a twin."

"Good," the little man said, beaming still, beaming till he could have lit the room all by himself. "We take all kinds here."

· ■ ·

TURCO WAS IN A COMMUNICATIVE MOOD THE FOLLOWING MORNING, chattering on about the suspect as if they'd grown up together, as if they'd shared a bed in the orphanage and married sisters. "He's a cagey one, this Nip—a whole lot cagier than we give him credit for, that's for sure. He got this bitch to feed him—two bitches, if you count the old lady—and then he has the balls to bust out of jail and make for the last place on earth we'd expect to find him."

He paused reflectively and scratched at his newly washed beard. "Still, they don't take to nature, the Nips—they're a city people, subways and pigeons and that kind of thing—and ultimately he's going to defeat himself, I'm about three-quarters sure of that."

They were in the Datsun, heading into the swamp. It had rained the night before and the road was slick, but the sun was up already and burning it off in a dreamy drifting haze. Abercorn had gotten about four hours of fitful sleep, while Turco, who'd strung a hammock over the second bed, had snored blissfully through the small hours of the morning and well into the dawn. They'd passed on breakfast, nothing open that early but Hardee's and a truck stop so full of potbellied crackers Abercorn couldn't handle it and ordered a coffee to go. It was no loss to Turco, who seemed to have an infinite supply of roots and jerky tucked away in the folds of his rucksack. At the moment, he had a plastic bag of what looked to be dried guppies in his lap. From time to time he'd dip a hand into the bag and crunch them up like popcorn.

"And if you're thinking disco and designer shirts, it ain't going to work on this character," Turco added, as if the ghetto blaster and Guess? jeans had been Abercorn's idea in the first place. "No: we're going to have to get a lot more devious than that." He scratched his beard and a gentle drift of flaked guppy settled in his lap.

Abercorn looked away. Ever since the interview with Roy Dotson, something had been troubling him. It was the question of Saxby. He liked Saxby, he did. And he didn't think Saxby would consciously aid and abet a criminal—and an IAADA, at that—but it did look pretty bad. Ruth was capable of anything—he knew that from personal experience—and she could have put him up to it. Easily. "What do you think of Saxby, Lewis—I mean as far as his involvement in this thing?"

Turco turned to give him a look. "Who?"

"Saxby. You know, Ruth's—I mean, Dershowitz's—uh—"

"Oh, him. Yeah. He's guilty. As guilty as she is. What do you think, it's just a coincidence that he brings this Nip out here and lets him go like Br'er Rabbit in the briar patch? Are you kidding me? The guy's as guilty as Charlie Manson, Adolf Hitler—and if he's not, then what's he doing camping out in the middle of the Okefenokee Swamp?" He dug into the bag of flaked fish. "The whole thing stinks if you ask me."

They'd passed the sign welcoming them to Stephen C. Foster State Park several miles back and yet there was no indication that anyone except a construction crew had ever been here before them. The road cut a straight and undeviating line through the wet and the green, a green so absolute that Abercorn had to glance up periodically at the sky to be sure what planet he was on. He supposed some people found this beautiful or inspiring or whatever, but to him it was just one more pain in the ass—they could make a parking lot out of the goddamned place as far as he was concerned. He couldn't stop thinking about Saxby and how embarrassing it was going to be to have to put the cuffs on him, if it came to that. And beyond Saxby, he was thinking of the Nip—and yes, he'd call a Nip a Nip and INS etiquette be damned—and wondering if he was going to spend the rest of his life getting sunburned three different colors and having his ears chewed off by mosquitoes the size of hummingbirds. (And that rankled him too—why the ears, of all places? His own ears, never exactly small by any measure, were swollen to twice their normal size and looked like slabs of salami stuck to the side of his head.) He drove on, trying not to look at himself in the rearview mirror.

Finally, buildings began to appear—long low wooden structures, a museum, a tourist center—and then he was pulling into a dirt lot behind a phalanx of police cars, two fire trucks and an ambulance. The lot was jammed with campers and pickups and there were people everywhere, though it was early, very early, so early it should have been the shank of the night still. People milled around the boats, peeked in the windows of the police cars, twirled binoculars round their necks, breakfasted out of picnic baskets, lifted brown paper bags to their lips. Bare-legged kids tore across the macadam, trying to lift kites into the lifeless air, an old man was watching TV in the back of a jeep and a woman with big meaty arms and breasts backed away from a battered Ford with a birdcage and set it down in the middle of the lot. It was crazy. It was like the Fourth of July or the beginning of a music festival, only worse. Abercorn felt his stomach sink.

"Lewis, you don't think all these people—?" he began, but the idea of it, the fear of it, locked the words in his throat and he couldn't go on. These people weren't just happy campers and holiday makers gathered here inadvertently at 7 A.M. on a weekday morning. No. They were gathered here as they gathered at the site of any disaster, patient as vultures. They were waiting for bloodshed, violence, criminality and despair, waiting for excess and humiliation, for the formula that would unlock the tedium of their lives. "But how in christ's name did they know? We just found out about the Nip—I mean, the Japanese—I mean, the Nip—ourselves. Am I right?"

Turco didn't answer, but he looked grim.

The moment Abercorn swung open the door a group of people detached themselves from the crowd and converged on him. He'd noticed them out of the corner of his eye as he maneuvered into the parking space—they were too well dressed for tourists and they seemed nervous, edgy, as if they were about to break into a trot, and what was that, a camera?—but now everything came clear: the press. They were on him before he could unfold himself from the car and there was his face, swollen ears and all, staring back at him in three angry colors from the dark eye of the TV camera.

"Mr. Abercorn!"—his name, they knew his name—"Mr. Abercorn!"

A woman with a plastic face and frozen hair had squared off in front of him like a wrestler. She looked familiar, looked like someone he'd seen on television, back in the days when he had an apartment, an office, when he was a member of society with a dull nine-to-five job like everyone else. TV, he thought, hey, I'm going to be on TV, and felt a little jolt of excitement despite himself. But then he understood that N. Carteret Bluestone was sure to see him there and he felt his stomach clench round the pool of cheap diner coffee that churned there, deep down, eating at him like battery acid.

What had begun as a little story, a six-line thing on page 28 of the *Savannah Star*, something to fill the odd space left over after they printed up the specials on boneless chicken and toilet paper, was now a big story, a TV story. He should have seen it coming. This was a real potboiler, after all, full of sex, violence, miscegenation, hair-raising escapes, swamps teeming with snakes and alligators, rumors of official incompetence and collusion on the part of a bunch of suspect writers and artists. Christ, it could be a soap opera, a miniseries. *As the Swamp Turns. From Here to Okefenokee. Jap Hunter.*

The woman with the plastic face wanted to know why it had taken the INS better than six weeks to capture this fugitive—and what about allegations of incompetence? She furrowed her brow in an investigatory frown, as if it hurt her to put such hard questions. Before Abercorn could frame an answer, a fiftyish man with a savage nose and forearms bristling with white hair poked a microphone at him and asked what the problem was with the security at the Tupelo Island prison facility—was somebody napping on the job? And if so, who?

And then the voices rose in a clamor: How did he feel about working with the local authorities? What was the suspect eating out there? Did they expect to catch him soon? Was he dangerous? What about quicksand? Snakes? Alligators? What about Ruth Dershowitz?

Abercorn found himself backed up against the car, feeling two feet taller than he already was, feeling naked and conspicuous, his face reddening like bratwurst on a rotisserie. There were too many of them and they were all jabbing at him at once. He'd never had to deal with the public before, never been asked a single question about a case, not even by telephone, not even the time the Hmong microwaved the chihuahua and the AKC compared them to Nazis at Auschwitz. His tongue thickened in his throat. He didn't know what to say. And he might have stood there eternally, looking stupid

in living color for N. Carteret Bluestone and half the rest of the
world, if it hadn't been for Turco. "No comment," Turco snarled,
slashing through the thicket of microphones with a homicidal leer
and jerking him by the arm. And then they were moving, briskly,
heading for the cover of the police cordon and the clutch of clean-
shaven men in uniform gathered beyond it.

Abercorn recognized the man at the center of the clutch: Sheriff
Bull Tibbets of the Ciceroville Police Department. If Theron Peagler had been something of a surprise—college-educated, soft-
spoken, intelligible—Sheriff Tibbets was just what he'd expected.
He was a grim-looking fat man with a wad of tobacco bloating his
cheek, a big-brimmed trooper's hat shoved back on his head and a
pair of mirror sunglasses masking eyes that were too small and dull
to be fully human. He'd given Abercorn a look of undisguised
contempt at the Ciceroville station the preceding night, and now
he didn't so much as turn his head as he and Turco joined the
group. There seemed to be a debate going on, but Abercorn couldn't
catch much of what they were saying—the accent was pure hell
down here, sounded like they were chewing on sweatsocks or
something.

"Gawl rawl, rabid rib," the sheriff said.

The man beside him—he was like a toy compared to the sheriff
and as slippery, low-browed and loose-jointed as a Snopes—pressed
the point. When he spoke, he sounded as if he were in great pain.

There was a moment's silence, and then the sheriff rolled his
massive head back on his neck, exposing a spatter of angry red
pustules just beneath his chin and flashing the heavens with the
light reflecting off his sunglasses. "Gawl rawl," he repeated himself,
"rabid rib."

Turco folded his arms. He looked bored, looked impatient. In
the distance, yet another bird, all legs and wings, swooped across
the cremated sky. "What's the deal?" Abercorn asked.

Turco lowered his voice. "The squirrely guy wants to bring the
dogs in, sheriff says no." He gazed out over the landing, the weeds
and muck and the mad growth of trees, narrowing his eyes as if

he expected to spot the suspect sculling across the horizon. "Dogs are prohibited here," he added by way of clarification. "Park regulations. Alligators go crazy for them, overturn canoes, jump right up out of the water to snatch them off the dock. It's like catnip to a cat."

Abercorn was dumbfounded. Alligators! Jesus. The more he learned about this place, the more he longed for Hollywood Boulevard.

They stood there another minute, listening to the sheriff and his men chew socks at one another, and then they were moving again, Turco leading, Abercorn following. "These guys are a bunch of cheesebags," Turco pronounced, spitting the words over his shoulder. Abercorn couldn't have agreed more, but wondered where exactly they were going and how it was going to help them capture, prosecute, imprison and deport Hiro Tanaka and get N. Carteret Bluestone off his back. And beyond that, how it was going to get him out of Crackerland and back to the mossy somnolent streets of Savannah and the attentions of girls like Ginger and Brenda who wanted only to sip juleps, eat oysters and fuck athletically on the rug in front of the air conditioner. Turco was leading him back toward the police cordon and the tourist center beyond it.

"Where are we going, Lewis—what's the plan?"

Turco paused on the steps, for once eye-to-eye with him. "I say we get hold of one of these powerboats and go bust this Saxby clown. He'll tell you where the Nip is, believe me."

Abercorn didn't know if he actually wanted to bust Saxby—what charge were they talking here?—but having a conversation with him sounded like a good idea. And he really didn't feature hanging around and dealing with the sheriff, who looked about as receptive as a guard dog. He shrugged and followed Turco up the steps and into the tourist facility, where six blondes of varying shades and ages stood expectantly behind a counter, each trying to outgrin the other.

Turco strode directly up to the youngest, a girl with big watery blue eyes and a nameplate that identified her as Darlene. "We need a boat," he announced, giving her his LURP-from-hell look. She didn't seem to notice. "I'm sorry," she said, and she was just as sweet as rainwater, though her accent was strictly bayou, "but I have orders from Mr. Chivvers and Mr. Dotson to not let any boats out."

"For all in-tents and purposes, the park is closed," the blonde beside her announced. This one looked to be about forty and wore her hair in an elaborate confectionary ball. "We regret the inconvenience," she said, "but there's a maniac a-loose in the swamp."

"An Oriental man," added another.

"Killed somebody east of here, is what I heard," said the eldest, who must have been seventy and had the gift of speaking without moving her lips.

"Three grown men and a baby. Strangled them all," the one with the hair said. All six of them froze their smiles.

This was Abercorn's opening. He'd been hovering in the background, but now he stepped forward. "Special Agent Detlef Abercorn of the INS," he said, flashing his identification, "of the district office in Savannah. We're after that very man." He tried a smile himself. "That's why we need a boat."

"Well," the first girl, Darlene, wavered behind her official grin, "I don't know . . ." She turned to the blonde next to her, a woman of indeterminate age in secretarial glasses and a bright-patterned scarf. "Lu Ann, what you think?"

Just then Roy Dotson stepped through a door at the rear of the office. He was dressed in his park ranger's uniform and a pair of hip boots. "It's all right, Darlene, give these men what they want."

Darlene gazed up at Abercorn. She couldn't have been more than seventeen and her grin was cavernous. Abercorn had one of those brief and inevitable sexual thoughts, and then the business came back into her voice. "I'll need to see a driver's license," she said, "and a major credit card."

· · ·

ROY DOTSON SAT AT THE HELM OF THE EIGHTEEN-FOOT FLAT-
bottomed boat, running the engine at full speed, which wasn't
much. Turco was crouched in the bow with all his jungle-fighting
paraphernalia, his entrenching tools and wire cutters and whatnot
dangling from the frame of his pack. In the middle, almost enjoying
the ride despite himself, was Detlef Abercorn. He was wearing his
waders and he clutched a satchel full of halizone tablets, sun block,
6-12, *Off!* and calamine lotion as if he were afraid it would sprout
wings and fly away. He was also wearing a bright orange life jacket,
though he felt a little foolish in it. Roy Dotson had insisted on the
life jacket and Abercorn had obliged him for two reasons. The first
was purely diplomatic. Turco had informed Dotson, who was after
all going out of his way to help them, that he would shove it—the
life jacket—up his—Roy Dotson's—ass if he said another word
about it, and so Abercorn, in the spirit of pacification, had meekly
slipped into his own. The second reason was more basic: he was
scared witless about going out amongst the alligators and snakes
and felt he needed all the help he could get. With the waders and
life vest, the only place a snake could get him, he figured, was in
the face, and he planned to keep that portion of his anatomy high,
dry and out of reach.

Still, for all that, the ride wasn't half bad. The breeze kept the
mosquitoes off his swollen ears and dried the sweat at his temples,
and the swamp seemed a little less threatening now that he was
actually out on it. Nothing crept into his waders to bite, sting and
gouge him, no snakes dropped from the trees and the only alligator
he saw was the size of a woman's purse. He was surprised too that
there was open water—quite a bit of it. If he squinted his eyes
behind the prescription sunglasses with the clear plastic frames he
could almost imagine he was a boy again, out on Lake Casitas with
his dad and mom and brother Holger.

Another surprise was the dock at Billy's Island. There was actually a dock there, nothing much more than two posts sunk into
the murk and a grid of weathered boards, but a dock nonetheless.
And beyond the dock, terra firma. Or almost. He began to feel a

bit overdressed in his waders and life jacket—he'd pictured something out of *The African Queen*, up to his waist in quicksand and slime, but this was just plain old ordinary dirt. Or mud. A little spongy maybe but nothing that would have ruined his day if he'd been dressed in jeans, T-shirt and hiking boots.

Roy Dotson led the way, closely shadowed by Turco, who stepped lightly, tense and alert and hulking under the weight of his pack. Abercorn brought up the rear, loping along with his big gangling strides, ducking away from the squadrons of insects that converged on his every step and fanned out to anticipate the next. They were following a crude trail to the far side of the island, where, according to Roy Dotson, Saxby had set up his fishing camp the previous morning. ("Pygmy fish," Turco had snorted when Dotson told them the story. "You ask me, it's a cover is what it is.")

They walked in single file for a quarter of an hour under a canopy of slash pine that cut the sunlight to a muted dapple. The air was heavy here, so thick it was like another medium, and the heat had them running sweat till they were as drenched as if they'd swum the whole way from the tourist center. Salt pills, Abercorn thought, and he cursed himself for having forgotten them. He was wondering what happened to you when you ran out of salt in your system—you collapsed, didn't you, something to do with electrolytes, or was that batteries?—when Turco took hold of Roy Dotson's arm and the three of them halted. "What?" Dotson said. "What is it?"

Turco tightened his grip. "The camp," he breathed. Somewhere a bird began to cry out, hard and urgent, as if some unseen hand were plucking it alive. Roy Dotson started to say something but Turco cut him off with a hiss. "Shhhh!" he said, and his eyes had gone cold. "Stay here, both of you. I'm going in alone."

Abercorn saw nothing but tree trunks and leaves. The waders were a sweatbox, the life vest constricted his lungs. He sucked in a breath and coughed out insects.

"Shhhh!"

"Lewis—" Abercorn warned, meaning to point out that this was not the Ho Chi Minh Trail, appearances to the contrary, and that Saxby was not an armed and treacherous communist guerrilla but a decent guy who loved fish and Ruth Dershowitz, not to mention an American citizen with inalienable rights, and who probably wasn't involved in all this anyway, or at least not too deeply, but Turco gave him a look of such uncompromising fury that he gave it up. This was what Turco was paid for, this was what he was doing here—there was no stopping him now. Abercorn exchanged a look with Roy Dotson as Turco shrugged out of his pack and darted off silently through the undergrowth. Though he still saw nothing—no camp, no tent, no sign whatever of civilization—Abercorn fumbled for his tape recorder and notepad, feeling the excitement rise in him despite himself. Maybe Lewis was right after all, maybe the Nip *was* hiding out there with Saxby and they could throw the cuffs on him, pack it up and get out of this shithole for good.

Roy Dotson didn't think so. His mouth was drawn tight and an angry crease had appeared between his eyebrows. "The guy's crazy," he said in a terse whisper. "Like I told you, Sax was as shocked as I was to see that man there in the trunk of the car." Abercorn didn't respond. He'd fixed his eye on the tangle of growth into which Turco had disappeared, and now he started forward, moving as stealthily as could be expected from a six-foot-five-inch albino in a pair of hip waders. Roy Dotson shrugged and fell into step behind him.

Nothing moved. The forest was still, locked in the grip of the heat. The bird cried out again, terrible, lonely, hurt in some deep essential place. Abercorn kept his eyes on a conjunction of branches up ahead, the waders grunting and squelching beneath his sweat-soaked feet. He stepped over the stump of a felled tree, and then another. Mosquitoes settled on his arms, his face, the backs of his hands, and he didn't bother to swat them away.

And then, what he'd been waiting for: a shout. It ruptured the silence, a single mad stunned bellow of surprise that rose up to steal the heat from the trees. Suddenly they were running and nothing mattered but the snarl of voices up ahead and the sudden sharp snap of branches and the thrashing in the undergrowth. *The Nip!* Abercorn was thinking, *Turco's got the Nip!*, and in his excitement he shot ahead of Roy Dotson, his knees pumping, the waders flapping like sails in a high wind. There! Just ahead: a tent—how could he have missed it?—a circle of charred rocks, a fishing net strung from the trees. Another shout. A curse. And then he was there, stumbling over the cold cookfire as the figures of Saxby and Turco materialized from the camouflage of briar and palmetto.

They were on the ground, rocking in each other's arms, their legs flailing at the bush. Turco was all over Saxby, though Saxby had six inches and fifty pounds on him. "Get . . . off!" Saxby roared, but Turco had him in some sort of secret commando grip, forcing his face down into the wet earth, the handcuffs flashing in a shaft of sunlight. "Lewis!" Abercorn shouted, but Turco jerked the bigger man's arm back and cuffed his wrists. "Lewis, what the hell—?" Abercorn's voice was high. This was all wrong. This wasn't the way it was supposed to be . . .

"Det, are you crazy?" Saxby was furious, thrashing beneath Turco's weight, a single smear of reddish dirt ground like a scar into his cheek. "Get him off me!"

But Turco had him, and he wouldn't let go. He crouched atop him like a gnome, knee planted in the small of the back, left hand rigid at the base of the skull. "Shut it," he said, and his voice was calm, even, not a hint of adrenaline in it. "You're under arrest, motherfucker."

Cheap Thrills

∎ ∎ ∎ ∎ ∎ ∎ ∎

EVERYONE ELSE SIMPLY READ IN THE FRONT PARLOR BENEATH THE ancient brass chandelier, informally, comfortably, with the lights up and the colonists settled into easy chairs or stretched out languidly on the rug. There was coffee and sherry and there was always something sweet—cupcakes or cookies, often baked by Septima herself. It was homey, unthreatening, an arena in which an artist— no matter his or her status in the world beyond these walls—could present work in progress in an intimate and supportive atmosphere. If anything, the bias was anti-performance. You simply stood up there and read. No tricks, no gadgets, no histrionics. You read in a flat, unobtrusive voice, letting the work speak for itself—anything else would have been inappropriate, a violation of the unspoken rules and an embarrassment to your fellow colonists. In a word, rude. And you read in the front parlor, beneath the chandelier. Everyone did.

Everyone, that is, but Jane Shine.

No. Jane had to read out on the patio in the black of night, a single spot trained on her from overhead while a second light, more stagey and diffuse, played off her gypsy features from a box located in the azalea bushes. Ruth couldn't believe it. The colonists were shunted outside and forced into folding chairs all marshaled in neat rows, as if this were Shakespeare under the stars or something. Three minutes in one of those chairs was like an hour on the rack. It was outrageous. What was she thinking?

Ruth came in with Brie just as Septima was working her way to the front to introduce Jane. She passed up the opportunity to sit with Sandy, Ina and Regina in order to take the seats directly behind Mignonette Teitelbaum and Orlando Seezers, who was stationed in his wheelchair at the end of the aisle. After a flurry of hushed hellos and some pronounced and disapproving mosquito-swatting, Ruth settled in to study La Teitelbaum from the rear. Did they have sex? she wondered. It depended on how far down the spine he'd been injured, didn't it? Teitelbaum wasn't much in any case. She was only a couple years older than Ruth, but she really showed it—and her hair, her hair looked like that stuff they pack crates with—what was it called? There were lines in the back of her neck too. But not just lines—seams, grooves, ruts you could fall into.

Ruth's reverie was broken by the amplified blast of Septima's voice—a microphone, she was using a microphone for god's sake! No one had ever used a microphone at Thanatopsis before, and now, because of Jane Shine, Septima—the power behind the whole place, its founder and arbiter of its tastes and traditions—was speaking through a microphone. It was sickening. A perversion of everything Thanatopsis stood for. Ruth couldn't fathom how everyone could just sit there as if nothing were going on, as if this, this sound system and lights, had anything at all to do with a sharing of work in progress. She felt her scalp tense beneath the roots of her hair. "This is ridiculous," she hissed at Brie while Septima's genteel tones roared out over the treetops.

Brie turned to her, enraptured, her expression as vacant as a cow's, her big watery eyes swollen beneath the skin of her contacts. "What are you saying?" she hissed back. "I think it's—it's *magical.*"

". . . my very great pleasure, and a personal three-ill," Septima boomed; she was clutching at the microphone as if it were a cobra she'd discovered in bed and seized in desperation. Ruth saw Saxby's eyes in her eyes, Saxby's nose, pinched with age, in her nose. She was wearing a tan linen suit, beige pumps and the pearls she never seemed to take off, and she'd had her hair done. "I repeat, a three-ill, to introduce an extraordinarily gifted young writer, author of a prize-winnin' volume of stories and a novel forthcomin' from"—here Septima paused to squint at a 3×5 card she held tentatively in her soft veiny hand—"from"—she named a major New York house and Ruth felt her jaws clench with hate and jealousy; ". . . youngest winner ever, I am told, of the prestigious Hooten-Warbury Gold Medal in Literature, given annually in England for the best work of foreign fiction, and the equally prestigious—"

Ruth tried to tune her out, but the amplification made it impossible: Septima's stentorian words of praise throbbed in her chest, her lungs, her very bowels, vibrating there as if on a sounding board. Septima went on to compare Jane to just about every female writer in history, from Mrs. Gaskell to Virginia Woolf to Flannery O'Connor and Pearl S. Buck, using the term "prestigious" like a dental drill. (She must have used it twenty times at least—Ruth stopped counting at five.) And then finally, after what seemed an eternity, she wound it up with a carnival barker's enthusiasm: "Ladies and gentlemen, fellow artists and Thanatopsians"—yes, she actually said *Thanatopsians*—"I give you Jane Shine."

A burst of applause. Ruth felt ill. But where was she? Where was La Shine? Certainly not sitting quietly up front or standing modestly to one side of the microphone. People craned their necks, the applause fell off. But then, all at once, a murmur went up and the applause started in again, stronger than before—as if just by deigning to appear here before these mere mortals she should be congratulated—and there she was, Jane Shine, sweeping through the French doors and out onto the patio.

Her hair—her impossible gleaming supercharged mat of flamenco dancing hair—was piled up so high on her head all Ruth could think of was the changing of the guard at Buckingham Palace. Dressed all in black—another one of those high-collared faux-Victorian things she paraded around in like a lost princess—she moved through the crowd with quiet determination, a small frown etched on her lips—oh, this was serious business, this was high drama—looking straight ahead of her, her back stiff, her steps tiny, delicate, the nibbling little mincing steps of a girl on her way to school. Flamenco siren, Victorian princess, schoolgirl: who was she kidding?

The light caught her face perfectly, exquisitely—even Ruth had to admit it. The overhead spot set her hair aflame, made a corona of it, a diadem, a glittering ball of light and highlight, while the second spot, the softer one, put a glow into her extraterrestrial eyes and lit her bee-stung lips from beneath. "Collagen treatments," Ruth whispered to Brie, but Brie was mesmerized by the spectacle of Jane Shine, La Shine, who'd fucked her way to the top, and Brie didn't acknowledge her. Jane bowed. Thanked Septima. Thanked the audience. Thanked Owen and Rico and Raoul Von Somebody for the lighting and audio, and then she fastened her eyes on the audience and held them, in silence, for a full thirty seconds.

And then she began, without introduction, her voice as natural and attuned to the microphone as Septima's was not. Her voice was a caress, a whisper, something that got inside you and wouldn't come out. The story she read was about sex, of course, but sex couched in elaborate and gothic imagery that made high art of painting one's toenails and having a monthly period. Three lines into the story Ruth realized that this wasn't work in progress at all—this was a story Jane had published two years ago and then polished—and repolished—for her first collection. It was finished work. Old work. Nothing from the "forthcoming" novel or the pages she'd presumably turned out here. Instead she was perform-ing, giving them a set piece she'd read god knew how many times at the invitation of Notre Dame or Iowa or NYU. Ruth was so outraged—so pissed off, rubbed raw and just plain furious—that she nearly got up to leave. But then she couldn't, of course. If she did, everyone would think she was, well, jealous of Jane Shine or something—and she couldn't have them thinking that. Never. It would be like being gored out on the African veldt, vultures swooping in, hyenas laughing in the bush.

So she sat there, seething. Orlando Seezers brayed with a rich too-loud laugh when Jane's story ran to what passed for wit, and toward the end, where the star-crossed fourteen-year-old lovers paint each other's toenails prior to parting eternally, Mignonette Teitelbaum had to hold his hand to keep him from blubbering aloud. Jane was shameless. Not only did she pander to the audience, raving like a madwoman and repeatedly pushing a carefully coiffed strand of hair out of her face, she even did a Swedish accent as if she thought she was Meryl Streep or something (the boy was Swedish, a Nordic demigod in short pants; the girl, of course, was a Connecticut ingénue with the hair of a Catalonian shepherdess and outer-space eyes). When she was finished, there was a stunned silence, and then someone—was it Irving?—shouted "Yes!" and the applause fell on her like a landslide. Brie had tears in her eyes, and Ruth would never forgive her that. Sandy whistled and pounded his hands together till they were red, and Ruth would never forgive him either.

■   ■   ■

THE RECEPTION AFTERWARD WAS JUST ONE OF THOSE THINGS YOU had to live through. The last thing Ruth wanted was to stand around and congratulate Jane Shine, but she had no choice really. If it came right down to it she could put on a face and play the game, no problem. She loved Jane Shine. She'd been to school with her. She wished her well. Right?

If only it was that easy.

Someone put on a tape of old Motown hits—Marvin Gaye, Martha and the Vandellas, the Four Tops—and Ruth almost let the beat infect her, almost let go, until she realized that the music was for Jane, who'd made a big deal of praising it in a recent issue of *Interview*, a copy of which had magically come to appear on one of the end tables in the parlor. Oh, yes, Jane had practically *lived*

Motown when she was a girl—a very young girl, of course, in kindergarten—or was it first grade? It was a beat and, she didn't know, *soul*, she guessed, that made it great. She tried for the same sort of thing in her writing, not that she could ever touch "Papa's Got a Brand New Bag" or "My Ding-a-Ling," but there was a rawness there, a sensuality, a *je ne sais quoi* that she strived for. Ruth had read the article surreptitiously. It made her gag.

After the applause had died down, Ruth wandered into the party with Brie—Owen had taken the whole thing inside because of the bugs, but the French doors stood open to the patio and the sound system was still wired out there in case anyone wanted to liberate the carnal spell of Jane's reading with a bout of groin-rubbing and hip-grinding. Ruth didn't. She planned to remain relatively incon-spicuous—a presence, yes, La Dershowitz after all, star of last night's dramatic scene on the patio, reigning queen of the hive, impresario of the whole Hiro Tanaka adventure—a looming figure certainly, but not the cynosure. Not tonight. Brie began to bob her head to the music and then she had a drink and before Ruth could stop her she was gushing over the reading. "I've never heard anything like it," she gasped, "I mean knock me down, blow me away, that's the best story I've ever heard. The best reading I've ever heard. Anywhere. I mean it."

Brie was goggling at her, vapid, open-faced, a little mustachio of pale sweat trembling atop her upper lip. Ruth held herself per-fectly still. "Bullshit," she snapped. "Cheap theatrics, that's all. You call that reading? You call that *sharing a work in progress*? I call it grandstanding. I call it an insult."

Brie looked stunned, lost; she didn't know what to do with her hands.

"And the story itself"—Ruth gave her a withering look—"it's the cheapest kind of melodrama. Fourteen-year-old Swedes, I mean give me a break."

"Ruth-ie"—the tone was admonitory, two attenuated syllables, a punch on the first and a long trailing tongue-cluck on the second—"you can't really mean that, can you?" Irving Thalamus had ma-

terialized at her elbow. He was wearing a chartreuse and yellow
shirt, open at the neck to show off the black creeping jungle of his
chest hair. Ruth realized with a jolt that this was the matching top
to the shorts she'd pilfered for Hiro. Irving was smiling at her, his
lips tight and sardonic, a smile that caught at the corners of his
mouth and pricked her like a goad.

Brie began to gulp for breath as if they were treading water in
the deep end of a swimming pool. "That's what I was saying, Mr.
Thalamus—"

He forestalled her with a raised palm and a tender squeeze of
the elbow that managed to be both fatherly and lewd at once.
"Irving," he said, "call me Irving," his voice rich and promiscuous.

"That's just what I was saying, Irving"—she gave him a smile,
cute, cute—"I mean I've heard a lot of readings at school, and in
New York, and this one just blew me away, I mean knock me
down with a stick, it's like she's possessed or something, I mean
talk about *act*ing, talk about dramatic interpretation . . ." Brie was
so worked up she couldn't go on. She just stood there, bare-
shouldered, wide-eyed, goggling and gasping like a goldfish.

"And how do you feel about it, Ruthie?" Irving's eyes were
hooded. Somehow he'd managed to work an arm round Brie's waist.
He was really enjoying this.

But Ruth wasn't about to give him a show. And she certainly
didn't want to talk about Jane Shine, let alone get drawn into a
debate over her trumped-up stories and half-witted histrionics. She
was going to be cool. Olympian. Above it. "Give me a break,
Irving," she said, leveling her eyes on him. "That wasn't a reading,
it was a premenstrual breakdown." And then she turned on her
heels and left them to their flesh-squeezing and body hair.

She went to Sandy for solace, but Sandy was as bad as Brie. He
sat on the far side of the room with Bob, tapping his fingers to the
music and basking in the afterglow of Jane's reading. Ruth tried to
turn him, tried to steer him away from idolatry and sow the seeds
of disaffection, but it was no use. He pulled blissfully at the neck
of a beer, glancing over at the little group around Jane—Seezers

and Teitelbaum, Septima, Laura Grobian, Clara and Patsy and half a dozen others—as if they were disciples gathered round the Messiah himself. Or herself.

She found Regina in the corner, scowling into a glass of rum, and she knew that at least she would have no qualms about calling shit shit and seeing Jane for the imposter she was. Regina had darkened her eye sockets with kohl and dyed her hair an interstellar black; she looked like a woman in purdah who's had the veil snatched away from her face. "So," Ruth said, sidling up to her, "do we bury her next to Wordsworth or what? Or maybe P.T. Barnum would be more like it." She gave a mirthless little laugh.

"Jane?" Regina snubbed out a cigarette in the potted palm behind her. She straightened up with a shrug, searched Ruth's eyes for a second and then looked away. "I don't know—she can be a real pain in the ass, a real prima donna, if you know what I mean, but I thought the thing tonight was at least dramatic."

"Dramatic?" Ruth echoed. She was incredulous.

"Half of this shit puts me to sleep after about six words—at least she, like, held my interest."

Ruth couldn't help herself—her voice got away from her. "Yeah, but with what? Fakery. Crap. The kind of trumped-up horseshit that hides the fact that there's nothing there."

Regina attempted a smile, but it faded as quickly as it bloomed. She fumbled in her leather jacket for another cigarette.

"Damn it," Ruth cried, yelped—she was going too far, she knew it, but she couldn't stop now—"can't you see that Jane"—she tried to lower her voice, tried to contain the damage—"Jane Shine is nothing but hot air and horseshit?"

Ruth became aware in that instant that Regina wasn't looking at her—she was looking just over her shoulder and she was trying to do something with her mouth and blackened eyes. Ruth turned as if she were caught in taffy, tar, as if she were up to her neck in the La Brea pits.

Septima stood there before her, her expression climbing up and down the ladder of emotion. Not ten feet away was Jane Shine, on the move, regal, her feet, hips and shoulders touched ever so gracefully by Motown funk, her face locked up like a vise beneath the towering shako of her hair. Between them, the ring of toadies and yea-sayers had opened up like a receiving line. All eyes were on Ruth.

Jane kept coming. When she reached Septima's side, she pulled herself up. "Yes," she said, and you could skewer meat on the edge in her voice, "I'm sure we're all holding our breath till you get up there, La *Ders*howitz"—she spat out the sobriquet as if it burned her tongue and then paused to let it gather force. "That is, *if* you've got anything to read—you do, don't you? You must have been working on *some*thing all this time."

Ruth didn't know what to do. Marvin Gaye was dancing all over her head and every face in the room was turned toward her. Her instinct was to lash out, slam the clenched white ball of her fist into those outer-space eyes, rip the lace collar from her throat, demolish the hair, call her out for the conniving leg-spreading literary whore that she was, but she hesitated and lost hold of the moment. Her face was working. Her brain was in overdrive. They were all—every one of them—waiting.

"Ruthie"—Septima had her by the hand and she began to chatter as if nothing had happened, as if the cold talentless bitch hadn't just called her out, humiliated her, smashed open the hive and stung her to death—"Ruthie, darlin', we was all—Orlando and Mignonette and Laura and I—we was all just sayin' what a pleasure it would be to have you read from your work too, and you know, as everyone here does, that while we don't require room and bo-ard from our artists, we do feel privileged to receive payment in kind . . ." She looked up at the ceiling as if it were transparent, a faraway smile fixed on her lips. "Some of the things we've heard in this very room . . ."

This was the challenge. This was it. This was the slap in the face, the gauntlet at her feet. She'd wanted to be inconspicuous, let Jane have her moment, fight her with subterfuge and innuendo, but she'd blown it. Her heart was going, her eyes must have been wild, but she knew her lines, oh yes indeed. "Septima," she said in her calmest, steadiest tones, and she looked into those milky old gray eyes as if they were the only eyes in the room, as if Jane Shine weren't standing there twelve inches to the right, as if she didn't exist, had never existed, as if this were a private tête-à-tête with the woman who could well be her future mother-in-law, "I'd be honored."

The doyenne of Thanatopsis House broadened her smile till her thin old lips were stretched taut. "Tomorrow night, then?" she said, and something flickered to life in the depths of her moribund eyes.

Ruth nodded.

"Same time as tonight's?"

Marvin Gaye: what was he singing? *Ain't no mountain high enough/ Ain't no river deep enough.* Ruth took a deep breath. "Sure," she said, "no problem."

.   .   .

IN THE MORNING, SHE CURSED HERSELF. HOW COULD SHE HAVE BEEN so stupid? How could she have let herself get sucked in like that? Jane Shine. She wished her an early death, wished her sagging breasts and pyorrhea, wished she'd explode like the puffed-up frog in Aesop's fable.

But wishes get you nowhere.

Ruth was in her studio, working hard, before anyone in the big house had even the vaguest semiconscious presentiment that morning had arrived and that breakfast and work and the slow miraculous unveiling of the day awaited them. She was working with an ease and concentration that would have amazed her if she'd stopped to think about it, hammering away at the keyboard and wielding her Liquid Paper like a sword while a stack of clean new perfectly wrought pages mounted before her. By ten o'clock she'd substantially rewritten sections of "Two Toes," "Of Tears and the Tide"— it wasn't so bad, not really—and the piece that had come back from the *Atlantic*, which in a burst of inspiration she'd retitled "Sebastopol," to suggest the sort of battle her main characters—two couples—were engaged in. What she thought she'd do was present fragments from each of the stories—real work in progress, the real thing, not some typeset and justified artifact—ending up with the section of "Tears" that described the very Hiro-like husband of the doomed woman. They would sit there—Irving, Laura, Septima, Seezers and Teitelbaum and E.T. herself—and they would think of her, Ruth, and her triumph over the sheriff and Abercorn and the macho little toad who'd given them a taste of real-life drama right out there on the patio before their wondering eyes. Then too, there was sure to be a certain prurient interest in the piece—what *did* she know about Japanese sex? Had she slept with him? Had she helped him escape? And she'd give them her enigmatic smile, the smile of La Dershowitz, regnant and unassailable, and let it rest. Yes, she'd show them what a reading was all about.

She worked through lunch, worked through the racket of hammering and cutting and banging as Parker Putnam—or was it Putnam Parker?—did his best imitation of a working carpenter. Hunched and sinewy, burned the color of tobacco, he showed up at eleven with a toolbox the size of a small vehicle, claiming in a halting rheumy voice that "Miz Lights" had asked him to come out and clean the place up. It took him most of the afternoon to knock the shards of broken glass out of the windows and nearly an hour just to get the old screen door off the hinges, but she hardly noticed. Normally, he would have driven her crazy, but today she welcomed him—he was there to test her, to lay one more stone atop the cart to see if it would tip over. But it wouldn't. Her concentration was complete.

It was getting late—four? five?—when he packed up his tools (a process that in itself involved half an hour) and left for the day. The hammering ceased. The splintering of glass, the wheezing and spitting and dull reverberant booming were no more. Silence fell over the studio, and it was then that Ruth felt the first faint stirrings of uncertainty. What if—what if the work was no good, after all? What if they didn't like it? What if she got up there and froze? She imagined the satisfaction that would give Jane Shine, and she felt her stomach clench. But no, it was hunger, that was all, and she realized in that moment that she'd skipped lunch.

She sat at her desk and ate dutifully—cherry tomatoes fresh from the kitchen garden, salmon mousse with Dijon mustard and a sort of cracker bread Armand had devised himself—and she began to feel better. She thought of her makeup and hair and what she would wear. Nothing pretentious, that was for sure, no lace collars and Edwardian brooches. Jeans and a T-shirt. Earrings. Her aqua heels, the ones that showed off her toes and instep. She would keep it simple. Honest. Genuine. Everything the Shine extravaganza was not. And if the stories weren't finished, weren't yet what she wanted them to be, it wouldn't matter one whit—she was reading sections only, and the sections were strong. The thought lifted her spirits— food, that was all it was—and she felt the strength seeping back into her.

She rose from her desk and gathered up her papers, inserting the new crisply typed pages in an old unpretentious manila folder. The room was still. The sun held in the windows. She was aware for the first time that day of the birds slashing through the shadows, lighting in the bushes, making music for her alone. She was standing there at the window, her back to the door, having one last cigarette before heading back to get ready, when a sudden noise on the front porch startled her. Turning, expecting to see Parker Putnam fumbling around for some tool he'd forgotten, she had a shock: this wasn't Parker Putnam. It was Septima.

Septima. Ruth's first thought was that she'd lost her way, an embarrassment of age, but the look in the old lady's eye told her different. Septima stood there on the doorstep, giving the place a tight-lipped scrutiny, Owen at her side. She was wearing her gardening clothes—a straw sunbonnet, an old smock over a pair of jeans, men's shoes. "Ruthie," she called in a voice that sounded harsh and strained, "I hate to disturb you, but I—may I come in?"

Ruth was so surprised she couldn't answer—Septima made it a strict rule never to visit any of the artists' studios, out of respect for their privacy, and Hart Crane was a long walk for a woman of her age. Ruth crossed the room wordlessly and swung open the door.

Something was wrong. She could see it in Owen's face, see it in the way Septima avoided her eyes as she moved past her and lowered herself into the cane rocker. "Whew!" the old woman exclaimed, "this heat! I swear I'll never get used to it, never. Would you have a glass of water for me, please, Ruthie?"

"Of course," Ruth said, and she poured a glass for Owen too, who remained standing in the doorway as if he hadn't really meant to come in. "Thanks, Ruth," he said, draining the glass in a gulp. "Think I'll just step outside here a minute and inspect the damage," he said to the room in general, setting the glass down on the windowsill. He focused on Septima. "You call if you need me."

When Owen had gone, the screen door tapping gently behind him, Septima lifted her head to give Ruth a long slow look. The air was still, heavy with a premonition of rain. The crepitating sounds of the forest rushed in to fill the silence. "I see Parker's been here," Septima said finally.

Ruth nodded. "He was banging around here all day—but it didn't disturb me, not really. I was lost in my work."

"It's a pity," Septima sighed, and Ruth agreed, though she wondered just what the old woman was referring to—Parker Putnam's dismal showing, the weather, the danger of being lost in one's work? "A real pity the way they shot up this place, Theron Peagler and all the rest of them. You'd think they'd know better. And the way they harried that poor Japanese boy—"

Again Ruth nodded. Again the old lady fell silent. Just outside the window a bird hit four notes in quick succession, up and down, up and down.

"Ruthie," Septima said after a minute, "I'm very sorry for disturbin' you out here, and especially at a time when you'd be workin' hard to pre-pare for your readin', but a matter of the utmost importance has come up."

Ruth had been fussing round the little room in an unconsciously defensive way, a proprietary way, but now she took hold of the arms of the other rocker and settled into it as if it might come alive at any moment with the shock of 50,000 volts.

"I want to ask you about this Japanese boy—and I want to know the whole truth of the matter. It's become somethin' of an embarrassment for the colony, especially since he's gone and escaped—the phone, Ruthie, has been ringin' off the hook all day, reporters from New York and Los Angeles, everywhere. Well, I want to know the extent of your involvement—the full extent. I think I have a right to that knowledge, don't you?"

"Of course," Ruth insisted, "of course you do, but like I told you—"

Septima cut her off. "You know I'm open-minded, Ruthie, and you know how I feel about the creative atmosphere at Thanatopsis and the artists' behavior as regards their personal ethics and standards of sexual conduct—"

Ruth could only stare at her.

"Well, when my son told me he was bringin' home a Jewish girl I didn't bat an eye—why would I, with all the talented Jewish artists we've had here over the years—but I'm gettin' away from what I want to say altogether. Whether you were more, more *intimate* with this foreign boy than you allow or not is really not at issue here . . ." She paused, and the silence could have engulfed ships and swallowed up oceans. "Ruth"—the sound of her own name made Ruth jump, she couldn't help it—"Ruth, what I want to say is that I had a call from Saxby this afternoon."

A call from Saxby, a call from Saxby. Yes? And so?

"He was in jail, Ruth. In the Clinch County Jail in Ciceroville."

"In jail?" Ruth couldn't have been more surprised had the old woman told her he was taken hostage in Lebanon. "For what?"

Septima gave her a close penetrating look. "My law-yers are seein' to that, don't you worry. He'll be out by this time and that sheriff down there and all the rest of them will be mighty sorry they ever tangled with Septima Lights, believe you me—but that isn't the point. The point is that they accused him of helpin' that boy escape and takin' him in my car, my Mercedes, down to that swamp. The point is, Ruthie, I wonder who put that boy in the trunk of that car and what you want to tell me about it."

Ruth was stunned. Paralyzed. She could feel her toehold at Thanatopsis slipping, her career in jeopardy, Saxby alienated from her, waitressing looming up like a black hole in her future. "I lied," she blurted, "I admit it and I'm sorry. But just about Hiro, I mean how much I helped him when he was . . . was at large. But I swear to you, I had nothing to do with his getting out of that cell, I knew nothing about it—and neither did Sax."

They sat there for half an hour, and Ruth fed the old woman the bits and crumbs of the truth about Hiro—but she'd never been intimate with him, never, she insisted on that—always circling back to the justification that she'd been using him for a story, for research, for art. That was it: she'd done it for art. And she hadn't meant any harm. She hadn't. Really.

When she was finished, the shadows beyond the window had lengthened perceptibly and the chatter of the forest had settled into an evening mode, richer now with the chirp of tree frogs and the booming basso of their pond-dwelling cousins. Owen was at the door. Septima cleared her throat. "They want you to go down there tomorrow, Ruthie—Mr. Abercorn does—and it's not a request. I know all about that shameful incident on the patio and I just kick myself for lettin' that class of people stay on at Thanatopsis, and I don't know how to be delicate about this, but *I* want you to go too." Septima fixed her eyes on her. "And I'm afraid it's not a request either."

"But—but what they did, grabbed me by the hair, called me names—" Ruth was angry now, she couldn't help herself. And then a little fist of fear clenched inside her. "What do they want with me?"

The old woman chose her words carefully. "I don't really know, Ruthie, but it seems to me the least you can do. My boy's gone to jail over this." She let the words sink in, and the moment held between them, bloated and ugly. "In light of all this—" Septima said finally, searching for the words, "—this emotional upset, I would understand if you'd like to postpone your readin' tonight . . ."

Postpone the reading! Ruth nearly came up out of the chair with joy and relief at the mention of it—off the hook, she was off the hook!—but then she caught herself. If she didn't read, no matter what the reason, short of nuclear war, they'd be on her like jackals. *Ruth backed down,* they'd say, *she's nothing but talk; did you hear what Jane Shine said about it?*

"You're sure Saxby's all right?"

"I've known Donnager Stratton for forty-two years and he went down there personally to set things right." Septima sighed. "He's a stubborn boy, Saxby, always has been. He's after those little white fee-ish, Ruthie, and he's goin' back into that swamp after 'em, manhunt or no manhunt. That's what he told me."

Ruth looked down at her lap. She was still clutching the manila folder. When she looked up again, she'd made her decision. "No," she said finally, "I'll read."

The Power of the
Human Voice

. . . .

THE FIRST THING HE WAS GOING TO DO WHEN THEY GOT HIM OUT of here was find that little paramilitary goon with the scraggly beard and kick his ass into the next county. And Abercorn too, that crud. The strong-arm tactics might go down with some poor scared hyperventilating wetback drowning in his own sweat, but he'd be damned if anybody was going to slap him around. Or Ruth either. It was unnecessary, totally unnecessary. It was outrageous, that's what it was.

Saxby Lights, scion of the venerable Tupelo Island clan, son of the late Marion and Septima Hollister Lights and lover of an obscure literary artist from Southern California, found himself in a concrete-block cell in the Clinch County Jail in Ciceroville, Georgia, guest of Sheriff Bull Tibbets and Special Agent Detlef Abercorn of the INS. The cell featured a stainless-steel toilet bolted to the floor and a cot bolted to the wall. Three of the walls were painted lime green and displayed an ambitious overlay of graffiti relating to Jesus Christ Our Savior, the probability of His coming, and the sex act as it was practiced between men and women, men and men, men and boys, and men and various other species. Crude drawings of a bearded Christ replete with halo alternated with representations of huge bloated phalluses that floated across the walls like dirigibles.

The fourth wall, which gave onto a concrete walkway, was barred from floor to ceiling, like the monkey cage in a zoo. The whole place smelled of Pine Sol cut with urine.

Saxby was on his feet—he was too angry to sit. In the interstices of his anger he was alternately depressed and worried, anxious for Ruth—and for himself too. Had she helped the kid escape? Had she concealed him in the trunk? He wouldn't put it past her, not after she'd hidden the whole business from him, not after she'd lied to him. Sure he was worried. He hadn't seen the inside of a jail cell since college, when he'd spent a night in the lockup at Lake George on a drunk-and-disorderly charge. But that hardly made him a career criminal. And while he could appreciate that the whole business with the Japanese kid looked pretty suspicious, especially after what Ruth had done, and he could understand that Abercorn was frustrated and beginning to look more than a little foolish, it didn't excuse a thing. They were such idiots. He was no criminal, couldn't they see that? He was the one who'd reported the guy in the first place. And yet here they'd sicked their commandos on him and wrenched his vertebrae out of joint, they'd handcuffed him and humiliated him and dragged him off to jail like some Sicilian drug runner. They didn't have to do that. He would have gone with them peaceably.

Or maybe he wouldn't have. On second thought, he definitely wouldn't have. That was the thing. Nothing could have gotten him off that island this morning—nothing short of physical force, that is—and the minute Donnager Stratton showed up he was going back, police cordon or no. What was he thinking?—settling the score with Abercorn and his henchman could wait.

The reason, of course, was *Elassoma okefenokee* (or *Elassoma okefenokee lightsei*—he couldn't resist appending his own name, though he knew it was a bit premature, and, well, a little childish too). He'd found them. He'd finally found them. And he'd just gotten going, just thrown his nets and discovered the mother lode, when that brain-dead little storm trooper came at him from behind. Talk about bad timing—he'd finally found his albinos, over two hundred of

them in his first six pulls, only to have them taken away from him.
Or to be more accurate, he was taken away from them.

But it was amazing. There they were, right where Roy said they'd
be. And the thing was, Roy hadn't even wanted him to go out—
not after the Nipponese escape artist popped out of the trunk between them and tumbled headlong into the swamp. "What in god's
name was that?" Roy had said, scratching his head and gaping out
across the boat pond to where Hiro Tanaka was cutting a clean
frothing wake to the other side. Saxby hadn't been able to answer
him. He thought he was hallucinating. It was as if he'd thrown a
ball up in the air and it hadn't come down, as if he'd turned on the
gas range and flames had burst from his fingertips. His mouth fell
open, his arms dangled like wash at his sides. But then he recovered
himself, then the impossible became possible and he connected the
trunk and Tupelo Island and the ground beneath his feet, and the
anger came up on him like a thousand little cars racing out of control
through his bloodstream. "You son of a bitch!" he bellowed, charg-
ing into the water like a bull alligator and shaking his fist at the
retreating swimmer, "you, you"—he'd never used the words before,
never, but out they came as if they were the very oleo of his
vocabulary—"you Nip, you Jap, you gook!" He was standing there,
knee-deep in the water, shaking his fist and waving his arms and
shouting, "I'll kill you, I'll kill you yet!," when Roy took him by
the belt and led him back to shore.

After he'd calmed down he told Roy the story, and that was
when Roy put on his official face, the face of the second in command
and de facto overseer of the Okefenokee National Wilderness Area
with his offices in the tourist center at the Stephen C. Foster State
Park and his unwavering allegiance to the mammals, birds, fishes
and reptiles of the swamp, not to mention the Secretary of the
Interior, a man who had more than a passing interest in law and
order and public relations. "We can't go out there now," he said,
"not after this."

"And why the hell not?"

Roy looked offended. "Why, we've got to call the sheriff, the authorities. They'll want to coordinate some sort of manhunt with our people on this end"—he was no longer addressing Saxby, but thinking aloud—". . . of course he won't get far out there before he's stung, bitten and chewed half to death, presuming he doesn't drown—and that in itself's a big presumption . . ."

"Roy?"

"Hm?"

"I'm going out there just the same."

Roy gave no sign that he'd heard him. "You say he's Japanese?"

Saxby nodded.

"Well, you never know. From what I've heard of the Japanese— they're pretty resourceful, aren't they?" Roy tugged at the bill of his cap, stroked his nose as if it were detached from him. "Still and all, I'd wager they haven't got anything like this over there, and resourcefulness can only take you so far, know what I mean?" He looked past Saxby to the low pine building that housed the tourist center and then back across the lagoon to the spot where Hiro had vanished in a vegetable embrace. "I'd say they'll have him back here by sundown."

"All the more reason to let me go—hell, the park's still open, isn't it?"

They both glanced at Roy's boat: it was canted back on the trailer, the gentle surge of the water baptizing its slick fiberglass hull in one long continuous motion. This was Roy's particular boat, the one he'd built himself for swamping, a marvel of poise and maneuverability. Their eyes fastened on the stenciled legend—the *Pequod II*—and both of them smiled. All round them were men with tackle boxes and coolers, their faces sun-inflamed, their eyes a squint of cracker blue. They glanced furtively at Roy and Saxby, the phenomenon of the amphibious Japanese no less marvelous than an eighty-pound catfish or a three-legged deer, but they went about their business as if it were the commonest thing in the world. Engines sputtered to life, boats cut the surface of the whiskey-complected water. For just a moment then, Roy relaxed his official face. "All right, go ahead," he said. "But you understand you're on your own. I won't be able to join you, not now. And if it gets bad," he added, "I'll come out there after you myself."

And so Roy walked off toward the office and the telephone that would summon Bull Tibbets, Detlef Abercorn and Lewis Turco and a whole chin-thrusting, neck-stretching pack of intensely curious people representing the nation's supremely curious press, and Saxby set out alone for Billy's Island in Roy's long low flat-bottomed boat.

It was early yet, and when Saxby got beyond the fishermen with their cane poles, straw hats and early-morning Budweisers, the swamp was still and silent, a place of immemorial wakings floating beneath a breath of mist. Roy's directions were flawless—for all his easy country ways, when you came down to it he was as precise as a brain surgeon—and Saxby had no trouble finding the crude trail that led round to the back side of Billy's Island. The trail was off-limits to anyone without a special permit, and since it wouldn't admit any of the motor-driven rental boats in any case, it was little used, overgrown with cascades of honeysuckle and cassena. Saxby had to pole his way through, stopping from time to time to cut back the vegetation with the machete Roy had thought to provide. By nine o'clock the sweat had soaked right on through to his underwear and the ribs of his socks, and the boat was a traveling salad of chopped leaves, twigs and fat disoriented spiders. The drizzle had cleared off and the sun was coming on strong by the time he glided out onto the titi-fringed pond Roy had described right on down to the last lily pad.

The pond looked ordinary enough—fifty feet across, six or eight feet deep, a prairie beyond it snarled with marsh grass, pipewort and lily pads, the slash pine of Billy's Island backing up on it from the rear. It was nothing more than an oversized gator wallow, really—in fact, an eight-footer hung in the water ahead of him, floating like a sky diver in the blue, its legs spread wide, the crenelated tail hanging motionless. Yes, the pond looked ordinary enough—no different from a thousand others—but to Saxby it was

entirely unique, the pond of all ponds, the place in which the albino
pygmy sunfish lurked in all its rare and recondite glory.

He could barely restrain himself. He wanted to toss out the
minnow traps, float the seine, make the water churn with the hard
flat caudal muscles of his quarry—but he knew better. Though it
looked clear, the sun hot, the sky arching electric overhead, he
knew the weather could change out here from moment to moment
and that he had to set up camp first—just to be safe. Half an hour,
that's all it would take.

When he drifted back out onto the pond, the sun had set it aflame
and the gator had gone (which was just as well—the last thing he
needed was tangling an angry gator up in his net). He set and baited
half a dozen minnow traps and then he floated the seine across the
pond. He wasn't particularly confident in the seine—if there were
too many obstructions the net would snag and the fish would escape—but he was hoping to get lucky. Short of dynamite, the seine
was the quickest and most efficient way to discover what lay beneath
the surface. And there was no thrill like it—as the two sides of the
net drew together like a purse, you could see the fish fighting it,
roiling the water and beating at the mesh, and then, as you pulled
it ashore, there they were, silver and gold, flashing in the bag like
rare coin.

The first pull produced nothing—the net fouled on a sunken
branch. But the second—the second hit the jackpot. There he was,
drowned in sweat and a paste of crushed mosquitoes, up to his
thews in the muck, the net sweeping closer, the neck of the bag
constricting, and he could feel the weight and the life of them. And
then he had the bag over the gunwale of the boat that floated beside
him, and there they were. His albinos. Two of them, three, five,
six and eight and ten, counting breathlessly as he plucked them
from the farrago of thrashing fish, casting aside the darters and the
bluegills and the ordinary dark-skinned pygmies like so much refuse. He put the good ones, the albinos, in an array of sloshing
buckets in the bottom of the boat, and then he cast the net again

and again. Finally, late in the afternoon, he forced himself to stop and take his treasure back to camp (he was like a forty-niner, a crazed old galoot onto the richest vein in the hills, and he didn't want to stop, couldn't, but he had to—the sun was slowly raising the temperature in the buckets and he was afraid he'd lose everything he had if he didn't). Yes, and then he went back to camp to set the buckets in the shade beneath the trees. Yes. And then Turco hit him.

All the long way back to the dock, all the way up the rough wooden planks, through the phalanx of reporters and photographers and into the tourist center where Sheriff Bull Tibbets sat chewing his cud and stroking his gut as if it were a crystal ball, Saxby protested his innocence. He raged, he wheedled, he reasoned, pleaded, threatened, but Abercorn wouldn't listen. Abercorn was angry. His jaw was set, his pink eyes were hard. "No more Mr. Nice Guy," he said, and his voice was cold and uncompromising, "I'm through fooling around." Saxby knew something he wasn't telling him, he claimed—and so did Ruth—and there were going to be some charges leveled. People were going to jail here. This was serious business. Deadly serious. On the other hand, if Saxby cooperated—if *Ruth* cooperated—arrangements could be made, charges dropped. All he wanted was this illegal alien. And he was going to get him.

Saxby was furious, enraged, frightened. No matter what he said, they didn't believe him. He knew nothing. But until he did know, until he told them precisely where Hiro Tanaka was and why and how he'd helped him escape, he was going to sit in a jail cell and work hard at remembering. For the longest while, Saxby couldn't even think straight—all he wanted was to spring out of the chair, snap the handcuffs like some superhero and pound that acid-washed face till it burst like a tomato. But then Abercorn waved him away in disgust and they shipped him off to the Clinch County Jail in Ciceroville and gave him his phone call. He phoned his mother. She was a towering presence, all-powerful, the mother he'd clung to as a fatherless boy trying to survive a Yankee accent in a Guale

Coast school. She honed her anger in the clearest tones of reassurance and threat: "Donnager Stratton will have you out of that cell inside the hour, I guarantee you that, and we will have the governor himself in on this by nightfall—really, I still cannot believe it— and those odious petty little agents will find themselves the ones in hot water, just you believe me."

"Mama," he'd said to her then, "Mama, they want Ruth down here."

"Ruthie?" she repeated, and he could almost hear the tumblers clicking in her head. "Certainly they don't think—?"

"They think everything, Mama. They want her down here to go out in the swamp with a megaphone or something and call out his name—they say she's the one he knows, the only one he'll listen to—"

"But that's absurd."

"That's what I told them." He thought of Abercorn, cold ridiculous Abercorn, and what he'd said: *You'd be surprised at the power of the human voice.* "But they're not asking, Mama. They want her down here tomorrow morning or they're going to lock her up too." He paused. He was in a big room with lazy fans and wanted posters on the walls. The deputy was watching him. "You tell her that."

. . .

SEPTIMA TOLD HER. AND SHE DIDN'T LIKE IT. NOT A BIT. RUTH FELT suddenly that she was losing her grip on Saxby, on Septima and Thanatopsis House and the whole wide brilliant world of celebrity and accomplishment that radiated out from it, felt as if she were clinging to a ledge above a yawning gulf while Jane Shine and Detlef Abercorn and even Septima herself beat at her fingers with their microphones and the hard flat unyielding plank of the law. She had no choice in the matter. In the morning Owen was going to drive her down to the Okefenokee Swamp and she was going to go out in a boat with Detlef Abercorn and Lewis Turco and anybody else they wanted to include and she was going to cry out Hiro's name and beg him to surrender. That was what she was going to do—for Saxby and for Septima too. And maybe even for Hiro himself.

But that was tomorrow. Tonight she was going to read.

. . .

AT NINE O'CLOCK THE COLONISTS GATHERED IN THE FRONT PARLOR and settled themselves into the familiar easy chairs, loveseats and sofas in the glow of the subdued and very ordinary light that emanated from the reading lamps stationed round the room. There were no spotlights and there was no microphone. Ruth appeared promptly at nine, dressed as if she were going to an outdoor barbecue. She'd spent some time on her face, her nails and her hair, but the clothes she kept simple—the T-shirt, jeans and heels she'd first envisioned. She was determined that every detail of this reading would stand in opposition to the one that preceded it. There would be no cheap thrills tonight, no Swedish accents and maudlin histrionics—just work, honest work, presented in an honest voice.

The first thing Ruth noticed as she took her seat in the big armchair beneath the chandelier was that Septima hadn't done her hair. She was wearing the same coif she'd worn for Jane's reading, and though she looked elegant, always looked elegant, her hairdo was a bit ragged round the edges, as if she'd slept on it. The next thing Ruth noticed was Jane. La Shine was ensconced on the damask couch between Irving and Mignonette Teitelbaum, with Seezers, in his wheelchair, perched at the far end. She'd let down her hair, the great frozen shako of last night's pelage combed out like a rug, its Medusan tendrils involved with Irving and Teitelbaum, woven into the fabric of the couch, providing cover for the icy glittering inhuman eyes. White silk pajamas—Ruth caught a glimpse of them beneath the typhoon of hair. Jane was relaxed, all right—she looked as if she'd been dropped into the couch from a passing jet. She was watching Ruth, a perfect little smirk of contempt ironed across her lips.

Ruth tried to ignore her, tried to ignore them all—but no, that wasn't right. She had to be warm, personable, overflowing with camaraderie and joy in their shared and collective talents. She forced herself to look round the room, smiling into each pair of eyes. And then Septima stood, put her hands together, and said, simply, "Ruth Dershowitz."

Ruth rose to a murmur of polite applause, and then she sat down again—she wouldn't stand, she wouldn't dominate them, she steadfastly refused to perform. This was the lesson of the reading, this was the corrective, the return to proper form, the example that would put Jane Shine in her place once and for all.

She began with "Two Toes," introducing the selection in a voice that was hushed, barely inflected, the voice of one-on-one conversation, easy and intimate. As she spoke she began to warm to the moment and she looked out into the faces of her fellow colonists and felt something swelling inside her, something like love. She told them the genesis of the story—perhaps in too much detail, perhaps she erred there—told them of little Jessica McClure, whom they all remembered from the news accounts of her heroic infantine battle for survival in that dark Texas well shaft, described the process by which she, Ruth, had attempted in her humble and modest way to transmute the bare facts into art. And then she began to read, investing all her strength and the strange tingle inside her that was a kind of love for them all, even Jane, in the quiet authority of the human voice—the naked, unassisted, uninflected human voice.

She began with the section that showed little Jessica grown into a recalcitrant teenager unable to reconcile her soulless Texas life with the climactic hours spent in that Freudian tunnel deep underground. There was sex in this section, plenty of it—here she'd out-Shine Shine—and a kind of fierce negativity that was sure to electrify the Thalamuses and Grobians. Then she read a longish section that took the well-shaft girl, the little heroine of the nation, and put her into a brutal marriage with a tattooed drifter fifteen years her senior. She looked up from the page when she'd finished and gave her audience the most spontaneous and heartfelt smile of her life. The only thing was, they didn't look exactly electrified—

more the opposite. Their faces were noncommittal, withdrawn, lifeless: the term "stupefied" came to her. Or no, she was misreading them—they were stunned, that was all. She held the smile and there was a flutter of applause.

"Thank you," she whispered, grinning blissfully, and she stirred her legs luxuriously, a cat waking from a nap in the sun. She could hardly believe it—here she was, La Dershowitz, holding them all, playing the role of the true and unpretentious artist, nearly drowning in the joy of it. "Next," she said, her voice small and modest and thankful, "I'd like to share with you a section of a work in progress called 'Sebastopol' "—and here she paused to irradiate Irving Thalamus with her smile—"a piece Irving has been generous enough to—how shall I say it?—to coach me on, for which I'm eternally grateful. Thank you, Irving."

Irving briefly extricated himself from the explosion of Jane's hair and gave her in return the great gleaming toothy Thalamus grin and said something that got them all laughing—Ruth didn't quite catch it, but she knew from the tone that it was something winning, small tribute to the modesty and humility of La Dershowitz, the artist, the sharer, the humble organ of her work. She went on—at length, too much length, she would see that in retrospect—with an introduction to this piece as well, and then she read a lengthy section that consisted in its entirety of an interior monologue. The wife of the second couple—Babe, her name was and she was thirtyish and delicately beautiful—was peeling shrimp and pounding octopus for a bouillabaisse and examining her unfulfilled life with Dexter, her lawyer husband, and the as yet unconsummated passion she felt for Marvel, the lawyer husband of her best friend Clarice, who together constituted the first couple. It was a story that featured more than a soupçon of sex—the story the *Atlantic* had turned down for its steaminess, in fact—but Ruth steered clear of it, selecting the section she did precisely because it was the only part of the piece that was relatively free of it. Jane had given them nothing but sex and Ruth had responded with her selection from "Two Toes"—no reason for overkill. Besides, the last piece, the tour de force and climax of the evening, was saturated with it.

She found herself drifting a bit during the "Sebastopol" selection—she was right there, reading carefully and with the proper lack of animation—but her mind took off on her, sailing back to the early evening when she was getting ready and Sax had called from Ciceroville. "Sax," she'd gasped into the phone, "are you all right?" Brie and Sandy—were they a thing?—had been sitting there on the window seat in the foyer, chatting about editors, astrological signs and writers they knew mutually who'd gone to fat, baldness and loss of affect, and they raised their voices to give her some privacy. It was the quintessential La Dershowitz moment, audience and all—this was real drama, real life, her lover in jail, a manhunt going on, the press beating at the windows (she'd had calls from six newspapers already that afternoon).

"I'm fine," he said. "Stratton had me out of here in two minutes and he's slapping a false-arrest suit on them, all of them"—he paused to draw a long disgusted breath—"but still he thinks we ought in good faith to deal with them, you know, cooperate. They've got nothing on us—Jesus, I'm talking like somebody in a movie or something—we didn't do anything wrong, and they're sure to drop the charges and beg us to withdraw the suit and all that, but still Stratton says we've got to cooperate."

"But Sax"—her voice was butter, honey, frankincense and myrrh—"why you? You're totally innocent, they know that."

"Abercorn's just being a prick, is all. He thinks we—you and I—have something going with this Japanese kid and that somehow we got him out of that old cell out back of Patsy's studio and hustled him into the Mercedes—and we didn't, did we, Ruth?"

"I love you, Sax," she whispered. It was a signal. When someone says "I love you," you say: "I love you too." It's like hello and goodbye, how are you and what's happening? Saxby didn't respond. "Sax," she repeated, "I love you."

"I love you too," he said finally, but there was no conviction in it and that scared her.

"I told you, Sax," she said, "I swear it: I had nothing to do with it. All I want to see is Hiro Tanaka in jail and this whole ordeal over with."

That seemed to mollify him. He was going to stay down there at the motel—he was worried about his fish: yes—and the spark leaped back into his voice, he was her Sax, boyish and enthused— he'd got them! They were out on Billy's Island in a couple of buckets and he hadn't had time to set up the oxygenator and he was going back out there first thing in the morning. After he met her, of course. She *was* coming, wasn't she?

"Yes, Sax," she whispered, "of course. I'd do anything for you." And then her voice had faded away almost to nothing. "You know that."

And so for a moment—a long moment, two or three pages at least—she was reading, but she wasn't focused, not fully. She came back to herself on the final page and took the story out with a muted, unpretentious, nontheatrical flair. She looked up. Smiled. The applause was like the faintest spatter of rain in the desert. Her fellow colonists looked grim, haggard. Laura Grobian might have been the survivor of a train wreck, Orlando Seezers was making some sort of peculiar clucking or humming noise deep in his throat, Sandy looked as if he'd just woken up. Had she gone on too long? The thought flitted into her head and she dismissed it—after all, the main event, the *pièce de résistance*, was yet to come. They'd had their cake, and now it was time for the icing.

Ruth trod delicately with "Of Tears and the Tide," trying to walk the fine line between capitalizing on the dramatic events on the patio two nights ago (and her attendant seduction of Hiro, Abercorn and the sheriff and her victory over them all), and emphasizing in her every phrase and gesture that she, unlike the histrionic Shine, was an artist toiling away at the deep stuff of fiction. Her introduction was like a chat with a sick friend. It was warm, intimate, unassuming, and it alluded to the events of the past few days (and the preceding weeks too) without directly mentioning Hiro or Saxby or the ceaselessly ringing phone in the foyer or the Clinch County Jail. She mentioned the Japanese, though, mentioned them repeatedly. Was she an expert? Did she have direct, hands-on knowledge? She gave them her mysterious smile, just as she'd planned, and then she began to read.

Halfway through the story Orlando Seezers began to snore. It was nothing outrageous, no tromboning of the breath through constricted nostrils, no deep flatulent blasts from the bellows of the lungs, but snoring nonetheless. Ruth glanced up from the page. Seezers was flung back in the wheelchair as if he'd been shot, his wiry goatee thrust to the heavens, the little plaid cap he never removed clinging to his scalp in defiance of gravity. His snores were soft, almost polite, but audible for all that—and everyone was aware of them.

Everyone who was awake, that is. When Ruth looked up she was shocked. Septima was nodding in her chair. Laura Grobian had snapped off the light beside her and drawn a thin comforter up over her shoulders, the famous haunted eyes staring out on nothing. Brie's head had come to rest on Sandy's shoulder; Sandy seemed to be having trouble with his lower lip; Ina and Regina looked terminally bored. In front, on the sofa, Irving was struggling, Teitelbaum looked embarrassed—should she poke Orlando or not?—and Jane, Jane looked triumphant.

Ruth caught herself. She glanced at the grandfather clock in the corner—no, it couldn't be—and realized with dawning horror that she'd been reading for something like two and a half hours. "My god," she gasped, and for the first time that night her voice achieved some animation. "I'm so—I didn't realize how long I've gone on . . ." A few of the colonists, sniffing change, sniffing blood, struggled up in their seats. "Well," Ruth murmured, covering herself as best she could but already hearing the new billiard room shtik—*Ruth's reading? Yeah, it was like three months on the chain gang*— "you've been very patient and I thank you all."

Dazed, the colonists shook themselves, shuffled their feet, rubbed their blasted eyes. Irving started up the applause—she couldn't believe it, the love she'd felt for them earlier, the joy, and now all she felt was shame and mortification and hate: she hadn't even finished—and a feeble stunned sort of involuntary applause startled the room into wakefulness. She could read it in their eyes—*cocktails*, they were thinking, *or maybe just one, and then bed.* Irving rose to congratulate her; Septima's head jerked up and the milky gray eyes struggled to come into focus.

"Hey, La D., Ruthie," Irving boomed, enfolding her in his arms, "that was some stuff. You're great, babes." She could see Sandy standing behind him, smiling weakly, a pre-ambulatory Brie clutching at him for support. And beyond them, she saw Jane Shine rise from the couch to stretch and yawn theatrically, yawing the mass of her hair this way and that and exchanging some nasty little witticism with Mignonette Teitelbaum and the gaping, blinking, eye-rubbing, nose-blowing form of Orlando Seezers. The three of them shared a laugh that was like shredding metal and then Jane swept back her hair so Ruth could get a look at her pajamas.

Ruth felt a sudden hot stab at her insides. These weren't lounging pajamas, this wasn't a tunic or a djellabah, this was no fashion statement—no, Jane Shine was wearing a put-down, a slap in the face, the decisive killing counterthrust to Ruth's feeble parry: she was in her nightdress. It was that simple: Jane had come prepared for bed.

Ruth looked away, but the damage was done. The night was a disaster, she was careening from the Thanatopsian heavens, burned to a cinder like a poor extinguished meteor, and all she could think of was the billiard room and how they would slaughter her over this.

H *a h a*

∎ ∎ ∎ ∎ ∎ ∎ ∎

THEY LEFT, THE JEFFCOATS, THE WAY THEY HAD COME, ON A shimmer of light. Hiro watched them till they were out of sight, till the moving paddles, the glistening hull and the strong square rhythmically working shoulders were swallowed up in the merciless bank of green. They were heading back to the dock, back to where the flame-faced *hakujin* crouched over their catch and the sheriffs and park rangers fingered their weapons beneath the wide brims of their hats. They were on a mission of mercy, violating the sanctity of their itinerary and scrapping their schedule for him, Seiji Chiba, the Chinese tourist attacked by crocodiles.

Hiro felt light-headed. He sat heavily on the platform beside the bundle of food they'd left him and languished a doleful look on the bend round which they'd disappeared. In an hour they would hate him. They would glide into the dock with their wide-open faces and confident eyes, gee-whizzing and gollying at the sheriff's convention awaiting them, at the baying dogs, revving engines and jaws set with hate. *There's a man in trouble out there*, they'd say. *Where?* the sheriffs would bark, *where is he? Red trail platform*, Jeff Jeffcoat would answer, *but what's the problem? Jail break*, the sheriffs would spit. *A Jap, and a arsonist into the bargain. Assaulted some people, mighta killed a poor innocent old black man. But no*, Jeff Jeffcoat would say, *you've got it all wrong, this man's a tourist, he lost his boat. For christ's sake*, Jeff Jeffcoat would say, *he's Chinese.*

They'd be after him soon, homing in on this very platform like heat-seeking missiles, like avenging angels. He had to get up. Had to slosh back off into the muck and neck-deep water, had to crawl back up the orifice of America the Primitive. But he felt enervated, weak, felt as if all the fight had been drained out of him and Jōchō reduced to the mad gibbering irrelevant monk he was. He was sick, that's what it was. He raised a hand to his brow and felt the fever burning there. And then it was in his guts, tearing at him like Mishima's sword, and he doubled over and vomited up the corned beef hash, the ketchup and coffee and eggs, the Cup O'Noodles, the potato chips and pound cake, vomited till he tasted the deep bitter purple-black berries and the gall of his bile. For a long while he lay there, unable to move, tiny iridescent flies settling on the mess even as it dripped through the slats of the platform to feed the massed and waiting mouths below. But then the pain tore at him again and he rose shakily and fumbled his way into the rough-wood cubicle of the toilet.

The flies greeted him. They rose from the chemical mouth of the thing, the crapper, in a miasma of dancing gnats and the reek of chemicals and human waste. He tore down his pants, the knife in his guts, the black steaming odor of shit—American shit, Julie Jeffcoat's shit—stabbing at his nostrils. "*Amerikajin,*" he cursed aloud as his guts exploded beneath him, the filth of them, flinging themselves down on plastic seats where a thousand others have flung themselves down before them, taking the dirt of the bowels to the table with them, sitting there over their food, as bland as stones, their buttocks and shoes reeking from the toilet. God, he thought, clutching at himself to keep from passing out with the pain of it, they were beasts, they were, and he hated them.

He didn't know how long he sat there—he must have dozed—but he woke to something boring at his ankle and the sick corrupt reek of his own bowels. A film of cold sweat clung to his temples. He was sick—yellow fever, dysentery, encephalitis, hookworm, malaria, the dirty diseases of a dirty place—and he needed medicine, a bed, his *obāsan*. But no, not his *obāsan*—his mother, his dead mother, his mom. *"Haha!"* he cried out like an infant, his voice strained and odd in his own ears, "Mama!" And then he dozed again, seated there on that plastic throne where Julie Jeffcoat had sat and Jeff Jeffcoat and Jeffie and the legion of nameless butter-stinkers before them, white faces that crowded into his dream like a conquering army.

When he woke again he felt better. He wondered briefly where he was, and then he knew and the fear of the *hakujin* and of the chase seized him. They were here, they were sure to be here, and he was trapped. He thought of Musashi, the legendary samurai who'd once hidden from his enemies in a latrine, buried in offal, with only a straw through which to breathe, and then he was in motion. He sprang up off the seat as if it were electrified, hastily fastening the cutoffs and peering breathlessly through the crack of the door. He expected demons, long-noses, *ketō*, the waking night-mare into which he'd plunged from the wingdeck of the *Tokachi-maru*, expected shotguns, bullhorns, the bared teeth and rending snarls of the dogs . . . but there was nothing. Nothing but the swamp, stultified with sun, the womb and grave of everything. He cracked the door. Edged out. And then the heat hit him and his head ached and his eyes swam with a fresh assault of the fever.

The door was shut behind him and the planks creaking under his feet before he realized how wrong he was. There *was* something there on the platform with him, unmistakable, too big to miss, something slow-blooded and antediluvian and muscular that even now was swiveling its long grinning snout to fix him with a cold eye. This was a thing that dwarfed the platform, the serrated tail and one clawed foot hanging over the far edge and dipping into the slough beyond it, the rippled belly stretching the length of the planks, and in the foreground, the hard pale lump of the jaw pinning down the sack of sandwiches and the rest with the weight of an anvil. Hiro looked at this thing and he felt the fever loosen its grip. His heart was hammering at his rib cage, there was an ache in his temples. He had to form the words in his head before he could understand: he was standing six feet from a crocodile the length of a canoe and it was looking at him and he was looking at it. This was not good. This was bad and dangerous. This was a situation that might have taxed Jōchō himself.

For a long while the thing merely regarded him out of the motionless eye, frozen in its length and mass, the statue of a crocodile, carved of stone. Hiro could smell it, its pores giving up a wild scent of the deepest bottom, of decay and solitude and the dark quiet seep of gas. He wondered, briefly lucid, if he should back into the latrine and pull the door shut, leap for the rafters and live out his life on the roof, fling himself off the far edge of the deck and sprint for the trees through the slurry of muck and water. None of the options really grabbed him. In the end, he stood there, sailing in and out of the port of consciousness, wanting one moment to reach out and stroke the thing, to ride it into the cool depths and share his lunch with it, and in the next, contemplating his death in its iron jaws, the rending of the flesh, the transfiguration and ultimate conversion to crocodile shit. Finally, as if it had had enough of the whole business, the bloated inert thing came to sudden life and slid off the dock and into the water with a swift surprising grace, inadvertently taking the sack of food with it.

No matter, Hiro thought. He wasn't hungry anyway.

■   ■   ■

THE NEXT TIME HE CAME TO HIMSELF HE WAS LYING ON A MUDBANK somewhere, and the usual things were feeding on him. He glanced down at his feet and saw that he'd lost the Top-Siders, and saw too that his feet were bloated and raw, nicked in a hundred places. The small shapeless things, the things he'd pulled from his legs an eon ago outside the Coca-Cola store, clung thickly to his calves and thighs. He sat up and pulled them off, one by one, and each left a livid wet spot of blood to mark its forward progress. He made a nest of his intertwined fingers, too much a part of things now to bother with the mosquitoes and green flies, and watched the clouds converge on the dying sun.

He had places to go, things to do: he knew that. But he felt light, not only in his head but in his bones too, felt drunk—gloriously, blissfully, rapturously drunk. Had he been drinking *sake*? Yes, he was in his bunk now and they were crossing the Pacific with its thick green skin and he and Ajioka-san had been drinking *sake* in the canteen and talking of America, the excitement of it, America with its movie stars and rock and roll and long-legged women and beef. Not to mention the exchange rate. An ordinary seaman, even a wiper, would be rich there. And there was so much room, the *Amerikajin* in their mansions with four bathrooms and their Cadillacs with whiskey bars in the back seat. The *sake* was hot because there was a blow and the wind had chilled him on his watch, and now he was drunk.

But it was wonderful. A whole circus passing before his eyes as he lay there, birds with feet bigger than their wings springing from lily pad to lily pad, the holy crane gangling overhead, frogs swelling and deflating all round him. He turned his cheek on its pillow of ooze and there was a frog right beside him, crouched big-bellied over its coiled legs. And then it inflated its *hara* magically and gave out with a booming eructation that startled all the other frogs for the briefest instant till they could inflate themselves in turn and belch back a response. It was funny. Hilarious. Better than a cartoon. He laughed till he felt the sword in his gut and then he sat up and struggled with his pants.

If the day was high comedy, the night was tragic. It closed in on him like a shroud and it was haunted and deadly. The cold settled in and the swamp rang with shrieks of protest while Hiro shivered in his wet T-shirt and his wet cutoffs. The insects feasted on him and he slapped at them now, but he was a pincushion, a blood bank, his skin swollen in its hills and valleys till it felt like a text in braille. Late, very late, when the moon was a frozen speck in the sky, a reptile, thick around as his ankle, nosed in beside him for warmth. He felt it there, nosing at his armpit, his crotch, poking its bald face at his nostrils for the heat of his breath.

In the morning, he was worse. He shivered in his bed of muck till the sun rose to redeem him and then he lay there like a cold-blooded thing, like an alligator hauled out on the bank, and the blood boiled in his veins. This time the fever took him back to Kyoto and he was a small boy clutching at his *obāsan*'s hand as they made their way through the festive Friday night crowd on Kawaramachi Street. There was a parade of neon, the smells of *gyoza*, *soba*, sweet broiled eel, people everywhere. His *obāsan* was taking him to meet Grandfather for a night out in celebration of his birthday—his sixth. They were going to have *udon* and tempura at Auntie Okubo's and then they were going to the coffee shop round the corner to have American sweets, chocolate fudge sundae and banana split. His free hand, the left, was thrust snugly into the grip of a new fielder's mitt with Reggie Jackson's name etched into the leather in flowing American characters. A pachinko parlor: "*Obāsan*, please, let me play, just one game," and he tugged her arm and he was off balance and staggered into a passing woman, an old woman, dressed not in western-style clothes like everyone else but in kimono and *obi*. She looked at him hard. "*Sumimasen*," he said, bowing deeply, "excuse me, please." *Obāsan* elaborated on the apology, but the old woman pinned him with her black hard eyes. "*Gaijin*," she hissed finally and turned to go, but Hiro lost his head, the insult stinging like vinegar on an open wound, and he snatched at the wide flowing sleeve of her gown. "*Amerikajin desu*," he said, "I'm an American."

But he wasn't. And he isn't. He'd seen the hate in their eyes. He pushed himself up from the mudbank, the sweat burning at his temples, and thought of the orange soda the Jeffcoats had left him. And where was it? Crushed beneath the mute unthinking weight of the thing on the platform, the beast, the dinosaur that was America. He saw it then, orange fluid leaking from beneath the wattled belly like urine, like pale diluted blood. But it wasn't blood, it was orange soda, and he longed for it now. The sweat stung his eyes and the fever blasted his throat: he could hardly breathe for thirst. He stood dazedly and saw the water all around him, an ocean, a planet of water. And then he bent to it, knowing he shouldn't, knowing it would only make matters worse, bent to it and drank till he could feel it coming up.

Sometime during the course of the afternoon the clouds began to bunch up in the west, bare knuckles of white shading to gray and blue-gray and black. The sky receded, the sun melted away. The wind came up then, moderate but steady and with a taste of the Gulf Coast on it. Aching in every joint, blistered and burned till he wondered if they'd mistake him for a Negro, Hiro lay there on his mudbank, and the mud accommodated him, molding itself to the cup of his head, the spoon of his shoulders and the ceaselessly working jackknife of his shrunken buttocks and wasted thighs. Rain was coming and another night of cold and wet, of shivers and fever and the sword in the gut, but Hiro didn't have the energy to move. And what would he do anyway? Put up his watertight tent and slip into a down bag? Fire up his hibachi and cook himself a cheese-burger—medium rare, hold the onion—over the glowing white coals of his charcoal briquettes? A dream, nothing but a dream. He watched the clouds bunch and spread and bunch again, and then he let his eyes fall shut.

He was back in Kyoto, eleven years old—a man, his *ojisan* said. His grandmother was at work, and he and Grandfather were watch-ing TV, an American show in which a collie dog with *hara* saves a straw-haired boy from the dangers of ten lifetimes, week after week, in a neat half-hour format. "Grandfather," Hiro asked, "tell me about my mother." Grandfather's legs were thin as fence posts beneath the folds of his *yukata*. They were sitting side by side on the *tatami* floor. Dressers crammed with clothing, soap, thread, mirrors and combs and all the other odds and ends of a household mounted the walls, one atop the other. "Nothing to tell." His grandfather shrugged.

"She died," Hiro said.

Grandfather studied him. On the TV, a long snaking line of

bare-chested Aryan men stood on a beach, lifting mugs of Kirin draft to their lips in perfect synchronization. "She died," he agreed. And then, because Hiro was a man now and because of the moving shadows the TV cast on the wall and because he was old and he needed to, Grandfather told him the story, and he spared nothing.

Sakurako was a failure. Some demon seed had got into her and she gave up her studies, the possibility of a decent marriage and family, the love and respect of her parents, for foreign music—and finally, a foreign husband. A hippie. An American. When he deserted her, as Grandfather knew he would, she sank into a shame worse than miscegenation, worse than the murder of her family. She became a bar hostess, "mama-san" to a hundred men. When she wheeled her bicycle through the old streets of Kyoto, her half-breed infant strapped to her back, people stopped to stare. She was doomed and she knew it. Worse: her child was doomed too. He was a *happa*, a *gaijin*, forever an outcast. Her only recourse was to go to America, to find Doggo and live there among the American hippies in a degradation that knew no hope or bottom. She had no money, no passport, no hope or knowledge of her hippie husband. She tried to come home. Grandfather barred the door.

Eleven years old, his hair cropped close and his eyes like two tortoiseshell beads, Hiro sat riveted. The television spoke to him but he didn't hear. He was that *happa*. He was doomed.

"And then," *ojisan* said, "and then one night she did what she had to do." Hiro knew in that moment what it was, the knowledge sinking into his blood like a stone in a pond, at once and forever engulfing the flimsy edifice of his grandmother's lies. His mother hadn't succumbed to some vague disease—always vague, never a name for it. No. She died by her own hand. But the shock of that sudden knowledge was a ripple compared with the rest of it: she'd tried to take Hiro with her, tried to commit *oyako-shinjū*, parent-child suicide, and she'd failed even at that. He knew the gardens at the Heian shrine, didn't he? his grandfather asked.

Hiro knew them well—his *obāsan* took him there to feed the *koi* in the pools and sit and contemplate the sculptured perfection of

nature. The mouths—his grandfather spoke and he saw the mouths
of the *koi* gaping at the surface.

And the bridge?

Hiro nodded.

One night, late—she was racked with an insomnia that fed on
her shame—she came back drunk from her barroom and strapped
the infant to her back. The gates to the shrine were closed, the
shaven-headed monks long asleep. She propped her bicycle against
the wall and hoisted herself over. In the dark she made her way to
the low covered bridge and she lifted the infant from her back.
Frantic, scolding herself in a nagging broken whisper, her breath
coming in gasps, she fought her way back to the path and dislodged
a rock, an ornamental boulder, tearing at it with her nails till the
rocks beside it were painted with her blood. She pushed at the
rock, strained against it, rolled and shoved and beat at it. Finally
she worked it across the planks of the bridge to where the infant,
where Hiro, lay sleeping. In a final mad superhuman effort she
lifted the stone to the rail, forced it into the breast of her bargirl's
kimono, pinned the child to her and gave herself up to the inexor-
able pull of gravity and the black transfiguration of the water
below.

Water. Hiro woke to it, rain on his face. His mother was dead,
but he was alive, flung from her arm as she hit the water and caught
up in the muck, the muck in which he was mired now, hopeless,
screaming, and the bald-headed monks came running. He struggled
to sit up. Lightning tore at the sky. The rain seethed across the
water, leaden pellets of it, beating the surface to a froth, hammering
at his cushion of mud. Monks, he thought, where were they when
you needed them? And he began to laugh, wheezing, delirious,
sick and starved and hunted, he laughed like a boy at a Saturday
matinee.

But wait: what was that? Out there, beyond the trees and the
crack of the storm? A voice. A human voice. The thunder rolled
across the sky, harsh and angry. The lightning sizzled. But there
it was again—he knew that voice. It was, it was—

*"Hiro, Hiro Tanaka, can you hear me? It's Ruth. I—Want—To—
Help—You!"*

Help me.

"Hiro. Listen to me. I—Want—To—Help—You!"

It was, it was—his mother, his *haha*, his mama!

He was on his feet, rain in his face, the silly grinning T-shirt
swirling round him in tatters. "Mama!" he cried. "Mama!"

A silence, deep and expectant, a silence that reverberated over
the swamp and through the storm. *"Hiro?"* the voice called and it
came from everywhere, from nowhere, ubiquitous as the voice of
an angel.

"Haha, haha!" he cried, over and over, till he was breathless, till
he was cold, till his brain locked up on him and there was no other
word in the language. And then he saw it, the boat breaking the
mist as in a dream, coming toward him, the anxious white face in
the bow—his mother, it was his mother, come for him at last—
and behind her, crouched there at her side, hippie hair and hippie
beard, he knew that face—it was Doggo, yes, Doggo, his own
Amerikajin father.

And he stood there, in the rain, and he called to them, called till
he was hoarse, called Mother, called Father.

Port of Savannah

PART III

Journalism

. . . .

THE DAY WAS HIGH AND CLEAR, WARM WITHOUT BEING OPPRESSIVE, and about as dry as Savannah gets. It was mid-September, the seasons grudgingly changing, the scorching humid endless days of high summer giving way to something milder, expectant, the rich long Indian summer that would push back autumn to the edge of winter. Ruth was unpacking, finding hangers for her things, clipping the tags from a new three-quarter-length Italian cloth coat with dolman sleeves and oversized buttons, and a drop-dead black-and-white suit that featured slashing triangles against a flowing field of parabolas. Saxby had called it a fish dress. Fish? she'd echoed, holding the skirt up for him to admire. They were in her room at Thanatopsis at the time and she was in her bra and panties, trying her new things on for him. It's the scales, baby, he said, punching the sobriquet with all the lewd innuendo of a disc jockey. Is that all you ever think about? she'd responded and he'd said No, I'm thinking about something entirely different right now. Prove it, she said, and she dropped the skirt to the floor.

But now she was in Savannah, for the week, a guest in the glossy bright high-arching home of Dave and Rikki Fortunoff, a home that had been featured in the pages of *Architectural Digest* and the *New York Times Magazine*. Dave was a friend of her father's from law school and he often stopped by the house when business brought him to Los Angeles—Ruth had known him all her life. Still, she hadn't really wanted to stay with the Fortunoffs—they were thirty minutes by taxi from the hospital where Hiro was gradually regaining his strength, under guard, and refusing to speak to the press, the police or his speckle-faced tormentor from the INS—but the advantage of the arrangement was obvious: she could stay here for nothing. A hotel would have cost her sixty or seventy dollars a night, minimum, plus meals, and she didn't have that kind of money. Not yet.

She studied herself in the mirror for a long moment, thinking she might just use a rinse on her hair before she left for the hospital. It would highlight her tan—and show off the new suit too. Outside, beyond the French doors to the courtyard, lay the bright vacancy of the pool, and beyond it the massed oleanders and potted begonias that fed off its reflection. She wished Saxby were here with her, but he was home at Thanatopsis, awaiting her return, his tanks and buckets overbrimming with pale little fish the size and color of a gum eraser. When she'd left for Savannah he was wearing a yellow hardhat and supervising the dredging of the reflecting pool, future home of the pygmy fish and their happy descendants. He'd waved as she pulled out of the drive, a look of pure rhapsody on his face.

Ruth dropped the tags in the wastebasket and crossed the room to hang the coat in the closet. The coat was brick red—not neon red, not flame red, not hello-are-you-acquainted-with-me-yet red— but a more restrained and dramatic shade. A more mature shade. In the course of the past week a sea change had occurred in Ruth, a change that saw her opt for the less flashy color, a change that had brought her to Savannah and required her to borrow fifteen hundred dollars from her father for three new outfits, two purses, a pair of scintillating (but mature) black snakeskin pumps and the Italian coat. What it amounted to was this: she was now a journalist. On assignment. Not that fiction wouldn't always be her first love and true métier, and she hoped to get back to it someday—someday soon—but she'd had an offer she couldn't refuse.

The whole thing began with Hiro. Began on that grim morning when she was impressed into the service of the INS, the morning after the single worst night of her life. Nothing could cheer her that night. Her reading had been a holocaust of disaster, a funnel of ridicule for as long as Thanatopsis existed, and Jane Shine had put her down with the finality of a gravedigger. Sandy had tried his best to distract her afterward, and Irving was especially solicitous, but she felt as if the world had fallen to ash around her. Worse: all she had to look forward to now was the wrath of Saxby, the intransigence of Septima and the contempt of unknown sheriffs, the speckle-faced Abercorn and his loathsome little factotum. She went to bed after a single drink, the other colonists looking shrouds at her, and she pulled the darkness down around her and plunged into sleep as into a bottomless hole.

In the morning, it was the swamp. And Saxby. He was angry, upset, resentful, his eyes full of accusation and hurt. She met him out front of the Tender Sproats Motel and threw herself into his arms like a war bride while Owen and a potbellied little brown man in a tractor cap looked on. They were on a tight schedule, the police were waiting, the pygmy fish languishing in their far-flung buckets, but she couldn't help getting the feel of the role. She was abused and misunderstood, she was self-sacrificing and courageous, giving herself up to her enemies so her man could go free . . . and she was a humanitarian too, going out into the pit of nowhere, fighting back mosquitoes, snakes, pygmy fish and worse, to save a poor misguided Japanese boy. She could feel her eyes beginning to water over the complexities of it. "Give me five minutes, Sax," she whispered, "that's all I ask. Five minutes alone with you."

He hesitated. There were fish in his eyes—and something else too, hard and vengeful. But then he took her hand, led her to his room and pulled the door firmly shut behind them.

It wasn't the time for love, though the thought of it came to her

in an involuntary little spasm and her pulse quickened just perceptibly. She moved into his arms and let the tears come. Again and
then again she reassured him that the thing with Hiro was nothing,
totally innocent, a mistake, and that she'd been using him for her
fiction and had no intention of helping him escape or find his way
into the trunk of that car. He had to believe her. He did believe
her, didn't he?

Three hours in the Clinch County Jail hadn't improved his temper any, but he was so fish-obsessed he couldn't really focus his
anger for more than a moment at a time. They were out there, his
albinos, in five plastic buckets, without protection. He had to get
to them and he'd worry about the rest later. "I believe you," he
said.

As it turned out, they drove down to the swamp together in the
Mercedes, Owen following in his Mazda. Driving, his forearm
slouched easily over the wheel, the radio up high, Saxby began to
relax, chattering on about his fish and his nets and his tanks until
Ruth began to think things would work out after all. When they
arrived, Abercorn and Turco were waiting for them, as were the
local sheriff, about two hundred sunburned gawkers with campers,
coolers and smoking barbecues, and a throng of media people who
came at Ruth with drawn microphones and flailing notepads. *All
this for poor Hiro?* she thought, and then the seed of it, the first
stirring: *And for me?* She ran a hand through her hair, put on a
committed and absorbed look for the photographers. Was she here
to save Hiro Tanaka? someone wanted to know. Was she romantically involved with him? Was he as dangerous as they said? She
knew this role, this one was easy. "No comment," she chirped,
and she stepped high, moving right along till the police cordon
opened up for her and the reporters fell away like so many flies.

In the next moment she stood face to face with Turco and Abercorn. Ruth felt Saxby tense beside her, but she clung to him and
he held back. Abercorn stepped forward, his patchy face and artificial hair hidden beneath the brim of the most ridiculous hat she'd
ever seen outside of a circus. He stood a head taller than anyone

else in the crowd. "Glad you could make it," he said, and there
was nothing friendly about it. "The boat's this way." She pecked
Sax a kiss, a kiss recorded by the click of lenses and the pop of
flashbulbs from beyond the police line, and then she went off
with him.

After that, it was the swamp. With a vengeance. There was the
stink of it, first of all—the whole place smelled like the alley out
back of a fish market. Then there were the bugs, legions of them,
of every known species and appetite, not to mention the snakes in
the trees or the blistered scum on the water. She looked out over
the matted surface to the ghostly trees beyond and to the trees that
shadowed them and so on all the way to the horizon and thought
of a diorama she'd once seen depicting the dinosaurs in their heyday.
But then the diorama was in a cool, dark, antiseptic museum, and
the trees were painted on.

And then a man she hadn't noticed till that moment was helping
her into the boat—he was clean-shaven, neither young nor old, and
he wore a baseball cap with a pair of fold-down sunglasses attached
to the visor. She sat up front beside a pair of loudspeakers—the
sort of arrangement local politicians favor as they Doppler up and
down the streets—while the man in the cap climbed into the rear
and busied himself with the engine. It was a big boat, long, wide
and flat-bottomed, and reassuringly stable. She looked straight
ahead as Abercorn stationed himself in the middle and Turco,
in his jungle fighter's costume, crouched down just behind her.
The motor coughed, sputtered and then roared to life, and they
were off.

By eleven o'clock she was hoarse, thirsty, sweat-soaked and sunburned, and bitten in all the key regions of her anatomy. Every
time she paused to catch her breath or take a sip of water Turco's
nasty little voice was there to fill the void, urging her on: "Come
on, come on, keep it up—I tell you it's going to work, I know these
people, I know them." It didn't take her long to realize that this
was his idea, yet another demented variation on the boom box and
the designer clothes. She wouldn't look at him, wouldn't speak to

him, wouldn't so much as turn her head, but she kept it up—for Saxby's sake, for Septima's sake, for her own sake and Hiro's— kept it up till she had no voice left.

It must have been about four when the sky clouded over and the storm came up on them. Abercorn and the man in the cap—his name was Watt-Something and he was one of the sheriff's men— wanted to go in, but Turco wouldn't hear of it. He was clenched like a fist, his face dark and angry. His tone was pathology itself. "I can smell him," he hissed. "He's out there, I know it." And then to Ruth: "Keep it up, goddamn it, keep it up."

She held the microphone to her lips and called out Hiro's name, over and over, though she knew it was absurd, hopeless, as asinine as serenading the bugs with Donna Summer. "Hiro!" she bellowed to the tree toads and turtles, to the birds and bears and the mute identical trees, "Hiro!," and the gnats swarmed down her throat and up her nose. She was still at it when the storm broke and the rain lashed them like a whip, windblown and harsh. And then all of a sudden Turco was pinching her arm and shushing her and there it was, thin and plaintive, the distant rain-washed bleat of subjection and defeat: "*Haha! Haha! Haha!*"

Hiro came to her arms, came running, awash in filth, bleeding from every pore, his clothes hanging in shreds, splashing through the sludge like a boy coming in off the playground. "*Haha! Haha!*" he cried, "*Okāsan! Okāsan!*" He was crazed, delirious, she could see that, could see it in his face and in the mad wide stare of his eyes. Turco crouched like an insect behind her and Hiro spread his arms wide, running, splashing, stumbling for her, and she felt in that instant that nothing mattered in the world but this poor tortured man, this sweet man, this man she'd kept and fed and loved, and she called out his name once more—"Hiro!"—and this time, for the first time, she meant it.

The rain drove down. The swamp festered and hummed. And then Turco was on him like some sort of parasite, choking him, forcing his face into the water, twisting his arms back till they went tight in the shoulders. They hauled him over the side like a fish and laid him face-up on the floor of the boat, and now his animation was gone—he looked half-dead lying there, his head thrown back and his sick tan eyes swimming in their sockets. They wouldn't let her touch him. All she wanted was to cradle him, hold his head in her lap, but they wouldn't let her. She lost control then, for just a moment, shoving at Turco, cursing him, and he came back at her with a ferocity that stopped her heart. He didn't touch her, not this time, but the look on his face was a thing she would never forget—only the very thinnest single played-out strand of wire was holding him back. All the long way back to the dock she sat there, staring out on nothing, the rain beating at her, feeling helpless, feeling like an apostate, feeling violated.

That was the low point.

When they got back to the dock, when the crowd overwhelmed the thin line of police and pushed their way through to get a glimpse of Hiro Tanaka, the desperado, the jailbreaker, the foreigner, their plain sunburned faces and steady pale eyes prepared for any extreme of outrage and shock, when a kind of frenzy consumed the press and even the police were hard-pressed to clamp down on their wads of Redman and retain their equanimity, that's when things began to turn. They were all over her, all over him. The police shouldered their way through, cleared a channel to the ambulance, the white arms and legs and sure hands of the paramedics, rain driving down and down and down. The lights flashed, the siren screamed and Hiro was gone, Ruth clinging dazedly to the picture of him laid out on the stretcher, Turco hanging over him like a vampire. They gave her five minutes, and in a fog she found her way to the ladies' room at the tourist center and wiped the mash of insects and sweat from her face, tied her hair up in a scarf one of the park girls gave her, and stepped out into the lobby to face them.

It was then, only then, that she began to realize just how big a story this was. And how big a part she'd played in it. And what she alone knew that no one else did. Forget Jessica McClure and the woman in the surf, this was the story of the hour and she was at the center of it. They jabbed microphones at her, there were lights and flashbulbs, and she knew that she had a story here, not a short story, not some labored fiction that strove for some obscure artistic truth, but a real true tough hard and painful real-life story—and what's more, she was the heroine of it. The realization hit her in a single glowing flash-lit moment of epiphany.

She smiled for the cameras.

．　　．　　．

THE FOLLOWING DAY, JANE HAD HER ACCIDENT.

Ruth was back at Thanatopsis, back in the good graces of Septima, back in the hive, the INS had their man and Saxby had his fish. She'd treated her inflamed epidermis to alternating hot and cold baths laced with Epsom salts, dabbed at each of her myriad swellings with alcohol and calamine lotion and slept till noon. Eating a very late breakfast on the patio—no one would have expected her to work after the ordeal she'd been through—she'd run into Irving Thalamus, who was nursing a hangover with the aid of a tall Calistoga and gin and the *New York Review of Books*. She had a long talk with Irving about her idea, about doing an extended magazine piece or even a book about the whole incident, and Irving had put her in touch with his agent, Marker McGill, of the venerable McGill Madden Agency. That was encouraging, but she was still feeling low over the disaster of her reading, though everyone assured her that it had gone off fine, even if it was a bit on the long side, and feeling lower yet over Hiro. She couldn't get the shock of it out of her head, the way he'd looked with his fevered eyes and wasted limbs, his sunken cheeks and lacerated flesh—and the leeches, leeches all over him like sticking plaster—and the way he'd come to her. That made her feel lower than anything. He loved her. He trusted her. And she'd betrayed him. But then they hadn't given her a choice. And in the long run it was for his own good—no jail could be worse than that swamp, and there was no question but that he would have died out there.

Ruth was in the front parlor waiting for Marker McGill to return her call when they brought Jane in. Earlier, it must have been about three or so, she'd looked up from the magazine she was numbly paging through to see Jane, in English riding habit, striding across the foyer as if she were auditioning for *National Velvet*. Already that afternoon Ruth had talked to the *New York Times*, the *San Francisco Chronicle*, the Atlanta, Savannah and Charleston papers, CBS Radio and Mr. Shikuma of the Japan-America Society, who wanted to warmly congratulate her on her part in the apprehension of his errant countryman and to apologize, at length, for any inconvenience or unpleasantness Seaman Tanaka may have caused her and to assure her that the vast majority of the Japanese—indeed, the entire country but for Seaman Tanaka, who was of course mentally ill—were great respecters of the law and proper behavior. The calls had made her feel better, and she began to warm to the prospect of a book on Hiro and had even begun to daydream about the amount of the advance and what she would do with it, when she looked up and saw Jane and felt incinerated all over again.

The Nordic slave was there at the door—or was he just a Swedish oaf?—and Jane pranced up to enfold him in a public embrace, looking ever so self-consciously cute in her jodhpurs and boots and that ridiculous little riding hat perched like a napkin on the spill of her hair. She was going riding. Ruth was at the center of a media storm, Ruth had risked her life in the swamps and assisted in the capture of a desperate fugitive and thumbed her nose at the law, but Jane was going riding. All the hatred Ruth had for her festered to the surface in that moment and she squinted her eyes to bore into her with a corrosive look. But Jane caught her out again—just as Ruth was about to drop her gaze to the page in her lap, Jane swiveled her head to lock eyes with her, to catch her watching, snooping, prying, envying the Nordic embrace, and gave her a perfect little bee-stung smirk of triumph.

Two hours later they brought her in. The horse had gone down on her and broken her right leg in three places. Jane's face was a snarl of pain, there was blood on her jodhpurs where the jagged face of the bone had sliced through the flesh. They rushed her into the parlor and laid her out on the couch, the Swedish oaf and

Owen, who came away with a smear of the anointed one's blood on his shirt. Jane shrieked like a woman giving birth to triplets, she shrieked breathlessly and without remit, save to break down in the occasional throaty rush of curses and sobs. Ruth moved aside while the whole colony fluttered round. She was horrified, she was, genuinely horrified. She could never take joy in another's pain, no matter how despicable the person nor how much that person had it coming, could she? No. No, she couldn't. And yet there was a thin tapering thread of satisfaction in it—even as Jane writhed and screamed and cried out for her mother and cursed the Swedish oaf: "Oh god, oh god—don't you touch me, Olaf, you pig, you—aiee, Mommy, Mommy, it hurts, it hurts!"—and the thread raveled out like this: now Jane would be out of action. At least for a while. It was a pity, a real pity. Ruth was already thinking up her billiard-room routine.

They took Jane to the hospital. Dinner that night was subdued, a joyless affair that ran to hushed conversation and furtive glances, the colonists numbly lifting Armand's lobster tortellini to their lips in a state of shock over the events of the past few days. Septima took her meal in the old wing of the house. Jane's place was conspicuously vacant. Somber rumors circulated—about Hiro, about Ruth, about Jane. After dinner, while Saxby—who alone of all the company remained ebullient and irrepressible—tended to his fish, Irving Thalamus took Ruth aside.

"So tell me," he said, swirling amber liquid in a snifter, "how'd it go with Marker?"

McGill had called just after the excitement over Jane's accident had subsided; he was taking Ruth on. He was sure he could sell the book. He'd made some calls and was fielding offers. "Oh, Irving"—she clapped her hands like an ingénue, like Brie—"he's taking me on." And then she gave him a look of such melting gratitude, such starry-eyed, humble and worshipful thanksgiving, that he set down his snifter and took her hand in both of his. "Irving," she repeated, her voice appropriately raw, "how can I ever—?"

"It's nothing," he murmured, and he was studying her, giving her a long sly look from beneath the hooded Thalamudian eyes. "Terrible about Jane," he said after a moment. He still had hold of her hand.

Ruth searched his eyes. What did he want her to say? Was he on her side after all, was that it? "Yes," she said. "Terrible."

He looked away then, patted her hand and set it free. He lifted the snifter to his nose, took a deep breath and then set the glass down. "Ruthie"—and he hesitated, went for her hand again— "Ruthie, I've been meaning to ask you . . . you know I'll be leaving in two weeks?"

Ruth nodded. Her heart began to accelerate. She was acutely conscious of the pressure of Irving's hand on her own.

"I've got this place I'm renting in Key West—greatest weather on earth—it's about three blocks from the beach. Big open room, windows all over the place. Hemingway lived there one winter."

She nodded again.

"Look," he said, watching her from deep within the folds of his hooded eyes, "what I'm saying is this: I want you to come with me. Live there—rent free, no obligations." He paused. "With me."

She couldn't help herself, the names just leaped into her head: Ruth Thalamus, Mrs. Irving Thalamus, Ruth Dershowitz-Thalamus. She saw herself at his side in New York, cruising the literary salons, sashaying into Bread Loaf on his arm, saw herself in bed with him, all that hair, those strong white New York teeth. Her pulse was racing, her eyes were bright. And then she thought of Saxby, sweet Sax, with his fish and his shoulders and the way he smiled out of the corner of his mouth, thought of Thanatopsis House and Septima, of Laura and Sandy and all the rest. She was queen of the hive: this was her home. "You're sweet, Irving," she said finally, "and I'll always love you. You'll always be my best friend, my mentor, my advisor—"

Irving had retreated behind his eyes, the meager bunch of his lips. "But—?"

"But"—she sighed, and she could look down now, and up, she could scan the room before she came back to him, all the time in the world—"but I can't leave Sax."

The first call the following morning was from Marker McGill. He had a deal for her and he wanted to know what she thought of it. He'd gotten an offer from a major publisher—he named the house—for a $500,000 advance against a fifteen percent royalty, first serial rights going to one of the leading women's magazines— he named it—for $75,000, to run in three installments. How did that sound?

And so, here she was, a guest of the Fortunoffs, contracts in the mail, new clothes spread out on the bed, a journalist on her way to the hospital to interview Hiro Tanaka and take some notes. It was warm, but she would wear the coat anyway—the fall season had begun, after all—and yes, she thought she would highlight her hair just a bit, to bring out some of the reds and golds. Then she would slip into her stockings and heels, don the new suit, collect her tape recorder, notepad and pens, and call a cab. There would be photographers outside the hospital and she would look smart for them—seductive, yes, attractive, yes, but in a mature way, a chic and businesslike way. She was a journalist now, after all—like Joan Didion, like Frances FitzGerald—and she had an image to maintain. Journalism—and she said it aloud to herself as she stepped into the shower—it was a noble profession.

. . .

AT THE HOSPITAL, RUTH RECONFIRMED THAT THE SAGA OF HIRO Tanaka was still very much in the public eye. There were reporters everywhere, pumping hospital staff, lawmen, doctors, nurses, even the janitors, for word as to Hiro's condition. He'd refused steadfastly to speak to anyone—not even his court-appointed attorney and translator. He was suffering from septicemia (which had elevated his temperature to 104 degrees), shigellosis and hookworm, and he was facing twenty-two criminal charges brought by the State of Georgia and twelve others at the hands of the INS.

Ruth posed for photos on the hospital steps—not to be mercenary about it, but they were money in the bank—but she brushed off the reporters. Why give them anything? This was her story now. She was aware of the trouble Hiro was in and she felt bad about it, and she knew that some people—the Jane Shines of the world— would say that she *was* being mercenary, capitalizing on his misery, sailing out the courtroom door while he was left holding the bag. Especially since the charges against Saxby had been dropped and she'd been given immunity, as per her arrangement with Abercorn and the district attorney. But that wasn't it at all. That was just a malicious distortion of the facts. Of course she felt bad for Hiro, but as she rode up in the elevator she tried to harden herself just a little. No one had asked him to jump ship or take up residence on her front porch, after all—they had to understand that. *He* had to understand it. And if she'd agreed to testify in exchange for immunity, she was going to go up there and do everything in her power to convince them how innocent Hiro was, how the whole thing was just an escalating series of misunderstandings, how he was nothing more than an overgrown boy, an innocent, a naif, how all he really wanted was to live in a walk-up in Little Tokyo and blend in with the crowd. It wasn't criminal, it was pathetic, that's what it was.

She found her way to Hiro's floor. The nurse on duty, a short black woman with cornrow braids and earrings that were like paper-weights, gave Ruth the sort of double take she might have lavished on a Di or a Fergie or Donna Summer herself, and then led her past a bored-looking deputy and into Hiro's room. Hiro was propped up in bed, looking wan, his skin and the whites of his eyes faintly yellowish, as if they were tarnished. His face, which seemed impassive, dead, the face of a stone Buddha, came to life when he lifted his eyes to Ruth's. "Rusu," he said, and though he was depressed, though he was hurt, sick and defeated, he couldn't disguise his pleasure, and he gave her a quick fading glimpse of his crooked smile.

Ruth had no illusions about the story—Hiro's story. Her story.

It probably had a half-life of about three days. It was one of those things that for some unfathomable reason gets the whole country worked up to a fever pitch and then dwindles away to nothing, yesterday's news, a dim glimmer in the collective memory. She knew that. But she was confident she could get the book done in six months—it was her own story, she was on the inside of it—and rekindle that glimmer into a spark. And so did her publisher, obviously. The reporters out front were giving them publicity you couldn't buy. "Hiro," she said, and she crossed the room to him.

She took a seat beside the bed. There was a silence. The deputy poked his expressionless face in the door and then took it away again. "How are you feeling?" she said finally, and she dug around in her purse for the little gift-wrapped box of sweet bean cakes she'd brought him. "I brought you something," she said, setting the package on the table. The deputy stuck his face in the door again, then he moved into the room, striding purposefully, and he took the package from the table and held his hand out for Ruth's purse. "Ah'm not gone frisk you," he said, "but Ah'm watchin'," and then he returned to his station.

"So, how are you feeling?" Ruth repeated. "They treating you well? Is there anything I can get you?"

Hiro said nothing.

"How about your grandmother? Do you want me to write her? Phone her?"

Hiro didn't respond. There was another silence. After a long while he turned his mournful eyes on her and said: "You lie to me, Rusu."

Now it was her turn. She waited.

"In the house," he said, and his voice sounded parched, dried up, torn out by the roots, "you are the one. You tell them I am here."

So that was it. She wasn't going to have to defend herself over the boat and the swamp and Turco—apparently that was lost to him. He was taking her back to Tupelo. All this time he thought she was the one who'd betrayed him. "No," she said.

"Yes. You never have any idea to take me to *mainrand*."

"No. It was Saxby. He saw you there on the porch and he went to the police without telling me. I never knew till it was too late." She lowered her voice. "I did want to help you. I do. I still do."

He gazed out the window. They were five stories up. There was nothing to see but dead clouds in a dead sky. "I'm tired," he said after a moment.

She wanted to tell him not to worry, that everything was going to be all right, that she'd look after him and get her father to help and Dave Fortunoff too—he was well connected in Savannah—but she couldn't. She felt awkward. He looked terrible. The deputy was watching her. "Okay," she said, rising from the chair, "I understand. It's all right. I'll come back tomorrow, okay?"

He glanced up at her, struggled to lift his hand from the sheets and spread his palm in valediction. "I say goodbye now."

She felt for him in that moment, a quick sharp flooding of the glands, and she bent forward to touch her lips to his cheek, guard or no guard. "See you tomorrow," she said.

He never answered.

The City of Brotherly
Love

. . . .

THE DREAMS WERE OF THINGS HE COULDN'T ADMIT, DREAMS OF torment and horror and hate. They came at him as he drifted in some disembodied realm where colors flashed in his eyes and faces bled into one another without reason or chronology. And a hiss, always a hiss, as of the air rushing from a punctured lung. He saw Chiba become Wakabayashi and Wakabayashi become Unagi and felt the slap of their multiple hands. He saw his mother at the bottom of the pond, her ravaged fingers, the rictus of her mouth, and the hiss became a scream, silent and prolonged. He saw Ruth and her face was the face of his captors and tormentors, and it was their hate that burned in her eyes. And then he saw himself, and he was at the bottom of the dead black endless American swamp, his flesh gone white, flaking, dropping from the bone, and then he was rising, apart from himself, above them all, rising toward the trembling aqueous light of the surface.

He emerged on a room in a hospital in the bright light of day. Above him floated a bag of clear liquid that fed its way through a tube and into his arm. He tried to lift his arm but found that he couldn't. There was a man at the door, a long-nose in uniform. A nurse—she was a Negro—hovered over him. "Well," she said, "at last. Feeling better?"

Better? He was feeling nothing, nothing at all. He'd been swallowed by the crocodile and he'd been living in its belly. He looked at the nurse and saw the grinning mouth and the serrated tail and his eyes fell shut and the dreams rushed over him again.

In the morning—at least they told him it was morning, and for lack of any standard against which to measure the information, he took their word for it—the great gift of consciousness was restored to him. Or perhaps it wasn't such a gift after all. He saw the long-nose at the door and understood, without recalling the details perhaps, but in a syllogistic way, that he'd failed, that he was a prisoner once again, that the world and his life within it were hopeless. A doctor examined him, asked inane questions: How did this feel? Did he know where he was? Who he was? It felt bad. He was in the custody of the *hakujin* police. He was a *happa*, a butter-stinker, half a long-nose. He didn't bother to answer.

In the afternoon another long-nose appeared, very well dressed, and introduced himself as his legal counsel. With him was a Japanese—a non–butter-stinker, pure bred, a member of the august and nonpareil Yamato race—the first such Hiro had laid eyes on since making his leap from the wingdeck of the *Tokachi-maru*. He was short and soft, this Japanese, with a puffy face, closely cropped hair and glasses that were too big for his head. His name was Hanada and he spoke with a northern accent and a breeziness that seemed inappropriate to the situation. But then the long-nose began to speak and Hanada-san became a machine, interpreting the *hakujin*'s words in a flat mechanical voice. Hiro, he explained, was too ill to go to court—there was no question of that—and so he would be arraigned here at the hospital, via videotape. (And sure enough, even as he spoke, three more butter-stinkers edged into the room, two fondling briefcases and another balancing a video camera on his shoulder.)

Hiro wanted only to hide himself. He was defeated, humiliated, a failure like his hopeless mother and his hippie father. He refused to speak to any of them, in English or Japanese. The first long-nose, his counsel, listened to a lengthy list of charges and entered a plea for him: Not guilty.

Well, yes, of course he wasn't guilty—that went without saying. Not guilty of any of their meaningless charges, anyway. What he was guilty of was stupidity, naïveté, guilty of thinking the *Amerikajin* would accept him in common humanity. He was wrong, and that was his crime. He had failed, and that was his fate.

The reporters came in the evening, and he experienced his one moment of weakness, the moment in which he wavered and came close to abandoning his resolve. They wanted his story and for a moment he wanted to give it to them, to rub their long noses in it, for a moment he imagined that story appearing in the newspapers and on TV, and somewhere, somehow, stirring Doggo from his slumber, and he imagined his father coming to his rescue like a cowboy on a horse. But it was stupid. Foolish. The burned-out core of a dream—ashes, that was all it was. The deputy held the reporters in the hallway while they fired their questions. Hiro looked up at the clamor of voices, and he turned his head away.

And then Ruth came. She was there in the chair beside the bed with the long white legs that had captivated and enslaved him and she was a reporter too. He looked into her eyes and saw that she didn't know him at all. She swore she hadn't betrayed him—it was Saxby, the *bōifurendo*, the butter-stinker: he should have known!—and he softened, almost broke. But she wasn't his Rusu, she didn't care, not really. She was playing another role, using him as she'd used him before. He told her he was tired. He told her goodbye.

What Ruth didn't know, what the attorney didn't know or the butter-stinker at the door or the nurse either, was that Hiro had a plan, that he wasn't down and defeated yet: he would escape them all, and he knew it and drew strength from the knowledge. They'd fed him the typical things, the *Amerikajin* Jell-O, the peach halves, the macaroni and cheese, but they hadn't given him chopsticks, hadn't given him a fork or a knife. They gave him a spoon, a poor pitiful thing not three millimeters thick. But it was rigid and cold and it would serve the purpose. He hid it under his pillow.

He waited for night. For the long pulsing dimly lit hours when the nurses tread with a lighter foot, when the stabbings and shootings and gang fights taper off and the terminal patients settle in for their grim solitary vigil. This was the hour when the *hakujin* guard, like the guards before him, would close his eyes, for just a minute . . .

Yes. And throughout the day, when they left him to himself, when the guard at the door followed a pair of legs and buttocks down the hall or let his eyes go slack with a dream of food or sex or violence, when the nurse was changing bedpans or doing her nails or crouching over a tuna-paste sandwich in the nurses' lunchroom, Hiro had been honing the cold stiff handle of his spoon against the concrete wall behind his bed. Just a stroke at a time. *Swish. Swish, swish, swish.* It was the hardest steel and it made the softest, most loving whisper. Yes. And now it was a spoon no longer: it was a shiv, a blade, a samurai's sword.

There was plenty of time, he told himself, no need to rush. Do it right. Do it with honor and dignity and elegance. He sat up in bed and braced himself against the wall. His hair was a mess, he knew it, and he regretted it. And his skin too—he wished he'd thought to ask Ruth for a bit of powder or rouge, anything to give him a little color. But he'd been sick, starved, hunted and abused: what could they expect? He wetted his fingers and ran them through his hair, again and again, until it lay flat. The guard sat in a chair just outside the door. His shoulders were slumped and his head propped up against the doorframe. If he wasn't asleep, he might as well have been.

What was it Jōchō had said?—*In a fifty-fifty life or death crisis, simply settle it by choosing immediate death.* Fifty-fifty. It was a joke. If only it were fifty-fifty, if only he had that much optimism, if only he had the foolish serenity he'd attained in the moment of his plunge into the oily black Atlantic. Ninety-five, he thought, ninety-five to five, all stacked the wrong way. It was a small matter, wasn't it?

He honed the blade once more, a deadly whisper, steel against concrete. *While we live, death is irrelevant; when we are dead, we do not exist. There is no reason to fear death.* A small matter. He studied the back of the guard's head, the arm that hung limp in the muted light from the hallway, and then he drew in a breath, lifted the thin cotton hospital gown to expose his *hara* and felt for the place, for the *kikai tanden*, for the spirit awaiting release. He held that breath and turned the blade, turned the shiv, the sword, to his flesh. One beat of the heart, two, and then he drove it in with all the strength he had.

It was like a punch, a terrible hammering blow, but worse, far worse, hot and invasive, a pain like nothing he'd known: he'd swallowed molten lead, burning lava, he was nothing but sweat and a brain. And a will. He drove deeper and he couldn't stand it; he slashed across, dragging the blade, hacking, and his arm locked with the shock of it. Again and again, forcing himself, digging deeper, on the edge of blacking out. And then he was giving birth, his own pale intestines bulging at the hole he'd torn in himself, the heat and the pain and the limp still arm of the guard still framed in its pitiful light . . . and the smell rose to his nostrils then, the heat of his blood and the corrupt rank fecal stench of the mud, the mud that had cradled him and brought him down . . .

And then suddenly he felt his *hara* lift—it wasn't actual anymore, it wasn't wet and hot and heavy in his hands, it was as light as air. He was going, but not to the city of Mishima and Jōchō, not to the city of his *ojisan* and his mother and all the generations of samurai and kamikaze and the pure unimpeachable Yamato race. No. He was going to the City of Brotherly Love: there, only there.

He closed his eyes. He was already home.